KANE WILLIAMS

Dust jacket and internal artwork by Anderson Magalhães from Design Unlikely.
Cover underneath (case laminate) by 100 Covers.
Edited by Sarah Chorn, Kathryn Harris and Nathan Hall.

A catalogue record for this book is available from the National Library of Australia

ISBN (e-book) 978-1-7637364-0-5
ISBN (paperback) 978-1-7637364-1-2
ISBN (hardcover) 978-1-7637364-2-9

First published in 2025 by Kane Williams.

kanew.au

To my brother, Lance, for the adventures behind us and the horizons awaiting.

AUTHOR'S NOTE

As a reward for not skipping over this page, I'll let you in on the origin of the chapter titles: each title is a word or phrase found in that very chapter.

Specific chapters lack a chapter number. There's good reason for this. I hope you appreciate a bit of mystery in your action-adventure fantasy novels.

This adventure takes place on a unique world, with its own fauna, flora and language. I've brought it to you in Australian English—which, in this context, is effectively British English.

Stylistic choices reflect my preferences as a writer and reader. For example, you won't find a thought tag (e.g., 'she thought') in this novel. You're already in the head of the point-of-view character, with select present-tense thoughts from them *italicised.*

Many thanks for reading.

Kane Williams

Notable Gods and Goddesses

Devtakaris, the god of magic

Heltorne, the goddess of agony

Lablias, the god of water

Preslina, the goddess of life

Reveth, the god of the harvest

Solisene, the goddess of love

Thelia, the goddess of sight

Ultinna, the goddess of the moon

Veritonan, the god of luck

Zentrina, the goddess of death and rebirth

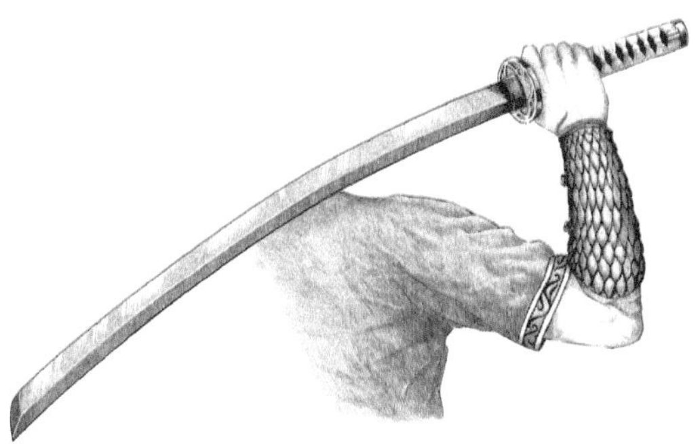

1. Window to Your Soul

Her past life clutched a secret. Tonight, she'd pry it free.

Antarna shuffled along a narrow ledge, keeping her back to the sheer mountainside. Her scarf, wrapped to the bridge of her nose, fluttered against her lips with each breath.

The hungry maw of the cave loomed ahead, many shades darker than night. Bluish-white icicles descended from its upper lip. The answers she sought were closer than ever. Antarna squeezed the hilt of her sword.

Her boot slid on the ice-crusted snow. As her toes left the ledge, her heel dug in and sent a cascade of white into the swirling clouds below. Antarna grounded the tip of her scabbard, finding reassurance in the additional point of contact. A long fall onto sharp rocks would've been an embarrassing way to go.

Enthriff loosened his grip around her wrist, smooth scales sliding over her skin. His fern-green head emerged from her cuff.

'It's nothing,' she said.

Her companion retreated into her warm sleeve and slithered up her arm to settle on her bicep.

Hunched against the lashing wind, she continued. The temple she called home grew smaller behind her and the gaping mouth of the cave larger. All around, jagged peaks reached for twinkling stars.

Antarna left the ledge and savoured the safety of the wide landing before the cave swallowed her whole. The wind subsided, its howl replaced by dripping water that echoed throughout the rock chamber. A two-tailed ice worm slunk into a crevice. She held her cancryst high, and the crystal's yellow light peeled away the dark. No larger than a candle, it blazed twice as strong. Still, the bulk of the cave remained steeped in gloom.

Icicles gave way to stalactites and stalagmites—the cave's longer, sharper teeth. She wove between them, heading towards a flat section of the rock floor where five concentric circles had been laid in pebbles. A spiral plant unfurled from the roof and started to emit a soft, sky-blue glow. Neighbouring plants awakened, unfolding and radiating the yellows and oranges of a sunset as if not to be outdone.

Antarna set the cancryst down on its hexagonal base and removed her cloak, scarf and gloves. She rolled up her sleeves, revealing a bloodsucker clinging to her arm, masquerading in white like a snowflake. Six thin legs and two transparent wings extended from its furry body.

'Enjoying your dinner?' Antarna stretched out her arm.

The insect removed its needle-like mouth and departed. As a child, she would've swatted it and taken pleasure in the red smear.

A bump grew on her amber skin. Her mother used to treat bites with the sticky sap of a carnivorous plant. Ten years had dragged by since Antarna had felt her mother's touch or heard her silky voice, memory ever a poor substitute. Hopefully her mother had been reincarnated into a life with loving parents who treated her bites with care.

The bite itched. Enthriff uncoiled, glided down her arm and nuzzled her. She petted him in reply. If the danger had been greater than a hungry insect, he would've warned her.

Antarna placed her left foot atop a chest-high rock covered in spongy lichen and leant forwards. A stretch spread down the trio of muscles at the back of her thigh. Last year, she'd spent every night for a month meditating on this ice-cold rock, searching in vain for a way into her soul. Tonight, it would all be worth it.

A patter of footfalls rose above the rhythmic drip of water. Antarna lowered her leg and turned to face the entrance. A man's silhouette emerged from the shadows. Light from her cancryst glinted off the enlarged eyes of her mentor, his golden irises stretching their length and width, absent the whites in her own. Gil held neither crystal nor lantern, having crossed the ledge to the cave by starlight alone—an advantage of being born in the cavern, an underground city almost as large as her birthplace. Age had taken the colour from the priest's beard, but he moved towards her with youthful energy and grace.

He freed the strap of his bag from his shoulder and lifted it over his shaved head. 'What's on your mind?'

'Why is it always the same vision?' She couldn't endure another night of failure, churned up and spat out by the same distorted fragments.

'Think of the soul like a diary that preserves a record of your every thought and action. Until you learn to turn the pages, you're stuck reading the last entry of your past life.'

'That makes sense.'

A droplet fell from the roof onto Gil's cheek. Captured by a deep wrinkle, the water ran down its length. He flicked it off and pulled open his bag to reveal a cylindrical drum of stretched shagrontin skin. A bundle of fabric sat on the top of the instrument. Gil unwrapped it to expose a dark ribbon with three silver bells tied along its length. It jingled as he attached it to his ankle. 'Shall we?'

'Yes.' She ran three fingers along the curved scabbard of her sword, smooth wood slipping by.

Enthriff constricted, causing one of her fingers to twitch.

Jealous? She raised her forearm to her lips and kissed his narrow body.

Antarna drew her sword, and the steel caught the light. She wrapped the hardwood scabbard in cloth and put it on a rock free from ice. Water, even frozen, forever played the part of steel's enemy.

Antarna removed an onyx vial from her cloak pocket. Careful to point the top away from her, she pulled the stopper free. A familiar shadow slid forth, more solid than any shadow should be. It crossed the five circles and took form in their centre, rising to mirror her height, build and weapons. There, it waited, motionless.

Her brother used to train in swordcraft against the shadow under Father's watchful eye. She embraced the nostalgia. The ebb and flow of the duel. The pride on Father's face as her brother took the upper hand. Their laughter at the elaborate flourishes her brother added to his celebration bow. What she'd give to hear that sound again.

Entering the circles, Antarna took her shield from her back and slipped it on—one strap across her forearm, another in her hand. The thin strap didn't impede her when she gripped the hilt of the stout dagger hanging from her belt. She unsheathed the blade, and it extended past the rim of her shield. Taking deep breaths through her nose, she rolled her shoulders and then adopted a fighting stance. The arcane shadow did likewise.

Gil adjusted his musical instrument. 'Remember, after you defeat the shadow and leap, you're looking through a window to your soul at events already written. Relinquish any sense of control and observe.'

The slow beat of the drum filled the cave.

The shadow launched forwards.

I am wind. With quick feet, Antarna avoided the strike, circling away.

Unrelenting, the shadow continued its assault.

I am water. Antarna retreated like the sea drawing back from the shore until the outer edge of the last circle was a step away.

The beat quickened. She was a wave crashing upon the beach, her sword an extension of her arm. Her steel blurred as she feinted and sliced. But for each strike, the shadow gave an answer. Sweat gathered upon her brow.

The shadow sprang into the air.

I am earth. Antarna stayed grounded. She met its blow with a hard block, her weight even and centre of tension low. Her exhale formed a white cloud that quickly dissipated, succumbing to the cold.

The pair separated. The shadow held the middle of the circle, controlling the space.

The drum rose to a crescendo. Harsh and fragmented, the beat rebounded off the irregular cave walls.

I am fire. She closed the distance. As her brother had done in a fight years ago, she turned her opponent's shield with her own, creating an opening. Her sword sliced through the gap and delivered the killing blow.

The shadow-form crumbled to the floor and disintegrated into a dark cloud. Tendrils of darkness slithered back to the vial.

Gil shook his ankle, the bells tinkling, marking the moment for her.

Antarna threw her sword to Gil and slammed her hand over her heart, feeling it pulse under her palm. Closing her eyes, she slipped into the vastness of her mind. A network of spheres joined by delicate silver threads stretched in all directions, like a young god had found an endless ball of wool and decided to link the stars. She settled softly within a sphere glowing with the fresh memory of her duel with the shadow. Orbs, vibrant with recent experiences, abounded to her right—a labyrinth she'd lost herself in before learning to clear away the noise and clutter through facing the shadow. Antarna rushed down a thread in the opposite direction, passing dormant memories of her early days on the mountain, bedridden and racked with pain. The sound of Gil's bells rose, and she chased it. Turn after turn, the spheres grew darker and bells louder.

Show me the way.

She ventured deeper.

Fierce, blinding light banished the darkness.

She leapt into her soul.

Antarna collided with her past life. Shock waves surged through her mind. Reeling, she fought to orientate herself in this foreign male body. His skin felt like a swarm of parasites crawled on it. Noises swept over her, loud and jumbled. Bright lights stabbed at her. A fathomless wrongness pervaded her brain's every nook and cranny. She refused to submit to the urge to return to her own body.

I belong here. Laughter and chatter emerged from the discordant sounds. The light dimmed.

She opened herself to her previous incarnation, lowering her walls. His thoughts invaded her own, wholly indecipherable. A blizzard that snatched her into its chaotic clutches and tore pieces from her. She'd been here before, more times than she'd like to admit. Instead of retreating in on herself, against her every instinct, she welcomed him in.

Tell me your name.

His thoughts continued to pummel her, and she lost touch with herself. Her memories slipped away. The link to her body frayed so thin it could be severed, leaving her detached and hollow. Antarna stayed dangerously open to him and repeated her request.

His voice reached her, 'Sal—'

The roar of his other thoughts drowned out the rest of his name.

Greetings, Sal.

The hazy outlines of a boy and his mother took shape.

Antarna tried to blink. Her eyelids didn't respond. They weren't her own. *You're looking through a window.*

Warm, humid air filled his lungs. The heavy perfume of nicarmia flowers abounded, their sweet fragrance familiar from her childhood.

The boy and his mother finally came into focus, garbed in cloth of rich reds and yellows. Bronze beads adorned the mother's braided black hair. They stood, like Sal, in the dappled shade of a nicarmia tree, one of many that lined a meandering pebbled walkway to the palace. Indigo flowers, fallen from the trees' generous canopies, carpeted the pebbles of the Purple Path. The dark walls of the bowl-shaped crater surrounded them.

A crowd stretched along the length of the path, their gazes on a procession with Antarna's grandfather in the lead—a man she'd never met. He waved to the crowd, his thigh-sized arms bulging. Behind him, her father and uncle followed, oddly young. Hunters pushed handcarts filled with their prey.

Her past life squeezed the hilt of his bone knife. *Just a little closer.* Brutality clung to every word. The thought overtook her. Became her own. His anger roiled, raw and hot and intense. And it saturated her. Bloodlust throbbed through them.

Today, he would kill. She would kill. They would kill.

Antarna fled.

She wrapped her arms around herself—around her familiar body. Her fingers brushed the crescent scar on her hip. Ever attentive, Enthriff unwound from her forearm and glided over her skin.

Gil leant forwards. 'You look pale. What did you see?'

'It's not what I saw but what I felt. He's furious and out for blood. My family's blood.' Antarna shivered. 'He could be …' She trailed off, unable to say the word "Resatrium" after what the rebel group had done to her family.

'But you didn't see him act upon his rage?'

'No.' It was true. He could've changed his mind. That would make more sense than her goddess allocating her the soul of someone who'd sought to murder her father, uncle and grandfather. She stood in the centre of the five circles of Zentrina, the goddess of death and rebirth. Zentrina would not have wronged one of her devotees, surely.

'You have only glimpsed the smallest fraction of his life. Don't judge him yet.'

'I won't.' And she meant it. 'As you suggested yesterday, I reached out for his name and got the start of it.'

'Excellent.' Gil put his drum back in his bag together with the bells. 'The rest will come. When it does, you'll be able to use that to ground yourself in the vision.'

She slid her sword into her scabbard, donned her cloak, and tightened her scarf. Gil led them out of the cave. Pale moonlight shimmered off the ledge that stretched like a delicate ribbon. Beyond it, the grey stone of Zentrina's five-storey temple melded with the mountainside. Light from a room at the top of one of the temple's towers poured into the night.

They navigated the narrow shelf in silence, absorbed in the task. A cloud engulfed Antarna, cool and damp. It blurred her surroundings. A bitter wind cut through her clothes, tugged the cloud away and sent it skittering alongside a cliff.

Before long, they left the ledge. Five concentric circles had been carved into the temple's wooden door. Elegant flowing text filled the spaces between the four outer circles. In the centre of these rings stood the image of her goddess in a billowing cloak.

Antarna ducked as she entered. The heavy door and stone dampened the roar of the wind to a meagre sigh. They descended a spiral staircase. Unlike her mentor, she leapt over every seventh step.

At the fork at the end of the corridor, Gil turned to face her. 'I almost forgot to mention, Priest Weslutch is looking for you. He's back from the crater.'

'Thanks.' She wasn't ready for Weslutch to pass along another scroll from Father.

Gil brought two fingers to the centre of his forehead, between his eyebrows, then lowered his hand to his chest. Antarna followed his lead, touching her spiritual third eye and then splaying her fingers over her heart. He turned towards the priests' bedrooms while she went in the other direction.

Reaching into a recess in the wall, she swapped her cancryst for a smaller one. 'Light, please.'

The crystal obliged.

At the armoury, she hung her Daslercian sword between one of bronze and another of bone. Steel was rarer than gold, for the secret of its forging had perished with the former kingdom of Daslercia. All blades pointed right, conveying trusting, non-hostile intentions; left-facing grips couldn't be drawn easily with the right hand.

On leaving, Antarna deviated around the library, not risking another run-in with its guardian, whose leniency had died years ago in the desert alongside her sense of humour. The walls gradually constricted until her shoulders brushed against them.

She opened a door. Against the wall, a full set of armour made of bone plates and wooden slats stood in shadow, complete with a face mask and crested helmet. Countless relics graced the temple. This one heralded from the crater, perhaps even having belonged to one of her ancestors.

As she passed the armour, it moved, a gloved hand grabbing her arm. The grip clamped down like a hunting trap. Her training took over. She twisted and raised her forearm, forcing the attacker's wrist into a position of weakness, and broke their grip with her free hand. Going on the offensive, she brought her elbow through, rotating her torso for greater power. The attacker ducked, and her blow glanced off their helmet.

The ancient headpiece slid sideways, revealing a mop of fiery hair.

'Tozias?' She extended her cancryst.

Her friend raised his hands. 'I surrender.'

She leant against the wall and chuckled. This had to be one of his better pranks.

'Help me out of this.' He raised his arms awkwardly.

'And miss the fun of seeing you struggle?'

And struggle he did, stretching for places on his body he could barely reach to pull at knots he'd tied too well. How he'd even got into the armour in the first place was beyond her. Halfway through, she took pity on him and helped remove the shoulder guards and chest piece. Underneath, he wore the thundercloud-coloured robe of their goddess.

Tozias led the way to the sleeping quarters, arms stretched wide, webbed hands brushing against the stone walls flanking him. His ivory skin—distinctive of lake islanders—contrasted against the ash-grey passageway. Thin, blond hair covered his arms, apart from a section near his wrist where lightning had struck. In gratitude for surviving, he'd joined the temple the next day. Now he bore Zentrina's mark on his forearm: holy text revolving within their goddess's circles.

'Priest Weslutch was asking after you.' Tozias looked back at her.

Antarna shed her cloak and slung it over her shoulder.

'But you have more important things on your mind.' He tapped two fingers against his temple.

She unwound her scarf. The soul of a cowardly man who had ambushed her family weighed heavy inside her, rotten and repugnant. A violation of her body. A perversion of her identity. A betrayal of the trust she'd placed in her goddess. *Unless Sal had second thoughts.*

'Your time with Gil left you with more questions than answers, again.'

'My past life may have done something unforgivable.'

'Did they?'

'I'll find out tomorrow.' She lengthened her stride. 'I must.'

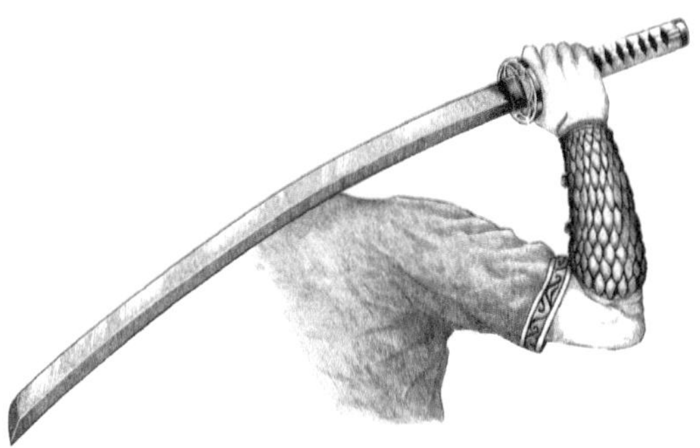

2. The Void

Rich notes resonated through the temple, hanging in the air like a guest reluctant to depart. Not yet done, the morning bell tolled two. With a final turn and a head tilt under the doorframe, Antarna entered the most sacred of places.

A domed ceiling stretched above the vast circular room. In its centre towered the likeness of her goddess, shrouded by a cloak cascading from head to toe. The deep hood concealed her face. Her cloak rippled; the liquid-like stone in motion was as wondrous as it was mysterious. An ancient scroll recorded that the first priest had carved this statue of Zentrina from the grey mountain stone and that the goddess had been so pleased with his work that she'd placed a tiny shard of herself in it. The less devout claimed the first priest had animated the statue with a powerful enchantment.

Robed devotees filed into the room and settled into one of the five nested rings around Zentrina's massive form. Antarna sat in the fourth ring on the cold floor, facing the form of her goddess, and Tozias joined the third. He rolled down his sleeve, covering Zentrina's mark. Everyone in the first three rings bore the same enchanted tattoo. The text rotated at different speeds, reflective of the heartbeat of its bearer.

Soon, she would take her vows and receive the mark of her goddess. Those vows of obedience and celibacy were nothing compared to the sacrifice of blood and body parts required by the god of magic. But before she could undergo the ritual, she had to tell Father that she wore the grey of Zentrina.

Last night, she'd had a nightmare of Sal chasing Father down the Purple Path with an axe, hacking at him and laughing maniacally. She could never escape him, not after inheriting his soul.

A trio of initiates took their places in the ring behind Antarna.

Three ... Three letters could be enough: Sal. She repeated the word in her mind and then, with her mouth closed, tried it on her tongue.

The Unjust Uprising had taken place on the Purple Path in the year before her birth. Odds were that her vision was of that day. *No event is more infamous. There'll be a scroll with the traitors' names.* Energy thrummed through her, making sitting still insufferable. Sal's full name could unlock his memories. She needed the scroll, but it had a particularly tough guardian.

High Priest Inhaloc entered the room, his steps slow and his back straight. The sky-blue trim on his robes added a dash of colour to the shades of grey. His piercing eyes, a shade darker blue than the trim, swept over his silent devotees as he advanced to the innermost ring.

Once there, he led the temple through the five expressions of thanks to Zentrina, voice resonant and solemn. Antarna struggled to pay attention, her mind fixated on how to access the scroll from the library.

Inhaloc turned to face them. 'Different paths have led you here, to the world's highest point, closest to the gods and to our goddess, Zentrina, weigher of souls. Some of you arrived here with hearts brimming with gratitude for the gift of life.' He looked in the direction of Tozias, who rubbed the patch of hairless skin on his arm. 'Others weathered a storm of loss, with wounds time had little chance of healing. Parsannon, please stand.'

After glancing at the boys on either side of him, the young initiate in the row behind Antarna did so. He'd arrived from the crater last year, a gaunt orphan in threadbare rags. Now he was starting to fill out the grey robe of their goddess. Parsannon pushed his short, dark hair off his forehead, then clasped his hands behind his back.

'You came to us alone, without hope and full of questions. I've been pleased to see you find not only solace and understanding, but also kinship and purpose. You will make an exemplary priest one day.'

Beaming, Parsannon bowed.

They concluded with a prayer, and almost eighty voices said the final line as one: 'With my soul as my eternal record, may my actions be honourable, ring true and serve others.'

Rising with the congregation, Antarna followed them onto a balcony level with the closest peak in the mountain range. She laid a woven grass mat next to Tozias's. The ends of his mat curled back on themselves. Bending down, she flipped it over. He gave a series of nods, each smaller than the last. *Like stones skipping across the crater's pond.*

Priest Yerkinfall stood before them. Behind him, the sweeping grass plains at the foot of the mountains emerged as first light ate the darkness. Swarms of four-winged reanildras swooped over the plains. Paying homage to them, Yerkinfall started with a series of five flight-inspired movements. He grounded his long, sinewy arms and, lifting his legs into the air, balanced his knees on his triceps. Yerkinfall was a paradoxical man: flexible of body and rigid of mind, especially when it came to following the rules.

Breathing deep, Antarna followed his lead. They returned to standing and began the next movement. As she folded over and pulled her face into her knees, a pleasant post-training burn spread across her lower back.

Antarna's legs framed the upside-down world. Blood rushed to her head. Her hair fell to the floor, as did everyone's. Dark of the crater, like hers; blond of the lake island, plus Tozias's red, of course. And tightly knotted and matted of the desert—believed to prevent energy from leaving their bodies. In contrast, sunlight glinted off the shaved heads of those of the cavern. The temple boasted a solid representation of all four races.

Following an assortment of poses to limber their bodies and clear their minds, the session concluded, and the congregation moved into an adjacent hall for breakfast. Rows of long tables spanned the room. After waiting her turn in line, Antarna found her berries and a filtinarid. The pyramidal fruit gave a little under the press of her fingertips.

Steam rose from two cups of tea on her usual table.

'Thanks.' Antarna took a seat and gave Tozias's left shoulder a squeeze.

He grimaced, having bruised it yesterday. 'I guess I deserved that.'

'Yes, you did.' Last week, he'd pulled the same stunt on her. Antarna peeled the filtinarid side after side. Emerald drops ran onto her hands. Before taking her first bite, she paused. Enthriff remained still.

Opposite, Letti blew on a steaming spoonful of porridge, her long lashes hiding her downcast eyes.

'Letti.' Antarna rested her elbows on the table. 'Oh, gorgeous Letti.'

A smile tugged at Letti's plump lips. She put her spoon down.

'I'd be forever grateful if you could help me access a scroll from the library,' Antarna said.

'When you sent Tozias last month, that dried husk of a librarian near skinned him alive.'

'Yes, but you have beauty and brains. It's not his fault he was born without either.'

Tozias choked on his food while they laughed. Afterwards, Letti changed the topic. Antarna would have to find another way to obtain the scroll.

Divislak passed by, drawing a tattooed finger across his tattooed throat. The ink on his hand depicted his finger bones. He joined a table of desert folk, taking a seat on the bench beside Revertika, a pain empath whom Antarna had no time for—he delighted in others' pain almost as much as he did in drawing power from it. The other three races sat intermingled throughout the hall.

The desert shades their own. She turned to Tozias and lowered her voice. 'When will he move past it?'

'Well, you did break his arm.'

'Fracture, thank you. And he had it coming.' Divislak had put Tozias in the infirmary a few months ago, stabbing him during a training fight. She'd challenged Divislak that afternoon.

An idea germinated, reaching for the scroll.

It wasn't long before the hall started to empty. Antarna cut a path towards Divislak. A tattooed snake climbed his neck and reared over his ear. She paused behind him. 'Haunted hall. Now.' She needn't say more.

There was only one reason initiates and acolytes met there: blood. He'd been thirsting to spill hers.

He cracked his knuckles.

Tozias followed her out, keeping any of his worries to himself. They climbed a crumbling staircase to a derelict hall. Dust blanketed the floor. Wind hissed through cracks in the stone wall, swaying tattered tapestries so faded that they'd lost all meaning.

Divislak entered, trailed by Revertika, who sported almost as much ink.

'Welcome.' Antarna spread her arms.

'Why would I fight you here?' He spun on his heels. 'No one will see me win.'

'Because in the training hall, they'd never let you fight me while I'm blindfolded.' She pulled a strip of black fabric from her pocket.

'The rules?' he asked in a slow, flat voice, feigning disinterest—but the intensity of his gaze gave him away.

'First blood.'

'The stakes?'

'Honour. And given I'm the only one blindfolded, a scroll from the library if I win.'

'There's scant honour to be gained with you blindfolded. I'll need something more valuable if I win.' He squared his shoulders and stood tall. 'Like ... your sword.'

Tozias stepped forwards. 'No way.' He knew what it meant to her.

Of course Divislak wanted to mete out as much pain and punishment as he could. She should've anticipated this. By goddess, she'd never be able to stomach watching him practice and parade around with her sword. And he'd be sure to use every opportunity to rub it in her face. She pushed such thoughts aside.

'I accept.' Antarna tied the blindfold around her head, plunging herself into darkness. She'd never forgive herself if she lost the sword. But she had a plan.

Divislak's fist smacked into his palm.

'Honour our mistress, yourselves and each other,' said Tozias.

She bowed, as Divislak would have. Raising her hands and sliding her feet, she took a fighting stance.

'Begin,' Tozias said.

In the ink-blackness, Antarna strained her ears. Clothes rustled. Feet shifted. Enthriff applied a gentle pressure to the left side of her wrist, warning her of Divislak's approach. Antarna stood statue-still with eyes closed behind the blindfold, waiting.

The pressure on her wrist increased, his sleek scales kind on her skin. *Trip? Body blow?* No. *You're not going to be able to resist going for my face.* She lowered her guard a little and tilted her head, as if listening for Divislak. The bait was set.

Enthriff stopped tightening, her opponent apparently worried she'd heard him.

After four breaths, the force on her wrist resumed its climb. *Almost there.* She kept her fists loose, shoulders down and face relaxed—despite her rising anticipation.

The grip on Antarna's wrist tightened sharply, constricting the blood supply and sending pain shooting up her arm. She responded by ducking. A fist rushed through the air where she'd been.

Antarna exploded skywards. Striking blind, she put the full force of her rise into her uppercut. Her knuckles clipped Divislak. Teeth smashed together.

Antarna readjusted the image of Divislak in her mind, with him a little further away. Seizing the moment, she followed up with a lightning jab. This connected, solid and satisfying.

'Blood is drawn,' Tozias said.

Antarna took off the blindfold, blinking against the light.

A red trickle ran from Divislak's nostril.

She bowed. He didn't.

'What scroll?' asked Divislak, as if the words tasted like his own vomit. He refused to meet her eyes.

'One with a list of names from the Unjust Uprising.'

When he turned his back, she stroked Enthriff.

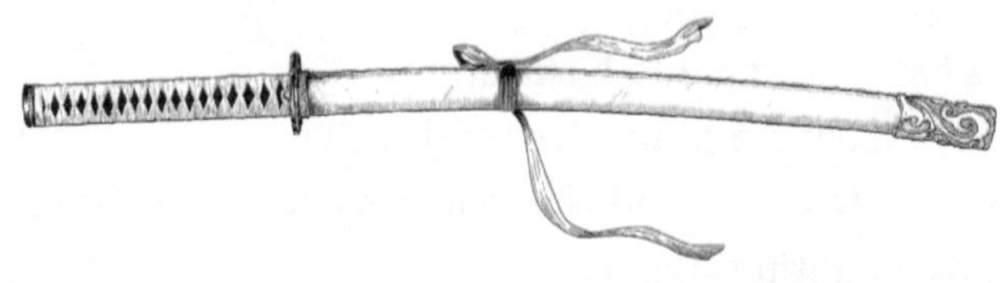

Divislak stormed out of the library, an old scroll clenched in his hand. He threw it at her, turned sharply and left.

Warmth radiated through her. She unravelled the parchment to reveal columns of names. Towards the bottom, under a list of known Resatrium traitors, she found it: Salorann. It rang true within her. She should've been overjoyed to learn his name, but to have him confirmed as a Resatrium member deepened her worry.

'I'm late for class,' said Tozias. 'You are too.'

'Go get some sun.'

'I know, I need it.' He looked down at his pale arms.

Together, the pair brought two fingers to their third eye and then lowered hands to hearts. As Tozias spread his hand, the enlarged membrane between his fingers drew taut.

Antarna bounded down the corridor. Most likely, she'd find Gil with his hands on his hips. He appreciated punctuality.

She turned the corner to find Priest Weslutch walking towards her. He raised his hand in greeting. The text in Zentrina's mark on his forearm revolved swiftly.

'Antarna, you look like you're in a rush. I'll keep this short.' He scratched his bony nose, which sat above a large mouth dominated by its lower lip. 'I saw your father during my trip to the crater. He'd love to see you.'

'He's welcome to teleport here.'

'How would you feel about returning home for a visit?'

Antarna blinked and, in her mind, was back there, in the crater, on the floor of the dining room, stretching an unsteady hand out to her brother. He convulsed just out of reach, foaming at the mouth. Her mother screamed until she collapsed.

With difficulty, Antarna pulled herself out. 'I am home.'

Weslutch stared at the ground and shuffled his feet. 'Sorry, I didn't mean—'

'I'm late to meet Priest Gilverson.' She passed him and did not look back. Her father should've known better. Weslutch should've too; last year, he'd appeared to take her rejection of her uncle's invitation personally.

Antarna met Gil outside the armoury. His hands indeed rested on his hips.

'Sorry I'm late, but I discovered his name.' She lifted the scroll, smiling. 'Salorann.'

'You almost had it yesterday.' He didn't return her smile. 'Don't rush this.'

She entered the armoury and collected her Daslercian steel sword from a wall crowded with stone, bone and obsidian weapons. After attaching her dagger to her belt, Antarna slipped her shield onto her back. She walked by her armour of scaled jadrossil hide on the way out. It had been a gift from Father, intended to help her feel safe. He'd killed the jadrossil himself, probably trapping the poor creature and then clubbing it to death—even steel struggled to pierce its scales. Her brother had had a similar set of armour. Enthriff's head emerged from her cuff. She ran her thumb over the scales on his neck; they were stronger than even a jadrossil's.

Gil shut and locked the door behind her. They snaked through corridors and ascended a spiral staircase. She took the deep steps one at a time but jumped every seventh.

'While I'm learning to control my visions, will I see anything other than the last entry in the diary of my soul?' she asked.

'Not unless there is provocation, a stimulus, so to speak. If you see, hear, smell, touch or taste something that had significance to a former life, that could allow you to go deeper.' He turned his attention to the lock on the door. It clicked. He exited the temple, and she followed, ducking under the doorway.

Her breath misted, and the dark mouth of the cave tied a knot in her stomach. The soul vision was a timely reminder: her family had targets on their backs. Thankfully, she was closer than ever to unlocking the power in her soul.

Sunlight reflected off the snow-capped peaks of nearby mountains. Above, a solid layer of clouds slid across the sky like a great white curtain. Her boot knocked a pebble, sending it over the edge of the ledge. It hurtled down the steep and rugged slope.

The drip of water welcomed them to the cave. Antarna took her place within the five circles, as she had last night.

Gil set the drum down in front of him. 'Today, may you echo your mother's grace and acknowledge your father and brother with your swordsmanship.'

And so, to the beat of the drum, she did. Body, mind and soul aligned. When her sword pierced her shadow opponent, she threw it to Gil hilt-first, followed the tintinnabulation of bells to her soul and leapt.

A cacophony of noises assaulted her.

Bright dots of light erupted, then faded just as quickly.

Salorann. She reached out to him.

He inhaled that warm, perfumed air.

After again intoning his name, their connection strengthened.

In front, the mother ruffled her son's dark hair.

Salorann. The soul memory sharpened until it was as though Antarna was back there, in the year before her birth, eighteen years ago.

Salorann shifted his weight. The crowd jostled around him.

Relinquish any sense of control and observe. Antarna couldn't move. Today, she didn't try to.

For the first time, she noticed her grandfather's crooked nose. It hadn't featured in the painting she'd stood before as a child.

Her father and uncle followed Grandfather, one over each shoulder. They'd inherited his size and his strong, square jaw, and they wore armour made from jadrossil hide. Her uncle grinned, his right cheek unmarked—unlike her every memory of him. Family to her, a target to Salorann.

Her past life was waiting for her family to draw a little closer. Dark emotions were tangled in his thoughts—foreign and hostile in her head.

Antarna kept her own perceptions close: *Hate will only breed further hate*.

Nine steps behind them, no more and no less, marched her family's guards. Salorann measured the distance twice.

A shrill cry rose above the noise of the crowd. Three crested littridons on leashes walked on two legs, slender tails swaying behind them. The picky plant-eaters sported hooked beaks on the tips of their snouts. Short, bony spikes covered their small triangular heads. The creatures advanced with heads bobbing, turning and tilting, their large yellow eyes unblinking and inquisitive.

Knives rose around Salorann in honour of the returning hunters. To blend in, Salorann did likewise. He brought his blade down upon his palm. Antarna felt his pain as if he'd cut her hand. Blood slid slowly along his little finger. A droplet splattered upon the ground. Salorann stood in a small circle of cleared dirt amongst a blanket of trampled indigo flowers. He continued to transfer his weight from one foot to the other—his nerves a snake constricting his insides and baring its fangs at his heart.

Those are his feelings, Antarna reminded herself. She could neither speak nor change the thoughts of a deceased man.

Hiding in plain sight amid the masses, Resatrium members waited. A force to be reckoned with, bolstered by the element of surprise. They had a mage, too: Layaury.

Close to the path, a Resatrium warrior held two wicked bronze daggers. Any longer and they'd be short swords. His face was all sharp angles, his eyes flat and cold.

Salorann resisted checking on the archer perched in the branches of the nicarmia tree above him, wary of giving his position away.

Ahead, dark blotches marred the armpits of a man holding a double-edged volcanic glass blade. A slight shake overtook his knife arm.

Grandfather drew close.

Relinquish any sense of control and observe.

On the precipice of violence, Salorann filled himself with anger. And he fed it with years of grievances: beatings from guards, the ransacking of his home, and tax collectors wringing him dry.

There was no calm before the storm. Parents cheered, and children laughed—innocent and unaware.

Stepping forwards, the sweaty man threw his blade. Spinning, it flew straight. The blade hit Grandfather in the chest and shattered upon his armour. Shards of glass took to the air.

Relinquish any sense of control and observe. Of all the things to observe ... The chaos of the Unjust Uprising swelled, contagious. The woman in front of Salorann screamed. The man to his side pulled his son off his shoulders, into his arms. Antarna clutched her composure, but it slipped through her fingers like sand.

'Let's take our glory, Salorann, before Layaury claims it all!' said the archer from his branch.

Salorann extended his arms. A bow and quiver dropped from the canopy, and he caught them.

A small orb sailed through the sky towards the Purple Path, soon to break upon the pebbles and release its smoke.

Salorann nocked an arrow and drew, arm strong, back taut. He released, and the arrow struck Grandfather in the meat of his thigh. Grandfather dropped to a knee. A grimace twisted his face. Her uncle ran forwards.

Salorann clenched and eased his fist. His delight clashed against Antarna's rage. He drew again. With the nock of the arrow between his forefinger and middle finger, Salorann brought the string back until it kissed the tip of his nose. He loosed the arrow, the motion as fast as it was smooth.

No, *please*, *no*. Antarna knew the fate of the ill-famed arrow. She couldn't look away. His neck was not hers to turn; his eyes were not hers to close.

Her uncle dropped to his left.

The arrow tore through his right cheek in a spray of blood. Her uncle screamed and fell to the ground, clutching his ravaged face.

With an arrow still protruding from his leg, Grandfather shuffled to his wounded son.

Father screamed over his shoulder at the guards. All around, panic reigned.

Salorann's smile broadened as the dual-daggered man charged Grandfather. Blue veins bulged along the attacker's neck, and one popped from his flushed forehead.

Grandfather used his sword to rise to his feet. Father rushed forwards, but Grandfather waved him back.

In a single practised movement, Salorann nocked and drew another arrow, sighting her father along the shaft. Fear shredded all thought.

No! No, you don't. A forest fire of anger roared through Antarna, and she drew upon its heat. The vision lost its clarity. She pulled at Salorann's arms and intention, fighting him with the entirety of her willpower.

He released the arrow.

Over my cold, soulless corpse. She refused to see it find its mark. Everything shook as if a powerful earthquake had struck.

The dual-daggered man leapt at Grandfather.

The arrow flew to Father.

Never! Antarna tore at the arrow—faintly aware she couldn't alter the past, but too furious to care. She'd watched Mother die, and she wouldn't stand by while the Resatrium attacked Father. She ripped a large chunk out of the sky, opening a dark hole. *What have I done?*

The vision deteriorated around her.

A savage force sucked sky, ground and people into the hole. Voracious. The more it consumed, the larger the hole became.

Salorann and Antarna disappeared into the void.

The cave blurred, and a scalding heat flushed Antarna. She turned away from Gil, losing her footing in the process. Her stomach contracted. Bile rose, demanding to be released. Vomit erupted, chunky viscous liquid splattering icy rocks.

Acid burnt her throat, and she wiped her lips. Enthriff gave her wrist a reassuring squeeze. Her stomach spasmed again.

Gil approached, eyes soft. She exchanged her dagger for his water bladder.

The cool liquid soothed her mouth. She swirled and gargled before spitting it out.

Gil sat and beckoned her to join.

Head throbbing, she did. 'That wasn't me …' *It can't be.*

'Not in this lifetime.' He squeezed her shoulder. 'Breathe.'

Deep inhale, pause, long exhale, pause, repeat. Her nausea faded. She checked her pulse; it still raced. Antarna rose and started to pace. *My past life is the reason for my uncle's terrible scar. Salorann almost killed my father, and if he had, I'd never have been born.* Zentrina had no right to give her Salorann's soul. She quelled a scream building within.

After several long moments of silence, Gil rose.

Antarna collected her sword, but instead of finding solace in its familiar grip, it reminded her of what she'd lost—of the lives the Resatrium had taken. Using the pommel, she chipped a chunk of ice off a rock and popped it into her mouth. 'It seems like a mistake for that to be my last life.' *Of all the lives …*

'You don't think our goddess had her reasons?'

No. Nothing could justify something so heinous. Her cheek lost feeling. She swapped the ice chip to the other side of her mouth. Frigid water dripped down the back of her throat. As if oil instead, it fanned the flames of her fury.

Tearing at her vision had been impulsive; nothing could change the past. Still, Antarna didn't regret it. She couldn't have watched another moment. If only she had the same power at her fingertips outside of a vision.

In no time, they arrived at the temple's outer door. Antarna turned to face the slope and tilted her head back. The mountain peak towered above, steadfast and unyielding—everything she wasn't.

'I'm going to take the climb.' She didn't trust herself to return to the temple and not hurt someone in the fighting ring.

'Of course.' He stretched out his weathered hands.

She handed him her weapons, her grip lingering longer than necessary.

'Remember,' said Gil, 'to access your soul's knowledge and power, you'll have to accept who you are, past lives and all.'

I'm nothing like Salorann.

They touched their third eyes and spread a hand over their hearts.

When he turned his back, she sought solitude on the mountain.

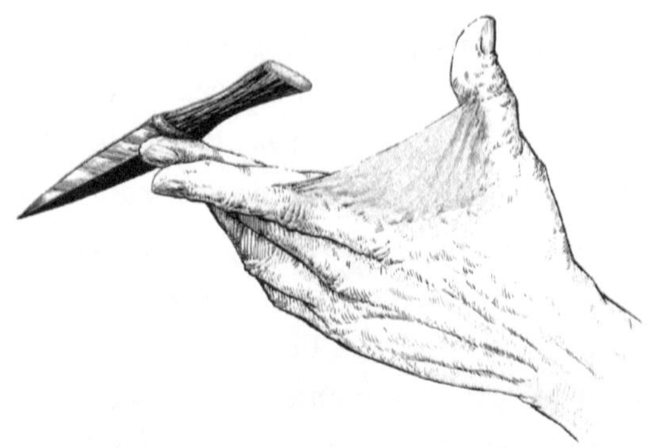

3. Red-hot Poker

It was an ungodly time of the day: sunrise. Blinding rays of light reflected off the lake. Cold sand yielded beneath his bare feet. He should've still been in a cocoon of dreams. But there was no going back to sleep after what he'd seen.

Cal crossed the beach and dived into the lake. Water rushed by, and the gnawing feeling in his stomach faded.

Silence engulfed him. He kicked and circled his arms, water tugging at the webbing between each of his fingers and toes. The temperature dropped as he descended; the light did too.

A school of dazzlers swam by, twisting and turning as one. Speed blurred the lustrous blues of their scales. As the fish's flexing bodies cut through the water, they painted a picture of curving lines and swirling blues, the lake their canvas.

A juvenile male dazzler trailed the group. He sped to catch up, but the school closed ranks.

Keep trying. It'll work out.

A frilled eel burst out from a dense bunch of kelp. Its jaws snapped shut over the shunned fish.

If that's a message, my goddess, I don't want to hear it. Not that Thelia, the goddess of sight, had cared what he'd wanted this morning when she'd sent Cal a vision of the chancellor stabbing a red-hot poker into his master's eye. But, armed with the foresight, he would ensure it didn't take place today.

With long kicks and a sweep of his arms, Cal rose to the surface. Sweet air awaited him. He glided through the clear water to shore.

A sandy boy with frizzy hair bounded down the beach. He picked a slimy, squishy morsel from his nose and popped it into his mouth. After examining his culprit finger, he locked his pastel blue eyes upon Cal. The child stretched out his arms. 'Future. Tell.'

You will not become a devotee of fine food. That much was clear.

Gesturing at his own neck, Cal showed that he didn't yet wear the necklace of seers. The boy missed the message. Maybe Cal needed to start carrying around a sketch of his master for times like this.

'You will grow even taller and'—Cal lifted his arm to expose his armpit—'hairier.'

The boy screwed his face up, staggered, then turned and ran back to his mother.

After drying himself and putting on his clothes, Cal turned for the city. A vendor on the edge of the street sold jellied eels from her cart, wobbling her cold chunks of eel set in hardened slime at passersby. The next cart displayed various items made from the shells of night turtles, from rattles and drums to masks and necklaces. Cal hurried past.

A man in tattered, soiled clothes sat staring at the sky. Maybe he knew a leaf protruded from his densely matted hair; maybe he didn't. No doubt there were bigger things on his mind. Two streaks of dark ink ran across each cheek, marking him as Disgraced. He'd wronged someone powerful, and only they could remove the stain. People gave the man a wide berth; most businesses would too. Cal patted his pocket for a coin only to find it empty.

As he passed through the streets, the feeling in his gut returned—like a pack of quill hounds had taken up residence, snarling, pacing and howling. Or maybe they were just rolling around on their needle-sharp backs. The vision that'd woken Cal had been fleeting but vivid, sickening in its details: a scorching metal rod burning through delicate eye tissues, turning watery fluid to hissing steam. It'd taken place in the chancellor's office. Unfortunately, that was where he and the seer were due all too shortly.

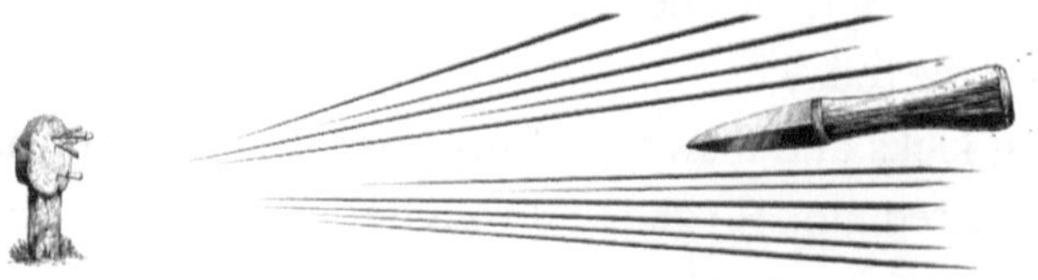

The wooden bench in the chancellor's waiting room had sung Cal's bum a lullaby. While the three oversized chairs standing against another wall would've been comfier, they were as dark and ugly as sun-dried kelp. Their appearance hadn't bothered his master, Brayan. He sat unnervingly still, not a silver hair out of place—well, apart from his unruly eyebrows. His years as the seer were etched on his face.

A spherical speck of light smaller than a fly passed through the wall opposite Cal, the stone no barrier. The madrilik drifted whimsically through the room. When he'd first seen them as a boy, he expected to become a mage. But try as he might, he could not control the life force of magic. Cal's ability to see madriliks was less useful than wings on a flightless bird. Still, they were enchanting.

A servant placed a crystal chalice of honeyed cider on the side table beside Brayan and then departed. Last year, when one was caught repeating something they'd overheard, not only did he lose his tongue, but the rest of the chancellor's servants did too.

Cal rose and walked stiff-legged to Brayan. 'I know we've had this discussion already, but you can't enter that room. You'll—'

'That was one possible future. It will be fine.'

'No, it won't. Let's postpone, say you're not feeling well. I'll paint some red dots on your face, and we'll arrange for Lady Rhodlin to see you. She'll tell the whole island before lunchtime,' Cal said, drawing a circle in the air with his hands. 'After that, there's no way the chancellor would see you.'

'Today is different. I can feel it.'

'Maybe it could be different. My training is going well; you've said so yourself. Let me take over the meeting.'

'And what if that's the reason I lost my eye?' Brayan chuckled.

If they were at home, Cal might have fallen to his knees and feigned a stab wound.

A priest strode into the waiting room, his presence filling the space. A crimson robe hugged his upper body, accentuating his distinct lack of arms—limbs he'd willingly surrendered for the god of magic. Flat, straight hair fell over his forehead. The priest's chest was bright with madriliks. These flecks of otherworldly light floated inside him like a swarm of translucent jellyfish. The armless swept by them.

Following the armless into the room, a servant carried a cider on a silver tray. The priest summoned a faint madrilik from his chest, drained its energy and used this to levitate the cup to his mouth. A couple of swigs later, the priest flew the empty chalice back to the servant. The light from the speck flickered and then faded away.

If the cider had been intended for Cal, and if it'd been an ordinary day, Cal still wouldn't have begrudged the priest. Truth be told, without the magic wielded by the armless, the four races would've been devoured by predators long ago.

The double doors opened, and the chancellor's herald beckoned the priest inside. Hopefully, the armless had news that would put the chancellor in a good mood. Their elected leader was as reasonable and patient as a drowning man.

With nothing to do but wait for a meeting that spelled certain disaster, Cal had about that much patience, too. The same servant returned to dust an elongated stinger that'd been severed from a beast and mounted in a recess along the wall—a gift from desert folk.

The doors opened once again. The armless exited, his face expressionless.

Cal put his arm on the back of Brayan's chair. 'This is a mistake.'

Brayan rose with a groan and stepped forwards.

The herald, Rayvic, waved them inside. Only the sides of his head held hair, short and white. Lifting his drooping eyelids, the herald turned to face the chancellor. 'Brayan Gerill, the twenty-second seer, and his apprentice.'

Trailing Brayan, Cal entered.

Behind a dark wooden desk, the chancellor filled his chair, a scowl bridging well-padded cheeks. The edge of his silk robe fluttered in the breeze streaming through the large windows. Behind him, the city spilled down the hill, ending at the lake.

A map of the island covered one wall. On another, a pompous portrait of the chancellor hung above a crackling fireplace. And beside the fireplace rested a gleaming bronze fire poker.

The chancellor inclined his head towards the pair of chairs opposite him, and they sat.

'I'm feeling flushed. Is there a chance you'd consider putting the fire out?' Cal asked.

'Who taught you manners, you tadpole? This is my office.'

'Yes, of course.' Cal lowered his head. 'My apologies.'

'You're getting married soon. You'll have to get used to the room being the temperature of another's choosing.'

Brayan engineered a laugh. Cal tried as well; however, it came out more like a cough.

The chancellor held up his hand. His small eyes held the reflection of flickering flames. 'Someone stole my urlire.' His voice was colder and darker than the deepest part of the lake.

'We will find it,' Brayan replied.

'With the gift of foresight, you should've stopped it before it occurred.'

'Yes, my apologies.'

'Our apologies,' Cal added.

Brayan shot him a look. A clear message: shut up. Cal crossed his legs. Few things were rarer or more valuable than a urlire. All mages coveted the storage jewel. After all, even the most powerful could only store so many madriliks in their chest. A mage with a urlire had that much more power for spells at their fingertips.

'I need you properly incentivised.' The chancellor gripped the armrests and pushed to stand. He shuffled over to the fireplace. Above a bed of white coal, flames leapt around a stack of cracked, blackened logs.

Cal cleared his throat. 'Sorry, Chancellor, the smoke is irritating my eyes and throat. Maybe we could continue this discussion on the balcony?'

'What is it about the fire that has you so worried?' His hand wasn't far from the gentle curves of the poker's handle.

Cal wrapped his arms around his body, fingers finding his ribs.

Brayan sat straighter.

The chancellor reached up to the mantel and grasped a jar of smoked glass. He carried it over to Brayan and opened the lid. A thick liquid drank in the light. Squid ink.

The seer dipped two trembling fingers in and smeared a line of ink across each cheek. The mark of the Disgraced.

Cal readied himself to do likewise, unsure how he'd explain this to his mum, much less anyone else. His breath came fast and short. Had he kept himself open to his goddess? Spent enough time in prayer? Visions were as predictable as dreams, but still, he couldn't help but feel he'd failed his master.

The chancellor closed the lid and returned the jar to its resting place above the fire, leaving Cal's cheeks unmarked. 'You will find my urlire.'

Rayvic opened the double doors.

Cal leapt up and scurried out, having to restrain himself from running. Life and freedom awaited in the fresh air outside. They never should've gone into the room. He'd had nightmares of being eaten alive that'd felt more pleasant.

'This'll cost you your wedding,' Rayvic whispered as Cal passed him. 'And so much more.'

So *much more*. That was a more effective twist of the knife by the herald. With ink on his master's face, they were a rung away from dead in the gutter.

Brayan emerged next, and his hands shook through Parliament's corridors and down its front steps. Cal struggled to find the right words to comfort his master. People passed them silently, deviating wide of them, and began whispering to themselves.

'I was clear,' Brayan said, a sharp edge in his voice. 'I would handle the meeting. I even warned you during it. Still, you opened that big mouth of yours.'

Cal hung his head. He'd disobeyed his master. It hadn't helped either. *Who taught you manners, you tadpole?*

The seer brought a hand to his face and glared at Cal through a cage of fingers. 'Look at my cheeks. Look what you caused.'

'I was trying to help, to save—'

'Not just my shame,' Brayan shouted over him, 'but yours too!'

And it was. The shame of a master fell upon their apprentice. Cal's thoughts swirled faster and ever darker.

Brayan stopped, his gaze transfixed upon a sun-bleached skeletal tree atop the hill. Long, twisting branches extended from its cracked, worn trunk.

There was something about that lonely dead tree. Something important.

They used to anoint seers there, but they stopped. Cal rubbed the roof of his mouth with his tongue, sifting through history lessons on past seers. When the sixth seer became deaf, he continued in his duties. But when the ninth went blind, he'd lost the gift of foresight. Cal dragged his feet. *The ninth hanged himself on that tree.*

If the chancellor took Brayan's sight, his foresight would be lost too. A blind seer was no seer at all.

4. Forbidden

Crisp, delicate snow crunched underfoot. Antarna pushed off a rough rock. Sunlight glinted off ice clinging to five stone columns to her right. She took the path to them, a small detour from the summit track. The gale tore at her cloak. For years she'd hungered for answers. *And now that I have them, I wish I'd never found them.*

The columns rose over her, an altar to Zentrina. She brought two fingers to the centre of her forehead, finding comfort in the pressure on her spiritual third eye. *My goddess, why him?*

Cold seeped through her boots. She didn't expect Zentrina to answer.

Antarna resumed her climb. The summit loomed over her. She passed a boulder carved to depict the mountain with a river of madriliks coursing through its heart and bursting from the peak. A single word had been hammered above the picture: D A N G E R.

A couple of dozen madriliks were fatal for a non-mage. Her grandfather had been murdered with them. Yet this source of power was also the reason for the temple's location.

The air thinned, and the whistle of the wind intensified into a howl, stealing her body heat. She pinched her nose and blew into it; her ears gave a tiny pop.

A unique tree crowned the summit. Transparent, it resembled an ice sculpture. Delicate branches absent leaves extended from a slender trunk. The plant sparkled as if to outshine the stars, basking in the torrent of madriliks rising from the peak—unseen except by mages and seers.

Death had a most beautiful signpost.

Red stones ringed the plant, a reminder of the threat. Antarna stopped before them. Lifting her hand, gentle heat from the tree permeated her glove. Enthriff unwound from her wrist and slithered down her waiting hand and between her fingers. After securing his tail to her middle finger, he lengthened and straightened. A glow spread down his body. Like the dazzling tree, he fed on madriliks. His body grew warmer. Her exhale misted the air. Finally satisfied, Enthriff withdrew back to her hand.

Grass plains stretched from the base of the mountain range. They gradually gave way to a dense rainforest. Above the vibrant canopy rose the dark rim of the crater. Some said it once erupted with lava, while others argued it was formed by the impact of a celestial rock. And, naturally, there were those that attributed it to the work of the gods.

Further on, a lake with an island in its centre sat surrounded by forest. Maybe someday she'd visit with Tozias. Then again, the Resatrium had spread there in recent years—*like the plague they are.* With their power growing, she needed to strengthen her own.

She'd come too far in her training under Gil to turn back now. From the moment, all those years ago, when Gil had harnessed the power in his soul to crush a rock larger than her head in his bare hands, she'd committed herself to the goal as if her life depended on it. And it did: the Resatrium assassin that had taken the lives of her mother and brother would strike again.

On a cloudless day, one could glimpse the ocean on the horizon. Today was not such a day.

Antarna pivoted and headed back. On the steepest sections, she gripped the knotted guide rope—never touching the seventh knot. Otherwise, with her hands deep in her pockets, her feet knew the way.

By the time Antarna returned to the temple, her breathing was laboured. She found Tozias on his favourite balcony, whittling a piece of wood into the shape of a shell like an open fan. Antarna had learnt many a fish name from enquiring about his carvings. The wind whipped by them, the balcony sheltered and secluded. She dropped down onto the rug beside him.

He nudged her with his shoulder. 'Want to talk about it?'

'Later.'

She opened his bag. Flatbread and cheese waited inside. Antarna tore a piece off, added cheese and fed Tozias; then she made herself one.

The sun dropped in the sky, tired from its labour. With each smooth, deft slice of Tozias's carving knife, a wood shaving fell to dot his robe. He added striations to the exterior of the shell.

Below, a lone figure ascended the path to the temple. Antarna blinked. The temple saw more shooting stars than visitors. An assassin? No, he lacked his upper limbs. The wind bent the trees yet didn't rustle the man's dark hair or snatch at his clothes.

A chill overtook her from the inside out. A decade had passed since the armless had teleported her to the mountains at Father's request while the bodies of her mother and brother were still warm. Questions from that day remained unanswered. Her father had promised answers and to apprehend the killer. He'd delivered neither.

Antarna leant towards the balcony's edge. The thin, golden chain around the priest's neck complemented his umber skin, darker and with fewer red tones than her own. His features marked him as one of the crater. The man wore a crimson robe, as all armless did. But his was notable for its black trim—signifying his rank as high priest of the temple of magic.

'You seeing what I am?' She scarcely trusted her eyes. 'The trim.'

Tozias squinted, then swore. 'That's Arric.'

'What's he doing here?' she whispered.

'Your guess is as good as mine. Here to see our high priest?'

'Yes, but why?' An in-person meeting of high priests was monumental. She couldn't take another unanswered question. And there was a way to know.

'No, not that look.' He dropped his head.

Antarna gave him her best expression of innocence. 'What look?'

'You're thinking of listening in. Are you ...'

Crazy? Looking to get expelled? 'Spit it out.'

'A woman with a plan?'

'Yes. Yes, I am.'

He pocketed his carving and spread his webbed hands towards the door, inviting her to lead the way.

She assigned Tozias to keep watch by the library and then leapt down the stairs, knowing just where to pick up the trail of the orphan-turned-hero.

Antarna followed Arric through the temple, maintaining her distance. She placed her toes and the ball of her foot down lightly before letting her weight come onto her heel—leaving a faint trail of footprints through disused temple passageways.

His feet never touched the floor. They landed close enough to stir the dust, though, encouraging it to dance in pale shafts of moonlight.

The mountain wind settled and whispered as though it had a secret to share. The man's robe swished softer still. The material was far too thin for the mountain. If he had a message from the crater, Antarna had to hear it.

Arric turned with confidence, as if well-acquainted with the convoluted route. By his direction, he was indeed headed to meet with her high priest.

She took another path. Striding down the passageway, she readjusted the thin string that kept her hair from brushing her shoulders.

Reserved for priests, the next passageway was forbidden to her. Antarna entered anyway. Incense hung in the air. Doors lined the right side. From the second one, candlelight escaped through a slender gap between the door and the floor, accompanied by murmured prayers. She slunk past. Someone shifted in their bed. If caught, she'd face extra duties or be relegated back to being a lowly initiate. It was almost enough to make her turn back, but something pulled her forwards.

A hoarse rumble emanated from the next room, startling her. She froze. The snore fell away before rising again. She continued.

The passageway opened into a larger corridor. A figure of the right height and build walked in the shadows.

Arric disappeared around a corner. Antarna turned too and strolled down a long parallel corridor. She stopped and bent down as if to tighten the straps of her thick-soled boots of kirikas fibre. Enthriff slithered down from her arm. He stopped before a crack in the wall and looked back at her. Eavesdropping on the high priest in his private quarters risked expulsion. Still, she waved him on—High Priest Arric could be here with dire news of the crater, like a Resatrium attack. Enthriff entered, melting into the darkness.

Rubbing her naked wrist, Antarna stood. The corridor contained nothing to hide behind. She was exposed, vulnerable. Fortunately, she wasn't solely reliant on luck tonight to avoid discovery. Positioned at the library's entrance, Tozias would signal if a priest inside headed to bed.

The wind gusted, rattling the shutters. Beams of soft moonlight snuck in, sliding across rough-hewn stones and illuminating an intricate carving of her goddess. Antarna outstretched her arm until her fingers brushed the cold grey stone.

She carefully unlatched the shutters, wincing at the soft scrape of metal, and opened them wide enough to lean her head through. Wind buffeted her face. Worn down by the elements, the outer walls had little purchase to offer. If someone approached, could she hide outside? Holding on long enough for a priest to walk the length of the corridor would be difficult, not to mention the risk of a gust ripping her free. Far below, large, pointed rocks awaited. Antarna closed the shutters.

She crept down the corridor and put her ear to a door. After a short, uneventful wait, she tried the handle. But it was locked. Antarna retreated, sank beside the crack in the wall and began to count. Better that than to guess at the conversation happening on the other side of the wall. She flinched at imagined movements, unable to overcome her deepening unease. *Come on, Enthriff.* Her count hit triple figures.

Chirps and whistles echoed through the temple, a barely passable imitation of an ice-beaked ripet. Tozias needed to work on his bird calls. Antarna tapped the wall twice beside the crack. *Time to go, Enthriff.*

As the warning faded, the sharp sound of boots on hard stone rang out. Her chest tightened.

Long moments dragged by.

She tapped again. *Hurry*. Antarna stood, back rigid.

At the entrance to the corridor, light chased away darkness, steady and unwavering. With each footfall, it grew brighter.

Priest Yerkinfall appeared holding a cancryst, his skin as pale as the moon. The cancryst in his hand bathed him in its harsh light.

He approached, his lips thinning. 'This is intolerable.'

'I'm sorry, I—'

'I don't want to hear it. You're under sanction.'

There was no talking him out of it. She groaned inwardly. No hot food. No leaving the temple. No practice fights. Extra cleaning.

Enthriff slithered up her ankle. She hid her momentary relief—easy to do when facing Yerkinfall's wrath.

'And we'll see what the high priest has to say about this tomorrow. I'd suggest packing your bags.' Yerkinfall sent her on her way.

He may as well have said the word: expulsion. He may as well have taken a knife to her. With footsteps slow and soft, Antarna moved through temple's corridors, preserving their solemn silence.

Tozias sat on the bottom step of a staircase, whittling. He looked up and sheathed his carving knife. 'Why have a lookout if you're going to chat with whoever comes by?'

'You needed the practice,' she replied, trying not to sound downcast. 'That ice-beaked ripet sounded as though it was choking on an insect.'

He laughed. 'How much trouble are you in?'

'We'll see tomorrow.' She didn't want to think about it, yet worry consumed half of her, at least. She couldn't leave now, not when she was close to answers about her past life.

'It better be worth it.'

'Let's find out.' Antarna sat beside him and extended an open hand to her ankle. Enthriff crawled onto her palm and curled into the shape of an ear. 'Yes, we're ready. What did you overhear?' She turned to Tozias. 'No guessing this time. You're awful at it.'

'Am not.'

'Just then, you thought his outline of an ear was a shell, didn't you?'

He shook his head, smiling.

'Last week, you thought a tree was a broom and a spear was a candle.'

He wagged a finger at her. 'I was close.'

'And when you worried that Enthriff's drawing of a bird returning to its nest meant a fly had died in your hair?'

Re-enacting that day, Tozias flicked his unkempt hair forwards. Strands narrowly missed her before falling to cover his face. He shook his head like a waterlogged animal trying to dry itself. Something small flew out: a wood shaving from his whittling. He leant closer, and she pushed him back, chuckling.

She lowered Enthriff to the stone floor. He formed a circle with his slender body, then constricted.

'Danger,' she whispered.

His body changed into the shape of a house. No, a temple.

'Danger to the temple. What kind?' she asked.

Enthriff dabbed his tail into the dust, leaving a circular impression. Above it, he curved his body into the remainder of a question mark.

'They didn't say. But the armless came to warn us. What did he want our high priest to do?'

This time, Enthriff drew two arches and then slithered through one to the other.

'Teleport away?'

He nodded.

'Abandon the temple ...' It was unthinkable, unfathomable. 'What did the high priest say?'

He crisscrossed his body into the shape of an X.

'No.' She scooped Enthriff up. 'Good. Nice work, bud. Thanks.'

She rose and paced the room—on stone laid centuries ago, in this most holy location where prayers to her goddess had been said every day since its construction.

Tozias dropped his elbows onto his knees and rested his chin in cupped hands. 'The danger has to be—'

'Cataclysmic.' She balled her fists.

'A flyer or other beast?'

'Up this high?' She waved a hand through the thin, cold air. 'And we've got the wards, walls and priests.'

'An earthquake, then?'

'The armless wouldn't know in advance.'

He shrugged.

She sat beside him and rested her head on his warm, solid shoulder—a comfort she clung to. His chest rose and fell with his steady breath. A calmness she wished for as her heart pounded.

The Resatrium's behind the threat. They must be.

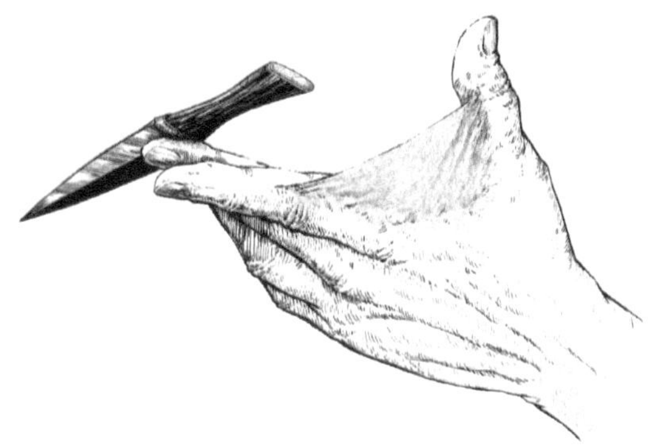

5. You'll Lose Everything

Cal stopped outside the only shop on the street without windows. He slipped his hand into his bag, and his fingers found the smooth jade statue Brayan had tasked him with selling.

Why here of all places?

Mustering confidence, Cal entered. Cabinets, tables and shelves overflowed with dusty scrolls, rare amulets, animal skeletons and a thousand curiosities. Cal gave the jar of preserved ears a wide berth. Incense hung heavy in the air, irritating his eyes. At least Brayan and he still had their eyes. Cal shivered, recalling the hot poker. His vision may not have come to pass yesterday, but it might today if they didn't find the urlire. And yet, instead of searching for the jewel, here Cal was, in the lair of an odious, slimy toad of a man—although a discreet one.

Gionco hunched behind the counter, his bulging eyes set beneath a prominent brow. Warts dotted his dry skin. 'Seeking or selling, seer-in-training?' His tongue darted out to wet his lips.

Cal put the jade statue of a crustrearon onto the wooden counter. Its eight limbs, spiked shell and tail with a pincer had been captured in striking detail. Gionco caressed the statue, akin to how a parent would stroke the hair of their slumbering child. Rings gleamed upon his fat fingers.

You'd sell the hair off your child's head for the right price, wouldn't you? Cal waited until Gionco raised his gaze. 'We'll agree upon fifteen bronze whirls.'

'Will we?' Gionco rested his pointy chin onto his hands.

Cal did his best to look bored, as if this was a foregone conclusion. It would've been easier if his heart wasn't beating so fast.

'We will,' conceded Gionco. He closed his hands around his purchase and disappeared out back.

Candlelight illuminated an array of artefacts mounted to the back wall. Gionco had a small section devoted to the Unjust Uprising. An old, stringless bow with a nut carved above the grip. A shattered knife: more than a dozen shards of volcanic glass painstakingly reassembled, slender and symmetrical. Another knife of plain stone. This called to Cal, silent but singing, still but shifting.

'You have a good eye,' Gionco said in a smooth voice as he slipped out of the shadows. 'That was Arric's.'

When he was a poor orphan. Before the fame and the power. Before he joined the temple of magic and rose through the ranks to become their high priest.

'A real prize.' Gionco withdrew a purse of jingling coins from his pocket.

Cal accepted the purse from him and counted its contents.

'You'd need more for the knife, but I have many treasures. Maybe I could interest you in another from the Unjust Uprising?'

Purse in hand, Cal made for the front door.

Gionco chuckled. 'Until next time.'

I hope not.

The door creaked shut behind him.

People streamed towards the foreshore. With the sun up and curfew over, they were eager to make the most of their day. Squinting against the morning light, Cal turned for home.

A group of three glanced at him, then looked away. A pair of old ladies whispered. Cal cut down a side street. A woman walked hand in hand with her daughter, shells swinging from her earlobes. Once, sand-dwelling snails with venomous barbs would have called those slender, spiralled shells home. As Cal drew near, she pulled her daughter into her arms and mounted the curb. Behind them, a couple broke hands and pressed themselves against the outside wall of the closest building. When they'd passed Cal, the couple stepped down, and their hands met again.

He emerged onto a main thoroughfare. Again, residents cleared a path for him, as if pus-filled boils and weeping sores claimed his skin. Well, more accurately, as if his face bore the same ink as his master's. It may as well have. But Brayan, with his elevated position, had so much further to fall than Cal.

Thelia, my goddess, I'll give up whatever you ask to make this right. Please let me make this right.

A woman waved men towards her stand of hair growth vials. 'Special price for a special elixir.' Her double chin wobbled as she spoke. It had more than a few strands of hair on it, as did her upper lip.

Been testing your wares?

Even with him holding a bulging coin purse, the vendors and hawkers left Cal alone. *What do you need the coin for, Brayan?*

Outside the tavern, two men played Glory. Each had a hand on the table—palm-down and fingers splayed—and held a knife at the ready in their other.

'Go,' shouted the game master.

The pair stabbed behind their thumbs, proceeding to the space between their thumb and forefinger, trying not to cut themselves. Around them, the crowd cheered and jeered. Cal rubbed the webbing between his fingers.

Front door after front door bore carvings of Lablias. The god of water rode waves, fought serpents, drowned villains and saved the feeble. One door in the street had carvings of Thelia, the goddess of sight. Cal approached the two-storey residence of seers and knocked. After nine months, it still didn't feel like home.

The door opened. Nalgrid stood hunched in the hallway, portraits of twenty past seers hanging down its length. Dust speckled the attendant's crisp, dark shirt. Perhaps Cal had interrupted him cleaning.

'Thanks.' Cal stepped inside. 'Brayan still in?'

'He is.' Nalgrid closed the door quietly behind him.

As Cal passed through the hallway, he touched the corners of the three portraits of the True Seers—those who had risked their lives and acted with valour to avoid a dark future coming to bear. He emerged into a sunlit courtyard.

A pile of bags, baskets and pots sat atop a handcart. Brayan's favourite broad-brimmed hat peeked out from the top of one of the bags.

A lump grew in Cal's throat. *And I'd thought foresight would lessen the surprises.*

Rounding the cart, Brayan extended his hand. 'How did you fare?'

The seer's fine hair should've been carefully combed and oiled back, yet it spilled over his forehead—as if it could act as a shield and protect his eyes.

'Better than you'd expected; almost what I'd hoped for.' Cal held the purse above Brayan's waiting hand. 'Are you going to tell me why we sold the statue? And what's with the cart?'

'Just some precautionary measures.'

Cal dropped the purse.

Brayan weighed the coins, shifting them in his palms. 'Not bad, my boy.'

Cal smiled. His father used to call him that.

'Come on,' Brayan said. 'The chancellor has summoned us.'

Naught but danger awaited. Cal felt faint. His vision hadn't come true the first time, but visions didn't come with precise timelines, as much as he wished they would.

'Did you foresee the urlire while I was out?' Cal asked, having tried and failed earlier. Brayan had promised he'd attempt it, too.

His master tensed. 'No.'

The chancellor can't expect us to have found it already. Yet the man was not known to be reasonable.

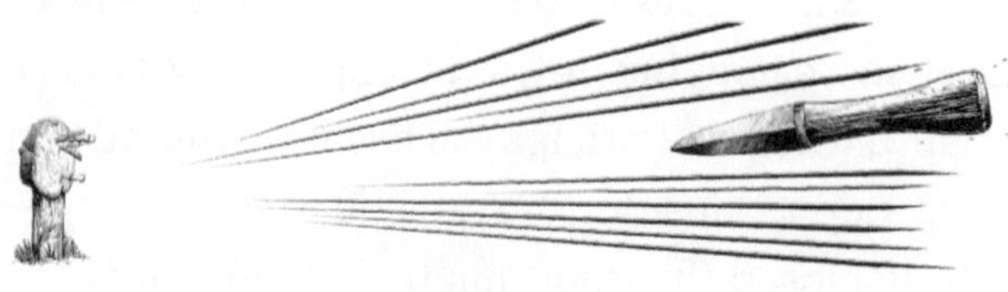

Out on the street, their presence brought as much cheer as curfew. Eyes looked away. Lips locked or voices dropped to a whisper. The path cleared before them.

'The power of fear,' Cal muttered.

Brayan ran his hand down his silver beard. 'I fear you'll be left cleaning up my mess.'

'I think you meant to say something like'—Cal cleared his throat and then resumed in a deeper voice—'fear is but an opportunity for courage, my boy.'

'That it is. We'll need it.'

Ominous.

The temple of magic cast a slender shadow upon the domed roof of Parliament Chamber—rather fitting given the temple's growing power. Its black stone made Parliament's pristine white structure that much brighter. The side wall of the temple bore a detailed carving of Devtakaris, depicting the god of magic from the waist up to highlight his lack of arms. The sculptor had carved away the stone around the god so that he rose out from the wall.

Brayan flicked a coin into the unlit alley between the buildings—as he did every day without fail. A filthy hand darted out and caught it. The hand of a beggar.

Pegnic emerged from the gloom, holding the coin aloft. 'My thanks, Seer.'

After fishing another coin from his pocket, Brayan tossed it over. 'In case I don't see you tomorrow.'

The coin spun end over end. Pegnic's long, dirty fingernails raked the sky, and then his hand closed around the copper. The coin disappeared into his tattered robe. 'What's coming?'

'Nothing good.'

Pulling a food scrap from his unruly beard, Pegnic flicked his gaze to the guards at the top of Parliament's steps, or maybe to Parliament itself. He melted back into the darkness of the alley.

Brayan took the steps one at a time, his back curved and his hands on his knees. The two steel keys on the necklace of seers, which resembled miniature swords, bounced against his chest. Keys passed down from seer to seer.

'Is there something you're not telling me?' Cal asked. 'Are you going somewhere?'

'Perhaps.'

To which question? Cal shook his head, recalling Brayan's words from their first day of training: "If you ask a second question before I've answered the first, you can't expect a straight answer to either."

Cal jumped a step to catch up to his teacher. 'Maybe there's good news. Maybe the urlire has been found.'

Brayan's tight lips and narrowed eye said it all: maybe not.

The guards at the front door let them through without a word. The pair stationed at the entry of the waiting room to the chancellor's office were no different.

Inside, Brayan wheeled on Cal. The seer fixed him with his hazel eyes. Brown flecked with gold swirled around his pupils, trickling into a stormy sea of green. 'When we get in there, don't say a word. Not a single word.' Brayan leant closer. 'Understood?'

'Yes.'

A servant entered carrying a silver tray with not one but two honeyed ciders. Cal accepted a crystal chalice and gave his thanks. With a drink in his hand and the waiting room empty, things were looking up, surely.

The double doors opened, revealing a slim man, his violet vest embroidered in golden thread with the face of the goddess of sight. His polished walking cane tapped against the hard floor—a ridiculous piece for a man in perfect health and only a few years older than Cal. Two bronze keys hung from a chain around his neck, imitating the necklace of seers. He'd had them made after Brayan chose to take Cal on instead of him.

'Mirogant, what are you doing here?' Brayan crossed his arms over his chest.

'You've got enough to worry about without adding that to your list.' The smug bastard ran two fingers over his cheek, imitating the ink staining the seer's face.

Cal bristled. 'What lies did you feed the chancellor, you water snake?'

'Shouldn't you already know? Is your training lacking, or have you fallen out of favour with our goddess?' He turned to the herald standing in the shadows of the chancellor's office. 'Thanks again for arranging access to the scene of the latest crime.'

'You're most welcome,' replied Rayvic.

Mirogant passed them without a second look, head high. If that try-hard would-be seer had the ear of the chancellor, then Brayan and Cal were replaceable. Expendable. Cal swallowed.

Rayvic admitted and announced them. The chancellor's scowl was deeper than yesterday.

Brayan stopped beside the chair he'd sat in the day before. Cal's hands rested by his sides. He moved to cross them in front of himself but then clasped them behind his back.

The chancellor indicated for them to sit.

With reluctance, they did.

A tongueless servant entered the room and added a log to the fire. Sparks kicked into the air. The log caught, the hungry fire tucking into its meal. It belched smoke. The servant departed.

'Who stole my egg?' The chancellor's hanging jowls wobbled as he spoke.

What egg? Cal bit his tongue.

'My urlire yesterday, my egg today.' The chancellor struggled out of his chair, then looked down on them. 'Who's behind it?'

'We will—' started Brayan.

'Provide an answer or nothing at all. I'll not take a mere promise to find the thief.'

Behind them, Rayvic lurked in the corner, his eyes wide and face flushed. His excitement only deepened Cal's unease.

The chancellor ambled over to the fireplace and took up the poker. 'I thought you'd be more useful.' He inserted the poker into the fire. Flames danced around the metal.

Brayan shrank in his chair.

The chancellor withdrew the glowing poker, twisted it, then inserted it back into the fire. Four burly guards stomped into the room, clubs dangling from their belts. The turquoise sleeves of their shirts extended from their boiled leather armour. They took their places around Brayan.

The heat from the fire washed over Cal. *Don't say a word.* He lowered his head. *Not a single word.* He'd disobeyed his master in the last meeting with the chancellor, and he couldn't repeat that mistake.

Carving circles in the air, the chancellor carried the poker over to Brayan, its bright yellow tip transitioning to red. 'How do you think I maintain my power?'

Lies, money and powerful friends. Cal held his tongue; he wasn't stupid.

The chancellor pointed the poker at Brayan's face. 'I don't tolerate failure.'

Brayan set his jaw.

The guards sprang into motion. One seized Brayan's left arm while another took hold of his right. A third guard secured his shoulders, and the last clasped the seer's head in his meaty hands. They'd done this before.

Cal scrunched his toes and tensed his legs, fighting the impulse to intervene—to do something to help.

The chancellor levelled the red-hot poker at Brayan's watering eye.

You'll lose your sight, your foresight, your position, your honour, your livelihood. Brayan, you'll lose everything. Cal opened his mouth, and then he shut it. Would speaking make it worse? Could it get worse?

The chancellor extended the poker.

Cal jumped to his feet. He couldn't let his vision come to pass. 'It was the Resatrium.' The words flew out before he could catch them.

The chancellor paused. 'You saw it?'

'Yes.' Lying wasn't strictly against the commandments of his goddess. And the rebels made sense. Well, more sense than the temple of magic or the crater. It also didn't hurt that the chancellor was known to be concerned about the rebels, who had spread to the lake island to oppose his use—his misuse—of power.

The chancellor lowered the tip of the poker.

Exhaling, pressure fell off Cal's chest.

Stepping forwards, the chancellor plunged the poker into Brayan's eye. Cal shielded his face and backed away, tripping over the chair. His shoulder broke his fall. The nauseating sizzle of flesh was drowned out by Brayan's tortured scream.

An acrid fog filled Cal's nose and mouth. Cal pushed himself up, swallowing bits of vomit. He rushed forwards.

A massive guard stepped in front and pushed Cal, the force lifting him off the ground. Cal flew backwards and smashed into something.

The chancellor stabbed the poker into the seer's other eye, which gave off a searing hiss.

Brayan would never see again. Not another sunrise or sunset, fish or coral. Not another person's face. Not even his own. And he'd never have another vision.

The chancellor plodded towards Cal, a sadistic smile upon his lips. The necklace of seers dangled from his hand, its keys clinking. He tossed it at Cal's feet. 'Find my egg, Seer.'

6. To Where it All Went Wrong

Zanth set the rectangular case down upon the boulder with the care he might show a babe.

An egg rested inside—beneath jadrossil hide stretched over a bone frame and nestled amongst feathers. A heating spell kept the egg at temperature, and he needn't recast it for a while.

Slipping open the false bottom of the case, he checked on the urlire. Its deep yellow facets stained the sunlight, and a horde of madriliks jostled within.

Soap of animal fat and wood ash clung to his beard. Zanth set to work with long strokes of his obsidian blade, shaving with the grain; he'd had enough adventure over the previous couple of days, and there was plenty more to come.

Clumps of black hair dropped to the ground, burying his feet. He shook the hair free, and it floated towards Silisa's cone-shaped headstone. Fine sky-blue veins ran through the black rock.

For you, my love. If she could see him now, she'd approve of the mission the Resatrium had tasked him with.

A north-easterly breeze stroked his naked cheeks. A few years of growth gone. Zanth cupped water from a rock pool onto his sensitive skin. When the water's surface settled, he found another man staring back at him, one with only a single triangle of hair below his lower lip, pointing to his chin. Dark, sunken skin lay under his eyes. Sleep often evaded those begging for it.

His night of tossing and turning hadn't brought him any closer to answers. Was he ready to return to the crater, where he'd lost Silisa? Could he infiltrate his former temple and avoid recognition? Would—

A piercing screech cut across the lake. Fury and loss clung to every note. Those he knew well. Maybe the creature's pain would fade; maybe it would fester. He'd left the mother with three of her four eggs.

The case lurched, and Zanth steadied it. The anti-magic trapped in the egg's shell was expected to bring down the ward to the inner chamber of the temple of magic's vault, granting him access to its most precious treasure. Assuming he got that far. First, he had to focus on getting to the crater.

Zanth changed into a light tunic with a thin band of royal purple on a sleeve—a robe of the enemy, recently stolen. Fifteen gems ran along the inside of his wide belt, orange specks of light floating within. Fakes, every one of them. On fastening the belt, one of the gems jabbed into his hip bone. He pulled the leather around, only for a gem to press against his spine. It took two more attempts to find a tolerable position. To finish, he wrapped himself in an old, coarse cloak. Zanth grabbed the rectangular case, a drawstring pouch, gloves, a knife and a scroll, then turned for the beach.

A madrilik danced along the shore, its light faint. Zanth's chest hummed with them already, his reservoir full to the brim, enabling him to cast even the most power-costly spells. If he were lucky, he'd get to melt the skin from his former master's face and boil the liquid in his eyes. *First, to the crater.*

His battered wooden canoe waited. With hands upon the stern, and straight arms and back, Zanth slid it through the sand and jumped in. Out on the clear water, the canoe was weightless. He immersed the blade of his paddle and leisurely pulled it alongside his craft. Rocks spanning every colour of the rainbow covered the lake bottom. Fish darted through pastel yellow forests of kelp. As the water grew deeper, the swaying kelp darkened to gold, then transitioned into greens. *Is this my last time on the lake?*

The bow of his canoe melted into the ring of thick fog that hid his tiny island. An ethereal white world swirled around him, cool and moist. After a series of sharp turns between treacherous rocks, he passed through the fog.

A spattering of canoes and boats dotted the water. Even so, the pier bustled with activity. Fishermen unloaded their catch. Several boats were docking, and others prepared to head out again. A group of boys gutted and scaled fish to a receptive crowd of birds. Girls lay salted fish on nets to dry. Fishmongers sold this morning's haul: an assortment of fish, clams, eels and water snakes, along with some night turtles.

Ancient, towering trees surrounded the lake. The forest harboured more ways to die than years it was old. Only those with a death wish attempted to trek to the crater—and the forest always granted their wish. Thankfully, Zanth had another mode of travel in mind.

He tied off to the pier. Frizzy algae clung to the wooden pillars. As he climbed onto the weathered platform, the rare nalitroite pendant on his necklace bounced against his skin. A necessary ingredient of his plan. Without it, there'd be no shortcut to the crater.

A group of children gawked, curious of his dark hair and skin when theirs was so pale. Most of the adults were more subtle, stealing sidelong glances. But some scrutinised him openly, eyes narrowed.

He left the shore, and the crowded streets moved well. Vendors lined the edges.

'Hot soup,' one called. Three pots bubbled in front of the man, kelp the strongest of the odours.

'Skewers. Buy two, get one free,' said the man beside him. Flames licked an assortment of meat and vegetables on the grill.

Further along, a plump woman pointed at him. 'Hello, handsome. Put some hair on that chin with a special elixir.'

Should've seen me this morning.

A pile of callamelons had been built on a rug, armpit high. Two halves rested on the corner of the rug, showing off the fruit's sweet magenta flesh encased in thick rind and tough peel. Zanth stopped at the stall beside it and bought a half-dozen boiled eggs, each dyed a different colour. He added these carefully into his case atop the egg he'd stolen.

Gradually, the streets grew wider and the buildings taller. Gravel crunched under his sandals, and the gems on the inside of his belt dug into his back. A temple to Devtakaris stood out from the other wooden structures, its black stone hewn from the crater's walls and painstakingly teleported to impress the lake islanders. They'd feel cheated if they saw the original temple of magic—carved into the wall of the crater from floor to rim.

A din rose, dozens of voices overlapping. Zanth turned the corner. A large group shuffled towards four guards clad in turquoise and leather. A guard inspected a woman's bag, another patted a youth down, and a third watched a fisherman remove his belt and then take off his shoes.

Flay me. Zanth adjusted his hood, hid an arm beneath his cloak, and put the other behind him, together with his case. Unfastening his belt would lead to questions he couldn't answer.

'Who are they looking for?' someone asked.

Not so much who, but what. They wouldn't be inspecting shoes if they were looking for the egg. So, they were after the urlire. For the guards to be this attentive, there must be an eye-watering reward on offer.

A baker rested his heaped basket against his flour-stained apron. 'I don't have time for this.' He turned and stomped off, the aroma of freshly baked bread trailing behind.

An apprentice blacksmith leant against his handcart, which gleamed with bronze spearheads and socketed chisels resting on a bed of straw. He turned to his master. 'Should we try another road?'

'No use. The guards have ringed the inner city, every street.' The smith dropped his huge hands to his hips.

Zanth fingered a fake gem pressing into his side. *I need a distraction.* A candle stood cold in a nearby windowsill. Smoke rose from a chimney a few buildings past the guards. Level with the guards, a man stood on his water-reed roof, making repairs. *You'll do.* The fall would break the man's leg, but he'd live. A small price when weighed against the importance of Zanth's mission to end the tyranny the Resatrium opposed. He focused on a madrilik in his reservoir, singling it out from the others and submitting it to his will—readying to use it to cast a spell.

Glancing over his shoulder, Zanth paused. Two mages approached with stores of madriliks bright as braziers of fire. Neither possessed more specks of power than Zanth.

Such comparisons had been the bane of his youth. He'd had the smallest store in the temple—and not a day had gone by without it being rubbed in his face. Hard work had fixed that, but then the acolytes had treated him like a short kid lucky to get a late growth spurt.

Zanth closed his hand over his nalitroite pendant. *Cloak me.* The veiling stone would hide his madriliks, making him appear as weak as all the regular people around him.

A respectful hush spread over the crowd, and they parted for the two crimson-robed priests of Devtakaris. Zanth's pendant dug into his hand, but he didn't loosen his grip. The pair of priests walked by him and continued past the guards, looking straight ahead.

The crowd lumbered forwards. A pregnant woman handed her bag over to a guard to riffle through. Next came the blacksmith and his apprentice, followed by Zanth. The priests proceeded down the street.

Still too close. You'll sense my spell. Zanth scrapped his intention to topple the man from the roof. Again, his hands found the fake gems running along the inside of his belt, and a new plan took shape. He dislodged a gem, nestling it in his palm.

The guard passed the bag back to the pregnant woman. Zanth advanced, aiming his foot for a rock that refused to sit flat amongst the worn gravel. The rock pressed through his sandal, digging into the ball of his foot. It wobbled under him. *You'll do nicely.* As Zanth transferred more of his weight onto the rock, it rolled, and he tripped, falling between the blacksmith and his apprentice. Zanth stretched out his arms. One hand caught the rim of the handcart; the other dropped the gem into the straw inside.

'Careful there,' said the blacksmith, his hand on the hilt of a fine dagger hanging from his belt.

'Loose stone, sorry.' Zanth took his hands off the cart. He would've raised them and spread his fingers, but his unwebbed hands would only attract attention. Instead, he stepped back. The guards, busy with their tasks, hadn't seemed to notice. Even still, Zanth's plan had risk.

The apprentice pushed the cart into the space between two guards. One guard patted the youth down. The other bent, rummaging through the cart.

Find it. Zanth tapped his fingers on his belt.

The guard straightened, something in his hand, and turned to the blacksmith. 'Who's this going to?' He lifted a bronze spearhead.

You useless sack of shit.

The blacksmith pointed to Parliament.

'Those guards get the best gear yet do none of the work.' He tossed the spearhead back into the cart. It landed with a clink, unlike the sound of metal on metal. He cocked his head to one side and dug back into the cart. This time, his hand emerged with the fake gem, orange lights twirling within. 'And what do we have here?'

'Uh …' The blacksmith stretched his neck towards the gem, eyes fixed on it. 'That's not ours. Never seen it before in my life.'

The apprentice shrugged. 'Maybe it fell into our cart?'

'It just happened to fall in there, did it?' The guard chuckled.

'This doesn't make sense,' said the blacksmith to himself.

'No, it doesn't.' The guard grasped the handle of his club.

The other guard grabbed the apprentice. 'You're coming with us.'

'No. This isn't necessary.' The blacksmith spun around as if he planned to appeal to the crowd. He stopped, locking eyes with Zanth. 'You.'

Zanth got ready to run.

The blacksmith drew his dagger. 'You—'

A club smacked upon the blacksmith's head. His eyes rolled back as he collapsed to the ground. Two guards threw him into his own cart and wheeled it off with the apprentice, now bound, in tow.

Halved in number, the remaining guards couldn't hope to get through all these people, not without reinforcements, taking short-cuts or long delays. One waved Zanth forwards. He remained stone-faced as Zanth slipped off his shoes and put his necklace on display without being asked. Only mages knew nalitroite when they saw it.

The guard's hands started on Zanth's chest. They slid down until they hit the belt, then checked the small of his back and his pockets.

Zanth did his best to look relaxed, even as he noticed a question brewing on the guard's lips.

'What's in the case?'

Zanth exposed the eggs, steam rising to greet the guard. 'Just cooked. Take one, please.'

'Don't mind if I do.' The man claimed his prize. 'On your way.'

That was close. Zanth strode down the street, adjusting his cloak so fresh air could get to the back of his damp neck. He passed a tailor, carpenter and weaver. The buildings abutted one another. By the entrance of a warehouse, a pair of hired muscle with spears stood, backs straight. The warehouse overshadowed the potter's narrow three-storey workshop.

On his pottery wheel, with elbows locked against his sides, Prann closed his hands around spinning clay. The mouth of the vase narrowed. The potter glanced up as Zanth entered his shop and mouthed, 'Be careful.'

The Resatrium would've told Prann just enough and no more. Aware of Zanth's planned intrusion into the neighbouring warehouse, Prann could deduce that Zanth was off to the crater, although the purpose would be a mystery. If tortured, the potter would have little to divulge.

Zanth climbed the stairs. On the second floor, towers of jars and vases rose to head height. Mugs, plates, platters and bowls filled the gaps. He weaved through to the left wall. Kneeling, Zanth removed a plug from a secret eyehole. The second storey of the warehouse sat empty, as it had been for the last week. He opened the concealed trap door, entered and tiptoed across the room.

Dust coated the wooden floorboards. Zanth lay down, crawled close to the stairwell and aligned his right eye with a gap between two boards. On the ground floor, four men worked in pairs, moving items from the back of the room into a square in its centre. The outline of the square pulsed a vibrant vermilion—the blood of starnakes thick upon the stone, too thick to have come from just one of the magical creatures. But, to the workers, it would've looked like red paint.

One pair carried a box of live crabs, their pincers and legs bound. The other pair moved jewellery, pearls clinking. Each were careful to step over, and not onto, the outline of the square. The pile grew, heaped with further delicacies and treasures that'd fetch a high price in the crater.

Two of the men went over to a large vase with the painted likeness of King Ithranned Tarlqua: a profile of his face, strategically from the left. The queen and their son were also featured, albeit on a smaller scale.

Careful with that. His mission hinged on hiding inside the vase. Prann had crafted it for him, though it looked smaller than expected. Would he fit?

They lifted it, took a couple of awkward steps and set it back down. After adjusting their grips, they tried again, waddling towards the square. As the pair crossed the vermilion border, one stumbled, and his grip slipped. The vase dropped, destined to shatter on the hard floor.

Zanth wanted to look away, but the looming catastrophe held him captive. He clawed the floorboard, powerless. Even if he could cast a spell in time, it'd give him away.

The blundering worker caught the ceramic rim with his fingertips. Grimacing, he halted the fall.

Zanth relaxed his hand.

'Lucky, you clumsy moron. If you destroyed this, Prann would've killed you,' the man said to his partner.

'Nah, he's too nice.' He kept his lips close together as he spoke. A huge moustache weighed down the top one.

'And how do you think the king would've taken the news?'

'Good thing I'm accountable to our chancellor, not their king.'

The pair finished moving the vase. Item after item was added around it until the square was full.

One of the hired muscles opened the door and leant in. 'Binyad's here.'

Right on time. His handcart followed the same route every day.

'Finally. I'm starving,' one replied.

The four workers put down their loads and exited with a spring in their step.

Zanth snuck downstairs to find the vase deep within the stacks. Too deep. With some items unstable and others unable to take his weight, he couldn't climb over them to reach the vase. Clearing a path with magic would rattle and clink the assortment. And, this close to the temple, any magic usage would have to be minimal.

The front door rested closed. It didn't take long to buy a pastry, though.

Specks of dust caught the light between the goods and the floorboards above. Zanth tuned in to the life force of magic and selected a madrilik from the tight ball within his chest. Drawing on its power, he rose into the air and floated over to the vase. As he reached for its lid, the door opened. With no time to hide, Zanth stilled his tightening, airborne body.

The moustached man entered with eyes locked on his pie. Zanth took cover behind a tall stack to his right, breathing easier.

Remembering the earlier stumble, Zanth formed a layer of ice ahead of the man. The worker's foot landed on it, and he slipped. Zanth removed the ice as the man landed hard on his backside. His pie took to the air before splattering on the floor.

Laughter sounded from beyond the door.

'We should rename you Graceful,' said one of the workers outside.

The man rose. 'Shut up. The god of luck hates me today.' He left, brushing pieces of pie off his clothes.

Zanth emerged from the shelter of the tall stack, floated to the vase, heaved off the lid and climbed in. With difficulty, and careful of his fingers, he lowered the lid back into place. His knees pressed against his shoulders, held in by hands crossed in front of his ankles. The case and scroll rested in the meagre space between his legs and chest.

As the wait lengthened, Zanth's back and neck cramped. Though, the discomfort paled in comparison to being torn limb from limb by a predator in the forest between the lake island and the crater.

To pass the time, he began to sort his store of madrilik, pushing the weakest specks towards his lower stomach, pulling the strongest to the top and leaving the rest in between. With his madrilik sorted into the three kinds—dulls at the bottom, brights at his heart and middlers fittingly in the middle—he could compare the proportions. A fifth were brights, releasing light of the greatest intensity. Half comprised of the commonplace dulls, useful for the least taxing spells. The rest, middlers.

If he could carry out the Resatrium's plan without a hitch, he'd barely need to dip into the reservoir of madrilik in his chest. But that assumed he'd refrain from killing his former master, Arric. He'd daydreamt so many ways to take the life of that putrid spawn of treachery.

The mission had to come first, though. The saphramurl gems were too powerful and dangerous for Arric to control. If they used them again to—

Footsteps punctuated the silence.

Four priests approached, with similar stores of madriliks. The clay-fired walls of the vase cloaked him in darkness but didn't block magical sight. Zanth took hold of his pendant.

The workers' conversation ceased mid-sentence.

'Is it ready?' asked a deep-voiced man. His tone commanded respect.

'Yes, Priest.'

The priests' soft shoes barely made a sound. They assumed their positions, one at each corner of the square.

A familiar chant rose. A few years ago—though it felt much, much longer—he'd practised the complicated teleportation spell with the others vying for priesthood. The demands it'd placed on his body and madriliks had almost killed him. Today, the priests would unknowingly do the work for him.

A powerful force rammed into Zanth from above.

Something tugged at every part of him. Fierce. Insistent. He focused on his right thumb, lest he be overwhelmed. The hairs and nail struggled to heave themselves free. The thumb kicked at its knuckle joints, trying simultaneously to sever itself in half and from the hand. The skin stretched from the muscle, and the muscle pulled away from the bone. It was like that all over his body. He was at war with himself.

Without noticeable transition, he separated. He wasn't ripped apart; there was no blood and no pain. Instead, he hung in multitudinous tear-shaped droplets, suspended in the air. Time had no meaning. After what could've been an instant or a decade, the droplets rushed together, coalescing. He reformed, and time applied once again.

The vase was as dark as ever, of course. Yet, on the magical plane, lights shimmered all around him. The square drawn in the blood of starnakes. Familiar temple wards. Bodies bright with madriliks.

He'd returned. To where it all began. To where it all went wrong. To where he'd lost his wife, Silisa.

The crater.

A nightmare in the flesh.

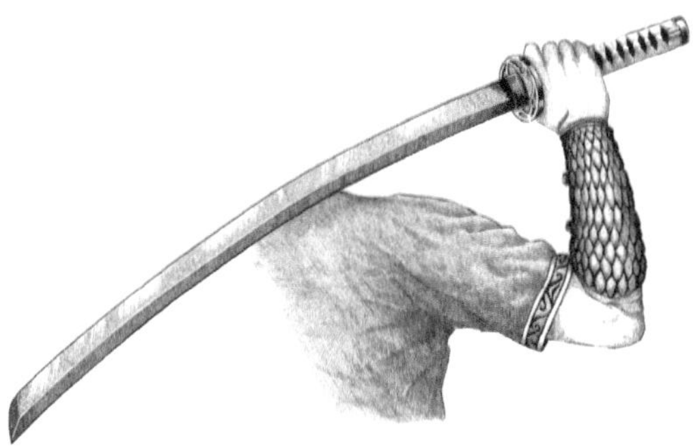

Darkness Massed

Antarna pulled the final bowl out of the darkening water and added it to the mountain of breakfast dishes she'd built to her left. The four initiates rostered on had been pleasantly surprised when they'd been told Antarna would handle the task alone. At least all she smelled was soap, unlike when she'd been assigned to empty chamber pots earlier this morning. One had been filled to the brim.

She smeared her water-soaked hands down her robe. The chores had given her too much time to think about her meeting with the high priest today and her pending punishment. Expulsion from the temple only seemed plausible if Inhaloc figured out she'd been eavesdropping on his private conversation. They had no evidence of that, but nothing got by Inhaloc.

She left the kitchen. Tozias was up the summit with Priest Chesare, but she couldn't leave the temple. With the temple under threat, he was safer up there.

Arriving at the training hall, Antarna removed her boots at the door. If the front shutters had been open, she could've seen out over the plains. The fighting ring took pride of place in the centre of the room. Priest Leharist supervised it, scars crisscrossing his strong, bare arms. On compacted sand, two fighters opposed each other, wrapped hands raised. Revertika circled broad-shouldered Uloron with quick foot-work. Uloron looked over his hands, waiting for his heavily tattooed opponent to come within range. Under sanction, the fighting ring was off-limits for Antarna today.

She grabbed two rolls of oil-softened jade wolf pelt. The thick brown fur had gentle hues of green from which the wolf took its name. Antarna wrapped her hands—leaving Enthriff uncovered—and made her way to a large strike bag. It hung from one of the many joists that spanned the room's width, supporting the pitched roof.

During this morning's pledges and prayers, the high priest had made no mention of his conversation with the armless. He'd chosen not to worry them. If she hadn't broken the rules, she'd be none the wiser. Evacuating the temple couldn't be necessary. Yet, Arric wouldn't have made the trip without good reason. Had the Resatrium threatened the temple?

Antarna unleashed upon the bag, determined to work up a sweat. Her jabs, crosses, hooks and uppercuts sliced the air at different angles. Each blow rustled the hulls inside the bag.

The snap of bone and a scream cut through the sounds of training. Eyes turned to the fighting circle. Uloron clasped his hands to his face. Blood seeped through his fingers and dripped down his chin.

Revertika stood taller, his chest expanding. A shiver ran through him as he licked his lips, the motion lingering as though savouring a sweet, forbidden taste. His eyes took on an unnatural shine, the pain empath revelling in Uloron's agony.

'A broken nose and you scream like you lost an eye. May it heal crooked as a reminder to keep your guard up,' said Leharist.

Antarna ran a few fingertips over the fibrous tissue that stretched down her right forearm. It was a powerful reminder not to extend her sword arm too far beyond the cover of her shield.

Leharist pointed over Uloron's shoulder. 'Get it tended to.'

As Uloron left the ring, Revertika bowed mockingly low. There was no greater victory for one of the desert than defeating another in single combat. The very best of them received the honour of having their tongue split, snakelike.

Leharist brought his staff down upon Revertika's back, and he fell face-first into the dirt. He rose and slunk away towards a grinning Divislak.

Enthriff exerted a sudden pressure upon her wrist. A dire warning.

She tensed.

Every shutter along the front wall burst inwards at the same time, latches snapping. The wind ripped weapons from hands and walls. It knocked people off their feet. These sounds mixed with cries of alarm and surprise.

Antarna dodged the bag as it swung for her. Then she braced, steadying herself with raised arms as an unnatural wind tore at her.

Something rammed into her gut, striking with more power than any punch she'd taken. Antarna doubled over, emptying her lungs.

The force didn't stop; it gripped her insides like a vice and twisted. Pain rippled out from her midsection.

Give her a foe to face. Was this magic? Yet that made little sense.

Antarna clutched her stomach, unable to breathe. Using the bag, she dragged herself upright. Her breath came back in gasps.

Close by, Divislak was on all fours, teeth clenched. Revertika emptied his guts. Behind him, Letti writhed on the floor. Her high-pitched cry joined a chorus of screams.

Antarna wished she could do something to help. Where was Zentrina while her loyal followers suffered so?

One by one, people raised hands to their temples. The pressure squeezing her head far surpassed that on her stomach. Antarna felt as if her eyes would burst, brain would liquify and skull would crack.

Don't scream. Antarna fought the pain.

The world blurred. She shook her head, closing and opening her eyes. Now even the light hurt, but she turned down the desire to shut her eyes again.

Mercifully, unconsciousness had taken Letti. Her chest rose and fell.

Blood oozed from Leharist's ear and ran from Divislak's nose. Drenched in sweat, Divislak continued to scream. Beside him, Revertika convulsed in a pool of his own vomit. His limbs jerked and spasmed.

Antarna had to get to him, roll him onto his side and protect his head. She released the bag, stumbled and fell.

A roaring boom resounded through the room, louder than any clap of thunder. It sounded like it had come from a floor or two below.

Shimmering zigzag lines snaked across her field of vision. Antarna brought her hands to her throbbing eyes. She'd expected the gentle massage to provide relief, but her fingers were flaming torches upon her eyelids. Her body responded, eyes welling and then dripping. Her vision cleared.

Revertika lay frighteningly still.

Agony was written on Divislak's straining face. He was covered in his own blood.

Bright red patches spread across the whites of Leharist's eyes.

Pain was nought but a flushed child throwing a tantrum for the attention. Its screams echoed through every part of her, and they only intensified with each moment she didn't act upon its message: this was life-threatening. It would not be ignored. Still, she crawled towards those needing her assistance.

Buried memories began to surface. She saw herself lying on a healing bed in the temple of the goddess of life, Preslina. There, she'd become intimately acquainted with suffering.

Antarna shoved the memories back and fought to regain control of herself. Her body demanded that she stop moving and make herself small.

All storms pass, Antarna said to herself, as Father used to tell her. She clung desperately to that thought, a buoyant flotsam in a sea of hurt.

The fury inside her tore at her mind. She tried to form another thought, but it was consumed. Her world was pain and pain alone.

Darkness massed within and stretched out an enticing hand. She knocked it back; she was no use to anyone unconscious.

Time dragged.

The darkness continued to reach its hand out to her, over and over. Each time, Antarna rebuffed it, pushing herself further and further beyond any limit she'd known.

Finally, the darkness took away her choice.

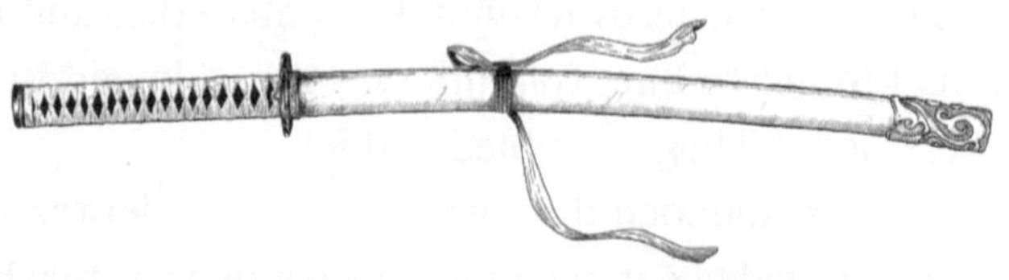

Barbed vines chased Antarna.

She sprinted in the dark, barely able to see more than six steps ahead.

A curling vine snatched at her ankle. Antarna leapt forwards, and it just missed.

She landed hard. Something grabbed her; she wasn't sure where, only that it had her now.

'Antarna.' The voice was soft and ethereal.

The vines were gone. The darkness fled. And a hand rubbed her shoulder.

'Antarna.'

She snapped her eyes open.

It was bright. A figure stood over her. Slowly, they came into focus. Sharp nose. Blue eyes.

Priest Leharist.

Antarna tried to rise, but her limbs were heavy and unresponsive. Enthriff applied gentle pressure to her wrist.

Leharist extended a hand. She took it and rose. The floor felt unsteady, as if she stood in mud instead of on smooth wooden floorboards.

'What happened?' Antarna asked.

'We don't know.'

Dried blood caked the priest's neck and ears. It stained the shoulders of his grey robe.

How much time for blood to dry? 'Was I out long?'

'Not much longer than me.'

Weapons littered the floor, together with hand wraps, pads, cups, water bladders and countless other objects. Most of the initiates and acolytes sat or lay down.

Divislak knelt over Revertika.

'Is he ...?' Antarna started.

Leharist placed a reassuring hand on her shoulder.

A young initiate lay unmoving, his arms and legs stretched at unusual angles. Another rested on his side, curled into a ball.

'Are they ...?' she asked.

Leharist squeezed her shoulder. 'They have passed on. I'm sorry.'

A tear ran down Antarna's cheek, swiftly followed by another.

TOZIAS? The thought struck like a lightning bolt. He could be injured, freezing to death upon the summit.

She staggered towards the door, her body sluggish. 'I have to find Tozias.'

'Be careful, please.'

In the hallway, a banner had fallen in a heap. She scooped it up and tied it around her waist. The fabric could form a handy sling or cape. Shards of broken cancrysts lay scattered across the hallway floor, sharp and gleaming. Antarna leapt over them, but her right foot landed awkwardly, rolling out. A jolt of pain radiated up her leg, bringing with it the fear of serious injury. With anything more than a minor sprain, she'd never make it to the summit.

Antarna forced herself to take a careful step, slowly adding weight to test the injury. Her ankle grudgingly took the burden.

Move.

Wincing, Antarna limped down the remaining length of the hallway. The image of Tozias lying bloodied and alone on the mountain burnt bright in her mind. She broke into a jog and entered the library. Toppled bookcases and upended desks blocked her route. Navigating them cost her valuable time, time Tozias might not be able to afford.

She palmed the door, and a strange red light entered through the gap. It filled the neighbouring passageway, flooding through the open shutters. Low blood-red clouds shrouded the mountain. They had none of the beauty of a sunset.

She left the temple behind her and pushed her reluctant limbs into a run. The steep gradient and loose stones troubled her ankle. If only she had time to be careful. She channelled the pain, urging herself to run faster. Her swinging arms helped to propel her up the slope. Strips of jade wolf pelt still bound her hands, and she struggled to unwrap them without slowing.

'Tozias!'

Rocks crunched under her feet, and her heart galloped in her ears. She couldn't catch her breath, the thin air no help, and she didn't care.

'Tozias!'

As she ascended, a weight grew upon her chest. At first, she'd passed it off as worry. But this was something more.

The rocks beneath her feet demanded her attention. But she couldn't help continually glancing up, hoping to see Tozias and the others making their way down the mountain track.

A figure emerged out of the cloud, lying on their side and facing away from Antarna. Her throat constricted.

It's not Tozias. Not Tozias. Please.

She couldn't take in what she saw. Antarna dug her nails into her palm. The details came to her slowly: their small body, thin limbs and dark hair. Clearly not Tozias—with his muscular build and unmissable red hair. The realisation brought no relief. A child of the crater and initiate of her temple lay before her, most likely dead. She sprinted the final steps.

Parsannon. He'd celebrated his tenth birthday only a few weeks ago, wearing a huge smile on his face the whole day. Within his open eyes, red filled the place where white should be. Blood had also escaped from his nose, ears and mouth. She felt for a pulse.

Please.

He was gone.

She closed his eyes, hung her head and brought her hands together. Inhaloc's words about Parsannon came back to her: 'You will make an exemplary priest one day.' If life was fair and just, he would have. How could her goddess take the young and the innocent? She sniffled.

'Zentrina, embrace him warmly.' It felt wrong to leave him, but she needed to press on to the summit. 'I'll come back for you.'

Within five steps, she accelerated into a run. Her ankle complained with increasing volume. Small, hardy plants with woody stalks clung to rocks and grew from crevasses. As she climbed higher, they became sparser.

Hope wavered inside her, but still, she nurtured it. Surely Tozias—older and larger and stronger than Parsannon—survived. Maybe he'd tripped and broken his leg ... That would explain why he hadn't descended.

The path steepened, and Antarna leant forwards against the incline, refusing to slow. Thick red clouds enveloped the peak, stronger in colour than when she'd set out.

'Tozias,' she cried.

A burning sensation spread across the skin on her arms. She'd felt it often as a little girl worried about whether her father would return from a hunt. Mother had sung to her to calm her down: 'Oh my child, don't let your imagination run wild. Rest, for I am here and hold you dear ...'

Rest was not an option.

A column of blood-red air stretched from the summit to the heavens and echoed throughout the cloud-enveloped sky. A sinister sight. The air shimmered, almost as if she was seeing madriliks for the first time, not that that was possible for her.

A gust pulled at the clouds. Bodies dotted the snowy ground, unmoving. Bloodied, frozen hands covered ears. Curled forms had made themselves small. The stench of vomit reached her.

Horror lashed Antarna, and hope died. The world reeled.

Off to the side, a tangle of red hair fluttered in the breeze. He sheltered behind a large boulder, arms around his knees and eyes closed.

'Tozias!' She dashed to him and extended a hand to his face. His cold skin met her touch. Blood marked his upper lip and chin but not his ears or neck. His chest did not rise or fall.

'Is he alive?' she asked Enthriff, her voice hoarse.

She prayed for two quick pulses from him—a yes. Anything but three pulses. Enthriff, however, was strangely still.

She lowered two fingers to Tozias's neck.

Please.

Live, Tozias.

Beat for me.

Please, Zentrina, please.

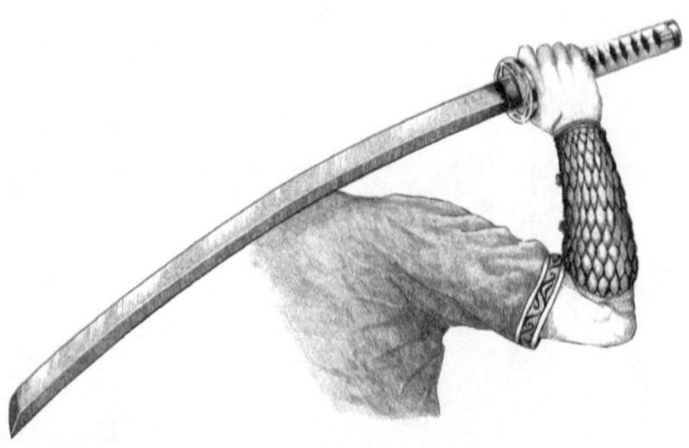

8. Burst its Banks

A faint pulse fluttered through Tozias's neck.

Sweet relief embraced Antarna, and dread fled before its light and warmth. *Thank you, Zentrina.*

She untied the banner from around her waist, unfurled it and put it around him. 'Hang in there, you hear me?'

She tore herself away from Tozias and quickly checked the others. Thick, dark yellow vomit covered the closest initiate. He'd passed on, as had the next two. Each were far too young to have died today. Her heavy heart threatened to crack.

Priest Chesare lay to her right, a deep gash running from his cheek to his crown. Copious amounts of blood pooled around his head and smeared the sharp rock beside him. She said a quick prayer for him.

Antarna shook her head, trying to clear it. A tear fell; she hadn't realised she'd been crying.

She still had bodies to check, and she went to them one-by-one. Only Tozias still clung to life, just. He needed warmth and a healer. Antarna returned to his side, pried his hands from his knees, looped her arms under his armpits and raised him to his feet. Her friend was heavier than he looked. While she embraced him, hug-like, his arms were limp, and his head lolled against her shoulder.

Antarna shuffled her leg between his feet and lifted his forearm over her head. Tozias's armpit rested on the nape of her neck—chilly when it should've been warm. She squatted and brought his body onto her shoulders. Standing, she adjusted him to better balance his weight.

Her first step woke her injury. Its anger spread to her foot and up through her lower leg. Her ankle looked as if it had swallowed another ankle.

With unequal steps, Antarna began the return journey. The steep gradient made for slow going. She only had her left hand to help her balance; her right held Tozias tight. Loose rocks littered the path, likely dislodged and scattered by the violent wind from earlier. She placed her feet carefully.

'I know you like a good nap.' The wind snatched at her words. 'But I need you to wake up, Tozias.' Maybe, even in his state, he could hear her. 'Remember when we hurtled down the slope on broken wooden panels? We skidded to a stop perilously close to that cliff edge.' How they'd laughed in the face of death. And what a glorious sound that had been. She'd give anything to hear him laugh again.

The next section was too steep to walk down. She tackled it facing backwards, with her left hand gripping the guide rope. By the end, her arm shook.

Parsannon's small form lay to the side. She again promised to be back for him and the others.

Her legs throbbed. Sharp bolts of pain ran from her knotted shoulders down her stiff back, but those had nothing on her ankle. Physical pain she could endure. Years ago, she'd arrived at the temple in agony, poison coursing through her veins. She'd hung in the hollow space between life and death.

Loss—further loss—terrified her. She wouldn't lose Tozias; she couldn't.

She had little breath and energy to talk, but if it could help, she had to. 'How about next week, you carry me down the mountain?' He'd probably drop her, then they'd laugh.

Zentrina's temple clung to the mountainside. The grey stone that blended in with the mountain was said to reflect that they were one with it, but maybe it'd been meant as camouflage, to hide them from danger.

Its infirmary saw plenty of cuts, stab wounds and breaks. But this was no ordinary case, and they lacked magic. Antarna continued down the path, heading for the place her father had trusted with her life all those years ago.

She passed the temple of Devtakaris, a squat, two-storey building constructed from dark stone. The four old armless who called it home rarely left its walls. They couldn't help her. While powerful, the devotees of the god of magic held no interest in healing.

One step, then the next. Finally, she arrived at Preslina's temple. In the current light, the white walls took on the colour of the sky. Antarna stepped over an uprooted babbling tree, much to her ankle's displeasure. These trees—named for their moans, murmurs and other sounds—had previously encircled the humble temple, their yellow-green canopies forming a halo overhead. Only a few still stood. The mountain breeze whistled through the fine slits in their trunks, and the sound was as eerie as the sky.

With the front door blocked by a fallen tree, Antarna approached the side entrance. The door didn't have a lock, and she opened it. Inside, heat gathered upon her cheeks. Jagged pieces of pottery lay scattered across the floor. She traversed them with care and made her way to a steep staircase—its steps simple, worn, and daunting in number. A cool stone wall called for her to rest against it.

'Almost there,' she said, as much for her benefit as his.

Leading with her left leg and with a hand on a wall for support, she found her first step manageable. Her right ankle wouldn't take the same level of punishment. So, instead, she lifted and dropped it beside her left foot on the same step. With her left leg responsible for the climb, her right limped along.

After the first six steps, Antarna paused. The seventh was too high and deep to skip. With Tozias across her shoulders, there was no way to jump the step. *It's just a number.* But it wasn't. It was at the heart of everything that had gone wrong that childhood day.

She rested against the wall, not bothering to scream for help. No one would hear. She hovered her foot over the seventh step. Tozias was far too still and cold.

Antarna took the step, getting on and off the unbearable stone as quickly as possible, and then left it behind.

Three-quarters of the way up, her left leg cramped. She refused to slow. At the top of the stairs, the corridor was empty. The next was as well. One turn later, she arrived at the infirmary. The injured filled the beds and lay on blankets on the stone floor. Blood marked faces, limbs and white robes. Groans and cries overtook her.

A flash of moss green broke through the red and white on the rim of a robe three beds away. Antarna limped over to the man who'd saved her life when she'd arrived from the crater. The high priest's long white hair was pinned into a top knot. He wound a cloth bandage around a wounded leg.

'Elgerin,' she said, her voice breaking. 'You need to save him, please.'

He turned, sending the dual plaits of his beard swinging. 'Let's get him down.'

They laid Tozias upon a double blanket on the floor. Elgerin held his hands over Tozias's body, starting from his head and working down to his toes. Afterwards, the high priest leant forwards to bring his torso directly over Tozias's. In a voice just above a whisper, he chanted. The ancient words took Antarna back to when she'd first been brought to the temple, close to death. *He'll save you too, Tozias.*

The chant finished, and Elgerin rose. Tozias's chest expanded and contracted, the beginning of a rhythmic cycle.

A great weight came off her. Antarna threw her hands around the high priest.

'Sorry.' She released the hug.

'That's quite alright.'

'I can't thank you enough. How is he? Will he wake soon?'

Elgerin took another blanket and spread it over Tozias. 'Let's get some fresh air.' He led the way to the balcony, from which he could still keep an eye on his packed infirmary. The wind was resting amidst the chaos. 'He's in a serious condition, but he's a fighter. We both know that.'

Antarna meant to nod but found herself shaking her head. 'I can't lose him too.'

'I know. I'll do everything I can.'

'What's wrong with him?'

'Overexposure to madriliks. He's been in contact with far too much of it. We all have. I managed to draw the residual madriliks out of him, but it's done a lot of damage.'

It explained why she hadn't been able to see what struck them, and how it had gotten through their wards. Everyone on the mountain knew the dangers of madriliks—reinforced by each trip to the summit, passing the boulder hammered with the word, D A N G E R.

'How is it at Zentrina's temple?' asked Elgerin.

'I don't have the words.' Antarna paused before continuing, looking out over the surrounding mountains but not taking them in. 'I didn't bring Tozias from there, though. He was up at the summit.'

'You carried him all the way down?'

Antarna nodded.

The high priest ran three fingers down a plait of his beard. 'He's lucky to be alive.'

'Why's that?'

'A strong river of madriliks runs inside this mountain and leaves at the peak, flowing into the sky. It's the reason that arm's length is the closest you can get to the summit. Today, the river burst its banks. Tozias should have drowned.'

'What caused it?'

Elgerin knelt before Antarna and gripped her ankle. 'If what I suspect is correct, this is going to hurt, a lot.'

Your healing never has before. She tensed.

Elgerin intoned five archaic words. His hand was a searing-hot coal. Something sharp stabbed at her stomach, not through the skin but from within. It was the first of many, as if her intestines were growing thorns. She exhaled slowly. Nausea overtook her. Pressure mounted on her chest and then started on her temples.

'There. We're done. I'm sorry.' Elgerin withdrew his hand.

Her pain made a quick retreat. 'Thanks.' A few pieces fell into place. 'Overexposure is why the healing hurt? Madriliks are stored in the chest and controlled by the brain, thus the two sites of the pain.'

'Yes, that's right.'

What caused it? But she knew better than to try her luck a second time. Instead, she said, 'I'll say my goodbyes before I leave.'

'Of course. And I'll send who I can over to your temple as soon as possible.'

'Thanks.' She brought two fingers to her forehead before dropping her hand to her heart.

He reciprocated.

Enjoying the freedom of movement in her ankle, Antarna returned to Tozias. 'You're in the best hands. You mustn't give up. Promise me.' She took his hand. Where before it was frigid, now it was cool. The mark of their goddess was strangely still on his forearm. 'I'll be back soon. Fight. You must fight.'

Enthriff travelled from her wrist, around Tozias's and then back to hers.

Antarna left the way she'd come. On the staircase, she avoided every seventh step. Outside, she rolled back her stiff shoulders, and they clicked.

Did that boulder save your life, Tozias? Or your distance from the summit? You were the oldest, apart from Chesare. The priest's bloodied face came to mind, his empty eyes open. She replaced it with the memory of him teaching her how to coax open a thistroll poppy.

With Tozias unconscious, she needed to see Gil—to know he was well.

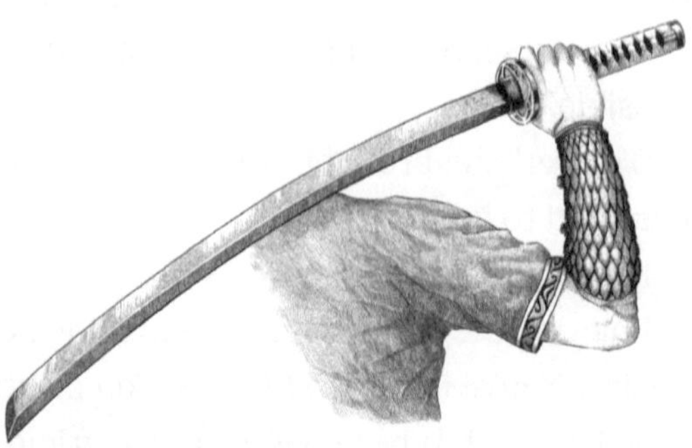

9. You've Been Warned

It was a short distance back to her temple. She'd always assumed that the priests only ever passed peacefully in their sleep. Priest Chesare's corpse proved otherwise. But if she could survive whatever struck, then Gil could, too. He'd probably been behind his locked door, poring over his hoard of literature on the former kingdom of Daslercia.

Antarna rounded the last corner. Smoke twirled skyward from Gil's third-storey room, escaping through gaps in the shutters. The charcoal-grey plume contrasted against the red sky. *Fire.*

Antarna broke into a sprint. All the paths through the temple to his room were convoluted, so she leapt upon the wall and began to climb. The stone sucked the warmth from her fingers. She slid her toes into a crack between stones and reached for a rough patch the wind was still smoothing. These holds got her to the first window ledge. With a swing, she jumped to the next ledge. Antarna skidded on the slippery stone and grabbed the sides to halt her. Given the lack of handholds and footholds, she went from window to window, horizontally at first, then vertically, grabbing the decorative stone above the window, hauling herself up, and jumping for the window ledge of the floor above.

Acrid smoke greeted her, pouring through the shutters on Gil's window. Wood crackled within.

'Gil!' she called.

Antarna kicked open the shutters, losing her balance for a moment in the process. Smoke engulfed her. A tongue of flame leapt up. She pulled away, covering her face, shutting her eyes and holding her breath.

'Is he in there?' She brought a thumb to Enthriff, praying for three squeezes: a no.

Enthriff applied pressure to her wrist and again. But no more. Gil was inside, which made no sense. She'd seen him punch through stone so thick she'd have struggled to shatter it with a war hammer. With the power he could access, he should've smashed through the door or a wall or leapt from the window. Unless he was severely injured. Or unconscious. Or dead. She swallowed her fear. If anyone could survive today, it'd be him.

After leaning wide and taking a gulp of fresh air, she launched herself into the room, feet first. Heat washed over her. Smoke stung her eyes, and blinking didn't help. She crawled into the room, the blistering stone searing her palms. Flames chewed at the bookcase spanning the length of the wall to her left and danced atop something beside the opposite wall—perhaps a bed. Charred remnants of Gil's beloved library hung in the hazy air, and sparks danced around them. She passed a wooden altar to her goddess, now a fiery pyre, and a table that had collapsed under its own weight. Her lungs screamed for air; she pursed her lips tighter.

With a thunderous crash, a bookcase toppled sideways, ablaze. She startled. Though Antarna couldn't make out the door, her recollection put it at where the bookcase had fallen. She'd have to move it to get out or leave the same way that she had entered.

Enthriff tightened his grip on the right side of her wrist. Antarna turned and scampered across the room on her hands and toes, bent knees just above the floor. Menacing flames licked her, hot and angry. Under a raised bed, a body lay unmoving. A white beard flowed onto the floor. Gil. Smoke invaded as she opened her mouth, and a cough racked her.

'Is he alive?' she asked Enthriff. If what she suspected was true, she didn't want to know.

Three pulses came the reply.

A scream welled within, and dizziness overtook her. The room spun. She dropped her head to the scorching floor and took a tentative breath through her robe. The bitter air was barely breathable. Resisting the urge to curl into a ball, she scrambled to his body, tears blurring her vision.

Gil's large eyes lingered open, bereft of their former lustre. Just this morning, they'd been more radiant than molten gold, full of life and deep with wisdom. Now, tarnished and dull and soulless, they exuded only death. Antarna closed them gently, and sound rushed back into her world. She hadn't realised she'd descended into silence until it shattered. The roaring inferno engulfed her senses.

I'll get you out of here.

She took Gil under the shoulders. His limp arms trailed on the floor, Zentrina's mark still. As she heaved him out from below the bed, her lower back tightened uncomfortably. Suffocating smoke deterred her from rising.

The climb down wouldn't be possible bearing his weight. She'd sooner die trying than callously tip his body out the window like a sack of flour. *If only I could access the power in my soul.* Not that that'd saved Gil from whatever had struck them. Bent over, she shuffled towards the door, dragging her mentor behind her.

The collapsed bookcase blocked the exit, half afire. Antarna laid Gil down, put her shoulder against the safer side of the furniture and pushed.

Out. Of. Her muscles strained. *My. Way.*

The thick wooden piece refused to budge. Her back foot slid further and further until she was forced to stand. The bookcase mocked her. May as well have laughed at her. What use was all her training if she couldn't move it? Gil needed her, and she was failing him. Antarna unleashed a front kick powerful enough to shatter a shin bone. Her boot met wood, and a jarring vibration reverberated up her leg. A satisfying splinter rose above the din.

Fire pressed her from all directions. Even climbed the walls, then rolled down from the ceiling. She refrained from looking to the window. *I will not yield. You taught me better than that, Gil.* Again, Antarna pitted herself against the charred wood and, channelling her swirling emotions, gave it everything she had. The bookshelf grudgingly slid enough for her to crack open the door.

She dragged her mentor from the room and slammed the door behind her. Flames gnawed at her robe, and she threw herself against the opposite wall, smothering them. Only when they were out did she realise she'd dropped Gil in her haste. *I'm sorry.*

Lightheaded and short of breath, Antarna gulped down fresh air between coughs. Her dry throat and ash-coated tongue craved water more than her throbbing hands and shoulder.

With faltering steps, she carried her mentor to the Sacred Hall, entering through one of the eight doors. In the centre, the liquid form of their goddess should have been tranquil, undulating with the gentlest of ripples. Instead, her cloak billowed behind her as if she walked against a gale.

A piece of folded parchment jutted out from Gil's pocket.

'Antarna.' Inhaloc's resonant voice carried to her with practised ease.

She snatched up the parchment, pocketed it and turned.

Her high priest swept towards her. Blood and grime flecked the sky-blue trim on his robe. His stooped shoulders, burdened with the weight of his responsibilities and the horrors of the day, contrasted against every memory she had of him.

Antarna stepped to the side to reveal Gil's body.

Inhaloc clasped a hand to his heart.

She bit her lip and fought back the tears.

'I'm so sorry.' His voice was soft. 'There was a fire?'

'Yes, in his room. It blazes still.'

'I'll have it taken care of.'

She told him of Chesare and the others up at the summit.

'We will get our people. Not today, though. The summit's too dangerous. How's Tozias?'

Antarna swallowed. 'He's unconscious, but in good hands.'

'You also need care. To the infirmary, please.'

'Yes, High Priest.'

They said their farewells.

Questions clawed at her. *Why didn't you evacuate the temple? How did the armless visitor know of the danger?*

In an empty corridor, Antarna opened the parchment. Gil had hastily scribbled, 'Happened before. At P'. When? She'd never heard of it. More importantly, where and how? She reread the barely legible words of her clue. The rounded loop of the P extended further across the stem than it should. This final letter only added to her curiosity and confusion. What place started with a P?

Antarna folded the parchment and made her way to the infirmary.

Uloron greeted her at the entrance. His broken nose had been reset. The infirmary was as packed as its counterpart at the temple of life.

'I'm on triage. You level?' He sounded almost like Tozias when he said it. The phrase was unique to the lake island, their equivalent of asking if someone was feeling well or doing alright.

She held up her blistered palms. When she'd asked Tozias about the phrase years ago, he'd replied, 'Embrace the level canoe, strong, steadfast and true.' Memories of him brought an ache to her chest. If he died, she'd be left with only memories.

Uloron pushed his blond hair out of the way to rub his forehead. 'I've got just the thing.' He led her to a shelf of jars.

'Have you ever heard of something like this happening before?' Antarna asked while he cleaned her hands with a liquid that stung.

'No. Can't imagine it ever has.' He applied a soothing grey salve to her blisters. 'There you go.'

'Thanks. Can I help?'

'We're fine. Go get cleaned up.'

Before leaving, Antarna found Letti on a nearby bed, comatose. Her complexion lacked its typical healthy flush, and a purple tinge clung to her lips. Instead of being serene, her unnatural stillness had a disturbing quality. As the fifth daughter of a pious family, a life with the temple should've been the safest path for her, and yet here Letti lay. If only there were a way to save her, Tozias and the others. *There must be one, right?*

Antarna headed to her bedroom, and Enthriff energetically circled Antarna's forearm. A lighter ring of skin was left from Enthriff's activity, showing the dirt and soot that marked her arms. She entered her room, closed the door and melted to the floor.

A collage of images whirled in her head. They flashed by, often several at once. She concentrated on her breathing, and the images slowed. There were so many of Tozias: laughing, scheming, training, lying unconscious at the summit. They were unordered. Came unbidden. Some arrived in pairs: Letti stretching this morning coupled with her writhing on the floor; Gil beating on his drum in the cave, then lifeless.

Antarna's eyes had adjusted to the darkness of the room. It was two steps to her wooden clothes chest and half a step from there to her sleeping mat. She'd find no reprieve from her memories here. With a clear mind, she also stood a chance to unlock the truth hidden in the parchment. Exhaling, she slid her back up the door, rising to her feet. Antarna collected a towel, a change of clothes and a thin strip of animal skin with wool on one side.

The corridor was deserted and eerily silent. She headed down a flight of stairs and then another.

An oval pool occupied the bath chamber, its deep blue water perfectly flat. Tozias had introduced her to it many years ago. She kindled a fire in the corner fireplace. As it grew, firelight licked the walls and reflected across the surface of the pool. Pops and hisses echoed off the stone yet were softened by the water. Sound had an unusual quality here.

Antarna scrubbed her hands and forearms in a bucket, churning the water black. Enthriff slunk to her upper arm. After stripping, she poured a clean bucket of water over her head and used a damp cloth to wipe herself down. Everything ached.

'Last chance,' Antarna said, looking down at Enthriff.

In reply, he wound the ends of his body together.

'Well, you've been warned.' Her voice was raspy from the smoke. She wrapped him in the animal skin, wool side against him and her skin. Enthriff could handle most things, but the cold wasn't one of them.

Antarna added more wood to the fire and hung her towel. A variety of cups, mugs and tankards adorned a nearby shelf. She ran two fingers down the line.

A bronze cup retrieved from Daslercia sat in last position. She filled it with water, added some tea leaves and placed it close to the fire.

Standing at the edge of the pool, Antarna took four slow breaths then one large and dived. Her hands broke the water.

One.

The frigid water stung her skin. It took three long strokes to reach the bottom of the pool. She pulled her knees to her chest and wrapped her arms around them. As she started to rise, she extended and raised her arms to stay down.

Light filtered down unevenly. The surface of the pool slowly settled. She wiggled her fingers and toes. The water had stolen their warmth but not yet their feeling. Antarna concentrated on her heart space, holding on to the heat therein.

Thirty-five ... Thirty-six.

Tozias's laughter echoed through her head, breaking her peace. She remembered him somersaulting into this pool. Parting her lips, she blew a bubble and thrust the memory inside of it.

Her body itched to move. Gradually, that was overtaken by an impulse to swim for the surface. Denial of that was equal parts pleasure and pain.

Ninety-eight ... Ninety-nine.

Her diaphragm fluttered.

Rays of light pierced the pool. The deeper they descended, the weaker and more diffuse they became. Their once-sharp edges blurred around her, gentle and at peace.

Her diaphragm contracted six more times.

One hundred and fifty.

Short of her usual count. But she hadn't come to set a new record. Today had tested her in more ways than one. Her lungs were on fire.

It's fine to not act stronger than I feel. Gil had taught her that.

She stretched out her legs and launched herself off the bottom. Her arms clawed for the surface. She kicked, short and powerful. Bubbles rose with her.

Antarna broke the surface. Second only to emerging from the inferno, never had air tasted sweeter. Shivering uncontrollably, she pulled herself out of the pool, rushed to the fire and grabbed her towel. It was warm, bringing feeling back to her hands. Running the towel over herself, she delighted in the fire, rotating slowly as if on a spit. Small bumps marked her skin.

The truth behind the folded parchment eluded her still. *When did it happen before? How did you know, Gil?*

The bronze cup was too warm to pick up with her hands. She wrapped the edge of the towel around it. Steam rose from its mouth. The distinctive aroma of black tea filled the air, earthy and floral. After blowing across its surface, she took a sip. As the tea cooled, her sips grew larger. The heat of the liquid awoke her lips and tongue, and it gathered inside her.

The firelight made the scar on her left arm seem to ripple. It ran down her forearm for half its length, straight and faint. More than once Elgerin had offered to remove it, along with those on her right shoulder, hip and lower back. But each held a lesson.

Antarna changed into her fresh clothes and returned to her room. She climbed into bed and shut her eyes. Tozias's bloodied face rose out of the blackness, then Gil's, his eyes dull. Her chest grew tight. Opening her heavy eyes, she sat up. But the plain stone wall could not hold her attention. She doubted that even a masterpiece would have.

Enthriff climbed her body and stretched across her forehead. He massaged her temples, and she lay back down. The stone roof was just as plain as the wall.

Something about the curving path Enthriff had traced upon her skin sparked an idea. The end letter on the parchment Gil had penned in panic could be a D instead of a P.

D for ... Daslercia. The object of Gil's obsession.

Could they have suffered the same fate?

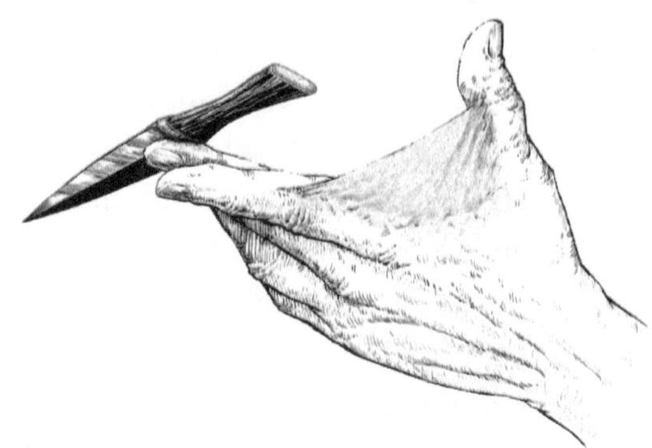

10. Don't Scream

BENEATH his eyelids, swirls of colour and flashes of light taunted Cal. Brayan's screams echoed in his head, accompanied by a searing hiss. He could smell it still: reminiscent of charcoal and bubbling fat with a metallic tinge, yet unlike any odour he'd encountered. Haunting. Sickening.

The necklace of seers dragged at his neck. *I'm wasting my time.* A vision required a calm mind and faith in his goddess. Cal had as much chance of that today as Brayan did of seeing again. He'd visited Preslina's temple, but the priests had refused to let him see his master—well, former master now.

Cal opened his eyes, uncrossed his legs and stood. A tingling, prickling sensation spread through his feet. He shook out his legs.

Thelia's shrine towered over him, silent and unresponsive. The statue of the goddess of sight knelt with her palms together in front of her face. She'd been formed from clam, mussel and oyster shells that overlapped like fish scales. *What a sick joke, to construct her of the shells of blind creatures when she abandons the blind.* Still, he should be thankful for the private shrine within the residence of seers.

Cal left the prayer room and stepped into the courtyard. The laden handcart sat undisturbed. In it, an armful of scrolls and books had been dropped atop two bags. A faded leather-bound book lay at an odd angle—Brayan's journal. While his former master had discussed most of his visions with Cal, some he'd kept to himself. To open it would be an invasion of privacy, but it could contain a vital clue about the thief his life depended on finding. He thrust his hands into his pockets.

Behind the handcart, a wooden training figure rested, even more battered and disfigured than the crater-pocked moon. Brayan had loved his throwing knives. It had taken Cal months to even hit the target.

His mum laid a scroll on a table covered with literature. Her white billowy dress hid her small form. 'Did you get a vision?'

'Flashes of light.' Everyone got those behind their eyelids, but "no" was far from reassuring. Everything hinged on him finding that stupid gem and egg—especially with Mirogant scheming to replace his bronze keys with the real ones Cal now wore. They were in a race, and the spiteful liar had a head start.

'Maybe you should go for a swim or lie down?'

'Maybe.' With the worry on her face, he regretted not putting more conviction into the word. Cal came alongside her.

'It could be the emerald egg that the lake island received from the cavern.' Mum pointed to a scroll. 'Or—'

The front door opened.

Cal raced towards it. *Brayan?*

Nalgrid entered and shut the door behind him. He appeared more hunched than usual.

'How's Brayan?' Cal asked.

'Still being treated at the temple of life.'

'Any word on a missing egg?'

'No.'

Unlike Mirogant, Cal wouldn't be getting access to the scene of the crimes. That much was clear. The servants couldn't help either, tongueless and illiterate. Cal rubbed the stubble on his chin. 'Guards can't hold their tongues. Where would they talk?'

His mum rested her elbows on the table. 'It's too early for the brothel.'

'Mum!'

'You could try Jescintra.'

'The jeweller?'

'Yes, her husband is the chief of the guards. You have a perfect excuse to visit her too.'

He groaned.

'Shall I come with you?' she asked.

'No.'

'Did you want to think about that?'

'Bye, Mum.'

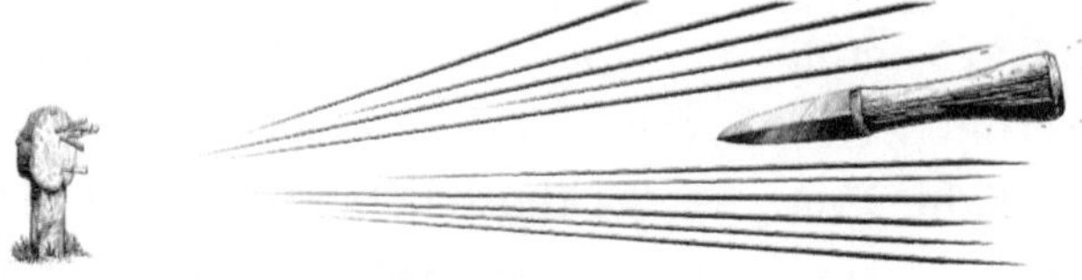

Antisocial white clouds hung still overhead, each enjoying a chunk of the blue expanse.

Two men played a board game on the deck of a tavern, manoeuvring wooden pieces. To the chancellor, Cal was such a piece. Still, with the right moves, Cal could knock Mirogant off the board.

He removed his shoes and entered the jeweller's. Every wall and table sparkled as if designed to paralyse and confuse.

'Welcome, Calik. Or should I say, my Seer?' said Jescintra. Big, bold, heavy earrings tugged at her unlucky earlobes. Her bangles clattered as she approached. 'I thought you'd be dropping by.'

'You did?'

'Of course. I knew you were a man of taste.' She waved a dainty hand over a selection of pearl necklaces and bracelets. White pearls rested beside black ones with green or blue overtones. Deep golden pearls gleamed in the centre of the table. 'What are you looking to buy your betrothed?'

He barely knew Kat. 'I'm open to your suggestions.'

Apparently, those words were tantamount to him saying that he had a fortune to spend and nowhere else to be. Jescintra led him through a head-spinning array of shiny things, her tongue tireless.

She put a second item aside. 'You're going to make such a good husband.'

'Uh, thanks.'

'How are the wedding plans coming along?'

'I've been too busy to make progress. You heard about the missing egg?'

Her pupils dilated, black circles wrestling space from grey-blue irises. Jescintra leant in. 'Yes. The mother serpent bit one of the guards.'

'Ouch.' *An egg from his rare ciltrilian serpent.* The chancellor prized the serpent for its unique anti-magic properties, probably because of his concerns about the temple of magic. He and his "snake" made a fitting pair: oversized, temperamental and deadly.

For my own sake, I better find it before it hatches. An egg, he could handle. What came out of it, now that was a different story.

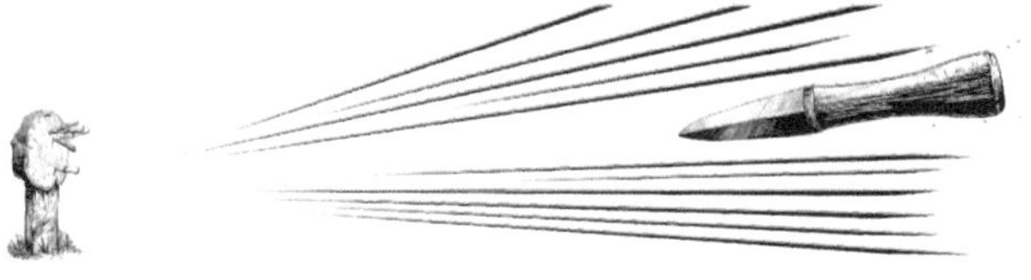

Four bronze spear tips bobbed above the crowd.

Cal ducked into the closest alley and approached home from the side, keeping to the shadows. *It's a busy street. There could be any number of reasons for them to be here.* He wrung his hands.

Lady Rhodlin's washing intruded into the alley. Gauzy rectangular fabric of different colours flapped in the gentle breeze. *Skirts? Tablecloths?* Whatever they were, it was better than seeing her undergarments again. Her wide-brimmed hat with its oversized pink ribbon hung by her side door. Lady Rhodlin could outtalk Jescintra; Cal had lost count of how many conversations he'd struggled to extract himself from.

Male voices drifted towards him. *You alright, Mum?* Cal crept to the prayer room's slit window on the outer wall of the residence of seers. Inside, three shrines sat side by side. On catching a flash of turquoise and leather in the courtyard beyond the prayer room, he ducked.

A pair of guards was common. Four meant trouble. The chancellor couldn't be happy.

Cal slunk down the side. The house ended and the back fence began. He pressed his eye to a knothole in the wooden fence. A tall guard emerged through the back door, another guard on his heels.

'I wouldn't want to be the seer,' said the tall man.

'The old or new one?'

'Either.'

His front door closed—a distinctive sound partway between a clunk and a thud. Moments later, a spear tip poked into the entrance of the alley. At the same time, the back gate opened.

Caught in the middle.

The litter in the alley failed to rise high enough to hide his shoes. Cal tried a door on his right only to find it locked. Lady Rhodlin's washing obscured her open window. Individually, the sheets of gauzy fabric were transparent. But ten of them were an entirely different story. As the two pairs of guards rounded the corners, Cal ducked under the washing. Thankfully, Rhodlin wasn't in her kitchen to see him lurking outside her window.

My outline's male.

Cal moved his legs together, grabbed her wide-brimmed hat and jammed it onto his head.

Lady Rhodlin entered her kitchen, balancing a cup of tea.

Don't look out your window. Cal felt his cheeks flush. He wanted to rip the silly hat off and duck down, yet the guards behind him were the greater threat.

Even at home, the pompous woman dressed in her finery. Perhaps, in her defence, she was about to head out—she was a socialite, after all. Lady Rhodlin put down her tea and riffled through a cupboard.

Footsteps passed his position.

Lady Rhodlin turned and stopped dead.

'Such a lovely hat.' He gingerly set it down. *Don't scream.* He pictured the guards running back, dragging him before the chancellor and a hot poker ramming into his eye.

She opened her mouth. But nothing came out.

Speechless for the first time in her life. Laughter bubbled inside him, and that's where he kept it. Cal hustled for his back gate.

He entered the courtyard. A heaviness descended, cold and oppressive. His mum stared at the sky, unmoving. What had the four guards said to her? She held a wooden box, her fingers longer than its sides. The chancellor's wax seal appeared on one face, where the lid met the base.

'Mum. You level?' He offered his hand. 'Let me take that.'

Her arms shot out and wrapped around him.

'It's fine.' Cal embraced her. 'I'm making progress.'

She squeezed him, released and then handed him the box.

'Exciting. I love gifts.' He put on a smile, directed her to a seat in the sun and found privacy.

On breaking the chancellor's seal, his fingers lingered on the wood. Even a box this small could carry any number of things, from ears to a male appendage. *This better not be someone's eye.* Could the contents be worse than not knowing? If it held a serpent waiting to drive its fangs into his skin, the answer was a resounding "yes". He nudged the lid open a fraction, but the contents remained hidden in shadow.

With his arms at full length, he flung the lid off. Inside rested eight triangular semi-translucent flaps of skin. He'd heard of someone who'd had his webbing removed for stealing. The man had been disowned by his family, lost his job and died alone in the gutter. The webbing in this box had probably come from another just as unfortunate.

Time was running out.

Cal entered the prayer room and started with the smallest of the three shrines. A grey bowl sat on a wooden board. He topped it up with lake water. Submerged at the bottom, an oval stone glinted a brilliant green. As Cal knelt, the colour danced for him. After a week of searching, diving again and again to pore over stones, Cal had found this one in time for his dad's funeral. The lake had taken the body, and the family kept a stone—a poor trade.

A portrait hung behind the bowl. Black and white worked for his cleft chin, soft smile and the freckles dotting his cheeks. But, of course, it couldn't capture the honey hues of his dad's blond hair or the deep-water blue of his kind eyes. At the time, all his family could afford was the black ink of a night turtle. Now that Cal had access to the finest paints, he intended to repaint it. He hadn't managed to find the time yet.

He moved to the next shrine: Zentrina's. Her hooded form had been carved from grey stone. Behind the shrine hung plaques for the deceased seers—apart from the disgraced fifteenth seer, whose painting was also absent from the hallway. Cal paid his respects, intoning a short prayer, and then rose.

Dropping to his knees before Thelia's shrine made of shells, Cal brought his palms together in front of his face, matching her form.

My goddess, hear me. Thank you for my sight. Of all the possible futures and all the moments within them, I know you guide me true. Guide me now. Please.

Time passed.

A black void opened in his mind. Darkness swallowed him. A pinprick of light appeared, followed by two more. Then the dots of light multiplied, as if each new one called upon a couple of friends, who in turn invited others. A force zigzagged Cal through the black. The light blurred around him, but there was no wind on his skin or in his hair. Three turns later, he collided with a bright light.

A vision awaited.

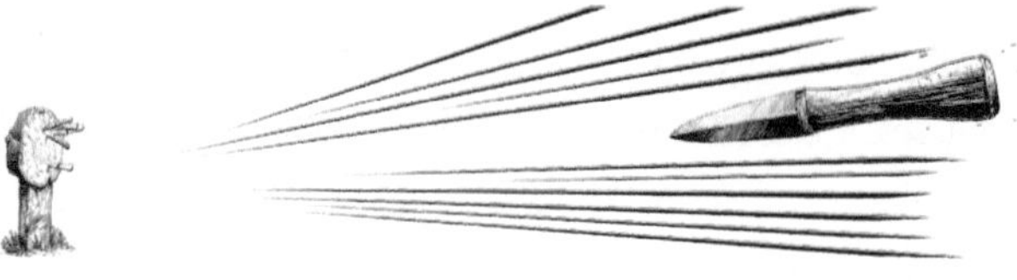

An armless in a crimson robe sat with his head hung, his short, dark hair thinning on his crown. He had a small nose and thin lips. Two floating liquid spheres massaged his temples. His torso held more madriliks than any man should rightfully have claim over, stored in dual reservoirs.

Arric, Cal guessed: high priest of the temple of magic.

Moonlight spilled through an arched window framing a striking view of the bowl of the crater. Far below, fields of golden-brown tivitania, ripe and tall, surrounded the palace. Few lights remained in the houses carved into the crater's walls.

A magical barrier stretched from rim to rim, keeping winged predators out—flyers, as those of the crater referred to them. A similar protective ward of a much smaller scale ensconced the high priest.

Magic sparked the hearth. The tinder caught flame and lit the kindling. Artefacts lined one wall and scrolls another. A golden mask gleamed.

A pressing quality accompanied the crisp vision, an imminence not to be ignored.

The door flung open. A fuzzy-haired priest stormed in, his crimson robe streaming behind him.

'Four of our brothers, dead!' His bushy eyebrows furrowed, deepening the creases along his forehead.

With magic, the high priest pulled a chair out from under his desk. 'Please, Brother Morsirel. Take a seat.'

'I don't want a seat. I want answers.'

'We can take solace in knowing that the four died to protect us.'

'There is no solace to be found here. Their blood is on your hands. I warned you.'

'You're understandably emotional. That's why I'll overlook this outburst.' The high priest stood, looking around as if he sensed something amiss.

The balls of madriliks inside both priests compressed in an instant, smaller and brighter—like a quill hound curling up in defence. Specks of darkness invaded the room, soaking up the light. One approached the ward around the high priest, and the spell collapsed.

'Anti-magic,' Arric murmured. The opposite of madrilik.

'The barrier!' Morsirel dashed to the window.

'Get it back up, then meet me back here to debrief. I'll find the cause.'

The pair left the room, and the vision sped up. If Cal had to guess, Arric would find the chancellor's stolen egg to be behind this. Would he catch the thief? The waning fire helped Cal gauge the passing of time. Flames faded to glowing embers, and the weakest of these died.

Morsirel entered and slumped into the chair he'd previously refused. Reestablishing the protective wards stretching over the crater had to have been taxing.

An ominous feeling descended.

A bookcase on the back wall sprang open without a sound to reveal a hooded figure. He called upon his plentiful madriliks.

Morsirel looked up, his shoulders raised. Two tongues of magic erupted from the hooded man and cut across the room—as thick as frilled eels and as dark as night turtles. Using his own magic, Morsirel propelled himself to his feet and raised a bubble-shaped shield. The attacks struck the bubble, which shimmered before shattering. Dark tongues curled upwards to strike Morsirel from either side. One collided with his temple, the other with his chin. Morsirel's neck snapped with a sickening crack. His ear slammed into his shoulder, and he collapsed limply. His eyes lost their focus, becoming vacant.

The hooded figure drew the madriliks from Morsirel's chest into his own. What started as a trickle became a torrent.

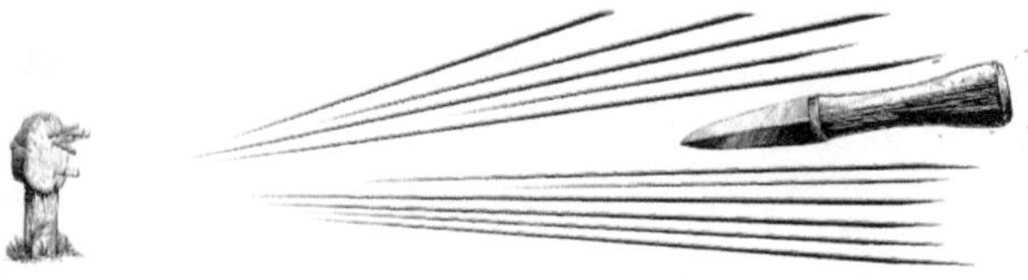

Cal bowed his head in thanks to the shrine to his goddess. The vision should appease the chancellor. The man had no love for the temple of magic, and an attack on them was unprecedented.

He left the prayer room. After composing himself and waving goodbye to Nalgrid, Cal headed for Parliament. Outside, lonely clouds still refused to make friends.

A snippet of the vision niggled at his mind. It'd happened so fast, but between Morsirel looking up and the hooded man snapping his neck, Cal could've sworn Morsirel had dropped his shoulders as if he'd recognised the murderer.

Whatever the case, in killing a senior priest in Arric's very office, the murderer had a death wish. There was a symmetry in that. And a lake-sized story for Cal to share.

On reaching Parliament's steps, he tamed his swinging arms. Maybe he should've felt sad for Morsirel or disturbed by his broken neck, but he'd never met the man and had seen plenty worse. Once inside, he progressed to the chancellor's waiting room. Rayvic stood beside the doors to the chancellor's office, again with drooping eyelids.

'How are you today, Herald?'

'You're late.' He opened the door and spoke into the room. 'Calik Dyterog, the twenty-third seer.'

How Cal had dreamt of hearing those words, though never like this.

A roaring fire filled the fireplace.

'About time,' said the chancellor without looking up.

Wonderful, everyone's in a good mood. Cal approached.

The chancellor shifted in his seat, and the chair gave a little groan. 'Well, where's my egg?'

'I had a vision of a death. But as you know—'

'Yes, I know your core commandment: you can't save a person you see die or allow another to. I won't. Go on.'

'In Arric's office, a senior priest named Morsirel will be murdered by a hooded man. Given the imminence underlying the vision, this will take place tonight.'

'Is that really all you have for me?' The chancellor eyed the bronze fire poker.

'No, not at all.' The words tumbled out. Cal took a breath, determined to take control of his nerves and the situation. He allowed himself a small leap of reasoning. 'The murderer is the same man who stole your egg.' The anti-magic had surely come from the egg.

'And who is the thief, the murderer?' With the usual difficulty, the chancellor raised his bulk from the chair. He headed for the fireplace.

Hooded *man* had already been a stretch: Cal didn't know their gender. Asking for more time would be like asking for his eye out. 'A mage.'

The chancellor paused, interest aroused.

'A Resatrium mage,' Cal said with false confidence. He'd already blamed the Resatrium. That had been a lie; this was an educated guess.

'Like Layaury?'

'Yes, just so.' Few names conjured more fear. If not for Arric, Layaury would've ended the crater's royal line during the Unjust Uprising.

How far would the murderous thief get tonight?

11. Death Catches the Stagnant

A faint halo of light crept through the imperfect seal of the vase's lid. Its clay-fired walls confined Zanth.

Priests of Devtakaris stood at each corner of a square. Unlike their lake island counterparts, these four priests had varying stores of madriliks. One was more powerful than Zanth. There'd be stronger mages in the temple though, especially Arric. That vile serpent of a man would be somewhere in the floors above, probably in his office.

The priests panted for air. Zanth didn't envy the exertion—few spells were more demanding than teleportation, even with the combined efforts of four priests in each location.

'What have we got this time?' the strongest of the four asked.

Zanth clutched his shard of nalitroite. With the element of surprise, he could kill two or three before they defeated him. But that was nothing compared to his mission.

The powerful one bled the energy from a dull madrilik and simultaneously lifted four lids, including from the vase next to his. The priest stepped forward, entering the square.

The lids hovered, the silence heavy between each rapid beat of Zanth's heart, before clinking back into place. He tensed, awaiting the priest's next spell.

'Just the usual,' an armless said.

The priests left the room.

Zanth dropped his head to his chest, which it was close to anyway in these cramped conditions, and he took a nasal breath with closed eyes.

Using his arms—limbs he'd come so close to giving up for this very temple—Zanth lifted the lid of his vase and emerged. His neck cracked as he stretched out his body. A high stone ceiling stretched overhead, the same black stone of the walls and floor. Delicacies and treasures from the lake island filled the vermillion square.

Safely masked by the remnants of the recent teleportation, he used a little magic to get himself out of the square. Wiping his brow, he shed his cloak.

Five floors up, the long window offered a full view of the crater floor. In his youth, fields of ripe tivitania would've filled him with excitement for the harvest festival. Back then, the palace had been something to dream about.

How naive I was.

Wooden stakes rose around Heltorne's statue.

The sun prepared to hand the sky over to the moon. A fleet of dark clouds closed in. *Slow down.* He needed moonlight to hatch the egg.

A ward stretched over the crater, maintained by his former temple. When the barrier came down tonight, flyers would descend and snatch people in their claws. In the chaos, he'd make his escape.

Zanth opened the top of the case. Inside sat an egg half the size of his hand—the green of young tivitania stalks, specked with white crescents. Reaching through the window, he felt for the ledge above. Even lifting his heels off the ground, it was too high. He stepped onto the windowsill. This time, his fingers brushed the ledge. Zanth carefully placed the open case upon it. Almost six floors high, small and painted black to match the walls of the crater, the case would not be seen from below.

He made his way to the door. Pausing before it, he checked for concentrations of madriliks. The hall was empty, as was the next. Zanth weaved through the back passageways. Instead of taking the spiral staircase, he used a ladder between storage rooms to ascend a floor.

He'd found the storage room years ago, as an initiate of the temple looking for a quiet place to write to Silisa.

The sixth floor was quiet, as always. It was the buffer between the upper floors housing the senior priests—including High Priest Arric—and the rest of the temple. Zanth quickened his steps as if he was in a rush. He wasn't.

Bronze bands and several spells reinforced the heavy wood of the arched double doors to the vault. An enchanted rope, thicker than Zanth's forearms, secured the doors.

Two acolytes stood before them. Patchy hair dotted the taller acolyte's face; the other had yet to grow any. Each contained pitiful stores of madriliks. Zanth took out the scroll and held it up. The scroll bore a seal of the same purple as the thin band on Zanth's sleeve.

'Urgent business from the king,' said Zanth. 'He heard from the seer of the lake island that the saphramurl gems were in jeopardy. I've been sent to check on them.'

'Where's your escort?' asked the older acolyte.

'I left the royal guards at the entry, and Priest Morsirel said I'd be fine without one.'

'Why?'

Zanth handed the scroll over. 'It's urgent, and I'm only checking on the gems, not taking them.'

'We'll still need to check with Priest Morsirel.'

'While you're at it, check with the high priest. No, let's call a meeting of all the senior priests.'

'Just Morsirel. It won't take long.' The older acolyte looked to his partner, then to the golden bell on the stand beside them.

Zanth threw his arms in the air. 'We don't have time for this. Morsirel understood the urgency. Why can't you? The gems are at risk. I'm the king's personal messenger, and you're holding a scroll sealed and signed by the king himself. It commands you to grant me access. If you ever want to take your vows, you'll let me pass. Now.' He stepped forwards.

The younger acolyte gulped, his neck yet to develop the male bulge. He moved to the side.

His partner took hold of the rope. 'Untie, unfasten, unlock, unbar.'

Nothing happened. If only he could see the embarrassed youth's face instead of his back.

'Untie, unfasten, unbar, unlock.'

The knot in the rope loosed and released. The pair pulled the heavy door open to reveal a long corridor.

As Zanth walked by, the older acolyte stiffened.

Confidence returning, even after you forgot the order to invoke the charm?

'While you're checking on the gems, we'll inform Morsirel,' the acolyte said.

'Of course. One question first.' Zanth turned, pouch in hand. He drew upon a madrilik. Using its energy, he pulled a powder from the pouch and hurled it at the acolytes' nostrils. The younger acolyte tried to reach for the bell but fell. The other fought his drooping eyelids; they opened and shut five times before he dropped to the stone. These two wouldn't remember a thing.

The hallway ran straight and long. An insect passed through a meagre slit of a window at the end. The clouds had taken the sky.

I need you, Ultinna. The goddess of the moon, radiant as she was, would want to shine and be seen.

After passing doors to priceless relics and treasures, Zanth stopped three-quarters down the length of the hallway. A ward blocked his way: a multilayered, crisscrossing network of woven strands. The structure resembled cobwebs laid one over the other. Far too intricate to unpick.

Zanth took a seat on the cold stone. If he broke the ward, all in the temple would feel it. Even feeble initiates would wake from their slumber.

'Ultinna, hear my prayers. By changing each night, you show us that change is possible. Help me reform and reshape the crater. I need your light tonight.'

Night deepened. One by one, the fires and cancrysts around the crater walls went out. The two acolytes lay motionless. Midnight approached, as did the shift change.

The stone had sucked the warmth from his legs. He stood, shaking them out.

Nothing pierced the layer of clouds, not one wink or glitter of a star. Despite fifteen more prayers—one for every stone he'd hidden on his uncomfortable belt—the moon refused to battle its way through. A large ward stretched over the crater with none of the complexity of the one in the hallway. One floor up, senior priests maintained it. This ward would come down, too. Zanth paced.

A beam of moonlight penetrated the cloud cover. It illuminated the rim opposite Zanth. *Thanks, Ultinna. Little closer, please.*

Voices drifted to him. Faint. Male. No doubt the shift change. Moonlight glinted off the pond, and Zanth smeared his sweaty palms down his tunic. The voices grew louder, words still indistinguishable.

Below, the blooming indigo flowers of the nicarmia trees emerged from the darkness.

'I'm blaming you for this shift,' said a voice.

The shaft of Ultinna's light slid over the temple of Devtakaris. A loud crack sounded outside the window, followed by a high-pitched cry. With a second crack, the egg unleashed a violent burst of anti-magic. Zanth stumbled under the onslaught of dark specks, taking hold of the wall to steady himself. The madrilik inside of him shrank from its natural opposite. Like an axe through kindling, the blast ripped the ward in two.

Zanth turned back towards the incoming acolytes, still a turn or two from his position. 'Protect the high priest! We're fine here.'

'We'll be back.'

Take your time.

Zanth raced into the inner chamber of the vault and threw open the last door.

The room was little bigger than a storage cupboard. On a wooden shelf, at eye level, sat fourteen saphramurls. They were far more than just precious gems.

He counted them again.

Fourteen. Not fifteen. One short ...

The largest rivalled the size of his eye. He took his belt off, flipped it over and laid it on the shelf. From the colour and size to the darting lights within, the two sets appeared identical. Of course, when close enough, anyone with magic could feel the difference.

Once he'd removed the fakes from the belt, Zanth braced himself to swap them for the real anti-magic gems. Picking up scorpions would be preferable. He dragged on leather gloves and pulled out a rag. Even using them, his skin sought to crawl away from the first saphramurl. Grimacing, he added them one at a time.

As he strapped on the belt now bearing saphramurls, the madriliks in his chest compressed. A grogginess overshadowed him. Other than his small knife, Zanth was defenceless.

He rearranged the fakes on the shelf. If all went to plan, the fakes would buy the Resatrium a couple of days, or, if luck held, maybe even weeks. When the temple did eventually discover the theft, the only thing better than seeing Arric's expression would be to watch him break the news to his beloved king. Not that Zanth would be anywhere nearby at the time.

A spell bathed the exterior of the temple in harsh light.

Wait for it.

The light flickered, then faltered. Anti-magic hung heavy in the air. Madrilik fled, repelled.

Zanth sprinted back—his feet unsteady—past the unconscious acolytes and into an adjacent room. Dust covered everything: the floor, chair, stout desk and scrolls. It sprang into the air with each step. Holding his breath, he unlatched and opened the shutters.

The crater lay unprotected, its barrier torn to shreds.

The balcony of the building neighbouring the temple of magic waited for him, cloaked in darkness.

Freedom. A jump away. Well, that, then through an unlocked door, down the hall, inside the third room, and into the secret room behind the shield.

Zanth climbed onto the narrow sill. A swirling wind whipped around him, seeking to pull him into the dizzying expanse of empty air below. He clenched the stone, vulnerable without his magic. The impulse to look down battled with a reasoned voice in his mind. He carefully released his grip on the stone, dipped his hands and bent his knees.

Shutters banged above him, thrown wide.

He froze.

'It came from outside,' a priest said.

'Really?' another replied. 'Wait, what's that?'

'Where?'

'There!'

'Oh, I see. Is it an egg?'

'Something's moving.'

Death catches the stagnant.

Zanth lowered from the sill and exited the room. He'd need to find another way, and quickly.

Shouts rang out through the temple. The thudding of boots on stone echoed down the winding stairwell. Zanth ascended.

A middle-aged priest rounded the corner.

Zanth squeezed the hilt of his knife but kept it hidden in his pocket.

'What are you doing here?' The man drew forth a dozen madriliks from his chest.

So close to the stolen gems, the priest's magic would be useless. Without arms or armour, the man had no chance against the knife. But he could still scream, even with his dying breath.

'He ran that way.' Zanth pointed down to the stairs.

'Who?'

'A traitor with a sword, covered in blood.'

The gullible halfwit rushed past him.

Zanth topped the stairs and then ducked into a narrow room with a slit for a window. From this height, the jump to the balcony of the neighbouring building would've broken his legs if not for the pile of straw.

A flyer plunged through a cloud, descending upon the crater, its huge wings tucked to give it a streamlined V-shape. Unless the temple did its job, there'd soon be a hapless victim clutched in its curved talons.

That and the baby serpent should keep you busy.

A magical rafter bridged the width of the crater, a new support for a replacement ward. The serpent egg's anti-magic hadn't lingered long, leaving Zanth especially vulnerable. The gems blocked his magic, but the priests could use theirs—not directly against Zanth while he had the saphramurls, but there were plenty of other ways. They could drop the ceiling upon his head. Or crack the floor. All the more reason to get out.

He steeled himself for the jump, practicing bending at the knees. The distance was daunting.

A priest entered the room above Zanth with an enormous store of madriliks, impossibly so. Only one had that much at his control.

Arric.

The walls felt as though they closed in around Zanth. His rapid pulse pounded in his ears. He opened the door, not remembering crossing the room. Zanth held it tight, gasping for air.

The staircase beckoned, as did the narrow window: up to kill Arric or leave with the gems he'd come for?

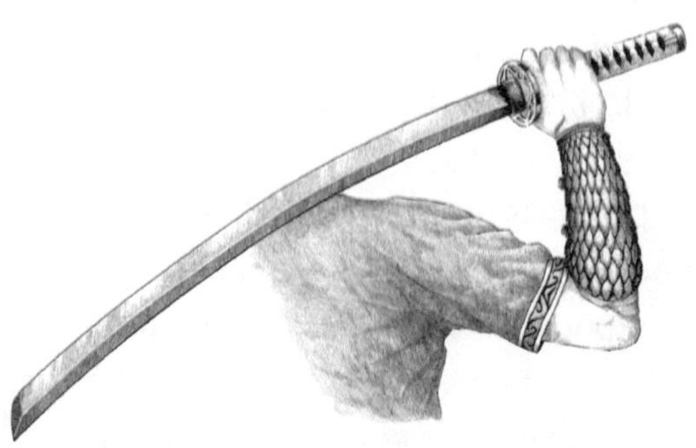

12. Whose Arm is That?

Antarna trudged through the temple of life, fresh snow slipping from her coat. The weather had laid a white blanket over the mountain, seeking to forget the recent horrors. It'd made retrieving the bodies from the summit this morning that much more difficult. She shuddered away the images of Parsannon and Chesare, their bodies cold and stiff and lifeless. The warmth of the temple seeped into her heavy limbs, numbness giving way to bone-deep aches.

She slumped down beside Tozias. The image and text of Zentrina appeared immobile on his forearm, as if but an ordinary tattoo. She took note of the position of the first word in the passage against a light freckle. His closed eyelids fluttered gently.

Hope it's a good dream. Nightmares had plagued her last night.

Elgerin took a seat next to her. 'Tozias is hanging in there.'

'But not improving?'

The high priest laid a hand on her shoulder. 'It's only been a day.'

'What can we do to help him?'

'We're doing what we can: giving him liquids and pulling out madriliks.'

Antarna picked up her chair and turned it to face Elgerin. 'You're still getting madriliks out of him?'

'Yes. The mountain is bathed in it, especially this close to the summit. Ambient madriliks are impeding his recovery.'

'Can you establish a ward to keep madriliks away?' she asked.

'Not a bad idea. A ward requires madriliks to cast and sustain the magic though, which would only increase the madriliks around him. While magic can defend against magic, it's not well-suited to repelling madriliks.'

'Sounds like an awful idea then.'

Elgerin smiled gently.

Repelling madriliks ... This tugged at the thread of something she'd tucked away in the back of her mind. She pulled on it, but the thread came loose without the fact.

They talked more about his other patients before saying their goodbyes. She touched Tozias's arm. Two words had overtaken his freckle. Only two.

Antarna jogged back, having found energy after seeing Tozias and reminding herself how much there was to do. The door to the armoury opened to the sound of metal rattling across stone. A large crack ran up the wall, and a chaotic jumble of weapons hid the stone floor. The walls had been rattled bare—every shelf, rack and stand. At least no one had been in the room when they'd come down.

She picked up a large axe and carried it into the changing room she'd come through. Item by item, she cleared the room. Handles were all that remained of some weapons. With the toe of her boot, she slid shards of volcanic glass, bone and stone chips out her path. The wooden scabbard of her sword had a small scratch in the shape of a downturned mouth. The mark irked her; the weapon was all she still had of her brother.

She took her sword and hung it in the usual manner, with the hilt on the left and the blade pointing to the right. After a long pause, she reversed the sword. The orientation of the grip now allowed for an easy draw. Antarna put the rest of the swords and knives up in the same manner. It gave the room a different feel, one that brought her both comfort and discomfort.

She turned to depart. By the sound of voices coming from the dining hall, though more subdued than the usual chatter, she was late for the midday meal.

Priest Leharist strode down the hallway, his eyes darting from side to side. His hand rested on the hilt of the bronze dagger attached to his belt. She'd never seen the powerfully built fighting instructor nervous before.

'Thanks for restacking the armoury,' he said.

'While hanging up my sword, I was wondering about Daslercia. What do you think happened to the former kingdom?'

'I'm not sure. Why?'

Antarna shrugged to conceal her interest, the parchment she'd taken from Gil's pocket on her mind. 'Just trying to distract myself.'

'Yes, we could all do with some distraction. Many say that they were attacked by a pack of hazzurus, and once blood was spilled, more creatures joined until no one was left alive. After all, the ruins of Daslercia are scattered with the skeletons of large beasts.'

They are, but none have been identified as belonging to a hazzurus. 'What did Gil think?'

'I'm sorry about your mentor. He thought Daslercia was a match for the hazzurus unless some kind of disaster struck first.'

Like overexposure to madriliks.

The pair headed to lunch.

After ladling soup into a bowl and selecting a few berries, Antarna took her usual seat. No cup of steaming tea awaited her. Without Tozias and Letti, the table was a barren, windswept desert. Uloron sat nearby, rubbing a puffy eye.

'Not sleeping?' she asked him.

'Not really.'

The first berry was sour. A sickening sense of loss clung to everything. The empty seats amplified the feeling, with one out of four either dead or in the infirmary.

'How strange was it without the bell sounding this morning?' Divislak asked someone behind her.

'They still haven't told us anything.'

Questions burnt a hole in Antarna's head.

An initiate threw a hisriloc into the air. Tiny orange marks marred the stone fruit's midnight-blue skin.

As a child, she'd seen gems filled with orange lights. *That's it!* Madriliks were repelled by their opposite.

Antarna dashed to the table of priests. 'Sorry, High Priest, may I speak with you, please?'

Inhaloc rose. 'Of course. I wanted to talk to you, too.'

They moved to an empty corridor.

'You go first, please,' she said.

'I am responsible for everyone here. Given what happened, the crater would seem to be—'

'I'm not leaving Tozias. And I'm not going back there.'

'I know it would be difficult.' He gave her a sympathetic smile. 'But this temple may no longer be safe.'

'You're going to abandon the temple?' Disbelief and challenge coloured her voice.

'We're discussing a few options, and that is one of them. At least, please think on a short stay in the crater. Now, what did you want to say?'

'The crater has saphramurls. There are what ... fifteen of them just sitting in a vault. They'd keep madriliks away so the unconscious could recover, right?'

He looked upward, weighing her idea, then his gaze returned to hers. 'Yes. And the anti-magic gems may even defend against another such event.' His brow smoothed, but then worry returned to his face. 'It would be most persuasive coming from you. We could have you teleported to the crater and back in a day.'

'You don't need me.' The words escaped with more force than she'd intended. Memories of the darkest day rattled the door of their confinement. 'The king will listen to any senior priest. It's his people up here, too.' Antarna shifted her robe so that the air could get to her hot neck.

Inhaloc took a step back. 'I'll send Yerkinfall and sound the bell once he returns.'

'Thank you.'

Breakfast concluded. The priests directed initiates and acolytes back into the Sacred Hall.

They formed five incomplete rings around the towering likeness of their goddess captured in liquid-like stone.

The high priest addressed the congregation. He spoke of loss, rebirth and cherishing life. Priest Ulican brought around a bowl of wet clay. When he reached Antarna, she rose and dipped two fingers in and smeared a grey dot on each cheek.

Inhaloc paused before continuing. 'The four races each have their own way to send off their dead. Those of the lake island weigh down the body—which has been twice washed and dressed in finery—and drop the deceased in the deepest section of the lake. The people of the desert bury their dead at a sacred site after tattooing the deceased's eyelids with their name and that of their family. It is a time of sorrow, a time to mourn. On the other hand, those of the cavern hold a festival for their dead. Under the first clear starlit sky, they emerge and burn the dead upon a pyre in a circle of dancing. Lastly, the people of the crater offer their dead to nature, to the carnivorous pirrocical plant.'

She hadn't seen the bodies of her mother and brother being given to the pirrocical, although she'd imagined it more than once.

'Here,' Inhaloc said, spreading his arms, 'we have a different tradition. No matter where we came from or who we were, we are one before our goddess. Zentrina judged your past life and rebirthed you into this one. We embrace this gift of life, honing body and mind with discipline, determination, courage and confidence. With our soul as our eternal record, we reach to fulfil our potential and act in a manner that makes us, our families, our goddess and our future lives proud.'

He talked of the pride he had for each of the fallen and how they would be warmly embraced by Zentrina. With her mentor and so many others dead, and Tozias and Letti in comas, Antarna wanted to believe that more than anything. Though her goddess had rebirthed Salorann into her body and let Gil die ...

When Inhaloc concluded, Priest Weslutch struck a small gong. It released a resonant echo.

Two priests and two priestesses carried Gil's body, cleaned of the fire, and offered it to the stomach of the animated statue of Zentrina; their goddess would've already welcomed his soul. The grey substance first claimed Gil's feet, absorbing him. Then, his legs, abdomen and chest. When his serene face—eyes forever closed—disappeared, Antarna held her breath. An ache grew in her lungs, and with her lips sealed, she waited for it to eclipse the pain in her heart. It never came close. Relenting, she drew her first breath in a new, darker world.

A grey seed no larger than a knuckle emerged from where his body had entered. Inhaloc stepped forwards and caught it before it hit the ground.

She held back her tears and kept herself motionless. Though if Tozias had been beside her, she'd have thrown herself into his arms.

The ceremony continued. Priest Chesare was the next one taken by Zentrina.

The youngest were especially hard to see off. When the image of Parsannon on the mountainside arose, she displaced it with one of him at a feast.

The high priest gave a final prayer. With the seeds in hand, he headed for the main tower with the two priests and two priestesses. Antarna followed the others to the balcony.

Intertwining vines crisscrossed up the tower. Several flowers budded and bloomed, each unique—just like every life. An elliptical petal spiralled to the floor, its golden flecks catching the light.

The priests and priestesses planted the seeds in the same order as their bodies were given to their goddess. From each, a vine would grow. They'd flower for five days following a rebirth. When Gil's seed entered the earth, she marked the spot in her mind.

At the earliest opportunity, Antarna excused herself. She sprinted to the temple of life as if being chased by a flyer. Inside, she tried to dampen the noise of her breathing. Avoiding the main thoroughfare, she weaved her way towards Tozias.

'Antarna, I can hear your heart hammering from here,' came Elgerin's voice from the next room.

She rounded the corner. The high priest sat at a small desk covered with books. The infirmary was the next room over.

'Sorry, I was ... I just need to see him,' Antarna said.

'After the funeral, that's understandable.'

'How—?'

'Inhaloc and I talk.' He rose.

Antarna followed him into the infirmary.

A blue tinge stretched across Tozias's lips; it hadn't been there this morning.

'He's getting worse. What can I do?'

'Just what you're doing now: visiting and praying.'

An initiate came for Elgerin, and he departed before she'd had a chance to speak to him about the saphramurl gems.

Antarna sat with Tozias. The fourth word of the sacred text on his forearm reached his freckle. The king had no reason to refuse the request for saphramurls: many of the temple had been born in the crater. Help was a short time away, surely. She patted Enthriff.

Shadows stretched in the infirmary. What was taking Yerkinfall so long? The seventh word drew even with the blemish on Tozias's skin.

When night descended, cancrysts cast stagnant shadows. Still, the bell was yet to toll. Something was wrong. Her conversation with Inhaloc repeated in her mind. Each time, her reasons seemed a little weaker.

She awoke beside Tozias, on top of the blankets. Her last memory was of trying to find a comfortable position in the seat next to the bed. His forehead felt overly warm against the back of her hand.

The moon and stars ruled, but not for much longer. She rose and paced, the feeling that she should've gone to the crater gnawing at her. If nothing else, she would've known what the holdup was. Antarna ran to the summit and back, then dived into the oval pool in the bath chamber of Zentrina's temple, but neither cleared her head.

The deep chime of the bell reverberated through the temple. Even knowing it was the morning bell, not the one signalling Yerkinfall's return, the sound stirred her aching heart. The bell tolled again, smothering her slender hope.

Yerkinfall wasn't in the Sacred Hall for prayer and didn't lead them for stretching. The delay defied logic. Teleporting happened instantaneously. Lengthy discussions weren't needed on the best ways to provide aid. The saphramurls gathered dust in a vault. The crater didn't need them.

Eggs broke her fast, a rare treat in the temple. Yet she picked at her food, finally relenting to eat without tasting it. The high priest didn't look her way, much less approach her. Classes and training resumed with a modified schedule.

During duelling, the bell rang once. A sweeter sound she'd never heard. She dashed out of the practice hall without an apology to Priest Leharist. She imagined rounding the corner to a gleaming pyramid of saphramurls. Darker thoughts crept up on her too. Maybe the king had refused the request.

In the foyer, Yerkinfall stood in conversation with the high priest. Both wore serious expressions, and neither held a box of gems.

She needed to know what had happened, but reluctance gripped her.

Inhaloc gave her a strained smile. 'I was just hearing the bad news.'

'The king refused to see me.' Yerkinfall looked at Antarna. 'His messenger said that he'd only speak to you.'

'Me?' Antarna clasped her hands behind her back to stop herself from throwing them into the air. 'Why?'

'That was all the messenger had for me after a day waiting to be seen.'

'Thank you for your effort.' Inhaloc raised two fingers to his third eye and spread a hand over his heart.

Yerkinfall reciprocated and departed.

Antarna leant against the wall. 'I don't understand.'

'He asked to see you last year, and you didn't go back.'

Both the king and her father had. 'This is life and death. The king must realise that.' But as he hadn't heard from Yerkinfall, she couldn't be sure how much he knew.

'Let's discuss this in my office.' Inhaloc turned and led the way.

Antarna had no choice but to follow.

His office would've been plain and grey if not for the elaborate stained-glass window. Morning light brought the vibrant colours to life, the stone floors and walls its canvas. The window artwork depicted madriliks ascending from the mountain summit and the lone tree standing proud.

They sat on simple wooden chairs. The room with its closed door and the chair with its high armrests added to her sense of confinement. Resigned to facing the difficult conversation, she began. 'I'm worried about leaving Tozias.'

'I appreciate that. Elgerin is taking care of him. The best thing you can do for him is to convince the king to loan us the gems. Your idea is the finest we have.'

A compliment. Don't think I don't see what you're doing. 'It's no longer my home. This temple is.'

'Speak to the king and come home. There and back.'

She'd do anything to save Tozias, Letti and the others. But this ...

'It's not safe for me.' Antarna rose and walked towards the window. The words had a horrid aftertaste. A guilt. She wasn't the same little girl anymore—not with her training, her weapons and Enthriff.

'It wasn't safe a decade ago. That doesn't mean it still isn't.'

'They still haven't caught the killer.' Her father had promised to bring the assassin to justice, a promise unfulfilled, adding to the chasm between them.

'Frankly, it's safer than here until we get to the bottom of this disaster and can ensure it doesn't happen again.'

Happen again. The words reverberated in her head. It'd happened before, too. The gems could keep the temple safe. Above all, they could save Tozias. Enthriff gave her wrist a gentle squeeze.

She sighed. 'I'll go.'

'Thank you.' Inhaloc rose. 'The mages should be sufficiently rested to teleport again by early afternoon.'

They exchanged farewells, and Antarna departed for the temple of life. White clouds floated above.

What am I going to say to Father? And to the king?

The second question was easier, so she started on her speech. By the time she was at Tozias's side, she had a rough draft.

His vivid hair was matted. With a damp cloth, she wiped down his face. His hair would have to wait.

'I promise to be back as soon as I can,' she said into his ear. After a quick glance around, she continued. 'I'll do anything in my power to get the saphramurl gems. Hang in there.'

She kissed his forehead, finding him still too warm, and departed.

Elgerin picked herbs from planter boxes in the main hallway.

'Have you heard the news?' asked Antarna.

'It travels fast,' he replied, tapping his head: telepathy.

She couldn't return in the grey garb of Zentrina, not when Father believed she lived and learnt in the temple of life under Elgerin's care. 'Could I borrow a white robe, please?'

'I'm not sure that's a good idea. The crater hasn't been taking kindly to our support of the poor and vulnerable.'

'Really? Why?'

'Just the normal: that the Resatrium are hiding in their ranks.'

Antarna shuddered. Without the strength of numbers, the rebels masked their identities, concealing themselves within the general population. 'I'll change shortly after I arrive. White is still better than grey.'

'We could make a trade.'

'A trade?'

'A white robe for your scars. You can't go back with them.'

She lifted her sleeve. The long scar was two shades lighter than her skin. 'You've been wanting to remove them for some time now.'

'That doesn't make me wrong. They don't belong on a—'

Antarna shot him a look. *Say it, I dare you.*

'—a young lady trying to pass herself off as having studied only healing for the last decade,' he said with a smile.

'Good save. Just the one on my arm. They'll never see the others.'

'Unless you wear something that shows your shoulder, or you bathe.'

'It's only a quick visit.'

'Will your father let you return if he sees a scar?'

'Fine,' Antarna replied. 'Where are we doing this?'

'Outside, so we keep the madriliks away from the patients.'

Elgerin made a quick detour. He emerged with a white robe in hand.

They sat on a rock, and the high priest spread his fingers along her first scar. He intoned several ancient words. Antarna committed the scar to memory and braced, noting his earlier mending of her ankle. Blistering heat spread down her arm. But nothing stabbed at her stomach, stomped on her chest or squeezed her temples.

Because madrilik levels are down and I've recovered from the overexposure.

The heat dissipated almost as quickly as it had arrived.

Elgerin lifted his hands. 'That wasn't so bad, was it?'

'Whose arm is that?' Her skin was unmarked.

'One down. Three to go.'

When the last of her scars had been removed, Elgerin handed her the white robe, and they said long goodbyes.

Antarna returned to her temple and met Inhaloc in his office.

He looked up from the scroll. 'I can recall at least three discussions about you telling your father.'

She adjusted her robe. The white was almost radiant against her amber skin and the grey backdrop. 'Yes, sorry.'

'This will be your first time teleporting?'

'Yes.' *Well, first time conscious.*

'Words can't prepare you, but I can try.'

He ran Antarna through what to expect as they took the path down the mountain. Three-quarters of the way to Preslina's temple, they turned onto a thin, winding track; it looked little more than an animal path.

The temple of Devtakaris was built from the black stone of the crater, as all their temples were, regardless of location. It was two storeys high, but only two or three small rooms wide and long. An initiate stood in the doorway, his black robe tied with a belt of crimson cloth.

'Best of luck, Antarna,' said Inhaloc. 'And thank you. I know this isn't easy.'

'I'll be back tonight or tomorrow. Take care of them and let me know if anything changes.'

'Of course.'

The young boy welcomed Antarna inside and led her to the second door on the right. The room had neither furniture nor windows.

'Please,' he said, extending his arm.

She entered and, as Inhaloc had explained, carefully stepped over the outline of a square that'd been painted in blood on the floor.

Four elderly priests of the Order of Devtakaris filed into the room. They took their places at each corner of the square. One had the golden eyes of the people of the cavern. Antarna focused on the floor in front of her. As a child in the crater, she'd had a hard time avoiding staring at their lack of arms.

The priests began to incant words foreign to her ears.

So much for never going back. Her nightmares and the Resatrium waited there—traitors one and all, as was Salorann.

Antarna prepared for impact with taut muscles and bent knees.

An invisible force struck from above. Had Inhaloc not warned her, she would've fallen.

Ten thousand unseen hands pulled at her. Her eyes watered as the force yanked at her eyelashes, eyebrows and every hair on her head. She pushed her tongue to the roof of her mouth and clamped her lips shut. No sooner had she done so than it snatched those parts, starting to rip her tongue from her mouth and separate her lips from her face.

One moment, she was being torn asunder. The next, she hung inside countless droplets, looking at images of herself.

She hung for an instant and then fell like rain.

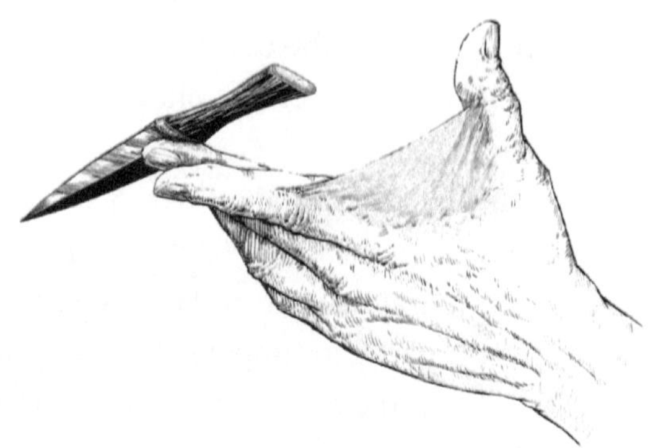

13. Deep Puncture Wounds

CAL scratched his jaw with the handle of his paintbrush. Brayan's leatherbound journal lay open in front of him. A necessary sin. Pushing his guilt away, Cal refocused.

He combined blue and red pigments to give purple. More blue than red kept the mixture cool. He added a third colour: yellow. This turned the paint grey. As he dragged in more yellow, it grew lighter. With fast and loose strokes, Cal returned to working on the river, though it had more in common with painting a waterfall. Strangely, though, the water didn't tumble from a great height. Here, it furiously climbed the mountain. After adding more yellow to his grey, he wove this new shade into the flow. He felt the twists and turns of the torrent of water.

Why's the river climbing the mountain? Is it to signify something impossible? If so, what?

Cal transitioned to white. This captured the water's energetic nature. It churned and frothed up the slope, crashing over and over. He didn't know what propelled it so. If Brayan knew what his vision had meant, it hadn't made his journal.

He took a few steps back, navigating the cushion-covered floor with practised ease. They came in all shapes, sizes and colours.

The painting of raging water ascending an imposing mountain stood on an easel in the middle of the room. It matched the detailed description in the journal. To finish, Cal needed to add mist and spray.

But what does your vision mean? Please be more useful than a callamelon that's all rind and no flesh.

He entered the courtyard. The laden cart glared at Cal after his trespass.

His mum cradled a cup of tea. 'You've come out to discuss the weddings?'

Cal turned and made a show of pretending to leave the room. He stopped before he hurt her feelings. 'Wedd*ings*?'

'Yes. I'm thinking one here for your people and one at the crater for hers.'

Someone rapped at the door: two confident strikes. All business.

Who is it? Since turning ten, he'd voiced that question once, and never again, after the person on the other side of the door questioned if he really was meant to be a seer.

Nalgrid answered it. A moment later, he shut the door and then walked stiffly down the hallway.

'Let me guess.' Cal patted his hair, but it refused to submit. 'Our chancellor demands my attendance?'

'Yes.'

He slumped his shoulders and hung his head. 'Nalgrid, we were about to discuss the wedding. Correction, wedd*ings*.' He turned to his mum.

She spoke first. 'Oh, so disappointed, are you? It'll be fine. We can discuss the weddings as soon as you return.'

'Lucky me.'

'And don't you forget it.'

'Yes, Mum.' He waved goodbye, departing for Parliament.

Curiously, the chancellor had declined to endorse his mum's first two choices of bride, each from a higher-born family. Something was afoot.

The sleepless moon clung to the heavens. Without the company of the stars, it sat lonely in the blue sky—dull and lifeless against the brilliance of the sun.

People swarmed around a new stall by a golden-eyed trader of the cavern. He had rare crystals, preserved wings, dried insects, glowing moss and healing mud.

Hope you're on the mend, Brayan.

Upon entering the waiting area outside the chancellor's office, Cal couldn't bring himself to sit in any of the bulky chairs.

Ugly chairs to make the chancellor's office more impressive when you enter or to better prepare you to meet the chancellor?

Rayvic emerged through a side door, one hand behind his back. 'Seer.' He dipped his head. 'The egg hatched. The baby serpent has been found and returned.'

The words took a moment to sink in, and Cal refrained from asking him to repeat them. 'That's the best news I've heard all year.'

The hint of a knowing smile slipped through the cold, blank expression Rayvic hid behind.

What aren't you saying?

Rayvic's arm twisted and unfurled from behind his back. A box of black stone sat on his palm. Thin veins meandered across the stone, the light blue of a clear summer sky—marking it as having originated from the crater.

'The chancellor received this and wants you to have it.' Rayvic held out the box. One side bore the crest of the crater's royal family.

Cal took it. 'What's inside?'

'Open it.' A flush washed over the herald's cheeks.

Cal's mouth went dry.

The stone lid rested in grooves cut into the sides of the box. With sweaty hands, Cal slid the lid free to reveal the coiled body of a baby serpent. A lifeless body.

Cal pictured the chancellor opening the box, rage consuming him, his clenched fists smashing down upon his desk. It was a wonder that the box hadn't been hurled out the window or into the fire.

'The chancellor looks forward to discussing this.' With that, Rayvic departed.

Cal tried to fit the stone lid back in place, but his hands were too unsteady. He put the box down and paced the room.

At six years old, he'd burnt himself on a pan fresh from the oven. How he had howled in pain. That'd be nothing compared to having a gleaming fire poker thrust into his eye. He'd never see the lake again. Mirogant would move into the residence of seers, leaving Cal and his mum in the gutter.

A sudden crack startled Cal, but then his mind caught up. He'd jumped at the sound of a door closing.

This is what the chancellor wants.

He wouldn't give the chancellor the satisfaction.

Think ... The carcass had come from the crater, so Cal had guessed correctly. And the chancellor still needed him to find the gem. Returning to the box, he slid the lid on and then deposited it in the corner of the room, behind the third seat.

A man took large strides into the room, his plaited beard interwoven with silver thread. Dripping in pearls, his wife followed, a baby in her arms. If the pair entered Jescintra's jeweller shop, she'd be counting her profit before they'd said a word.

Rayvic ushered the man in to see the chancellor, and he entered, his back straight and chin up. His wife took a seat, eyes on her baby. Wrinkles appeared at the corners, blossoming from joy, not age—she was only a few years older than Cal. Her baby snuggled deeper into a fur pelt.

The lady held the bundle with practised care. As Cal stepped closer, she repositioned it for him. The infant had plump cheeks, closed eyes and a few strands of hair.

'What a gorgeous baby ...' *Boy or girl? Too late, too long a pause.*

'Thank you. Yes, she really is,' replied the lady. 'You're the new seer, right?'

'Yes.'

She glanced at the door, perhaps worried about what her husband would think of them talking. 'Would you mind doing a reading?'

'I can try.' Cal sat and took off a glove.

'I don't have a fish.' Worry had crept into her voice.

'Sorry, a fish?'

'Yes. For you to split open.'

'Thank you, but no. I don't read entrails. All I need is your permission to place my hand on your daughter's head.'

She nodded.

Cal lowered his hand. A door slammed nearby, and the baby let out a cry.

The woman gave him an apologetic smile and swayed her daughter in her arms. The little one refused to settle, her protests growing ever louder. If the power of her lungs was any indication, maybe the baby would become a singer.

A short time later, the door opened, and the woman left with her husband. Despite the fact that the chancellor was guestless and the waiting room only held Cal, Rayvic did not admit him.

Failure weighed like an anchor in the pit of his stomach. He had no way to know how Mirogant fared. But the conniving liar already had a head start, and, with all this waiting, Cal slipped further behind.

Another couple entered the waiting room. The herald ushered them in to see the chancellor.

Cal resumed his pacing, determined to focus on something constructive. *Mountain ... large, immovable, solid, tall. Symbolises ... firmness, stillness, constancy.* Shy of the wall, he spun around. *What about the river? Motion, life, the flow of time, a path to take, change.*

If Cal wasn't admitted soon, he'd violate curfew. The sun dropped further, and the murmur of voices drifted from the office.

Ascending a mountain. A tough journey? A challenge? Inner elevation? He stretched his arms over his head.

The couple reappeared, and the doors to the office banged shut behind them.

In a corner of the room—the furthest one from the box—Cal crossed his legs and lowered himself to the floor. He prayed to Thelia. Eventually, darkness reached for him. Specks of lights appeared, then transitioned into streaks.

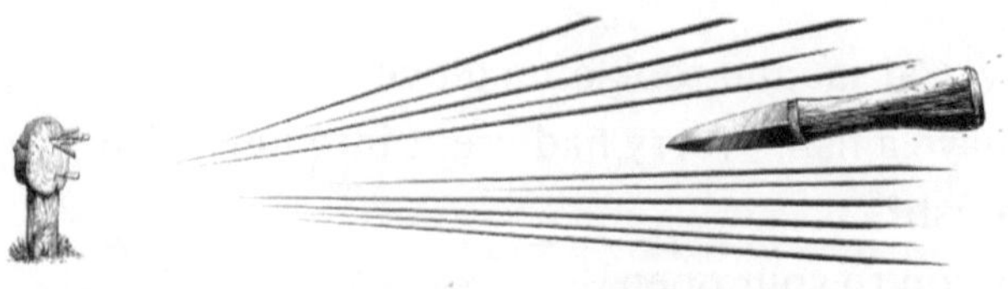

A camouflaged, stocky woodsman stood in high grass, a hand over most of his smirking mouth. An irregular bite-like scar ran along the outer edge of the hand, finishing where the little finger should start, but the digit was missing.

Buildings had been reduced to piles of rubble. Seven columns rose to the side, covered with silver flowers—delusians.

The man screamed and disappeared into the greenery, face-first. The scream was short-lived, ending at the same time as a sickening thump. Grass rustled, and a flicker of movement betrayed a tail within.

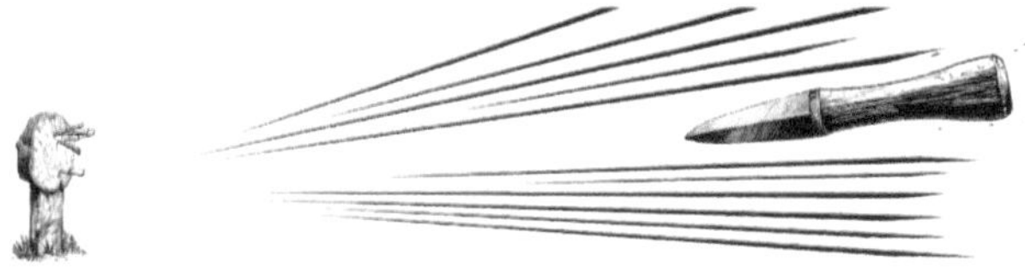

Strange. *It's not hunting season. And no columns close to the lake island.* Cal turned and sank back against the wall.

The sky darkened. Cal rose and again walked the length of the room. His stomach rumbled. Hunger was the least of his concerns.

The guards outside changed shift. The chancellor wouldn't keep him past curfew, would he?

The passage of time provided an unwelcome answer.

Dim firelight from the chancellor's office seeped through the gap between the door and the sill. Heavy footsteps approached.

Here we go. Cal drew himself up and clasped his trembling hands behind his back.

But the footfalls fell away. Apparently, the chancellor had left his office through a side door.

This may have been the man's plan from the outset: have Cal stew in his own worry all day and night, then torment him tomorrow. Cal retrieved the box and exited the room. The guards didn't raise a hand.

Gloomy clouds hid the moon, too thick for moonlight to brighten. Cal stood in the doorway, turning his head left, right, left, right. At this time of night, cold-blooded threats could be anywhere. The street was empty.

Above, the rafters were evenly spaced and unoccupied, excluding a spider clinging to its web. Getting down on his knees, he checked under the benches. Nothing there. He rose.

Cal turned back. He hastened towards a bearded guard twice his age. 'It's past curfew. I need an escort home, please.'

'I can't leave my post.'

Cal turned to the other guard, searching his blue eyes for compassion. He found none. Returning to the exit, Cal measured the distance to his residence. His fingers had found his lips.

A quill hound's bark sent Cal into the air and back to a time he'd locked away.

He was eleven and three-quarters, out past curfew after waking from a vision. Fluffy barked, not happy or excited, but scared. Cal sprinted to his quill hound. A stick lay in his path, and Cal scooped it up without slowing. He leapt over a hedge. Fluffy growled at a dusk snake, his sharp quills raised. The snake bared its fangs and hissed, its green hood with eye-like markings on full display.

'Help!'

'Cal, where are you?' The voice was close and familiar.

'Dad?' Cal swished his stick at the rearing snake. 'I'm here.'

The dusk snake struck out, and Cal leapt back. As the reptile recoiled, its flattened tail rose into the air and forked tongue darted in and out of its mouth.

Dad hopped over the hedge. 'Son, step towards me, slowly.' His tone was firm but not icy.

Cal extended his back foot. It landed on a twig that snapped.

The snake launched at him.

Stumbling, Cal lost his balance.

His dad sprang forwards, arms extended.

The dusk snake sank its curved fangs into his father's forearm.

Releasing a piercing cry, his father hit the ground, hard.

'Dad!'

The reptile slithered into the hedge.

'I ... I can't move my arm,' his father said, voice wavering. Blood dribbled from a pair of puncture wounds. 'Where are you, Son?'

Cal was standing right over him.

'Help,' Cal screamed at the top of his lungs.

Fluffy came up to his father, whimpering.

A hound howled. It wasn't Fluffy. It wasn't right.

Cal clung to the front doorframe of Parliament, every muscle tensed. After burying his face in his hands, he set off for home.

A Snake with Two Heads

Zanth sat in a secret room, his ear pressed against the back of the door. Muffled voices and footfalls faded. A faint ray of light snuck between the door and its frame, not even enough for him to see his feet.

The door rested behind a wall-mounted shield in a prestigious house a stone's throw from the temple which Zanth had escaped from. The king's guards and hunters would be ransacking the poorer districts and applying pressure to known Resatrium members. Staying secreted in this room while Zanth's brothers and sisters of the cause were beaten bloody felt cowardly, but if the plan worked, the pain would come to an end, the cycle broken.

The belt of saphramurls lay curled opposite Zanth in a corner of the room. There was something fitting about the dark to contemplate justice and revenge. Arric's death would achieve both: justice for his people and revenge for his dear Silisa. He massaged the tattooed skin over his heart, his ribs firm and bumpy.

Zanth had met Silisa in the dark. A hushed silence had spread across the gathered crowd as the moon swallowed the sun, swathing the land in shadow. A mesmerising halo encircled the moon, like the sun had bestowed a crown upon it. In the dark, a hand found his, delicate and warm and comforting. When the eclipse passed and light retook the land, she introduced herself.

Three soft knocks on the shield echoed off his four walls. Zanth counted the silence that followed, dropping four fingers, one after the other. Two more taps on the door followed. With the secret knock complete, he unlatched the door.

A tall, slender man entered, ducking his head on his way in. A younger, smaller woman slipped in behind him, thin like she'd been starved. Given the fresh brand marking her face, she probably had been, and worse. The dim light of the cancryst in her hand hurt Zanth's eyes, but they adjusted. Of the two, he knew only the man, Lisoun. They'd met at a Resatrium meeting before Zanth moved to the small island on the lake.

'You did it, brother.' Lisoun embraced him. 'You really did it.'

The physical contact felt odd; it had been some years since he'd had arms around him.

Zanth allowed himself a smile before they separated. 'Where's your blood brother, Ezro?'

'They're holding him for questioning. He won't break. They're ripping the crater apart, searching for you.'

'Mainly for them.' Zanth pointed to the belt studded with saphramurls in the corner. 'I'm safe here?'

Lisoun chuckled, taking a seat against the wall. 'The owner of this place is the one who leads the search for you, and they have no idea he's one of us.'

The woman strode towards the belt. Of all in the Resatrium ranks, she seemed like a strange choice to transport the most valuable asset they'd ever held.

'I don't know you, sister.' Zanth didn't hold back the challenge in his voice.

She picked up the belt regardless. 'They're paying attention to the people you know.'

That made him sick.

'You're far from inconspicuous with that brand on your face,' Zanth said.

'It's fresh. They think they broke me.' She looped the belt around her tiny waist, pulled her shirt over it and left, closing the door behind her. At least she was confident.

The room felt larger without the saphramurls. But he found no comfort in their absence.

Lisoun leant forwards, excitement building on his features. 'We can weaponise the gems, right?'

'No.' This was *not* why Zanth had stolen them.

'They did. We can turn their weapon against them. You could. You could destroy the palace.' His outstretched arm swept in a violent semicircle.

So often consumed by his own feelings, Zanth had forgotten how much others had lost under three generations of oppressive rulers. Of Lisoun's once-large family, only Ezro still lived.

'Don't look at me like that.' Lisoun tucked his hands under his armpits.

'We're fighting a snake with two heads: the king and Arric. You kill the snake by cutting off its heads, not blowing up a building and killing servants.'

'But it's—'

'No.' Zanth summoned a ball of fire in his palm. 'We stick to the plan. We kill Arric, then the king.'

'You're sure Arric will come? He'll meet us on the ridge, alone?'

'I'm sure.'

'Then we'll make the trek soon.' Lisoun stood and departed.

The darkness was no longer peaceful or poetic. Lisoun's anger lingered in the room.

When Silisa died, he'd wrapped himself in fury. Zanth had not let go of it since, and he'd need it for what was to come.

15. How Thick are Ya?

The room spun. Antarna extended her arms for balance. Nothing pulled at her. There was no pain.

She squinted at the light flooding through a window that had most certainly not been there a moment ago. Strange—to have travelled so far without having moved a muscle. Focusing on her hand, Antarna wiggled her fingers. Enthriff was curled many times around her forefinger. She rubbed him with her thumb.

Four armless stood at the corners of the square, breathing hard, the youngest more so than the others. Antarna dipped her head in thanks.

Hot air, heavy under the weight of humidity, draped over her. The crisp air of the mountains awaited her return, as did Tozias. She rolled up the sleeves of her thick robe. The white fabric contrasted against the black walls, floor and ceiling. It was peculiar to be robed in white after so long in grey.

Stranger still to be back here. Her grief rose closer to the surface, draping its leaden presence over her heart, weighing her limbs, clogging her throat, misting her mind.

The room's long, narrow window afforded a limited view of the dark crater walls, bustling with activity. Leaving the square on the floor, she approached the window. People flocked to the trade district and temples. Fields of mature tivitania stood tall in the bowl of the crater.

They'll be harvesting soon. She'd played many a game of hide and hunt with her brother in the fields.

The four priests exited. Another entered, his back straight and stride purposeful—the armless that'd visited her mountain temple. There was a confidence about Arric, the kind that came with power. And, aside from the king himself, none were more powerful. If she could see madriliks, then the magnitude of that power would be on full display within his chest.

He made eye contact, his gaze as intense. 'Welcome, Prin—'

'Antarna, please,' she said, breaking protocol. 'It is an honour to finally meet you, High Priest. Your reputation precedes you.'

'The honour is mine.' He looked her over. 'It can be a rough trip. We have tea steeping in the next room, if you please?'

Light filled the neighbouring room. Antarna drifted over to a large, unshuttered window. Below, the Purple Path ran to the palace—the only significant structure on the crater floor. In her early years, there had been something enchanting about the meandering walkway carpeted in indigo flowers and dappled shade. Now she recalled Salorann's arrow striking Grandfather amidst the horror of the Unjust Uprising.

A new wooden tower near the pond rose as high as two people. People lined up for water. *How odd.*

She must've been four or five floors up. If her memory served her correctly, the sixth floor housed the vault. *Where the saphramurl gems are.* She wanted to ask for the high priest's support with the king, but they'd just met.

Arric poured her tea.

'Thanks.' She remained by the window. Despite the passage of time, the crater looked largely unchanged from her childhood. To her right, between the edge of the crop fields and the crater wall, a statue of Zentrina and the eye-catching pirrocical plant made a suitable pair. The funeral of her mother and brother had taken place there, while she had lain in a mountain infirmary. She'd visit after she saw the king. 'You can see it all from here.'

'We can. If you look down, you'll spot your escort.'

At the temple's entrance waited a palanquin, four bearers and ten members of the royal guard. The lacquered palanquin featured a host of white stars in a sky of royal purple. Intricate geometric patterns adorned each end of the bronze poles.

'I was hoping to walk.'

Arric chuckled, innocent and scorn-free.

She sat, steam rising from the cup in front of her. 'The king will receive me when I arrive?'

'No, he has important business. The earliest you'll catch him is tonight.'

No business could be more important than saving the lives of the injured and comatose in the mountain temples. She'd break down the doors to the palace if she had to; Tozias needed her.

She took a breath. There was nothing to be done. Interrupting the king's business would only work against her. Like landing a strike in a duel, asking for a favour was as much a matter of timing as it was delivery.

After they finished their tea, she politely declined his offer to walk her to her escort. The pair parted in a wide and long hallway. Rectangular recesses covered the walls. They featured vases, sculptures, paintings, masks, ancient weapons and jewels. It reminded her of the palace.

She took the stairs to the ground floor. A pair of initiates stood in front of a heavy gate, the sole passage in and out of the crater.

Antarna turned away from them and left the temple. The bearers rose to their feet. The royal guards straightened their backs and tightened their grips on the shafts of their bronze-tipped spears. They cast glances at a man in the centre of their front line, whose angular, elongated face tapered to a pointed chin. His short, manicured beard and long hair framing his face added emphasis to its narrow shape. A ruby ribbon flitted on the shaft of his spear, below a spearhead of Daslercian steel.

The question written on his face made it clear he didn't know if she was the person he'd been sent to collect. This presented an opportunity to visit the pirrocical plant in peace and anonymity.

'She's arrived and should be ready shortly,' Antarna said before they had a chance to ask the question.

'Thanks, Acolyte,' replied the leader of the royal guard. A wide, flat animal tooth, larger than her hand, rested on his armoured chest, dangling from a vine around his neck.

The bearers sat back down under the shade of the nicarmia trees.

The pebbles of the Purple Path crunched under her feet. Screams of panic and pain from the Unjust Uprising surged in her mind. She shook her head and pushed the memory aside with a fond one of a hunting party returning to the crater; her brother, Kyrak, had proven himself on his rite of passage, making his first kill. That day, the trees had already dropped their flowers.

Today, the nicarmia trees were heavy with sleeping flowers; they bloomed only at night. Ahead stretched the ivy-covered front of the palace. She turned right and stretched out her arms. Head-high tivitania brushed against her hands. The path was narrow enough for her to reach the edge of the fields on either side.

The dark statue of Heltorne, goddess of agony, rose above the crop. Suffering contorted her face and stretched along her body, pronouncing the muscles in her neck and twisting her limbs. Her pitiful clothes put starvation on display. One hand missed a couple of fingers, and those remaining lacked nails. The other bore three deformed claws. Long wooden stakes rose from the ground around Heltorne's statue.

These are new. A dramatic touch?

Antarna kept walking, passing into the shade of the crater's rim. A list of names ran down the crater wall, chiselled in large letters. Names including her grandfather's and great-grandfather's. Father's name would no doubt be added when he passed. Her brother's chance to earn his place had been stolen from him.

A sickly sweet, fruity perfume gathered in the air. The pirrocical plant's sunset-orange leaves formed pitcher-shaped traps, vibrant against the dark backdrop. The cavities were filled with viscous liquid that digested its prey. The central pitcher dwarfed her. Around it hung smaller versions of itself, for which a finger would be too large of a meal.

Next to the carnivorous plant stood a statue of Zentrina, lifeless in comparison to the liquid-like version at the mountain temple. A stone scroll rested at the goddess's feet. Antarna sat to read its list of names—highborn names, few of which had the honour of being also carved on the crater's wall. Patriket Tarlqua, her grandfather, was three quarters of the way down. The last two names were her mother's and brother's, Veronique and Kyrak Tarlqua.

Numbness spread over her.

A decade ago, she'd cried a lifetime of tears. Fresh ones tumbled down her cheeks. Her arms were too heavy, too depleted, too unresponsive to wipe them away.

For some time, she sat unmoving, shoulders slumped, head bowed.

I'm sorry I haven't visited. Not that you're here. You'll have been deservingly reborn. I hope our paths cross. I could support you, as you supported me.

If you're still up with Zentrina, some friends of mine will have just joined you. Make them welcome.

Listless, she rose and started out to the pond. Her face begged for a splash of water.

She passed out of the shade.

Crops rustled ahead. A boy glanced up from pulling weeds. Hair was yet to grow upon his chest. Sweat glistened from his skin, darker than bronze, lighter than a trenn nut. Under his eye perched a splotch of deep purple.

Any number of reasons could explain the bruise, from carelessness to being disciplined by a figure of authority. Or it might have happened during training. Members of the Resatrium could be anywhere, though they wouldn't know she was back in the crater. Even her own father may not recognise her.

A group of five girls walked towards her, clay pots of water on their heads. The pots were scuffed and chipped. The oldest looking of the group, who seemed about the age of the boy pulling weeds, held the largest pot.

The pot was balanced on her head, leaving her hands free to hold a basket of washing. The others needed at least one hand on the pot to steady it. They had bare feet and birdlike legs: straight and thin, with no fat and little muscle.

'His leather was a bit snug,' one said with a giggle.

'Is that why you batted your eyelashes at him?' another replied.

'You're going to make me puke.'

'Enough talk of watchmen, unless you want a brand,' said the eldest.

Quiet fell down the line.

Watchmen? Antarna hadn't heard the term before.

She had the path to herself until a trio of ladies approached. Each had a baby wrapped snugly against their chest.

The fields on either side of her came to an end. The pond marked the centre of the crater floor. On its surface floated snow-white acoako nuts from a tree on the pond's edge. A boy on a small raft was collecting them. Another was busy picking up those that littered the ground. Inside each white leathery shell would be a pair of filling, earthy seeds.

Insects buzzed around the uplaful vine that curled around the trunk of the tree. White and blue flowers with radial filaments like a halo adorned it. The vine stretched down into the lake to drink, but the flowers stopped well short—never trespassing beyond the high-water point of recent years, as if afraid of the water.

A line of people, sixteen long, ran to the pond's edge. All except the youngest child held a pot or bladder. It didn't make sense to Antarna; the pond could easily fit a few hundred around it at any time.

They conversed in whispers, with eyes to one another or downcast. Not a laugh nor a smile to be found.

Two men sat close by on tree stumps in front of the wooden tower. Leather covered their torsos, shoulders, forearms and shins.

The girl had been right. The armour was tight on both, but the second man was almost bursting through his. She pictured him struggling into it each morning and pitied his wife, who would've had to help.

The purpose of these watchmen escaped her.

As she drew closer to the pond, a few in the line glanced up. The watchmen turned. One had grey, lifeless eyes, a squashed nose and almost no neck. Dull. The other had hard dark eyes shuttered by squinting eyelids. His eyebrows were pulled together and lowered. Angry.

'Hey! And what do you think you're doing?' asked Angry.

The pair rose and approached her. They each brandished a cane.

Antarna raised two fingers to her third eye. 'It's nice to meet you. I'm—'

'I didn't ask your name,' said Angry. 'Why aren't you in line?'

'Sorry, do I need to be?'

'How thick are you?'

Dull sniggered. 'Ay, how thick are ya?' The words came out slowly.

You're a beacon of intellect.

'Sorry, I've just arrived at the crater. I'm after a handful of water.'

'Get!' Angry pointed to the back of the unnaturally straight line. Discipline becoming of the royal guard—not the women, children and one old man who currently made it up.

Maybe not the time to ask why there's a line.

A pungent smell assaulted her nose: mature sweat and grime, baked in the sun.

No one spoke. A child tapped his mother's arm; she shook her head in reply and held a finger over her lips. The old man wasn't breathing well. Each exhale was prolonged and low-pitched, like a snore or a moan. He coughed, and it sounded throaty and wet.

After advancing a few places, hushed conversation resumed. The hands, arms, neck and face of the lady in front of Antarna were dotted with thick, crusty patches of skin. Ahead of her was a boy with an itchy-looking rash that tracked down his back.

Who is caring for these hapless people? She wished Elgerin was closer.

If she had food, she would've handed it out down the line. The boy's shoulder blades were pronounced, and his rib cage showed through his back.

A shadow passed over them: a flyer. Enthriff slithered from her finger to her wrist. Halfway down the line, a small girl wrapped herself around her mother's leg and squeezed.

The mother patted her daughter's hair. 'There's nothing to fear. The barrier is back up.'

Antarna turned to the lady behind her.

A scar dominated her cheek. It was made up of four parts that almost touched and resembled a broken knife. Each raised area was lighter than her normal skin tone.

She recalled what the girl had said: *Enough talk of watchmen, unless you want a brand.*

When did they start branding people?

Realising she was staring, Antarna quickly found her words. 'Sorry, do you know when the barrier went down?'

'Uh, must have been three nights ago.'

'Thanks. And definitely at night?'

'That's what they're saying.'

'Thanks.' So, *not connected to what struck us? But they were both three days ago and magic related. That can't be a coincidence.*

Antarna pointed at the large open space between the pond and the fields. 'What happened to the market?'

'Where have you been? That was shut down years ago.'

'I've been away and missed a lot, it seems.'

Antarna had fond memories of the vibrant market; it had set fire to the senses. The soft furs and smooth scales. The smell of spices and flame-kissed meat. Vendors hawking wares of all descriptions and children playing tag or skipping stones across the pond. She missed the mouth-watering fruit-nut-honey sweets, as well as the jugglers, musicians and puppeteers.

The line swelled faster than it moved.

The watchmen dragged themselves off their well-padded backsides to walk down its length. All eyes quickly found the ground. The silence was broken only by the old man's wheezing and Dull swishing his cane about.

Angry paused beside Antarna.

Can I help you? I'm standing quietly in your damn line.

He whacked the cane into his hand, releasing a sharp sound.

Swing it, I dare you.

Dull overtook him, and the pair moved on.

'What's your name?' asked a watchman to someone towards the back of the line.

You'll ask theirs but not wait to hear mine? His words were fast and clear. *Angry*.

'Evireny.' The reply, from someone young and female, barely carried to Antarna.

'What are you hiding?'

'Nothing, I promise.'

'Show us.'

Antarna glanced behind her, but the line was too straight with many people between them.

A woman looked at Antarna and shook her head.

Antarna nodded and returned her eyes to the pair of bare feet in front of her.

'I said show us, not twirl on the spot. Take your clothes off,' said Angry.

What? No!

The people in front didn't raise their eyes or open their mouths.

Antarna took a small step to the side and turned her neck.

A girl in a long, loose dress stood with her arms outstretched. The sleeves of the dress stopped short of her elbows. Her arms were nothing more than twigs. Antarna could have closed her thumb and forefinger around either her forearm or upper arm. The girl wasn't any older than Antarna. A fresh brand sat upon her cheek, red and weepy.

Evireny kept her body still, which accentuated her trembling lips and rapid blinking. One eye was dark brown while the other was green with flecks of yellow. The man behind her had the same eyes and brand.

Angry took a step towards the girl. 'Strip. Now!'

Antarna turned back around. What did they think she was hiding?

Clothing rustled.

'Too slow,' said Angry.

A cane struck exposed skin.

Antarna flinched. She slid a hand into her pocket, touching the onyx vial she'd brought with her from the mountain temples. But the shadow wouldn't just intimidate the watchmen, and these poor people were frightened enough. Antarna risked another look.

Evireny stood in her meagre breechcloth. The girl hugged her dress over her otherwise bare breasts.

'There's nothing there,' Angry said while poking his cane towards her torso.

'Nah, nothin',' Dull said.

Her chest was all rib cage, the curve and bump of every bone visible. Below it was a sunken cavity where a stomach should have been. Her hip bones jutted out unnaturally, giving something for the skin to hang off. Too much space separated her thighs.

Antarna clamped her teeth over the tip of her tongue and turned back around.

'Drop ya dress.' Dull had joined in giving orders.

Fabric fell to the ground.

Antarna squeezed her wrist, drawing the skin over her knuckles taut.

'What are you hiding under that?' asked Angry.

Antarna pictured the girl. Other than her dress, she only had a breechcloth: a single piece of cloth passed between her thighs, held up by a string around her waist.

'N-nothing,' the girl replied.

'Prove it.'

Antarna tightened the grip on her wrist. Enthriff joined in.

'Take it off, spread your legs and bend over,' said Angry.

'Now,' added Dull.

Again, a cane smacked the girl. It was louder this time.

Evireny screamed, high and short.

'We didn't tell you to open your mouth.'

Antarna could feel a third whack coming. *Over my cold, soulless corpse.* She took a step out of the line, then another.

The girl's back was rounded, and her shoulders were pulled forwards. It protruded her vertebrae further; they were a straight line of rocks upon a beach. Her legs quivered. Red welts marked her lower back and bottom.

'Can we talk?' Antarna asked.

Angry's wicked grin became a scowl. He pointed his cane at Antarna. 'Shut it. Get back in line!'

'We need to talk. It's important.' She walked towards the open area.

Angry's mouth narrowed. 'Stop!'

Antarna obeyed.

The pair advanced.

'I'd prefer to keep this between us. Could we talk about this privately, please?' Antarna glanced to the open space.

Angry pulled himself up to his full height. He had to lift his chin to meet her gaze. She may have been taller, but he was at least double her weight and armed.

He dropped a hand to the knife on his belt. 'I couldn't give a kennturia shit what you want. There is no privacy, not for your likes. We're not going to talk. You're getting the beating of your life. On your knees.'

'I'd like to talk first about why you're searching her.'

His face flushed. 'How dare you! Kneel, or we'll have you impaled.'

She took half a step back. 'Before Heltorne?' *You haven't been impaling people on those stakes, have you?*

A smirk returned to his lips.

That wormed its way under her skin. Antarna got in his face, determined to put him in his place. 'I'm going to tell you my name. Then, you're going to bow and apologise to me and her.'

Angry's eyes bulged, and Dull's jaw dropped.

She allowed herself satisfaction at their shock.

Enthriff squeezed her wrist.

Angry launched, striking at her head with his cane.

Antarna sidestepped.

Angry drew his knife. Dull pulled a small orb from his pouch and threw it onto the ground. Red smoke rose. No doubt a signal for reinforcements. This was escalating.

Antarna put her hands up. 'I don't want to fight.' By goddess, part of her wanted nothing more than to beat some sense and humility into them. But she shouldn't. 'Let's talk. I'm—'

'I don't care who you are!' Spittle flew from Angry's mouth.

Drops hit her cheek. She wiped them away. 'You will. You should. I—'

'I should? I should, should I?' Angry advanced.

Dull unsheathed his knife and looked over her shoulder. 'Gotcha now.'

A trio of watchmen approached. One carried a club, the other a spear and the last an axe. With Angry and Dull, they formed a circle around her.

Five, the number of my goddess.

'What we got?' asked the spearman.

'A sympathiser.' Angry drew mucus in and spat it at Antarna's foot.

She moved out of the way. Before this turned into a bloody melee, she had to lower the tension. 'I'm—'

'Dead!' Angry leapt at her, slashing with an arc that cut from his shoulder to his hip.

The spearman thrust with all his might.

Time slowed.

Perhaps the spearman thought she was focused solely on Angry. Maybe he just wanted the glory.

The point rushed towards her liver.

Antarna sprang backwards and to the side, putting the spear between Angry and her.

The tip slid past her.

Angry's knife raked the air.

When the spear reached its full extension, Antarna grabbed the shaft with one hand and slammed an open palm down with the other. The wood snapped with a loud crack, splinters flying. She kept hold of the end with the point.

Before the spearman could react, Antarna kicked his knee joint. He cried out and bent forwards.

Antarna threw a hook, her arm at ninety degrees. Pivoting as she punched, she rotated her hips for greater power.

Her two leading knuckles crunched into his jaw. He collapsed, unconscious.

The man with the club tried to take her head. She ducked and sliced open his thigh. Blood flooded the gash before running down his leg. He couldn't hold the wound closed with one hand, so he dropped the club.

The three uninjured watchmen converged upon Antarna, clearly oblivious to proper footwork. Priest Leharist would've been horrified.

The man holding his bloodied leg teetered on his feet.

Antarna pushed him into Angry's path.

Dull was close, his knife raised at head height in reverse grip, point down.

Attack low, away from the knife.

She kicked at his front leg. Her shin connected with the side of his knee, which buckled inwards. Dull fell into the last watchman, who tried to catch him with his free hand while keeping the axe clear. The weapon poked out awkwardly from the entangled pair.

Avoid the artery.

Antarna engaged, cutting the axeman's extended forearm with precision. His grip failed and the axe fell. In constant motion, Antarna circled around to Dull's back and stabbed him behind the shoulder blade.

Angry tossed his fellow watchman out of his way, frothing at the mouth. He sliced an X into the air as he advanced. As she'd done against Divislak, she changed her guard. This time, she raised it, giving Angry a good look at her unarmoured midsection. Two cuts later he went for it—the shift in his weight and gaze telltale, even before the tense of his arm. Antarna evaded with ease, flanking him as she did so. She stabbed him between a joint in his ill-fitting leather armour.

A pack of hunters arrived, each heavily armed and armoured as if they were leaving the crater. People dropped to their knees. Antarna threw the broken spear into the ground, point first. It buried deep.

She raised her hands. *How am I going to explain this*?

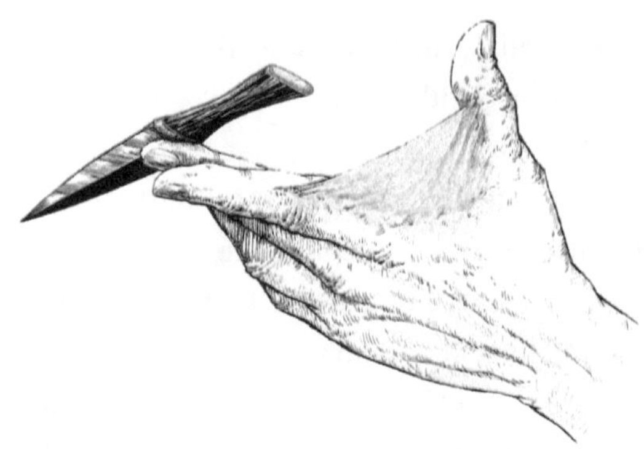

16. Bold, Stupid, Strange

A line of people extended from Devtakaris's temple. Most carried coin, jewellery or art. Only the poorest held perishable gifts. Cal bypassed the line and entered a spacious prayer hall. It was large enough to accommodate them all, yet the line crawled. Only once one person had finished did the next begin. In seeking protection, they wanted maximum attention from the god of magic.

A boy in a black robe with a crimson belt crossed in front of Cal.

'Loyal initiate,' Cal said, 'the high priest summoned me.'

'My Seer, of course. Please, follow me.'

How long would it take for him to grow accustomed to being called the seer? Not that he should be getting ahead of himself: if he didn't have news to share when the chancellor finally saw fit to see him, people would be using the title to address Mirogant.

The high priest's chamber was on the highest floor, up six flights of steps.

Another initiate stood in front of a heavy set of double doors. The young pair swung the doors open and announced Cal.

High Priest Josmark sat behind a desk large enough to seat two families. He rose for Cal. His crimson robe contrasted against the dark stone wall behind him, like fire in the night.

The initiates closed the doors behind them as they left. They still had their arms, for now.

'Take a seat, Seer.' A weak madrilik leapt from Josmark's chest. Energy flowed from it to the chair in front of Cal. The chair slid out from the desk. The listless speck left through an unshuttered window. On the horizon, the black rim of the crater jutted out above the rainforest.

Cal sat and brought his hands together in his lap.

Josmark pursed his lips before opening them. 'Your predecessor failed to stop the theft of the serpent egg. You failed to apprehend the thief before he used it to steal the saphramurls.'

'How tragic.' And it was. *All fifteen saphramurls*? Cal hadn't seen that in his vision. Using anti-magic trapped in a rare eggshell to steal anti-magic gems was fitting.

'That's not all. While in the temple, he tried to murder High Priest Arric in his study. Instead, he mistakenly killed Morsirel and then drained his madriliks.'

Cal's vision had been accurate. *Maybe that's why I've still got my eyes*. The chancellor would be gleeful with the crater and temple of magic, the two biggest threats to his power, weakened and embarrassed. Cal reclasped his hands. Murder and theft in the same night seemed ... bold, stupid, strange.

Madriliks churned inside Josmark. 'Have you got nothing to say for yourself?'

'I apologise. What can I do to help?'

'You can find the thief. We've already identified him. His name is Zanth. He was born in the crater and fled here a couple of years ago. We're not sure how long he's been with the Resatrium, but likely for some time. It's in both our interests that he's found, quickly.'

'Of course. What does he look like?'

'Dark hair and skin. He posed as a royal messenger to steal the saphramurls, so was clean-shaven with a triangle of hair under his lower lip. Around twenty summers. Still has his arms.'

Odd thing to add, unless he trained at your temple? 'I'll commence my search today.'

'Good. Keep me updated.'

Cal left the room and descended the stairs. The ridiculous line to the prayer hall had grown. More than a few in it stared openly at him.

On the street, Cal pictured his bronze throwing knife in his hand. Transferring his weight to his front foot, he released the imaginary knife. Of course, it flew true. Throwing nothing but air seemed to have also drawn a few stares.

Something called to him, neither a feeling nor a sensation. Hard to describe. Contradictory: silent but singing. He turned down an alley, only to realise where his feet were leading him.

Cal entered Gionco's shop. He ducked under a chieftain headdress from the desert, red feathers extending like a set of wings. An ancient bronze helmet from Daslercia stood on a stand, a relic of a bygone age.

Gionco flashed him a grin, stained teeth filling his mouth. 'Knew you'd be back. The knife?'

'Yes.'

'Of course.' The swindler took Arric's old knife down. Stone. Simple. He laid it on the counter.

Cal hovered his fingers over the blade. Memories bubbled below its surface. Part of him wanted to turn around and leave. A larger part needed to touch the knife. He lowered his hand and fell into infinite darkness. Light appeared, like stars in the night sky. The dots became streaks as Cal hurtled *backwards*—for the first time. He weaved between the lights until he collided with one.

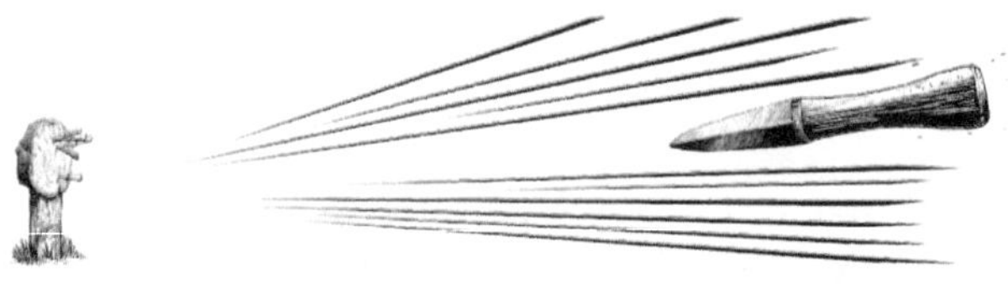

All held a knife; all bore a smile.

Arric carried a stone knife. Dark, untamed hair covered his ears. A single dull madrilik resided in his chest. He couldn't be older than twelve or thirteen.

Until now, Cal had only read of seers having rare visions of the past.

A dense crowd shuffled forwards, laughing and shouting over the steady beat of the drums. Arric squeezed through a gap between two families, ducked under the arm of a vendor selling a wine skin and avoided a row of colourful, fluttering banners.

The boy slid and pushed his way to a nicarmia tree. Its trunk was terribly twisted, as if it had learnt to grow by watching someone climb the spiral steps of a tall, narrow tower. Arric scrambled up. He settled onto a low-hanging branch that offered a full view of the procession.

King Patriket Tarlqua marched down the Purple Path, flanked by his two sons. Behind them, seasoned hunters pushed handcarts filled with the bounty of the hunt: a dismembered kennturia.

The royal trio drew their swords and offered them to the gods, honouring those of the hunting party that had left as boys and returned as men.

Arric raised his knife with the crowd and then brought it down upon his palm. Around him, red droplets fell like rain.

Cal prepared himself for the bloodshed and death to come. He'd read accounts of this infamous day. Never had he thought he'd see it.

The king elevated his blade once more, this time for the three fallen, never to become men.

A knife struck the king square in the chest, point first. The dark glass blade shattered against his scaled armour, sending fragments ricocheting.

Screams filled the air. An arrow buried into the king's thigh, and another sliced Prince Ithranned's cheek. The screaming intensified into a maelstrom of sound.

Two royal guards fell.

While Arric clambered higher up the tree, pandemonium reigned. People shoved, jostled, knocked one another over. They even trampled the helpless.

The royal guard surrounded the royals, a wall of shields.

A hammer cracked a skull. An axe lodged into a neck. A club dropped a man. A spear impaled another. Death, everywhere.

Madriliks filled the chest of a thin, hooded figure emerging from the tree line. He outstretched his arms.

Layaury: the notorious Resatrium mage.

The guards around the prince rose into the air, eyes wide and limbs flailing. They hung, helpless, before being hurled away. One hit the ground headfirst; he did not rise.

Specks of light raced from Layaury like a stampede of shooting stars. A beam of raw power swept over the royal trio. The younger of the two princes, Barrass, shrieked, dropping sword and shield. As each moment dragged into the next, the sound escalated. Prince Ithranned fell, his screams joining his brother's. The king dropped to his knees and planted the sword into the path, knuckles white and teeth gritted. Layaury focused the madriliks on him.

Arric climbed back to a low-hanging branch, dangled from it and then dropped to the ground, landing with bent knees and wide arms. The masses ran away from Purple Path. Not Arric: he walked towards it.

The king collapsed, lifeless, and the beam turned to the princes.

Arric stepped into it. Bright light flooded him. A party of shooting stars in his chest and upper abdomen.

Cal recalled reading a description of this from Arric. Something like: *Heat, blazing heat. As if standing too close to a roaring bonfire. Instinct told him to move back, yet something stronger held him there. The heat gathered inside him, growing hotter and hotter. Pain spread from the centre of his chest until soon all his nerves shrieked in unison.*

Arric let out a frantic cry. Heltorne, goddess of agony, had welcomed him into her arms. He burnt from the inside out.

The end did not come.

His reservoir burst, overflowing into a deeper one in his lower abdomen—the envy of most mages. Arric opened his arms wide, like a bird preparing to take flight. By his face, the pressure and pain had eased.

Arric gripped the beam like he would a rope and pulled. The bright specks rushed towards him.

The world flickered.

It flickered again.

There was nothing but darkness.

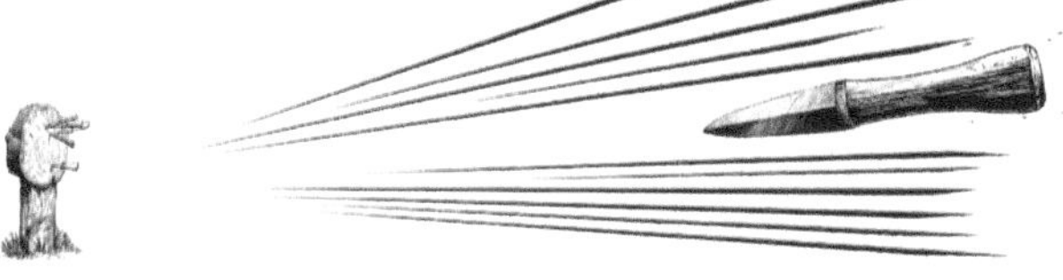

Cal tore his hand from the knife.

Everyone knew the end. Arric wakes a hero, having saved the princes and stopped Layaury.

'Are you level?' asked Gionco. He stood so close that Cal could smell betricil berries on his breath.

'Yes, thank you.' Cal took a few steps back.

'What did you see?'

'The Unjust Uprising.'

'See, it's authentic.' With a flourish of his hand, he invited Cal to admire the knife. 'Did you bring enough coin?'

'No.' Cal left the shop to Gionco's curses.

Why a vision of the past? Why that vision? What are you trying to show me, Goddess?

He headed east, taking his first of many turns. By the time he reached the beach, his feet hurt. A dozen or so people lay upon the pale-yellow sand, and at least twice as many were enjoying a dip. Further out, fishermen worked from their canoes and boats. Wind filled the lapis-coloured sail of a boat, a father and his son aboard.

I miss you, Dad.

After taking off his shoes, Cal stood on the tops of them, the sand hot underfoot. He pulled off his gloves and stripped down to his underwear. A young couple spun around and turned for home. A woman grabbed her daughter and hastened down the beach.

The clear water of lake called. He hoped the chancellor wouldn't.

Did I see Arric defeat Layaury because Zanth's a Resatrium mage like Layaury was? Where are you, Zanth?

17. In This Prison

Zanth rubbed his stubble. It'd be months before he'd have a full beard again. Well, if he lived through today. Either he or Arric would die; it was that simple. He should have been thankful that he hadn't crossed paths with the high priest during his theft. They'd meet on Zanth's terms today.

Three knocks broke the silence followed by two more. He opened the door. Light assaulted him, stabbing his eyes.

Lisoun and Ezro stood tall, packs on their backs. The brothers shared the same broad foreheads topped with tight curls. Colour came back to Zanth, his eyes adjusting. Purples and reds dominated Ezro's face, and his lip was split.

Ezro touched his jaw. 'Don't worry, just a bit of extra motivation for today.'

'We've each experienced a lifetime of motivation,' Zanth said.

'That we have,' said Lisoun.

Zanth stepped out and shut the door behind him.

A tapestry of a javelin protruding from a horned beast masked in mist dominated the back wall. No one had seen more of a hazzurus than its horns and lived to talk about it. The javelin featured a ruby ribbon tied to it, a splash of colour in the otherwise greyscale piece.

The trio had a long climb ahead.

Zanth sat atop the crater's rim, massaging his tired legs. The urlire in his pocket created a faint bulge. His breath had returned to normal. Below, the pond almost large enough to be a lake looked akin to a puddle.

Wood clinked behind the thicket as Lisoun unpacked the sharpened stakes. Water sloshed into a hole.

Ezro cast a handful of red dust high into the air, signalling to the Resatrium that they were ready. The cloud quickly dispersed.

Swallowing the lump in his throat, Zanth rose to his feet. He'd relieved himself before he'd sat to rest, but the urge came again. Ignoring it, he lifted his necklace over his head and handed the necklace to Lisoun. Without the nalitroite, Arric would be able to make out Zanth's store of madriliks.

Will it be enough? Will I?

It must. I must.

Zanth called upon a madrilik. Draining its power, he manipulated the light in front of him, allowing him to see far-off objects. Before Arric had become the high priest, he'd taught Zanth this spell, beginning with the act of focussing sunlight upon a leaf to start a fire.

On the crater floor, a young boy jogged up to the entry of the temple of Devtakaris, scroll in hand. Two initiates halted the boy, and he handed over the message for the high priest.

Zanth was on his second piece of jerky when Arric emerged. People scurried out of his way, and guards straightened. The high priest paid them no more attention than a child chasing a ball gives to ants on the path. He hadn't changed.

Old feelings welled in Zanth, as dark and sharp as ever. 'It's time.'

'Finally.' Lisoun grabbed his ear with his opposite hand and drew his head down until his neck cracked. His other hand held a rainbow orb.

'Is he alone?' asked Ezro. A bow rested in his lap.

'Yes.' Zanth licked his lips. The message had been clear, but there had been no guarantees it would be heeded—none, bar Arric's arrogance. Meeting on the rim would isolate Arric from his priests, and the king's hunters, watchmen and royal guard.

The brothers took their places behind a boulder.

Arric scanned the rim of the crater, turning his neck and then his body until he spotted Zanth. A bright sun of madriliks resided within the high priest.

Three times my supply? Not that it'd matter. The best way to race a distance runner was in a sprint. The fight would be over fast.

Arric crossed the crater floor. Drawing on his own madriliks, he floated in the air. Arric rose without haste in a spiral pattern, like a bird catching a rising current of warm air.

Dropping the sight spell, Zanth conjured a defensive barrier. His leg jittered. He'd waited years for this fight. Finally, it was imminent. Justice and revenge. His late wife deserved nothing less.

Arric drew level with the rim and stepped onto the dark rock. He had not one but two madrilik reservoirs in his torso, like overlapping suns, one below the other. 'This ends here. Give me the gems.'

'What, we're not going to reminisce about old times?' Zanth pulled open his robe. The word SILISA was tattooed over his heart.

'We've been over this. The plague spread faster than any could have imagined. Sadly, lives were lost. But many more were saved. The king did the best he could, as did I to support him.'

'You supported him in directing healers and medicine to the rich and powerful. You locked down the crater, confining us with the sick in crowded conditions.' Heat flushed through Zanth's tense body. He recalled the angry, weeping boils covering his love's skin. 'I sent for your aid, and none came.'

'Even if I had given it, we'd be here now, facing off as we are. You still would've run from the temple on the night before your test, afraid of the pain and the sacrifice. Bitter, you still would've turned on us.'

'That night, I couldn't sleep.' Zanth clenched his fists. 'Not at the thought of committing my life to serving you!' It shouldn't have taken him a few months to see where the rot was, but his mind had been clouded. When he'd lost her, he'd lost everything.

Deep down, years of agony and grief had festered. It surged upwards, dark and bitter and twisted. He would swallow it no longer.

A mighty torrent of fire gushed from his outstretched hands, bright and deadly. Streaks of violet twisted through the yellow-orange flames. As they drew near, the high priest took to the air. Zanth redirected his attack, twisting it towards his target. Nothing would keep him from incinerating Arric.

The blazing flames raked the sky, ever closer to the fleeing figure. They tore through Arric's defensive barrier and licked the hem of his robe. Never had revenge been closer.

Arric spun to face Zanth and cast a powerful spell to divert the course of the deadly flames overhead. Drenched in sweat and gasping for breath, Zanth fought for control of the fire—it was his, after all. Yet it refused him. Tiny tremors spread along Zanth's arms and legs. Blistering heat from the inferno burnt his skin and seared his lungs.

But pain, he knew. Just as he knew this fire, understanding it in a way Arric never would. Zanth had tested and perfected it. The spell had proved itself when it ripped through his enemy's defensive barrier. So, he wouldn't stop now.

Wild spirals of flames continued to erupt from his palms. Zanth pitted his will against his former mentor's. The fire arched over Arric's head, responding to the man's power. Though it heeded Zanth too, at times descending dangerously close to consuming the high priest.

Zanth felt his control slipping. His legs wobbled, as the body often did close to the finish line. And the line was within sight. The fire wanted to be free to consume Arric, surely.

His legs betrayed him, collapsing. As the hard ground met his knees, Zanth ceased his spell. His head fell to his chest. Where before it had been bright and full with madriliks, now it was nearly empty. And all for nought. Though he had more than one trick up his sleeve.

Arric descended, his dual reservoirs barely depleted. 'You never stood a chance against me. Give me the gems.'

Breathless, Zanth shook his head. Arric's need to recover the gems was the reason the high priest hadn't sought to land a killing blow. A mistake he would dearly pay for.

'I don't know how you've slept the last few nights, after what you did.'

Zanth snorted. *I know what you did.*

'You brought down the barrier. Flyers got three before I got it back up. Their deaths are on *you*.' The loose rocks around Arric rose briefly into the air. 'If a pack of hazzurus got in, we'd be dust like Daslercia. You endangered every life here just to steal the gems. Need I go on?'

'It was safer than letting you keep them. The king's reign must end, as must yours.'

Arric came closer. 'We keep the people safe. Your Resatrium brothers and sisters have lost sight of that truth.'

'What's next—you'll tell me the crater is a paradise?'

Arric scoffed. 'It's anything but. Daslercia had a real name to go with a real city. Of the four races, none have that. We've named ourselves after the piece of nature we cower within.' He inclined his head towards the crater to make his point and continued to close the gap.

Just a little closer. 'With all that wealth and power, it must be so hard for you and the royal family.'

'Lose the sarcasm and wake up. When we send a hunting party into the forest, who is the hunted and who the prey? It wasn't steel that kept Daslercia safe, but magic. Too few are born with magic. Look down, tell me what you see.' Arric turned to face the crater.

Lisoun and Ezro leant out from behind the boulder. After taking aim with his front arm, Lisoun released his orb. Ezro's arrow overtook it in flight.

A shimmering magical shield rose around Arric. The bone arrowhead shattered against it. The orb arched through the air, closing in on its target—and it'd make short work of the high priest's defensive barrier.

Zanth pushed himself to his feet and hurled a bone-breaking curse.

Arric took control of the air, veering the orb wide of him and looping it around his body. At the same time, he dismantled Zanth's curse as easily as untying a bow.

The orb sped back the way it had come.

Lisoun and Ezro dived behind the boulder. The orb smashed into it and exploded, obliterating the rock and shaking the world. Wind tore at Zanth's hair and clothes. Dust consumed everything. When it cleared, his brothers lay dead—bodies crumpled, bloodied, broken. A heaviness draped itself over his shoulders and nestled inside his chest.

Arric strode forwards. 'Two more deaths. Who's responsible? You stole the gems. You weren't brave enough to face me alone. You ambushed me.' He drew level with the thicket.

Zanth had enough madriliks for two small spells. He summoned a clap of thunder and split the blue sky. At its loudest, at the height of the intended distraction, Zanth launched the sharpened stakes.

Arric separated the stakes with a quick spell, despite Zanth trying to force them back on path. They flew by him in two packs.

Without his nalitroite, Arric would know he was out. This wasn't how the fight was meant to go. He'd pictured it so many times over the years, but never like this.

'I'll give you the gems.' Zanth reached into his pocket and closed his hand around his urlire. Falling to his knees, he smashed it against the rock. The jewel splintered, releasing its stored madriliks. He dragged some of the sweet power into his chest. With the rest, he lifted the water from the hole, froze it into sharp icicles and propelled them at his enemy.

Arric countered the spell, melting the ice. Water splashed upon the rocks. He flung a potent curse, using more madriliks than Zanth had used in his last four spells.

C.U.B.E. It had been drilled into them as first years. Zanth didn't have enough power to Counterattack or Block. More intricate than a spiderweb, the curse was too hard to Untie.

Evade. Zanth turned and sprinted, swirling up the dust behind him for cover. Not that there was anywhere to run to, high atop the crater's rim. He adjusted course, only for the curse to do likewise. It cracked the rock it rushed over.

The edge of the crater's rim loomed ahead. The forest stretched out in all directions. This high, he was closer to the clouds than the ground.

The curse split the rock half-a-step behind him.

Death catches the stagnant.

He leapt off the edge, arms pumping, legs spinning. Wind tore at him—from his clothes and hair to the liquid in his eyes. Never had the mass of air felt so substantial. He hurtled towards a bunch of boulders, soon to break his every bone. Soon to crack his spine, collapse his lungs and paint red the outer slope of the crater. But that wouldn't avenge Silisa.

Dipping into his small store of madriliks, he selected one. The boulders appeared ever larger. Using the chosen middler, he hastened to slow his fall. The spell failed to take. His heart quickened its desperate beat. Mere body lengths from a gory splatter, Zanth tried again, mustering all his focus to picture marionette-like strings lifting him to safety. The jolt threatened to tear his arms from their sockets and dislocate his legs. He landed in a heap, nursing his shoulders most of all.

Energy gathered above. His enemy would give no respite.

Sparce vegetation clung here and there. Nothing that could be counted on for cover. Zanth sprinted down the incline towards the forest.

Arric unleashed a devastating spell. It soared down the slope and impacted where Zanth had been moments before. Zanth flinched as a sound split the air—mightier than thunder, more blood-chilling than a pack of velengoric. Rocks erupted, and the ground shook violently. He fell, hands extended, and righted himself with magic.

Rocks slid and bounced, stampeding down the side of the crater. His former master hadn't missed: he was going to crush and bury him under an avalanche.

Zanth grabbed his only bright. Siphoning its energy and directing this into a spell, he rose into the air and rushed towards the forest.

A flowerpot-sized rock nicked his ear. The next was larger. Zanth manoeuvred out its way, breathless. Rocks tumbled around him. He screamed, and the reigning chaos consumed it. Dust stung his blinking eyes, filled his nose and lined his throat.

Something struck his shoulder, sending pain radiating down his arm and back. This broke his concentration, and he fell.

Casting anew, Zanth formed a protective sphere around himself. Inside it, and after a bounce, he skidded down the seething slope. A headache squatted between his temples, poking the back of his eyes with pudgy fingers. The world blurred, from the pain or sheer speed he knew not. Rocks pelted the back of the sphere. He gritted his teeth, struggling to hold the barrier. The madrilik faded.

Zanth shifted left, lining up with a gap between two tall trees.

Almost there.

He entered the dark forest and veered around a tree, only to smash into another.

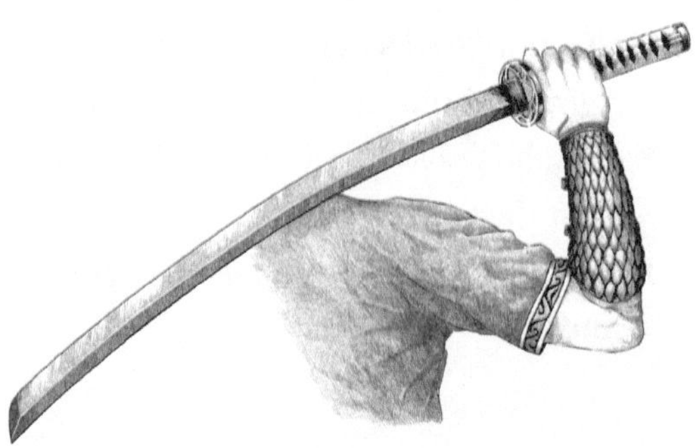

18. I Swore Never to

Antarna extended her arms, offering them to a toned hunter holding a coil of vine, two body lengths long. He bound her wrists securely with layers of the supple vine and finished with a complicated knot that sat between them. The excess hung from this knot, forming a leash to control her with.

She had not resisted. He hadn't stripped a starving, defenceless girl naked and beat her. Nor had he attacked Antarna. If only the watchmen had let her speak—let her tell them who she was. By goddess, she'd tried. But still, could she have done more? Deep down, some part of her had wanted the fight, had hungered for it in the name of justice and all that was right.

But her mission was to secure saphramurls for the mountain temples. For Tozias and Letti and all the other injured. For her high priest who'd trusted her. Not to protect a girl she didn't know, in a land now unfamiliar.

Back for a mere fraction of a day and already arrested. What did that say about her? Or did it say more about the crater?

Angry had both hands pressed against his injured side. Blood dribbled from between his fingers. The snarl on his face twisted as he winced. 'Whore, they are going to stake you and your family for this.'

You attacked me. I'd suggest you worry about what my family is going to do to you.

'Look what ya done, bitch.' Dull struggled to reach his wound.

Acolytes of Preslina arrived. They wore white robes like hers but of a lighter fabric, and pristine. Red splattered Antarna's. She couldn't look any worse for Father and the king.

The acolytes rushed to attend the watchmen and stem the bleeding. Bandages were liberally applied—to Angry's side, Dull's upper back, the axeman's forearm and the gash in the club-man's leg.

The spearman was out cold. It took four to lift him onto a stretcher. A second stretcher was brought for the club-man.

Dull gritted his teeth as he took an assisted step. He almost flattened the poor acolyte he leant on.

The hunters formed a square around her—one on each side, four in front and four behind—and led her away. The acolytes followed with the watchmen. Evireny was brought along too. A runner was dispatched.

A decade had passed since she'd been to the palace. If what she'd seen today was any indication, much had changed. But, from the outside, it looked the same. Green ivy sheathed the front wall, shiny, three-pointed leaves overlapping like Enthriff's scales. Lavish golden flowers bloomed on vines stretching the width and height of the right-side wall. Such beauty seemed incongruous with the events of the day.

She started working on her speech to the king. It'd be crucial to swiftly explain the facts, then shift the focus to why she was here: the gems. Yet that seemed doomed to fail. She'd accepted that she couldn't interrupt the king's business upon arriving in the crater, and now she was doing just that.

They turned onto the Purple Path. The royal guard and bearers were still waiting in front of the temple of Devtakaris. A guard pointed at her. After hurried conversation, they jogged towards the procession. Soon, they overtook it. Their leader with the rare steel-tipped spear gave her a long, hard look on his way past.

The path sloped up; the palace had been built on the highest ground. The records detailed that the crater had flooded no fewer than seven times. Antarna had read that the tunnel to the outside, on the bottom floor of Devtakaris's temple, was first built to let the water out. Later, it had been expanded to allow for expeditions and hunting. The risk of flooding was also a reason the temples and residences were all in the crater walls—that, and it maximised the land available for farming. Old history couldn't distract her from what awaited her.

The huge twin doors of the royal palace loomed ahead. As heat arose along her arms, she took deep breaths.

The servants' entrance had been too much to hope for. She couldn't have made a louder entry. If only she'd climbed into that palanquin. She'd have been dressed in finery, ushered to the king at a time convenient to him, heralded, and they would've discussed the aid needed for the mountain temples.

Although a palanquin ride would not have revealed the gross mistreatment of people happening every day within the crater. Her gut told her that what she'd seen today barely scratched the surface of the horrors being committed. She'd have to take this up with the king and with her father.

Every eye in the foyer looked their way. Antarna bent her knees and rounded her shoulders, taking a little off her height. The square of hunters provided reasonable cover, as did the royal guards in front of them.

A young woman carrying a platter of food passed by. Her dark hair cascaded down her back in a waterfall of thick curls. The provocative neckline of her dress framed more than her collarbones. If that's the look they'd expect of her, they would be in for more of a shock than Antarna had thought.

The group turned right.

So, *the king's at court.*

The leader of the royal guard stopped before a set of doors carved with the core commandments. He stood tall, with muscled shoulders squared and chest proud. Something in his demeanour—not just his overly manicured beard, glossy hair and clean nails—suggested a fondness for his own reflection. Someone like that wouldn't tolerate embarrassment, which is exactly what'd happen if the king asked why he hadn't collected her on her arrival in the crater. I *made another foe.*

Angry's confidence had returned. She couldn't wait for his smug smirk to be wiped from his face. Judgement would be swift and terrible, and it wouldn't go the way he was expecting.

The doors opened, and the herald stepped forwards. 'Announcing Hunt Commander Farikarr with an accused and injured in tow.' The herald's voice projected through the vast room.

They entered, and her hand twitched, anxiety coursing through her veins.

The imposing figure of King Ithranned Tarlqua sat on a throne of rare deep-purple rock carved with the heads of the deadliest of forest predators. Ilunger snouts for armrests. A pack of velengoric roaring for the backrest. The preserved wings of a flyer adorned the intricate chair, each three spears in length. A scar ran down the king's cheek.

Zentrina, why rebirth me to this life? Salorann almost killed him ... and my father. The weight of her past pressed upon her.

She dropped her chin to her chest. The centre aisle was uneven under her feet, a mosaic of bones from creatures beyond the crater. Small bones filled the gaps between larger ones.

Her father, Barrass, sat to the king's right—as each hunt master had done before him. He no longer looked the younger of the brothers. Horizontal wrinkles stretched across Father's forehead. Similar lines bracketed his mouth, running down from his nose. There were more grey hairs on his square jaw than dark ones.

With each year apart, the chasm between them grew. It was now so wide she couldn't be sure he'd even recognise her. Especially not bound and dragged in by guards.

Sunlight poured through generous windows. Father's jadrossil-hide armour and the heavy gold chain around the king's neck caught the light. Antarna appreciated the two vacant seats to the left of the king, as the presence of the queen and their son would only add to the scrutiny upon her.

The procession halted at the end of the aisle. To her left was a zarrleck's rib cage. Each rib was thicker than her thigh. An accused would kneel within the structure while awaiting the court's judgement.

Everyone took to their knees before the king, except for Antarna who struggled to rearrange her bound hands so the tips of her fingers ran up her forearms. She bowed, sliding one leg behind the other. On her rise, she lifted her chin, revealing her face.

The wrinkles on Father's forehead deepened. 'Antarna?' Her name seemed to hang in the room, weighty and thick with things unspoken.

The sound of his voice tugged her back to a version of herself long gone, when she'd been soft and innocent. 'I'm sorry. This was not the entrance I'd hoped to make. It's nice to see you, Father. And you too, my king.'

The king's expression darkened, lips flattening, eyes cold.

Her father stared, blinking on occasion.

Say something, please.

Father pointed to her. 'Hunter, cut those bonds from my daughter, now.'

The man hastened to comply, his knife sliding through the vines with ease. 'Forgive me, Princess.' His voice shook.

'You performed your role.' She clasped her hands behind her back, rubbing her red wrists out of sight.

The king gripped the armrests of his throne. If they'd have been made of wood, he'd have reduced them to splinters. 'Do you realise what you've done by assaulting *my* watchmen?'

Realisation hit her—harder than the slap of his words and fiercer than his demeanour. The watchmen were an extension of the king. By opposing them, she'd publicly challenged his authority. Treason. She'd all but raised her fists against her uncle, the rightful ruler of her people.

A tremor ran down her arms, and Antarna tensed them. 'Please accept my sincere apologies.' She bowed again to her uncle.

The most powerful man of the four races sternly raised his chin, rejecting her apology. He looked like only blood could placate him.

The air grew heavy.

Father broke the silence. 'Farikarr, why didn't you accompany my daughter as requested?'

The leader of the royal guard stepped forwards, grounding the shaft of his steel-tipped spear beside his foot. 'I attended the temple with a palanquin. But we had a'—he paused as if struggling to find the right word—'misunderstanding.'

The king shifted his piercing gaze to Antarna. 'You misled him?'

Harmlessly. 'There was something I needed to do first, urgently and unaccompanied.'

Father cleared his throat. 'What did you need to do first?'

His feet were bare, as with all hunters: silence was paramount outside the shelter of the crater. Greaves of jadrossil hide protected his shins and tibia.

'I needed to visit the pirrocical plant.'

'That's understandable.' Father emphasised the last word, likely seeking to calm his brother.

'Perhaps.' The king stood. He had a bulging waist like Angry but solid legs and arms. 'What I can't understand is why you're covered in blood, and there are five injured watchmen in my court.'

'Two watchmen cruelly strip-searched one of your subjects in line for water. I asked to speak to them and tried several times to tell them who I was. They wouldn't let me talk and attacked me. I refused to engage. Three more watchmen arrived. The five tried to kill me. Unarmed, I defended myself.'

'Well?' said the king, looking down the aisle.

'I am Watch Leader Cassian, Your Majesty,' said the man she'd dubbed Angry. 'A branded Resatrium member was acting suspiciously, and so we conducted a search.'

Evireny is Resatrium?

Branded with a broken knife. Of course, the knife that shattered against my grandfather's armour at the Unjust Uprising.

I defended a Resatrium member.

Antarna had missed a good part of what he'd said, so consumed by her thoughts.

Angry continued, '—we had cause to think that she was just another troublesome sympathiser. After she failed to comply with our directions on multiple occasions, we sought to carry out your justice. If only we had known she was of royal blood ... We apologise.'

The king nodded. 'And the part where a skinny unarmed girl defeated five of you?'

'She's had advanced training. She must have.'

The king spun on his heels, turning to Antarna. 'Is that true? I wasn't aware that those of Preslina practised fighting.' He tilted his head as if trying to picture members of the temple of life in combat.

'I also spent some time at Zentrina's temple.' *And if I didn't, you'd be offering my body to the pirrocical plant.*

This stopped the king. 'At the temple of the goddess of death?' He looked to her forearms as if expecting to see Zentrina's mark.

'And of rebirth. The goddess is often misunderstood. Like Preslina, Zentrina values and cherishes life. You'd agree that each life is invaluable?'

'No, I don't. Take those of the Resatrium, for example.'

'Does the ideology of a person change their worth?'

'People's actions certainly do. What about the Resatrium member that killed your mother and brother?'

How dare you use them to try to win an argument! She craved to stomp and smash the old bones of the centre aisle. Steam gathered within, knocking ever louder to be released.

'Why did you start learning at Zentrina's temple?' asked Father, changing the topic.

'The clash of weapons reminded me of you training Kyrak.' She swallowed; it'd been far too long since she'd voiced her brother's name. 'His sword is all I have of his. Training with it made me feel close to him.'

And I swore never to be helpless again.

'We're almost to the bottom of this,' the king said. 'Watch Leader, bring the branded one into the rib cage.'

Her name is Evireny.

Angry shoved the girl inside. She fell to her knees.

'And you've reasonable cause to suspect that she's concealing something?' asked the king.

'Yes, Your Majesty.'

'Then complete your search.'

Has the world gone completely mad? She looked to her father, expecting him to intervene. His mouth was set.

After having Evireny open her mouth and lift her tongue, Angry ran a fat, grimy finger along the inside of her cheeks.

Antarna pictured herself breaking the man's horrible fingers. They were lucky she had left her sword in the mountains.

Evireny's dress came off, again. Her breechcloth dropped to the floor.

Inside, Antarna screamed—at the dignity being stripped away, at her father's silence, at the ruler who had ordered this. The violation could never be justified. Her stomach churned.

Angry bent Evireny over at the waist. With a thin cloth covering his hand, he reached into her rear. She scrunched her face, eyes squeezing shut.

'Traitor.' Angry pushed her to the floor and thrust his hand high. Something coloured and spherical caught the light.

It can't be.

19. Vertical Pupils

Zanth reached for his pounding head, but branches ensnared him. One jabbed his ribs. Another poked his back. Heavy, his eyelids slid shut.

Get up! He peeled his eyes open. Arric didn't appear to be pursuing, but priests or hunters may have been on their way. His arm stung. A bloody gash ran down its length. No smell was more alluring than blood to a predator. Maybe one already had his scent.

Zanth slithered backwards, willing his weary body over stout roots and out of the branches. The bottom third of a tree trunk stretched above his head. The rest of the tree had formed a shelter over him. Rubble lay in mounds on either side.

He coughed, bringing up dust and aggravating his back. Black dust smothered the forest and coated his ripped clothes.

Grabbing the trunk, Zanth hauled himself upright. His dry throat and headache demanded water. Only a dull madrilik remained in his chest.

The glade had plenty of water and madriliks, and he could sense its power close by. His stomach grumbled. *Yes, food too.*

Not that he deserved food with his people starving. Even three-on-one, with a urlire and chosen terrain, they'd been no match for Arric. Years of training and months of planning, only to fail. He'd led Lisoun and Ezro to their deaths. A heavy grief should have been smothering him. His chest should have been aching with sorrow. Instead, it was as if his heart had been hollowed out, leaving just an empty space.

Zanth trudged through the forest. Low-hanging vines sought to entrap him. Roots reached up to catch his feet. He passed a tree laden with dangling seed pods. These, like its limbs, were covered in sharp thorns.

Further on, two neighbouring trees offered more promise. Round purplish-black fruit grew on their trunks. He recognised some of the trees around him—oparitoons, yellow haripens and gendikrils—but not these. Insects swarmed the tree on his left, but there were none on the other. Trusting his instincts, Zanth picked three from the left-hand tree. The sunlight-yellow pulp was sweet and juicy.

Few options remained. Without his nalitroite, the crater wasn't one of them; he'd be a danger to any who hid him. Zanth needed to get a message back to the Resatrium, but a dull was insufficient for the task.

Zanth pushed a fern frond out of his way. Wind stirred the canopy, sending the shadows into a dance. Sunlight glinted off a spiderweb that arched from tree to tree. A colony of spiders hid in the darkness above.

Neglendiers.

A solitary spider was deadly enough. But these worked together, like spitting ants under their queen.

After backtracking around the web, Zanth continued. Fallen trees and soft moss called to his tired legs, but he'd already lost too much time. Zanth couldn't tell how low the afternoon sun was. The glade—with its potent energy—wasn't far now.

A dark bird specked with grey landed on a branch high above him. The deathdealer twisted its head one way and then the next, examining him.

Zanth stood straight and stretched his arms wide, making himself as big as he could.

I'm no easy meal. That's what the deathdealers found: the wounded, sick, elderly, and young separated from the pack.

The deathdealer squawked, loud and harsh. Zanth threw a stick at the bird, but it passed harmless under the branch.

Death catches the stagnant.

Zanth urged himself into a run. The scavenger followed, shrieking. Another deathdealer joined it, wings and fan-shaped tail spread. They landed on a branch ahead of Zanth and squawked in unison. Their call would attract the worst of attention. A death sentence for him.

A cramp grew on his right side, under his ribs. Every step provoked it. He wiped his forehead, but his damp sleeve just smeared the moisture. The still, humid air trapped the sweat on his skin.

The wretched birds overtook him and resumed their call. A fallen branch snapped under his heel. Leaves rustled. His chest heaved and heart pounded.

This is what they want.

He slowed, picking his footing with care and controlling his breathing.

The carrion-feeders grew silent.

Zanth froze.

Pronounced nostrils emerged from heavy foliage. Long jaws followed. Two eyes sat atop the ilunger's head, and each side held another. Each milky, yellow-green orb held a black slit. These vertical pupils were trained on Zanth. He could feel the creature measuring him. It stood on two legs, at twice his height.

Back to the spiderweb? Even if he could make it that far—which seemed doubtful—the beast could take a path wide of the web, or the spun threads mightn't contain it. Zanth needed a different plan.

The ilunger raised its crest of blood-red feathers, a striking contrast to its dark-green scales. It roared, blasting Zanth with a breath of rotting flesh. He gagged, ears ringing. The creature charged. Vicious curved teeth filled its wide jaws.

Grabbing his only dull, Zanth gathered an intense light within his clasped hands and thrust this at the ilunger. A brilliant white light consumed all, even having turned his head to protect his eyes. Blinded, the creature staggered back. With the last energy from the madrilik, he ripped a thorn off a bush and propelled it into one of the four eyes. The ilunger bellowed, raking its claws through the air in front of its face. Blood oozed from the puncture, followed by a clear liquid.

Zanth turned and sprinted. He ducked under a low-hanging branch and leapt over a shrub. *If* he could make it to the energy-rich glade, the beast shouldn't follow.

The deathdealers arrived on the tree in front of him, squawking. They were not ready to give up their meal; ilungers always left enough on the corpse for them. Zanth cut left. A branch tore at his shins.

The ilunger gave chase. It weaved between trees, head low and long, segmented tail extended for balance. A row of feathers extended along the tail's centre line.

Zanth stumbled but caught himself on a tree. Its coarse bark ripped open his hand. The ilunger roared and closed the gap.

Snapping jaws came for him. Zanth pictured these closing around his leg, its many teeth sinking into his flesh. He dived sideways into a copse of oparitoons. The tall, straight tree trunks were too densely packed for the ilunger to pass through. It snorted and went around as Zanth pulled himself through. His stinging palm had nothing on his throbbing head or burning lungs. Sweat rolled down his back.

Ahead, sunlight flooded an open space and reflected off its central pool. Madriliks frolicked around the water. Spurred on by this, Zanth pushed his fatigued limbs into one last burst of speed.

The ilunger gained on him, its clawed feet pounding the earth.

I won't die here.

Zanth jumped for the viridian glade. The ilunger launched itself after him. Its terrible mouth snapped shut just shy of his sandal. Zanth fell upon the soft grass, rolling over and over before coming to a halt.

Standing at the edge of the trees, the creature snarled. It put one foot on the grass—as if to show it wasn't afraid—and then turned its back and disappeared into the forest.

Zanth lay panting. Alive. The sky dimmed, preparing to don its black dress, as his wife used to say. Sometimes, she seemed so far from him. Other times, she was close enough to breathe her in. He started to crawl towards the pond, but it was too much effort. Instead, he found it easier to roll there. The sweet scents of water and moss filled his nostrils. Dizzy, he cupped the liquid in his mouth. When he could drink no more, he dragged himself in, clothes and all.

The cold pool deepened quickly. A throng of lively madriliks swirled at the bottom, bright and brilliant. He sank his head under, surrendering to the embrace of a quiet, weightless world. Zanth rubbed himself down, clouding the water with dust, dirt and blood.

Six years ago, he'd loosened his crimson belt, shed his black robe and dived into the pool under Arric's watchful gaze. Immersed in the madriliks, they'd filled his reservoir far quicker than he'd anticipated. A searing heat had struck, and an immense pressure had rammed his chest. Clinging to the image of a second reservoir inside him, Zanth had strived to locate it. He'd dug his nails into his legs and screamed as pressure and pain mounted, sending bubbles rushing by his face. When blood spilled from his nose, he'd swum for the surface, only for Arric to turn away. Back then, he'd given in to agony and fear.

Enough. He dragged himself out of the memory.

Faint shafts of light penetrated the water. Submitting to his anxious lungs, he kicked twice and broke the surface. Madriliks spun and swayed above him, though nothing like the quantity at the bottom of the pool. Zanth floated. A middler skimmed the surface. He called to it, and the middler was drawn into his chest like a moth to a flame. The more he collected, the easier it became—not that it was a challenge in this place of power. Sated, he slithered from the pool and summoned a fireball for warmth. There was not a creature in sight to capture and roast, and he certainly wasn't willing to venture back into the forest. He submitted to exhaustion.

20. Afraid to Fly

It made no sense. None at all.

Angry held an orb aloft. A rainbow of colours swirled within, a slow-motion whirlwind.

Antarna needed a seat. And fresh air. And, by goddess, some answers.

Her hand grazed her chin, moving to cover her mouth, which had apparently fallen open. She struggled to compose herself.

'Summon Arric,' said the king.

Feet scampered away.

Angry pulled out his cane. 'Where did you get it?'

Evireny curled into a ball. The cane whistled through the air and cracked against her naked back.

'Who was it going to?'

Antarna averted her gaze, wincing in anticipation of the next blow. When she'd fought Angry, she should've broken his dominant arm or, better yet, severed it in a spray of hot blood. He administered another brutal stroke, and Antarna drove her nails into her palms.

'What is it?' Angry hit Evireny again.

You didn't even give her time to answer. The resonant slap of the cane against flesh lingered, tearing at Antarna's resolve.

Arric entered.

'Perfect timing,' the king said.

A servant brought the orb—which had been cleaned—to Arric.

'I've seen this once before,' he said. 'It contains a hex and heralds from the people of the cavern. However ...' He levitated the ball to eye level. 'The colours are too slow. The spell has been tainted.'

'How would that happen?' the king asked.

'That's a delicate subject, Your Majesty.'

'Everyone out except Arric, Barrass, Farikarr, the prisoner and Antarna.'

The courtroom cleared. Farikarr entered the giant rib cage with Evireny, taking over from Angry.

'I sense the work of anti-magic, as if it came too close to a saphramurl gem,' said Arric.

How's that possible? The only saphramurls in the crater were kept in the vault of the temple of magic.

'Well, that is an interesting development,' said the king. 'Girl, you'll tell us everything. Now, or after experiencing excruciating pain.'

Evireny started to hyperventilate. The rapid breathing shook her tiny body.

The king nodded, and Farikarr unleashed a brutal kick to her thigh. A shriek escaped Evireny's lips.

The king walked over to the rib cage. 'Last chance. Where are my stolen gems?'

Antarna reeled at the implications. Without the saphramurl gems, there was little hope for Tozias, Letti and the other injured. They'd never wake from their comas. Zentrina would welcome their souls, and her animated statue would take their bodies, just as it had taken Gil's.

Why hadn't the king told Yerkinfall? *What am I even doing here?*

Evireny's lips sank into a thin line.

'So be it. Farikarr, take her for questioning.'

'Yes, Your Majesty.'

He hauled her up with ease and dragged her from the room. Her dress and breechcloth lay on the floor.

'That's enough excitement for one day,' the king said. 'Antarna, join us for breakfast tomorrow.' Without waiting for a response, he turned and strode away with Arric a few steps behind.

Father approached, scratching the skin under his forearm guard. 'How do you fare?'

'After that, I don't even know where to begin.' She stilled her head, realising she'd been shaking it.

'I understand. There's been a lot of changes. These are difficult times. I'm sorry you had to see that.'

Sorry I had to see it. But not sorry that it happened?

A messenger arrived with a wax-sealed scroll.

Behind him, a servant girl ambled by carrying a stack of ceramic plates. She peeked in.

'How about you take a nice hot bath, change into some clean clothes and we talk over dinner? On the rooftop, at sundown?' Father massacred a smile. 'I know you've got questions. I've got answers. I'll see you tonight, yes?'

She managed a nod.

A pair of servants passed the door, glancing her way. Word of her return—not to mention what she'd done to the watchmen—had spread already.

Antarna hurried to the rear of the winged throne. It offered a way out few knew about.

Skulls covered the back wall. The velengoric's serrated teeth became progressively smaller as they neared the back of its mouth. She'd be no more than two bites. Five dozen or so curved white daggers filled the ilunger's long, narrow snout.

Only one had the flat teeth of a grazer: the kennturia skull. While its four-horned head was still impressive, it'd been mounted for another reason. This was the animal brought back by the hunting party on the day of the Unjust Uprising.

Images from Salorann invaded her mind.

He'd wounded her uncle but failed to kill him or Father. It was Layaury, not Salorann, who had murdered Grandfather. If Arric—just a poor, young boy at the time—hadn't stopped Layaury, her family's line would've ended.

The pattering of footsteps reminded her that she wasn't alone.

Antarna lifted the back of the throne, whispered to a cancryst and bounded down the stairs two at a time. She had ample space. The royal family had always been tall and heavyset, which the labourers had accounted for.

Taking the right fork, she was surprised that, after about a decade, her feet still knew the way. She resisted the temptation of a detour via the larder and slunk by the guardhouse. A few turns later, she arrived at the back of a rectangular wooden shield. Unlatching the clasp, she swung it open and stepped out.

She emerged from an apparent dead end, deep in the royal sleeping quarters. Her room was the third door on her left. If she knew her father, it'd be kept for her even after all these years.

On opening the door, a punchy, zesty scent with a touch of ground spice greeted her. A candle had been lit; the wax at the top was still heating and had yet to drip. It pulled her back to her childhood. She saw her mother, with her dark, straight, waist-long hair, reading to her by the window. She recalled Kyrak leaping up and swinging around the posts of her bed.

Carvings of flowers, vines and leaves spiralled around the bedposts. From them hung a delicate, sheer canopy. It fell around the extravagant bed, rivalling the size of her temple room. She hadn't slept on a real bed since leaving the palace—unless one counted the months in the infirmary of Preslina's temple upon arrival. The same infirmary Tozias lay comatose in, drawing ever closer to meeting their goddess. How had it all gone so wrong?

A wooden minderel, with sleek feathers painted white, sat facing her on the shelf. Nesting inside the carved hollow toy would be another one, exactly the same but smaller, and, inside that, a final bird. The room was exactly as she'd left it but for her bare wardrobe.

She headed to the dressmaker. Isebellyn was two floors down, on ground level. Her room was a maze of fabric and fur. Clothes, in various stages of creation, hung from racks and the rafters, draped over furniture and overflowed from chests. Light scattered from beads and precious gems. Antarna rang a diminutive bell by the open door, its notes high and clear.

'Princess.' Isebellyn emerged and clasped her hands to her chest. 'I've missed you.'

'Missed you too. Nice hair.' Today, Isebellyn's short, curly hair was dyed teal. It used to change as frequently as the weather.

She fluffed it and looked Antarna up and down. 'Too kind. Having to see you in *that* is not.'

'Sorry.'

'White, so impractical. Am I right?'

A giggle burst from Antarna. 'Yes. And thanks, I needed that.'

'What can I do for you? A new wardrobe?'

'To start, just something simple to wear to a casual dinner tonight, please, and then breakfast with the king tomorrow.'

'Simple?'

'Yes, please. One or two colours. No fur or gems. More on the conservative side.'

'Hmm ... Out of that. Show me what I'm working with.'

Antarna untied and dropped her blood-splattered robe.

Isebellyn began to take her measurements with practised efficiency. She used string that was marked at regular intervals.

'So, what's the latest news? I know you're across it,' said Antarna.

'Last month, Kathrina got engaged to Calik Dyterog, and he's just been named as the lake island's seer.'

'Kathrina?'

'Farikarr's daughter. Now, arms up.'

Antarna obeyed. If that man's daughter took after him, she'd be vain and self-absorbed. 'How have things been with the lake island?'

'Tense. But the marriage should help to put things back on track.' Isebellyn wound up her string. 'I have what I need. What's next on your list?'

'A bath.' Maybe it'd clear her mind and allow her to formulate a new plan.

'Good. Take a long soak, and I'll have something ready for you by the time you get out.'

'Thank you. One day, you'll have to share your secret.' No one knew how she turned around a dress in the time it took most to prepare a sketch. Enchanted needles were a popular guess. 'It's so good to see you.'

'And you. Take this,' Isebellyn said, handing her a loose robe. 'Now, I've work to do.'

The baths lay behind the palace, nestled around and within a sprawling hedge. Antarna progressed into the winding, twisting network of passages. The hedge stood taller than the tivitania. She passed several baths, their black-rocked bottoms drinking in the sunlight. Vines heavy with violet flowers climbed a pair of columns ahead.

A huge circular bath dominated the space. Faces of past kings adorned its sides, regal expressions artfully carved into the stone. She climbed its steps and dipped her toes in. Warm water greeted her, inviting her further. In comparison to the frigid pool of her temple, this one felt like it should be bubbling and steaming. She unrobed and entered. The black rocks were smooth beneath her feet and then comfortable on her back. Heat enveloped her. Blue sky stretched above.

Her mind wandered from Angry and Evireny to the king and Father. It settled on the saphramurl gems as waterlogged wrinkles overtook her hands and feet.

So, the Resatrium stole them from the Order of Devtakaris, right from under Arric's nose. Why? And what can I do now?

Father would never let her take part in the search for the gems—kicking in doors and interrogating suspected Resatrium members. Not that they'd see eye to eye, given what they were doing to Evireny.

The sun dropped, and shadow overtook the pool. It would soon take the whole crater floor. One thing was clear: Father knew more than he was letting on. Pulling answers from him would be like dislocating an arm—actually, that'd be simpler and preferable.

She opened her eyes to find a cobalt dress draped over a chair. The colour was gorgeous. Antarna got out and quickly ran a thick, heavy towel over her body, all the while resisting the urge to touch the dress. Only when she was dry did she permit herself to lift it. Sumptuously smooth material slipped through her fingers. Yet all she wanted was to be robed in grey with Tozias whittling by her side.

By the time she'd returned to the palace and climbed the stairs to the roof, the sun had retired. Paved winding paths meandered through lush greenery. A central tree soared overhead, shining with the light of countless cancrysts. The canopy was a giant bouquet of flowers, the oranges and yellows of a good hearth or a glorious sunrise. Father sat under it. He'd changed out of his armour into a deep-purple tunic embroidered with silver thread. No servants waited in the shadows.

Father rose. 'I'm glad you came. Please, sit. Can I pour you some wine?'

I don't drink; none from the temples do. Although, let's see if that still holds by the end of the night.

'Water would be great, thanks.'

He filled her cup. 'That's a lovely dress.'

They stumbled from topic to topic: the temperature of her bath, the weather, the upcoming harvest. If their conversation was a bird, then it was afraid to fly and instead would totter along on its short legs, fall over, struggle to rise, then do it all over again. Her questions stuck at the back of her throat; the moment never felt right.

Father rubbed his short beard. 'I was hoping last year you would finally change your mind and visit. Our king was too.'

You could have come to see me. And he wasn't just after a visit.

'Yes, it would've been nice. There were a few reasons. Good reasons. If I'm honest, I wasn't sure that I could handle the memories from this place.'

'I understand. Although the desert chieftain's son was here.'

And there you have it, the real reason: to marry me off.

Four servants arrived.

Perfect timing.

The table was laden with steaming dishes. The centrepiece was a stuffed, spit-roasted herangtin.

'How is the food at the temples?' he asked. His real question was clear, though: had she been getting enough to eat?

She fixed upon him a look, direct and unambiguous. *How about you worry about the people of the crater that are starving to death outside the walls of your palace?*

'Sorry.' He smiled, warm at first, but then sadness crept in. 'Your mother used to give me that same look. Often, I might add.' He gently shook his head. 'I deserved it then, too.'

I miss her. The words died behind her teeth, or maybe they never made it that far. A longing ache reverberated through her.

Antarna filled her plate with vegetables and checked her wrist.

Father must have noticed. 'I'm glad you still have the lilreneer. It's grown.'

'*He* has, yes. I'm very attached.' Enthriff rubbed against her.

They busied themselves with the meal.

After an awkward silence, Antarna asked the question that'd long been on her mind. 'What struck the mountain temples? What happened?'

'I'm not sure this is—'

Antarna gripped the table.

'You can't tell a soul.' He rolled his lips back to the point where they almost disappeared, looked away from her and then affixed his brown eyes to hers. 'Near the glade, Arric's priests defended the crater against a hazzurus. All four died.'

Really? If he thought staring into her eyes would help to convince her, it was having the opposite effect. 'What does that have to do with the mountain temples?'

'They're built above a river of madriliks, right? The same river that feeds the glade. The shockwaves from the magical battle caused the river to flood, and you almost died.'

'I'm fine.' She took a sip and kept hold of the cup, readying herself to give voice to the grim reality. 'My best friend, Tozias, is close to death. Like so many others, he lies in a coma. He's …' Her throat tightened. 'He's getting worse. Most of them are. That's why I'm here.'

'That's tough. I'm glad you're back, though. It's not safe up there.'

She slammed the cup onto the table. Water slopped from it. 'I'm not back to stay safe. I'm not back to stay. We need to save them. They need saphramurls to keep the madriliks away.'

Father raised his hands. 'I'm sorry. My comment was … insensitive. I've just been worried about you up there.'

'First, you told me to stay there while I recovered from the poison.' *The poison that killed Mother and Kyrak*. 'Then, it wasn't safe to return. You said that year after year. When I was happy and settled, you started asking me to come back.' The table was suffocatingly close. She thrust herself to her feet.

'I—'

'I've been back for half a day. Watchmen tried to kill me.' She extended her thumb.

'That should have never—'

'The gems are stolen.' She dropped her forefinger. 'People are starving. You're torturing people! Zentrina forgive you, you're staking people.' With each line, she had flicked down another finger. She held up her hand, all fingers spread.

'It's the Resatrium. If we are soft, we'll be crushed. You don't understand what we're dealing with.'

'How'd you want me to be treated if I was in that girl's shoes? She has an older brother. Did you know that?'

'Antarna, you saw her orb. It's—'

'You're stoking the fire, not putting it out. What else don't I know?'

'A lot.' He rose, planting both hands on the table. 'They're not just amassing weapons like that orb. They haven't just stolen the saphramurl gems. They have a mage akin to Layaury. He brought the barrier down. He murdered Morsirel, a senior priest, in Arric's office the other night. We're lucky Arric wasn't there.'

A *Resatrium mage murdered a senior priest. In Arric's office*. It was too much to digest.

She threw her hands into the air. 'The end justifies the means, does it?'

'I questioned the methods at the start. But they're getting results, as you saw today.'

'Results. Is that what we're calling that?'

'We have the orb and a lead. We'll find the gems.'

You still haven't even found their murderer. It's been ten years.

'I ...' Antarna turned her back. 'I can't do this.' She fled from the rooftop and leapt down the stairs.

In no time, she was inside her old bedroom, slamming the door behind her.

'Light.'

The cancryst chandelier came to life.

Antarna threw herself onto the bed. It sank under her weight. She pictured Evireny, suspended from the roof of the dungeon, bloodied and screaming as her teeth were pulled. Or her flesh burnt. Or toes severed.

In what world is that right?

A line from Father reverberated in her head. "*You don't understand what we're dealing with.*"

Clearly, she didn't. She'd been wrong about Evireny and unaware of the murder of Morsirel.

The voice of the king wasn't far behind Father's. "*What about the Resatrium member that killed your mother and brother?*"

She kicked the fur throw onto the floor. The bed was too soft. Antarna rose and paced the room.

A full-length sleeveless dress hung in the wardrobe. It was the green of a dark forest and teemed with small white flowers sculptured from fabric. Next to the dress, a dewgem necklace glinted in the light. It was in the shape of an inverted triangle. Each gem resembled a translucent dewdrop about to fall from a leaf or branch. Or a collection of tears put on display like trophies.

How many meals could you buy with something like that?

She saw the faces of the people from the line for water.

The room was too bright. She was used to a single cancryst or a candle, if she was lucky.

'Light off.'

Gentle moonlight spread over the room and then danced in the dewgems, as if to taunt her.

Antarna bolted from the room and down the corridor. Two flights of steps and another corridor later she strode through the main entrance.

'Princess, where are you going?' asked one of the royal guards.

Away from here.

She turned off the Purple Path.

The dewgems also reminded her of the droplets during teleportation.

Not that I'll be able to get back tonight.

Not that I can go back without the gems.

Not that we know where they are.

The stars were out in force. Most of the crater's populace had turned in; only the odd square of light marked the high rock walls that otherwise melded into the backdrop of the night sky. High on the wall, a statue of her goddess was underlit by a brazier.

A combination of stairs, landings and ladders led to the top. She might have enjoyed the ascent had it not been for her afternoon, topped off by her evening. The dress didn't help the climb either.

Outside the temple, a priest was sketching the moon by her own light. His grey robes were trimmed in sky blue.

'Antarna, welcome. Inhaloc's told me all about you.' Effain put the parchment and charcoal down.

'It's nice to see you, High Priest.'

'You seem upset.'

'A thief stole the saphramurl gems.' She couldn't bring herself to voice that, worse yet, the Resatrium were responsible.

'That's disturbing and the first I'm hearing of this.' He raised a hand, motioning her inside.

'I don't know what to do.'

'When I don't know what to do, I meditate or seek guidance from one of my past lives. But, right now, can I suggest sleep? Let's find you a room.'

'Thanks.' *Guidance from a past life ... if only.*

Bleak. Lifeless

Zanth woke to find dawn preparing the sky for the sun's arrival. Another forthcoming sunrise under the rule of King Ithranned Tarlqua, with Devtakaris's Temple controlled by Arric. The snake still had both of its heads; yesterday had been nothing short of a complete catastrophe.

He looked for something good in this world. Underground, beneath his body, a powerful river of madriliks rushed towards the mountain temples. To watch it burst from the summit would really be something.

A flock of minderels chirruped as they flew past in an arrowhead formation. They had a direction, a purpose. More than that, they worked together, as the Resatrium did, and as he had with Lisoun and Ezro. A burning stirred within him, fierce and familiar. One way or another, he'd find a way to take down Arric. Not just for Silisa, but for the sake of his people.

After washing his hands and face, he stretched. Nearby, blackened branches devoid of leaves clawed the sky. Curiosity mingled with an unease.

Zanth steeled himself and entered the forest, stepping over broken limbs longer than he was tall. Fern leaves reached for him; each had been bent or snapped to face away from where Zanth headed. Insects buzzed and chirped, but nothing larger made itself known. A charred skeleton of a tree loomed over him. Zanth passed it and skirted another that'd been ripped out by its roots. Despite the area's proximity to the glade, not a single madrilik floated by.

A blackened plant crunched underfoot. The forest parted, scorched earth stretching out before him. Bleak. Lifeless. The clearing harboured a sinister cavity at its centre. An unsettling wrongness pervaded everything. The ball of madriliks in his chest tightened in on itself.

Zanth approached the edge of the gaping hole—large enough to be a burial pit for every man, woman and child of the crater. In fact, it resembled a small crater: a circular depression with smooth, steep walls. He knelt, cringing at the bitter tang in his mouth and the unclean feeling that swept through his body.

So, it happened here.

He pictured the explosion: earth flying, intense fire and wind, and magical shockwaves rippling out. This close to the madriliks beneath the glade, of course, the mountain temples suffered. The flood of madriliks that'd hit the mountain temples originated here.

If the Resatrium report was correct, Arric had lost four priests. *Pity it wasn't more.*

The priests' deaths and the tragedy at the mountain temples couldn't go unexplained. The king needed a believable story to conceal the terrible truth from the masses. A natural disaster wouldn't cut it.

What lie will you try to sell?

The possibilities were limited. A training accident would bring embarrassment to the temple of Devtakaris, and Arric wouldn't stand for that. Blaming it on the gods would also weaken the temple's standing. Four priests were too many for a hunting party, and no hunters had been lost. They'd have to have died as heroes.

Zanth rose to his feet and clasped his hands behind his head. The crater's walls protected its people from the land creatures, and the magical barrier stretching over it kept flyers out. What new threat could the king and the high priest claim they protected the people from? A *hazzurus*? A *demon from another realm*? They'd think of something, that's for sure.

Zanth turned back for the glade, needing to get a message to the Resatrium.

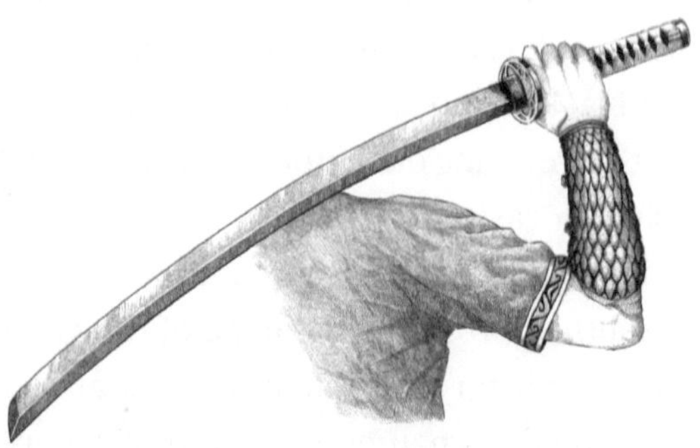

22. A Familiar Shadow

DAWN prayer and stretching were held in the fresh air before the statue by the entrance. As the instructor concluded, the high priest approached Antarna.

'Is your mind clearer?' Effain asked, indicating to a seat in the sun.

She sat. 'A little. It's full of questions. How did the saphramurl gems get to be stored in Devtakaris's temple?'

'Long ago, Daslercia mined the gems for their anti-magic.'

'In a cave swallowed by the passage of time: the Lost Cave.' She'd read about it. Gil had loved Daslercian history. At times, it didn't feel like he was gone. On other occasions, the void of his absence left her hollow. She turned her face from Effain.

'That's right. As their civilisation ended, it's recorded that a Daslercian mage teleported into the crater with the gems. For a time, the gems were split between the temples. After the Unjust Uprising, they were worn by the royal family for protection. However, before long, the royals began to feel unwell. So, the gems were locked in what was thought to be the safest place in the crater.'

Workers took to the fields below. A line started for water. From her elevation, the people appeared no bigger than insects.

'Why did it make them sick?' she asked.

'Just as too many madriliks are dangerous, it is thought that too few may be as well.'

'And before the royals wore them, you had a gem here?'

'Yes.' Effain looked up. 'In the room above us. It's unlocked, of course, if you'd like to look.'

'I would, thank you.'

The sizeable room above was new to her; she'd only visited the temple a few times as a child and never past the entrance hall. Antarna opened the shutters. The view of the crater bowl had nothing on the rainforest that stretched beyond it. Only from this height could one see out beyond the crater walls. Shades of green ran to the horizon.

A stone statue of Zentrina stood in her customary cape, facing out. On the cape's hood was a shallow indentation, perfectly round. Of all the statues of her goddess, this was the first Antarna had seen with such a depression. It sat around Zentrina's third eye.

This must be it. Where the gem sat before the king took it back.

Now that she'd found it, she didn't know what to do next.

What did Effain recommend again? To seek guidance from one of my past lives.

If it was only that easy. There was something disconcerting about the thought of leaping for her soul without Gil—without his wisdom and reassuring presence, without the beat of the drum to assist her into a meditative state and the sound of the bells to mark the memory. Entering the soul was also not without danger; you could lose your way and be trapped forever without someone to guide you back. She'd never succeeded without him, and doubt clawed at her: maybe she couldn't.

And yet, Gil would want her to leap, even if she fell short. She couldn't let her grief or fear stifle her from even trying. Never attempting again wouldn't protect her from failure, it would crystallise it.

Gil, I'll do you proud.

Antarna pulled an onyx vial from her pocket and unstoppered it. A familiar shadow slipped forth and took shape.

Her hands ached for her sword. A selection of bone and obsidian knives hung on the wall. She ran her fingers over them. A pair of obsidian blades spoke to her. They were a hand and a half long—the second longest set on the wall, but still shorter than her dagger. She lifted them free. The morning light played off their lustre as she got used to their feel and weight.

In silence, keenly missing the sound of the drum, Antarna faced off against the shadow. Her opponent attacked, unleashing a flurry of blows that forced Antarna to retreat. It advanced, aggressive but not reckless, ready for her counter.

Soon, Zentrina's statue was at her back, and behind that, the window. The shadow struck. Antarna ducked under the strike and swept its front leg. Diving onto the fallen shadow, she plunged a knife to the hilt.

She rose next to the statue, leaving her jet-black blades on the floor. Impulsively, she reached out and touched the indentation on the hood of the cape as she closed her eyes. The memory darted ahead, and Antarna pursued it to her soul.

A rumbling, booming surrounded her, loud and unceasing, yet unthreatening. There was something calming about its consistency.

Her past life stood in a cave or tunnel with rough, grey rock walls—not the colour of the crater. Armour weighed upon him. Cancryst light gleamed on his steel forearm guard.

Steel? Only Antarna's royal blood had blessed her with her sword, one of less than a dozen steel weapons recovered from the ruins of Daslercia, and armour had never been found intact. Salorann would never have gotten access to steel.

You're not Salorann. The answer fitted. This man felt nothing like Salorann. She'd turned the diary of her soul to a different page, a much older one.

Beyond curious, Antarna reached out to his mind and asked for his name. His thoughts didn't pummel her as she'd expected. He didn't resist.

A male said, 'Horcil.'

She settled into the memory.

Horcil glanced over his shoulder at two men in steel armour. Well-known to her past life, their names came quickly to her: the taller,

Waslok, and the shorter, Redgwid. Behind them, a powerful waterfall tumbled down a sinkhole. Its mist scattered a strong shaft of sunlight. A vine ladder with cylindrical, wooden rungs dangled near the entrance to the short passage. Horcil turned his attention back to the rock wall before him. He ran his finger around the inside of a circular and smooth hole, so shallow that it didn't even reach the first knuckle. Moisture gathered on his fingertip.

'The answer you're looking for is "yes", that's a good size for your dick,' said Redgwid.

Waslok laughed and added, 'It's generous for you.'

Redgwid slapped his thigh. 'And it's going to be the most willing orifice you'll find.'

'Apparently it's as deep as your thoughts can get,' Horcil shot back. 'You know it's where they found the first gem?'

'What I don't know is why we couldn't wait at the top,' Redgwid said.

Horcil spun around. 'You worried the damp will fuzz your hair?'

Waslok brought his hand up to cover his widening mouth.

Redgwid took his foot off the flat top of a stalagmite and stepped toward to Waslok. 'I don't know what you have to smile about, given your receding hairline.'

Self-conscious, Waslok dabbed the naked scalp above his temples.

Redgwid rounded on Horcil. 'If only your necklace could also keep your jealousy away.'

Horcil shook his head. This moved the saphramurl gem hanging from the black, braided string. It was of a blue darker than any water. Orange specks frolicked within the stone.

'I don't know how you wear that,' said Waslok. 'Mine made me sick. I—'

The heavy, wooden door swung open. Tiny saphramurl gems studded the surface. It was out of place in the cave, as was the man-made stone wall that it stood in. Abulap stepped through. Two steel keys jingled on his waist, shaped like swords with teeth on one side of each blade. He dropped a small sack, the contents clinking together.

'Careful with those!' said Redgwid.

The gem below Horcil's neck jumped and began to vibrate.

A blast of wind tore down the shaft, launching water droplets at them. The breath was knocked out the men.

Redgwid grasped his stomach. 'What's happening?'

Antarna fought to hold the wall between her thoughts and Horcil's. Wave after wave of his confusion broke against her barrier.

Waslok knelt, groaning in a strained manner. His pupils were dilated. Abulap and Redgwid gasped for air. At the same time, each of them brought their hands to their heads.

I know what this is! So, it has happened before.

The saphramurl gem grew hot on Horcil's chest. Part of him was tempted to rip it off his neck.

No, don't!

With blood leaking from his ear, Waslok screamed. Abulap joined him. Redgwid had put his leather necklace between his teeth and was biting down with all his might.

Horcil rushed to Waslok's side. 'What can I do?'

Abulap dropped to hands and knees. He heaved. Stomach acid and half-digested food splattered the cave floor.

The ground shook violently, throwing Horcil off his feet. He landed on his elbow, sending a sharp pain shooting down his forearm. The sharp tip of a stalactite wobbled above his head.

Redgwid wasn't moving. Neither was Waslok. Horcil was too focused on Waslok to register the vine ladder dropping down the shaft in the background.

Abulap pushed himself out of his pool of vomit, eyes watering.

A thunderous crack resonated through the passage. The cave trembled again. Rocks slid free from walls and bounced along the floor. The door swung shut. Stalactites snapped, raining down from the ceiling.

Horcil covered his head with his armoured forearms. A rock tip shattered against the steel.

Abulap's hand slipped on his own sludge. Above, a leg-sized stalactite broke free from the roof. It tore through Abulap's neck. Blood spurted from the space between his shoulders and ran from his head, which was only loosely still connected to his body.

Antarna recoiled, and the vision spasmed.

Horcil's horror tore down the thin wall between them.

23. Cuddling Those Worthless Intentions

Antarna opened her eyes to the statue of her goddess. Two of her fingers still rested on the round depression on the cape's hood. Enthriff circled her wrist, clearly worried about her.

She shuddered, trying to banish the image of Abulap's nearly decapitated body.

Why didn't I see Salorann? Not that she was complaining.

She struggled to recall what Gil had told her. With just one hand, she could count the days since that conversation had taken place, but it felt like months had passed.

A ...

... stimulus! Something of real significance in one of my former lives.

The hole on the statue before her was like the one the man had teased Horcil for touching, and each used to hold a saphramurl gem. His life had centred around those gems, as a guard with one around his neck.

Antarna made her way to the window. The rim stretched overhead, a crown of dark rock. She'd been there once, as a girl with her father and brother, and the view had made her feel small. An ancient forest stretched around the crater in all directions. The mountain range had been little more than a collection of hazy, blue serrations on the horizon.

Below her, a mob fifty or sixty strong encircled the watch tower overlooking the pond. Not a single person approached for water. Dots of light appeared as people lit torches. Flames had no business being so close to the crops—and weren't needed for light or heat during the day.

Her stomach lurched. A riot would be met with swift force; the king had no mercy.

Antarna raced down the stairs. No matter how many she jumped, it was never enough. Even as she slid down the ladders, the descent dragged on.

If she hadn't intervened with Evireny, this never would've happened.

A dozen priests emerged from the temple of magic. Five packs of hunters advanced towards the pond, each taking a different path.

She passed the halfway mark of her descent. The path narrowed and twisted. Did Father lead the largest group of hunters? Antarna pushed aside the temptation to skid to a halt for a breather and a better look, opting for glances instead. The man at the front of the pack appeared taller than the others, and, though it was hard to tell from this distance, purple or red graced his shoulders. While Father had faced much worse than an angry mob, age wasn't on his side. A farmhand could land a lucky blow; it only took one. Her actions had put the only family she had left in danger.

Fire engulfed the watch tower. A rotund watchman stood trapped on the tower's balcony, the ladder broken, its bottom half sprawled on the ground.

On reaching the crater floor, sweat plastered her light robe to her back. Shouts from the mob jumbled together. With long strides, she drove her legs into the dirt. Her arms cut the air, propelling herself onwards. Tivitania fields blurred as she sprinted by. The tall, mature crop blocked her view. Ahead though, a plume of smoke rose into the sky.

Words stuck out from the chaos.

'Down with the Crown!'

'Free Evireny!'

'Free us!'

At least the fighting hadn't started yet. Maybe they'd listen to her. She had to try. First, she had to reach them in time. She fuelled her legs and arms with the dire reality of the situation. If the watchman burned to death, the hunters would show no mercy. If the watchman jumped, he'd at least break his legs—and be an irresistible morsel for the angry mob. That too would leave the hunters little choice, or so they'd see it.

Her legs ached and her insatiable lungs screamed for relief. Each breath came thinner and less satisfying than the last, leaving her gasping. With lives on the line, she refused to ease up. The source of the smoke drew closer.

Antarna turned the corner. Flames had enveloped the roof of the tower and spread down its walls. The stranded watchman used his arm to shield his head from the intense heat.

Father and his hunters faced down the mob who thrust farm tools and knives above their heads. Bone and stone in untrained hands against bronze-armed warriors had an inevitable ending.

'Lay down your arms!' commanded Father, his voice rising above the ruckus.

From within the mob, someone threw a multi-coloured orb—like the one secreted within Evireny. It arced towards her father.

If it struck, the hex the orb contained would ravage him. And, from this distance, she was powerless to save him.

Three-quarters through its trajectory, the orb stopped mid-air. A couple of breaths later, it soared to an armless in a crimson robe trimmed in black. Arric.

The high priest met her gaze.

Antarna lost contact with the ground. An invisible force lifted her higher. Her feet still bore the weight of her body, despite the air under them.

Magic.

'High Priest, put me down!'

She stomped, surprised to meet something solid. Antarna slid her foot forwards, and her toe hit an unseen object. Her hands told her that a firm, smooth, solid form rose in front of her eyes.

Like a wall.

She worked her way right only to discover another wall intersecting the first. A corner.

I'm in a box!

With a lap and a jump, she confirmed it.

The rectangular box stopped rising. It floated towards the royal palace.

'Get me out!' She wasn't sure her words could carry beyond the magical walls.

With a collective scream, the mob charged.

Father led his hunters, their lines tight and neat.

The two forces crashed together. The hunters were a boulder rolling down the hill; they scattered the assailants. Father flattened one with his shield. That poor man would've been lucky to be a third of his weight. A knife-wielder lunged. Father severed his arm at the elbow, his blade making the cut with ease. Antarna flinched at all the blood. Father's steel sword was next matched up against a spade, its triangular head made from the scapula of a medium-sized animal.

The scene gradually lost its details, even with her face pressed against the magical barrier. From a distance, without the gory specifics, it should've been less horrifying. Yet her vantage point showed off the gut-curdling scale of the violence. Enthriff tried to comfort her.

A pair of royal guards awaited her.

'Princess,' one said, 'the king has requested you.'

She grounded a foot at last. 'Lead the way.'

The guards led her to a waiting room across from the dining hall. A soft rug cushioned her steps, while Father carved a bloody swath through field hands.

'The king will call upon you at the appropriate time. Please, make yourself comfortable.' The guard closed the door and locked it.

The window offered a view of the fields and crater wall. It didn't look towards the pond where her people killed each other.

A girl brought her tea, a pretence of a civilised society.

How had it deteriorated so much? She recalled her history lessons. The Resatrium had started out as a peaceful group of citizens advocating for better working conditions and more rights. As time passed without meaningful progress, the voice of the more bitter and radical members gained power. Her grandfather's uncompromising reign culminated in his assassination. The divide and hatred remained to this day.

And she'd contributed. She'd challenged Angry, unaware of the theft of the saphramurls or of the Resatrium stockpiling magical orbs—like the one that had come close to killing her father today. Antarna hadn't known what Evireny's facial brand meant, nor had she intended to fan the flames of rebellion.

Still, there was no justification for strip searching Evireny in full view of others or for torture. Antarna would have to make her uncle and father see that.

A butterfly fluttered above the tivitania fields, small enough for the barrier to allow it into the crater. Its four wings reminded her of the reanildras near her mountain temple and of the people there depending on her.

After a chunk of a butterfly's lifetime, the door finally opened again.

'The king's ready for you,' said the guard.

They crossed the hall to the dining room. It had been dozens of moons since the room had haunted her nights and a decade since she'd stepped foot in it—where she'd lost her mother and brother. Still, her hair stood on end.

Deep breaths. She patted Enthriff.

In an ornate chair beside the king, Father sat tall, his back rigid and hands formed into fists. Tension radiated from him, and he avoided her gaze. Thankfully, he had no visible injuries, although he could have been bandaged under his white, finely woven garb. He'd washed off the blood, but the battle clung to him still.

The polished wood of the grand dining table gleamed under the cancryst chandelier's glow. Four dignified men occupied the far end, Arric amongst them.

She took a seat opposite Father. 'You're unhurt?'

'Yes. Though I can't say the same for some of my hunters.'

'I feel terrible. I never meant for any of this.'

'The weak and the short-sighted cling to their good intentions,' said the king. 'You need to make clear to everyone whose side you're on. You're a royal, and we will not show the Resatrium any leniency.'

'When I confronted the watchmen, I clearly didn't do so to support the Resatrium,' Antarna said. 'I acted out of basic decency. We can never sacrifice that.'

'What do you know of sacrifice?'

She bit back her retort. 'We need to deescalate this situation. Have you considered announcing a release date for Evireny?'

'That would be a show of weakness, not strength.' The king pointed a finger at her and opened his mouth. 'You're the cause of the escalation. So, you will stake the girl.'

He couldn't be serious. But he most certainly was. Antarna pushed herself upright against the back of the chair.

The king smiled at this. 'Yes. After a long night, the prisoner told us what little she knew. You need to demonstrate your loyalty. Your action needs to be loud and unequivocal. You will impale her.'

'That's against Zentrina's every teaching.' Antarna started to rise, compelled by an urgency within.

'Sit!'

She obeyed, then resented having done so. If this had been a sword fight, her opponent would have just caught her off-balance, leaving her mere moments from death.

'You were born in this crater and have our blood flowing through your veins.' The king looked to her wrist. 'You will obey the head of this family and your king. You *will* place her on the stake.'

Her hand craved her sword. In a fight, sometimes one had to give ground. At other moments, one had to stand firm. She would not take another step backwards. Not in the face of something so vile and perverse.

Antarna leant in. 'I'd sooner cut out my own heart.'

The silence that followed was as deep as the crater's walls were high. Maybe she shouldn't have been so blunt.

The king spoke slowly. 'Then your father will impale her brother and then her, and you will watch and applaud.'

Siblings to be put to the stake by Father's hand. One to watch the other die horrifically, knowing they'd soon suffer the same fate. A nightmare that'd scare her worst nightmares. 'The punishment does not fit the crime. Lock her away for a year, maybe. But not this. And what did her brother do?'

He scoffed. 'The brother also bears the mark. He probably talked her into joining the Resatrium in the first place.'

'Father!'

Her father turned to the king.

But the king spoke first, ignoring his pleading look. 'Stake the girl or be responsible for the death of her and her brother.'

An impossible choice. One she couldn't make. The weight of the moment threatened to crush her. In the tense silence, the smothering pressure only grew. She couldn't breathe. Couldn't think.

Antarna leapt out of her chair and bolted for the far exit. Father got up after her.

'Guards. The doors!' commanded the king.

Heavy bars slid into place.

Father caught up to her and whispered, 'Antarna, calm down. It will be—'

'Alright? No, it won't. Not in the slightest.' It had all gone so wrong.

Father glanced back to his brother. 'You need to—'

'I need to avoid an atrocity.' She wouldn't make either choice; there had to be another way. One that would keep Evireny alive. So many lives depended on her. 'I also need to save Tozias, Letti and others at the temple.' She couldn't return empty-handed.

'As you know, the Resatrium stole the saphramurls. Even if they didn't, we'd need them for defence against their mage who killed Morsirel. All of this is beside the point.'

'No. It's exactly the point.' Her mind cleared, and her confidence returned. The king needed the anti-magic gems more than having her stake the poor girl.

Antarna spun and strode back to the king, who wore a smug grin. 'I can locate the saphramurl cave. I've seen it. I've been there in a past life.'

The king's jaw went slack. 'The Lost Cave … Where it is?'

'In a sinkhole with a waterfall. Behind a stone wall installed by Daslercians with a thick door studded with tiny saphramurls.'

'And the sinkhole is where?'

'When I'm closer, I'll get another vision with the rest of the details.' She hoped, at least. 'To start with, we need the keys. The legend is true: they're passed down from seer to seer of the lake island.' The steel keys she'd seen in her vision matched a drawing she'd seen of the seer's necklace.

'No.' Father drew himself to his full height. 'The lake island, then where? The forest? The ruins of Daslercia? For days, maybe weeks. You'd never make it back, even accompanied by a full hunting party. It's suicide.'

'It's the only way,' Antarna said. 'The only way to save Tozias, Letti and the others of the mountain temples. And to protect the crater against the threat.' *The Resatrium threat.*

Father's face refused to soften.

'Tozias is like a brother to me,' she added. He wouldn't survive for weeks. Antarna would have to make it quickly there and back.

'You've never stepped foot in the forest. It's forbidden because it's a death sentence.'

'It's forbidden without my permission.' The king turned to her, enthusiasm in his eyes. 'You could get a vision with the cave's location at the lake island?'

'Yes.'

Father bristled. 'Brother, you cannot be entertaining this madness.'

'Arric, what say you?'

Antarna had nigh forgotten the four seated advisors. While she'd piqued the king's interest with the Lost Cave, Father's concern had curbed it. Everything hung on Arric's advice.

The high priest paused before speaking. 'The forest has many dangers, but is anywhere safe these days? The mountain temples are not, and neither is the crater. With an experienced leader, hunters and a priest from my order, the risks could largely be mitigated.'

'Wise counsel.' The king inclined his head. 'Hunt commander Farikarr can lead the trip. None know the forest better. Plus, his daughter, Kat, is marrying the new seer, and we need that key. In fact, let's send Kat, too.'

'Brother—'

'It is decided. Antarna, what will you need?'

'My weapons and armour from the temple. When I'm successful, a dozen gems to save the injured in the mountain temples.' She took a breath, pausing to give her third and final demand the impact it deserved. 'And your solemn vow to keep Evireny alive and to never stake another of your people. It's reprehensible and there's been enough bloodshed.'

The king weighed her words. 'Impalement will deter further bloodshed.'

'No. Those are my conditions. You'll never find the cave without me.' She was gambling with Tozias's life, and Letti's and the others'. But with good reason and solid prospects—the king had shown his desire for the gems.

'You have my vow; now find the gems.'

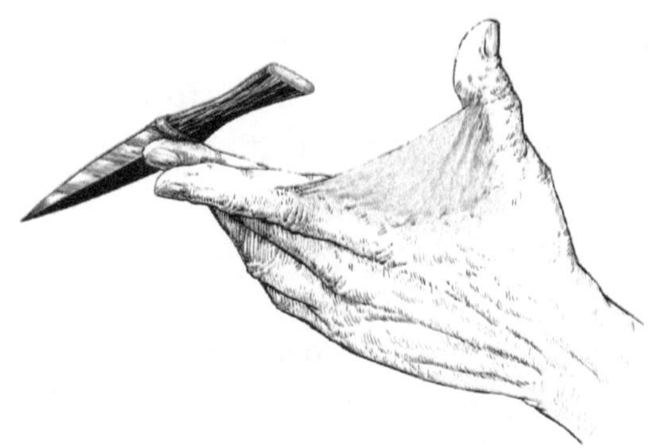

24. No Heroic Ending for Me

Cal took a seat on the first of two U-shaped benches opposite the open door to the teleportation chamber. The four armless inside took their positions, standing at the corners of a square outlined in vermilion upon the floor. The closest priest called upon a dull and shut the heavy wooden door. Strange carvings covered its surface.

His left eye twitched again. Last night, Cal's mattress had felt like a bag of rocks. He'd held back the chancellor's wrath by recounting visions of Zanth ambushing Arric and of a riot in the crater. Both had been brief and blurry, but they'd done the job. Of course, the chancellor hadn't shared these with the crater. Cal rubbed the webbing between his thumb and forefinger, all too aware he needed more good news to share soon.

This morning, his bed had been a soft cloud and his thoughts just as nebulous. Nalgrid had come in three times before he'd grudgingly risen.

He fingered the vague note in his pocket from his betrothed. It failed to explain why Kat was arriving with so little notice or with a princess in tow. A secret lay behind the elegant calligraphy and ornate expressions.

Cal stuffed cushion after cushion behind his back and leant into them. His silk shirt tugged at his shoulders. He'd only met Kat twice.

She'd smiled, laughed politely at his jokes, and touched his arm. They were yet to have a meaningful conversation or find common interests.

An initiate entered, levitating a pot of tea and a leaning stack of eight cups. He acknowledged Cal and put them down on a small table between the two bench seats.

A foreign chant rose within the adjacent chamber. Great stores of madriliks poured forth from reservoirs.

Familiar words were muffled by the stone. The guests had arrived. Cal pulled the cushions out from behind him and threw them back into position.

Look alive. He picked up the bouquet of golden flowers next to him.

A steel spearhead poked out through the doorframe. Cal winced, but he'd plastered on a smile by the time its wielder emerged. The man in his late forties had a high nose and a long, narrow face. His shoulder-length hair hid his ears; it was said that he'd lost half an ear during a hunt.

'Farikarr, welcome back to the lake island.'

'Flowers, for me? You shouldn't have. But not my colour.' The older man looked up to the ruby ribbon on his spear.

Cal engineered a chuckle for his future father-in-law.

Her perfume announced his betrothed like a herald. There was nothing subtle about it or about her. She emerged in a glittering dress the colour of sunshine. The fabric crossed diagonally, forming a deep V-shaped neckline. Her father's wealth was on display around her neck: yellow diamonds nestling in her ample cleavage.

Eyes up.

Emeralds hung below each earlobe, orbited by enchanted specks of cancryst.

'Kathrina, you're radiant this morning.' *Why's your dress so bright?* Cal handed her the flowers that his mum had bought.

He was rewarded with a perfect smile, teeth white and straight, full lips a deep red.

'Thank you. You're too kind.'

Next through the door was a tall lady in a high-necked dress that tapered to her slender waist. Green and dotted with lifelike white flowers, it was pretty without being loud. She had toned arms, like a swimmer, and gave off a strong sense of self-assurance. A thin, scale-patterned armband circled her wrist, her only jewellery. Before he could discern the unusual material, she covered it with her long fingers.

'It's lovely to meet you, Princess.' And he found that he meant it; there was something intriguing about her.

'The pleasure is mine, Seer.'

Her dark, impenetrable eyes held his gaze, then fell upon his neck or chest as she moved aside for four priests of Devtakaris. Of the four, only High Priest Josmark wasn't sweating profusely or breathing heavily from the effort of the casting.

Josmark led his priests to the furthest bench while Kat and Farikarr sat on the other. Antarna beat Cal to the teapot and poured first for the priests. Farikarr toyed with the oversized animal tooth hanging from the vine around his neck. If he lost the saucer for his cup, the wide tooth could double as one.

They waded through pleasantries with not a hint of the true reason behind the visit. By Antarna's stiff posture and forced smile, she was either impatient and trying to hide it or as bored as he. The tea, a blend designed to calm the stomach after teleportation, didn't help to keep him awake. When the cups sat empty, the priests entered the chamber to bring three hunters through.

Cal led the guests down the stairs. The narrow heels of Kat's leather boots struck the hard floor to the clink of her jewellery.

She paused on a landing after a couple of flights. 'They couldn't have teleported us onto the ground floor?'

In front of her, Antarna sauntered silently down the stairs. Periodically, she'd skip a step, springing off the ball of one foot to land gracefully on the other.

A morning person. How untrustworthy.

Stepping outside, he raised his hand to shield his eyes. 'This colossal building is Parliament Chamber. Its dome roof is self-supporting; there are no internal columns.'

Kat opened a colourful parasol. She glanced at the building before turning her attention to her pointed nails.

Right—not into architecture.

Cal cleared his throat. 'There are two islands on the lake. This one is by far the largest. The other is said to be haunted.'

Kat turned to him. 'Really?'

'A couple of years ago, a child went there on a dare and returned a blabbering mess. I've heard bloodcurdling screams emanating from it. Mysteriously, the tiny island is always shrouded in fog, dark shadows dwelling within.'

As he spoke, Kat compressed her lips and ran her fingers through her hair. It fell to the small of her back in curled ribbons.

'How spooky,' she said.

'So, you believe in ghosts?'

'Of course.' Her voice was melodious.

'What about you, Princess?'

Antarna paused before speaking. 'Ghosts, no. All manners of creatures, hazzurus included, yes.'

Cal kept a straight face.

'This is us.' He indicated to the building on their left. 'It's been passed down from seer to seer.'

Nalgrid must've heard Cal's voice, for he opened the front door. His mum hurried down the hallway.

Introductions and more pleasantries were made, shoes removed and steel left outside. The group moved into the internal courtyard. Brayan's cart had been wheeled away yesterday by a strange, unkempt man. Maybe Brayan couldn't forgive Cal for intervening. Or, as his mother had said, maybe he kept clear because it was safer for everyone that way.

Antarna stood and took a step towards the prayer room. 'May I pay my respects to your father?' Hers was a face of compassion.

'That's thoughtful. Of course, please.'

She departed for the prayer room.

'It's not too soon to start planning the wedding, is it?' asked his mum, her arms gathering energy.

Save me.

'Not at all,' replied Farikarr.

His mum clapped. 'Wonderful.'

She dived right in. They quickly settled upon the two unimaginative wedding locations: the temple of the goddess of love in the crater and here on the foreshore. After trying several combinations of dates, his mum squealed when she learnt that her father's birthday was the day after the wedding day of Farikarr's parents. It was on the next moon, too. They locked it in.

Antarna returned, taking a seat.

'Excellent, time for presents,' Kat said.

The flowers count, right?

Kat handed him a palm-sized gift, beautifully wrapped in long, bright leaves. He said his thanks and opened it. Inside was a bracelet of yellow diamonds and emeralds.

'Oh, we'll match,' said Cal.

'Yes. I'm glad you like it. Here, let me put it on you.' She fastened it around his wrist, her fingers lingering to caress his skin.

As Kat sat back down, Antarna handed him a present wrapped in simple cloth. It was about the size of a cup, but ever so light. He opened it carefully to reveal a large flower on a short stem. Each layer of its ruffled petals was a different colour. He touched them in turn—gold, orange, pink, maroon and mauve—working his way towards the pistil.

'I understand that you like to paint. Maybe you could use it as inspiration or for a dye?' said Antarna. 'The petals glow at night.'

'They glow? I certainly will. Where'd you find such a beauty?'

'These flowers grow on the rim of the crater. This was the only one I could get to.'

You picked it from the crater rim? 'Well, thank you, it's stunning.'

Farikarr's expression became serious. 'There is a sensitive matter that King Ithranned was hoping to secure your assistance with.'

'Why, of course,' said Cal, careful to keep anticipation from his voice. This explained why he'd received so little notice of the visit. Was Kat's presence a cover?

Farikarr put a hand on his daughter's arm. 'Perhaps you and Lady Dyterog could visit the foreshore and discuss decorations?'

Kat uncrossed her smooth legs and rose, her beige skin noticeably lighter than her father's and Antarna's.

'What a marvellous idea,' said Mum, more excited than a quill hound receiving a new bone.

When the pair were out of earshot, Farikarr continued. 'Earlier this week, the Resatrium stole the saphramurl gems.'

Cal couldn't decide whether to fake looking shocked or admit his knowledge of this. He leant back instead. 'And your king is after my assistance?'

'Yes. The theft of the gems could not come at a worse time. The king needs them for the defence of the crater.' Farikarr looked to Antarna.

She took over. 'The anti-magic gems are also needed to save many clinging to life in the mountain temples after a magical disaster.' Her voice wavered. 'We can't wait for the gems to be recovered, if they ever will be. However, we have a lead on the saphramurl cave. Its key is around your neck.'

He touched the keys passed down from seer to seer—or, in his case, ripped from his blind master's neck and thrown at Cal's feet. 'I thought the knowledge was lost. How did you learn of it?' *And what disaster?*

'In a past life, I guarded the Lost Cave. I've seen the memory, something I was learning how to do at the temple.'

He had so many questions about that, but he kept on point. 'So, where is it?'

'In a sinkhole with a waterfall, in the forest. I'm expecting further details shortly.'

Cal noticed his hand moving before it had a chance to scratch the back of his head; he rubbed his neck instead. 'That's not a lot to go on.'

'We're confident we can find it. We wouldn't be here otherwise.' Farikarr looked Cal in the eyes.

'It's more than it first appears,' said Antarna. 'A river must feed the waterfall, and the scrolls suggest that it's not far from their city, which I understand is only a two-day walk from here.'

'Only?' *Trust royalty to be so naive.* 'Two days there and two days back is a lifetime's worth of danger in the forest.'

A faint smile graced her lips—free from fear. 'We'll take hunters and a priest. All we need are the keys, which I'll guard with my life.'

'We'd greatly appreciate your support, as would the king.' The Hunt Commander's voice was smooth and rich.

The king could keep his thanks. How would the chancellor feel? He'd be furious if the crater found the Lost Cave and the lake island didn't share in the credit and the spoils. But the chance of success was remote at best.

'I'm sorry, I can't part with the keys. As the seer, they must remain with me.' He had a compromise in mind, though. 'After you find the Lost Cave, you can come back here for the key.'

'It'd take too long. The injured at the mountain temples are barely hanging on.' The tension in Antarna's posture revealed the burden she carried.

'And double the amount of time in the forest,' said Farikarr.

Double the risk. While he made a valid point, the larger risk was that they'd never find the Lost Cave. 'My hands are tied, sorry.' They weren't, but it sounded better than the alternatives. He waited for her to protest.

Antarna unlocked her ankles. 'We understand.' She glanced skyward. 'Then come with us?'

'I've too many responsibilities here, sorry.' Again, he expected her to object or plead.

'Of course. It was a big ask. Could you please show me the lake before I leave? Maybe point out that haunted island?'

'Absolutely.' She didn't seem the type to give up easily. Would she venture into the forest to the find the Lost Cave and come back for the keys? Or was she getting him alone to change his mind or steal the keys?

They left the house. The best view of the small island was in the opposite direction to the foreshore that Kat and his mum were looking at for the wedding—which suited him just fine.

'See that building?' Cal pointed at the tallest one. 'That's Lablias's temple. It's right by the lake. I had my first vision about it.'

'What did you see?'

'A man set fire to it at sunset.'

Antarna laughed, a sound full of warmth and life. 'You saw the temple of the god of water on fire?'

'Yes, the irony. A distraught fisherman had lost his son.'

'What did you do?'

'I told Mum I was going to pray and went there before sunset every night for two weeks until he showed. I tried to talk to him, but he was distraught. He pushed me down and set fire to the temple.'

Antarna halted. 'What?'

'Yes, no heroic ending for me. The priests came out and quickly put out the flames. There was little damage and no lives lost.'

'How old were you?'

'Ten. At the time, I didn't know if it was a dream, a vision or if I was going crazy.'

'That's tough. But you found your answers and your path.'

'I did.'

Ingosils glided between packs of trees on either side of the street. Large ears dominated their four-eyed heads. Their brown and green fur had a hint of orange from the toxic beetles they regularly consumed.

Antarna made an about-face and proceeded to walk backwards, looking at him. 'Of all the futures, why do you see the parts that you do?'

'Great question. Out of the possible futures and the moments within them, we see those that we have good reason to see.'

'Do you ever struggle to understand that reason?'

'All the time.' *Why see deaths I can do nothing about?*

'What do you do to work it out?' She kept a straight line, despite not being able to see where she was going. The street was quiet, and those on it gave them a wide berth.

'I paint. Why?'

'I've been struggling to understand Zentrina's choice for ...' She gestured to herself. 'Of all the possibilities, my last life was a member of the Resatrium who scarred the king's face and tried to kill my father.'

'No way. You scarred the king.' *And saw the Unjust Uprising, just as I did when I touched the knife.*

'Certainly did.' She spun on her heel, returning to walk beside him. 'Up at the rim of the crater, in addition to your flower, I found an answer. I realise that I've been put here to right the wrongs of my past. To do so, I need to find the gems.'

Well played. 'I'm sorry.'

'No, I am. I didn't mean for this walk to turn into an ambush. Although, while I'm at it, I'd like to add one more thing.'

He spread his fingers.

'As I mentioned earlier, the mountain temples are in dire need of them too. We were exposed to a flood of madriliks. Dozens are lying comatose or weak, unable to recover without the gems. My best friend, Tozias of the lake island, is amongst them.'

He hung his head. To think that she was willing to risk her life for a lake islander ...

'I'm sorry,' she said, 'I wasn't trying to make you feel guilty, just to provide a fuller picture. Well, that's enough of that.'

They nattered about the surroundings as they drew closer to the temple of the god of water. People kept clear of them—well, of him—but Antarna didn't seem to notice.

Half of the temple sat on stilts above the lake. Three storeys rose above its square base, each narrower than the one below. In the water out front, Lablias was carved from wood, spearing a colossal serpent.

There was not a breath of wind. It must've tired itself out while rattling Cal's shutters last night. Clouds floated in the sky and on the still water. *If clouds could see, would they be vain and spend the day checking out their reflection?*

They were white and fluffy, which reminded him of his bed this morning. He yawned.

Antarna looked over the lake. She didn't turn, but the corners of her lips rose. 'Sorry we got you up so early this morning.'

'All good. That's the haunted island.' He pointed out the shadow within the veil of fog.

'Not how I pictured it.'

'Yes, little roar but plenty of claw.'

That drew another closed-lipped smile.

'I need to ask. Is it me? Everyone is ...' Antarna looked to a family that tiptoed through scattered animal droppings instead of getting close to them.

'Giving us a wide berth. It's me.'

She tilted her head.

'The chancellor was displeased with my predecessor and gouged out his eyes. Understandably, they've been wary since then.'

'How horrible. How savage and cruel. Is he alright? Are you?'

He shrugged. 'People have been wary ever since the fifteenth seer broke his oath by saving a person who he saw die in a vision. In my goddess's displeasure, algae bloomed over the lake, threatening everything. So, the chancellor of the time had the seer drowned.'

'How did the chancellor know the seer was the cause?'

'Because it was the chancellor's life that my predecessor saved.'

Unsurprisingly, that killed the conversation.

After taking in the view for a while longer, they returned home. Kat, Farikarr and Mum were waiting, enjoying some sun in the courtyard.

'How was the foreshore?' Cal asked.

'Perfect,' said Kat. 'It's going to look gorgeous at sunrise, especially with what we have planned.'

'I have no doubt.'

Farikarr shuffled onto the edge of his seat. 'The upcoming wedding is another reason for finding the cave now. We can be there and back before then.'

'Imagine finding the Lost Cave and bringing back the gems,' said Kat. 'You'd become a hero for your people ... and for me.'

'You might even get made True Seer,' Farikarr added.

His mum gave him a reassuring smile. She stood in the spot where they'd hugged after the four guards had burst into their home and delivered the box with the webbing.

We'd be safe. It'd also put Mirogant out of the picture for good. That sly scoundrel would be forced to beg for scraps. If Mirogant hadn't made the chancellor feel like Brayan was replaceable, then maybe his former master would've still had his vision.

Kat looked at him expectantly.

Cal couldn't help but laugh. 'I surrender.' He raised his palms. 'I'll talk to the chancellor, and we'll see what he says.'

Amidst a round of thanks and clapping, Kat leapt from her chair and gave him a warm hug. Her skin was soft and perfume delightful but overpowering.

Kat ducked out to powder her nose, and Mum left with her.

Cal took a seat and turned to Antarna. ‘Let’s say we find the saphramurls. How do we get them to the mountain temples?’

‘The armless will teleport them, just like the last Daslercian mage who teleported into the crater with them. This is confirmed in our records, and High Priest Effain told me of it.’

Something about that didn’t seem right. ‘And, before I take this to the chancellor, what was the disaster that hit the mountain temples?’

Antarna dropped her gaze and touched her face. ‘Four priests died near the glade, defending the crater against an apex predator.’

A *half-truth or lie*? ‘I’m sorry to hear that. What was the predator?’

Farikarr answered before she had the chance, ‘Given they died, we’re not sure.’ His voice was confident and unwavering. ‘An explosion destroyed the bodies too.’

How convenient. He’d always struck Cal as a slippery one. ‘And an explosion at the glade resonated at the mountain temples, as the madriliks from the glade flow there?’

‘Exactly.’

They knew more than they were saying. One way or the other, he’d find out the truth.

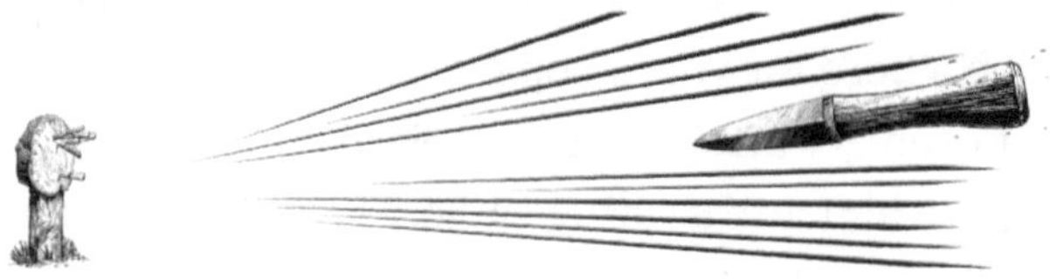

Cal sat on a log bench half a street away from his residence, mulling over the chancellor’s words. *Can’t say I’m surprised.*

He ambled back and found them all still in the courtyard.

‘Well, don’t keep us in suspense,’ his mum said.

Cal sat. ‘Do you want the good news or the bad news?’

‘Good first,’ said Kat.

‘We’re off to the forest.’

Kat put her hands together in prayer, looked up and mouthed, ‘Thank you.’

‘Was it divine intervention’—Cal glanced upwards, imitating her—‘or brilliance on the part of your betrothed?’

She twilled her fingers around a lock of her hair. 'That depends. What's the bad news?'

'We're off to the forest.'

Kat threw a pillow at him.

Cal ducked under the fluffy projectile. 'I surrender, for the second time today.' He raised his hands, fingers spread. 'In all seriousness, the chancellor was agreeable, subject to the lake island receiving an equal split of the gems.' *But he wants us to betray you and take all the gems.* Cal cursed himself for not having anticipated that. 'The lake island will contribute three woodsmen and me.'

'That's fantastic. Thanks, Cal,' said Farikarr. 'And yes, those terms are fine.'

'Who's hungry?' his mum asked.

Nalgrid entered, balancing a huge platter.

'This morning just gets better and better,' said Kat.

Cal helped Nalgrid set the platter down on the table. 'Thanks. This is great. Please send a runner to the chancellor to say that the terms are agreed upon and that we'll be leaving shortly.'

'Of course, my Seer.'

Cal extended a hand towards one end of the platter. 'Here, we have smoked mriout on fresh bread. It's one of my favourite fish. The smoke flavour really comes through, and the sauce is to die for.'

Kat bit her lip.

'Now at this end,' Cal said, 'we have omelettes with a mixed seafood filling.'

Antarna's faint smile wavered.

'Is this fine, Princess?'

'It looks lovely, but would you happen to have any fruit, please?'

'Seafood is not for everyone, I understand. I'm sure we can find you something more exciting than fruit, though. How about kelp soup? It's nourishing, hot and far tastier than it sounds.'

'Thank you, but fruit would be perfect, please.'

'Of course.' *Wait ... Soup!* Her mother and brother had died from poisoned soup. She almost had too.

'When can we be ready to leave?' Antarna asked.

'By lunch,' he replied, knowing that was the answer she was after and needing to make it up to her.

'Great. We know that the cave is close to Daslercia. My visions need a stimulus. We'll get one in the ruins. That's one place we know my past life was in.'

Are you sure you can find it? It's known as the Lost Cave for a reason. Visions are unpredictable—I know.

When they had finished breakfast, Cal accompanied Kat back to the temple. Her rounded hips swayed as she walked, accentuating her curves. Discussion of the upcoming trip and their wedding passed the time quickly. Kat was talkative, to say the least.

Standing before the stone structure, she put a steady, plump hand on his arm. 'This quest is very brave of you. Please stay safe.'

'I will.'

'Also, there is something that you should know.' She gave his arm a gentle squeeze as she rose to her toes to whisper into his ear. 'You can't trust the royals.'

Cal put his hand on hers. 'Why? What do you know? You can tell me.'

'Just what my father told me: something secret is afoot, and you can't trust them.'

'That's ominous.' Cal's head spun. He took a seat on a nearby bench.

'Sorry I brought it up.' Kat sat next to him. 'Focus on the expedition. Just be careful.'

25. Pus-filled Boils

Zanth materialised and collapsed.

'I'm here,' said Prann.

The potter's face was out of focus. One moment, he had four eyes; the next, he was back to two. Squinting made no difference. Blinking didn't help either. Everything was blurry. At least he'd survived the casting. On shaking limbs, Zanth struggled to rise.

Prann took his arm. 'No, stay down. Oh, your lips are blue.'

His chest was tight. Unable to draw a full breath, he had a hunger for air he couldn't sate.

Prann pressed a cool, damp cloth onto his forehead and offered him a drink. The rubosberry juice was sweet.

Zanth handed the cup back to him. 'Thanks. You told them about Ezro and Lisoun?' Their names echoed off the walls of his heart.

'Yes. Initially, leadership said to rest up and lay low. But everything has changed.'

'How?'

'They're going after the Lost Cave.'

That'll be our ruin. Zanth sat up, regretting it instantly. 'We can't let that happen. Who's going?'

'Princess Antarna, Farikarr and the seer, with hunters, woodsmen and an armless.'

'Farikarr? Really?'

Prann nodded. 'Yes.'

'When are they leaving?'

'Any moment now.'

Zanth extended his arm. 'Help me up.' The spell had cost him half of his refreshed supply of madriliks and almost all his energy.

'Leadership is massing a group, but it'll take a day or two. They need you to pick up the trail. Once you find it, let me know where to send them,' Prann said.

'Will do.'

His vision resolved. Zanth stood in an empty section of Prann's basement. The rest was stacked high with logs for the potter's kiln.

Prann held out a slender azure nalitroite.

'Thanks. Do you have a sharp knife?'

'Of course.' From under his apron, Prann fetched a small blade made of knapped obsidian and handed it over.

Zanth pursed his lips together and took to the triangle of facial hair that pointed to his chin. 'I need to visit the seer's residence.' With something that belonged to the seer, he could perform a location spell. 'Can you fetch me provisions for a couple of days in the forest? Dried fish and the like.'

'Sure.'

'Thanks. I'll meet you back here.' Zanth pocketed the knife.

They took to the street and parted ways. Weavers knelt, one end of their looms around a post, the other secured by a strap around their waists. A carpenter worked on a chair, whittling its leg. Zanth stepped around a handcart laden with earthenware jars, swashing with wine.

On the next street stood the two-storey residence of the seers. He knocked on the door. A hunched man with a polite smile answered. The left-hand wall was lined with portraits, mostly of old men. A collection of capes and cloaks hung next to the open door. How was Zanth to know which belonged to the seer? He ruled out a pink one, another covered in beads, and a third with a feminine brooch.

'Good day. My name is Taltio, and I seek an audience with the seer,' Zanth lied.

'Welcome. I am Nalgrid. Sorry, the seer is not available. We generally take appointments a month in advance.'

'Of course. May I book one, please?' He slid a hand into his pocket and clasped his knife.

Nalgrid reached behind the door and took off a parchment mounted on wood. It had sixteen squares, one for each month.

Zanth had narrowed his choices down to two capes: one deep blue, the other pale green. The green one was finer, newer and had a more stylish cut. It would appeal to a young man.

With a paltry dull, Zanth snapped the rope holding up a portrait of an oversized seer. Nalgrid turned at the snap and rushed to catch it. As the portrait hit the floor, Zanth grabbed the edge of the green cape and cut it clear.

The knife and the piece of fabric were back in his pocket before Nalgrid looked up. Zanth booked a time with the seer and left. People scurried hither and thither. He bought a pungent clam soup, blew across the top and took a slurp. The liquid was thick, the flavour deep. It would be his last hot meal for days.

Prann had beaten Zanth back to his pottery. He sat throwing clay, alternating between shaping it and kicking his wheel. Wetting his fingers, he ran them up the inside of the pot, gracefully extending its circumference.

A sack sat to his side. Zanth could tell Prann he'd be back soon, but he wasn't sure he believed that. The forest had any number of ways to claim its victims. Plus, stealing from hunters, woodsmen, an armless and a seer that could see you coming was not without risk. Though, anything had to be safer than duelling his former mentor.

Zanth collected the provisions, said his thanks without making promises he couldn't keep and made for the shore. His canoe was where he'd left it. A delicate breeze wrinkled and creased the surface of the lake. With each stroke of the paddle, his island grew larger. It had been home for a bit over three years. One lonely night, drunk on wine, he'd howled over and over at the moon. A few days later, purchasing supplies at the main island, he'd laughed on hearing a group of boys fighting over whether there was a ghost or a monster on his little island.

He pulled his canoe ashore, leaving half in the water. Stripping, Zanth dived into the water, scrubbed his face and walked out. There was no time to swim. The rocks were smooth beneath his feet.

After drying himself and changing, he knelt in front of Silisa's headstone.

I almost passed on, my love. Maybe then I could have found you again. Looked down and seen you reborn into a lovely family. But I can't let you be raised in this world, not as it is.

What face did she have now? When they'd first met, her eyes had twinkled above the strong cheekbones of her heart-shaped face. He couldn't help but stare. This image was sullied by her last days. A lump the size of an egg had grown upon her neck. Spots joined her freckles. These were replaced by pus-filled boils. Her sunken eyes had fallen dull and then closed forever.

His magic had been useless; the Order of Devtakaris did not teach healing. If he'd joined Preslina instead, he could've saved her.

Zanth got up, fetched his water bladder and hurried back to the shore. A vermillion leaf floated on the lake, its edges curling to trap a droplet of liquid within. He picked it up and put the leaf on top of the piece of the green cape. Drawing a middler, he focused on the fabric, holding the image of the seer in his mind.

The leaf rose into the air. It swayed from side to side before cutting a straight line towards the main pier.

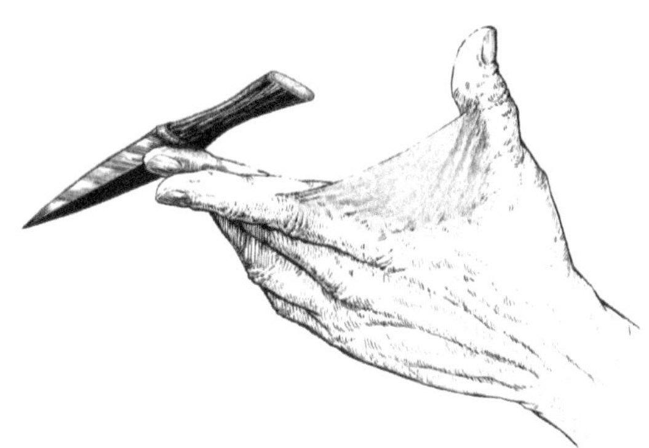

26. Brave Not to Shed a Tear

CAL stood on the pier facing Farikarr, pretending to listen to a story about a hunt. Woodsmen and hunters packed two canoes with supplies and weapons. Antarna conversed with the armless, who was joining them to provide magical protection.

You can't trust the royals. Kat's vague warning came back to him. If only he could ask Farikarr what the royals were hiding. But there was no easy way to weave that into the conversation. Even if Cal asked, Farikarr had no reason to answer him, and maybe the man didn't even know himself. One possibility was that the crater planned to betray the lake island and claim the saphramurls for themselves, just as the chancellor intended for the lake island. As if the mission wasn't dangerous enough.

Biesan, a stocky woodsman he'd met earlier, greeted his slender wife and young twin girls who shared their mother's shade of coppery ash-blond hair. The girls ran to their father, wrapping their tiny arms around him and burying their heads into his stomach. Grinning, Biesan stroked their hair. His hand lacked its little finger, and an adjacent scar puckered his skin, irregular and bite-like.

Cal drew a sharp breath. Unable to pull his gaze from the empty space where the digit should have been, he scratched the skin above his eyebrow. A sickening thump reverberated in his mind. The looming forest on the other side of the lake was reminder enough of the life-threatening danger awaiting them.

'I'll be back before you know it,' Biesan said.

Cal turned away. His goddess would've had her reasons for showing him the vision, but he was clueless as to what those were.

When Biesan died, the hunters of the crater would outnumber the lake islander woodsmen. It would make it that much harder for the lake islanders to betray the crater and claim the gems for the chancellor. Under the chancellor's plan, the betrayal had to occur in the cave, when the anti-magic gems rendered the armless powerless.

Cal climbed into the front of the five-person canoe, which swayed gently, and nodded to the two woodsmen at the stern. Biesan and Antarna followed, taking neighbouring seats in the middle of the vessel.

Hinn, the lanky young man next to Garlin at the stern, untied them and pushed them off. The woodsmen's names—Garlin, Hinn and Biesan—all sharing the same ending letter made them that much easier to remember. A small coincidence but one worth savouring.

Biesan and Hinn already had paddles. Two more rested at Cal's feet. He kept one and extended the other to the oldest woodsman, Garlin.

Antarna took it out of the air. Instead of passing it back to Garlin, she placed one hand on the top and adjusted her other hand on the shaft. She turned her face to Cal, as if daring him to suggest that she needn't contribute or that she'd better enjoy the passage if she just observed. He kept his lips closed.

Antarna, what did you expect? His choices for the last paddle were an experienced woodsman who'd grown up on and around the lake, or a princess on her first visit. Some part of him knew the answer though: she would've liked to have been asked. Too late for that now.

Kat strutted onto the pier in a bold pink dress that hugged her curves. Eyes turned her way, and Kat pretended to be oblivious to the attention. She gave Cal a generous smile as if she thought he was doing all this for her and then blew him an exaggerated kiss. Reluctant to blow one back but wise enough to know a smile wouldn't suffice, he plucked the kiss from the air and pressed it to his cheek. Farikarr smirked, and Cal curled his toes. In fairness, Cal hadn't expected her to come down, not after he'd told her there was no need to see him off. When the father and daughter embraced, Antarna turned to the forest.

The crowd on the pier swelled. Families waved their loved ones off, and spectators gossiped. Amongst the faces, towards the back, sunlight reflected off a bald head, highlighting its unforgiving, recognisable contours. The chancellor's herald nodded to Cal. His message couldn't have been clearer, well, unless he'd brandished a fire poker.

Cal dipped in his paddle. The twins' adorable smiles turned to frowns, but they were brave not to shed a tear. Their father would die. Cal couldn't break the solemn oath he'd made before his goddess when his master had taken him on. No seer could; some things were beyond the laws of the universe.

The laws of the universe ...

Antarna's plan to magically teleport gems that were valuable because they repelled magic made no sense.

27. Sucking my Blood

Out on the lake, lively noises from the dock faded behind them. The flat expanse of water separated civilisation from the wilderness. Antarna sank her paddle into the water in unison with Cal.

It troubled her how sceptical the seer had looked when she'd told him that they'd teleport the saphramurls. The records, verified by none other than High Priest Effain, were irrefutable. Further, the plan had been sanctioned by her uncle, the king. The crater only benefited if the gems could be teleported. A small voice at the back of her head pointed out that the king may have just wanted to get rid of her after the mess she'd created. But that was ridiculous, and she quickly quietened it.

Twisting around in her seat, she addressed the leader of the woodsmen. 'Garlin, how many trips have you made to the ruins?'

'I've lost count, which is probably a good sign.' He smiled.

Hinn shook his head. 'What else have you forgotten?' He had a playful glint in his eye.

'I haven't forgotten how long and painful it was to train you,' Garlin replied.

'A fault of the student or of the teacher?'

The group laughed.

Cal finished another long, smooth stroke, his shoulder and back muscles relaxing, the tension easing from his form. Water trickled down the blade of his paddle and back into the lake, sending out circular ripples. The sleeves of his shirt were bunched above his elbows. Prominent, bulging veins ran down Cal's arms like forked rivers, an intense blue against pale skin. His striking eyes were an even deeper, otherworldly blue. They'd been the first thing she'd noticed when they'd met.

'What did you think of the lake island?' Cal asked over his shoulder.

'It's pretty. I wish I'd had time for a swim. The water is more inviting than the snowmelt I'm used to back home.' Antarna leant over the side and immersed two fingers into the clear, tepid water. Shimmering fish wove through a field of undulating kelp, tall and golden.

He chuckled. 'That's for sure.'

'I didn't see a redhead today. How rare are they?'

'Very. Just a couple a generation. Otherwise, it's shades of blond.' Cal shook his messy mane.

Knew you were a shooting star, Tozias.

The second canoe drew level with them. It also held five—the most auspicious of numbers. Paddles hit the water at different times, not a single webbed hand holding them. Farikarr dipped his in every now and again, content to let the three hunters under his command steer and propel the vessel despite the impracticality of an odd number doing the paddling. It matched his air of arrogance. The fifth member of their canoe, an armless called Orrsin, sat at the back. Thick, fibrous and shiny skin ran up his neck onto his jaw, stopping short of his cheek. She missed her scars, each one a potent reminder.

Burnt by fire or magic? The smell of Gil's smoke-filled room came back to her, overpowering and toxic.

Her canoe pulled away from the one manned by those of the crater. Brown and green paint camouflaged the face, neck and hands of the lake islanders in her vessel, hiding their pale skin. Something told her that there was plenty being hidden amongst them.

Ten people, one mission, but how many different allegiances?

It was too simple to think that those of the lake island were loyal to the chancellor and those of the crater were loyal to her uncle and father—assuming none were Resatrium. While she'd only met him recently, it was clear that Farikarr cared most about himself. Orrsin, the scarred priest, would hold his vows to his temple above any duty to the crater. No doubt he'd keep High Priest Arric updated on their progress by telepathy. She wasn't sure what had motivated Cal. Perhaps he'd agreed to join them to impress Kathrina, but she liked to think it was to help the wounded lake islanders in the mountain temples.

The canoe jolted as its nose grounded. Cal hopped out and offered her his forearm.

'Very kind, but I'm good, thank you.' *I'm no Kathrina.* She landed with bent knees. Her dagger hung from her hip, and she held her shield and sheathed sword.

The seer rolled down his sleeves.

Fallen leaves of yellow and gold crunched under her feet. Antarna leapt onto a tree stump. The new boots she'd had to don rubbed against the back of her heels. Exposed skin anywhere below the shoulders was too dangerous in the forest.

'Yes, we clear a few trees,' Cal said, 'so we can see what's approaching the lake.'

'Makes sense. Have you been there before?' She indicated to the looming rainforest. It was the setting for every bedtime story told to scare her as a young child.

'A few times. What about you?'

'No.'

'But you've come prepared.' He indicated to her weapons. 'I hear you know how to use them.'

There was nowhere to hide. She raised her shield in front of her face to conceal her pained expression. 'You heard?'

'Oh, I think everyone has.'

'Perfect.' *Just perfect.* She took a moment before lowering her shield. 'Your throwing knives are stunning. How proficient are you?'

His hand fell to the pair of bronze blades strapped across his chest. Two more rested against his thighs. 'They're a great stress relief. I'm decent, but not sure how'd they'd go in a fight. Could be useful to wound or distract.'

She'd heard that steel interfered with visions.

The second canoe landed. Farikarr climbed out, followed by his three hunters. She reminded herself of their names: Nol, Eryx and Rundlud. Like Farikarr, each wore an animal tooth around their neck. Nol's was long, slender and curved, and Eryx's serrated. The youngest hunter, Rundlud, had a plant eater's tooth, broad and flat.

'To the ruins?' asked Farikarr.

Antarna jumped down from the stump. 'Yes.'

Garlin led the way. They proceeded in single file. Antarna savoured the sunlight on her skin prior to stepping into the forest. By goddess, it felt good to be on the move with a plan to save Tozias. Time was not on their side. Decaying leaves—slimy, battered and brown—clung to her boots. They were less slippery than the moss that otherwise blanketed the forest floor. She stepped over a troop of mushrooms, cups of scarlet close in colour to the ribbon on Farikarr's spear.

Throughout the forest, mushrooms were on the march. Orange ears climbed trees and white nets traversed branches. Purple and pink ones striped like tiny parasols consumed rocks. Importantly, there was not a honey horn to be seen. Those poisonous golden amber mushrooms were always found in horn-shaped pairs.

A picture formed in her mind of horns rising through swirling mist. That was all they knew about hazzurus: horns and mist. *That's a very convenient creature to blame, one that's feared but never been proven to exist.* She'd read a report of a purported sighting, but even a tree limb could look awful scary in the mist.

Cal stopped and she did likewise; Garlin's hand was raised. The woodsman knelt, examined an impression in the earth and then continued. As Antarna drew closer, the footprint took shape. It exhibited three toes splayed in a V-shape, each longer than her hand. A faint mark behind the heel suggested an additional toe, backwards facing. She patted Enthriff. *I'm glad you're looking out for me.*

Flies buzzed around a pile of scat large enough to lose a foot in. Further on, two large horizontal marks had been scored through the thick bark of a tree, exposing its yellow trunk. She pictured talons rivalling her dagger.

They stopped under a gigantic tree that'd punched through the canopy and just kept growing. Its crown of needles was too thick for sunlight to pierce. Antarna took her pack off, and she sat against a twisting root that rose high enough to support her back and head.

The twisting, gnarled roots strangled the earth, guarding the tree's territory. Cal hesitated before joining her.

Curious. She held her tongue.

They drank from their water bladders as the priest constructed a magical barrier around the group. When he finished, they were permitted to talk for the first time since entering the forest.

'Thanks, Orrsin,' said Antarna. 'You look like you've done that before.'

'Yes, when I'm not accompanying hunting parties, I help tend the barrier over the crater. It's the same spell, keeping creatures out and sounds in.' He sat on a root.

'Did you help restore it after it went down?'

'I did.'

'What brought it down?'

Orrsin crossed his legs.

'You can tell her,' said Cal. 'The theft of the ciltrilian serpent is common knowledge.'

The priest shifted in his seat. 'Well, yes, when the baby serpent hatched from its egg, it released anti-magic trapped in its shell. This brought down the barrier to the vault and over the crater.'

'Because madrilik and anti-magic are opposites that can't stand one another. I've read that the closer they get, the greater they repel.'

'Correct. The two can't come into contact.'

'What if they did?'

'Not possible.'

Something seemed off. She couldn't put her finger on it.

Orrsin stood. 'I should check when we're leaving.'

When he left, Cal broke into a wide smile. 'I could see you setting that up. Bait went into the water. You got a bite then reeled him in. Impressive.'

'It was good teamwork. Thanks for jumping in with the serpent.'

'Yes, not a bad guess.'

'You guessed? I'll have to keep an eye on you.'

Orrsin pulled down the barrier, and Garlin led them on. They didn't speak, but the forest did. Gliders called, birds sang and insects buzzed.

There was no telling whether the cave would be close to the ruins, or if she'd get another vision of it. *Hold on, Tozias.*

They came to a clearing. Enthriff squeezed her wrist. She put a hand on her curved scabbard, ready to pull her sword free. A pride of yalluts raised their heads from grazing. There were seven females, a smaller male with proud antlers and four young ones. The broad, curving antlers were all the more impressive with the knowledge that they fell off and grew back each year. Along the backs of the adults ran a double row of short, narrow plates.

A large female stepped forwards. She reared onto her hind legs and swung her spike-adorned tail.

'Step back, slowly.'

Orrsin's voice had come into her head, bypassing her ears. Telepathy—her first experience. The words were just as clear. What they lacked in tone, they made up for with feeling.

The group withdrew from the edge of the clearing. Yalluts were aggressive if provoked, especially with their young around.

As the light faded, the air grew cold and damp. Ahead, a tree looked to have black leaves. When Antarna was closer, she realised that they were not leaves but bizeracs. The bloodthirsty creatures covered the skeleton branches of the dead tree. When the sun finally fell, they would wake and leave their roost.

Antarna held her breath at the putrid smell of a rotting carcass. It had probably been dragged into the nearby bushes, thick and thorned. She felt something watching her, but Enthriff was silent.

They halted in a gap between four trees and Orrsin again raised a barrier.

Farikarr pulled out a cancryst. 'Time to check yourselves for bloodsuckers.'

As tunics came over heads and belts were undone, Antarna headed behind a bush and crouched, holding her knees. Thanks to Enthriff, she didn't have to strip and search.

'Two leeches for me,' said Hinn with a deep, distinctive voice.

'I got a star leech,' another said.

'Exotic. Five tackulas on me.' The voice was young, perhaps Rundlud's.

She'd only seen a drawing of a tackula. They had large swollen bodies, often the size of a thumbnail. With eight legs, they were more closely related to spiders than insects.

'They know who's boss. None for me,' Farikarr said.

Cal muttered a curse. 'I've an anchor leech.'

'Didn't see that coming, did you?' someone replied.

The man was rewarded with a chorus of laughs.

Antarna turned and stood. There were naked bodies everywhere. She dropped back to the ground. 'Do you need help, Cal?'

'There's no helping him,' said Garlin. 'He's just going to have to wait for it to drop off. You try anything on that leech, be it salt, fire, magic or a knife, and Cal will get a nasty dose of poison.'

'I might have a secret weapon,' Antarna said.

Cal joined her behind the bush. His tunic was back on, but his pants were draped over the crook of his elbow. The anchor leech had attached to the inside of his thigh.

'Sit,' she said.

He did, stretching his legs and laying his pants over his undergarment.

She extended her arm. 'Cal, I'd like to introduce you to Enthriff.'

Enthriff slithered from her wrist to her palm.

'What the?' Cal scrambled back and drew one of his bronze blades. 'Is that a snake?'

'No, he's not.'

'I'm ... not good with snakes.' His hand shook.

Is that why you paused before the twisting tree roots? 'He's a lilreneer.'

Cal didn't seem to register the word, but then, the creatures were beyond rare.

She held Enthriff up. 'See, no fangs. He won't hurt you.'

Cal sheathed his knife and exhaled.

'Sorry. You alright?'

'Yes.' Cal shuffled closer but kept his legs bent. His face was even paler than normal.

Antarna rested her hands in her lap. 'Let me tell you a story, the first part of which you would've heard. I was almost seven. We were having soup in the dining room as a family. I took my first spoonful. A hunter entered, and my father had to leave before even starting. I refused to eat anymore. My mother and brother weren't so lucky. While they lay dying, I was teleported to the mountain temples for care.'

She drew a breath. 'I was in the infirmary for months, constantly in pain, hallucinating and burning up. I refused to eat and barely slept, worried that the poisoner would find me again. My father visited and gave me Enthriff. He can sense danger, including poison. This gave me the confidence to eat and sleep; *he* did.'

'I'm sorry, Princess.'

'Antarna or Tarna, please. And thank you.'

'I'm also sorry for offering you soup earlier. I wasn't thinking. That was insensitive; no, plain stupid.'

'It's fine. Didn't bother me, really. Don't think twice about it. Now, let's get that leech off you.'

Cal extended his leg. The anchor leech looked like it had legs of its own. At least ten appendages extended from each side of its elongated body. They didn't rest on his skin, but pierced it, anchoring the leech by more than its teeth.

Antarna held out her hand. 'You ready?'

'Yes.'

When Enthriff touched his skin, Cal squeezed his eyes shut and crumpled his face. He may have been biting his tongue.

'Breathe. You can do this,' she said. 'He's a lilreneer, not a snake.' *Did something happen to you as a child?*

Enthriff circled the leech. It withdrew a few appendages from Cal and thrust at her lilreneer, who was just out of range. Each appendage came to a fine point, ideal for puncturing skin and hide. Engaging, Enthriff coiled his body around the leech. It stabbed at him. The point broke upon Enthriff's tough outer layer, oozing vibrant green.

'What's happening?' Cal asked. 'Is it working?' His eyes were still shut.

'Yes, almost there. What shall we name your new friend?'

'What?'

'It's ... no, *she*'s a hanger-on. How about we call her Clingy?'

Enthriff squeezed. The leech struggled against his grip. She released her mouths from Cal and tried to bite Enthriff. But, in his tight coil, Enthriff had control.

Antarna flicked the pair off Cal and dived to cover them with a cup.

Cal stood and shook himself off. Two bloody circles marked his leg, surrounded by smaller punctures.

She tilted the cup for the briefest moment, and Enthriff slithered out. Antarna picked him up and patted him.

'It's trapped under that?' Cal pointed to the cup and drew his knife.

Antarna stepped between him and the cup. 'Yes, but there is no need to kill her.'

'What? It's been sucking my blood.'

'That's what leeches do. Clingy's off now.'

'I ...' He slammed his knife back into its sheath and walked away, hands on his hips, muttering to himself.

With Orrsin's help, Antarna dropped the leech in a bush outside the barrier. *And that's the last I expect to see of you.*

She picked a flat area free from roots. A smile grew on her face as she pictured Kathrina being asked to sleep on the ground. *Why do I keep bringing her up*? She cleared away the fallen sticks and laid out a thin blanket.

Cal returned. One arm crossed across his body. It held his other arm that was stuck to his side. He took small steps.

'I'm sorry, Antarna. And thanks for getting it off me, you and Enthriff.'

'Our pleasure. And it's fine. It was drinking your blood. I get it.'

The light and smoke from a fire posed too much danger. They ate cold food, then settled in.

Lying down, she stretched her hands above her head. 'Cal, my father told me that a traitorous mage brought the barrier down. Orrsin confirmed it was the serpent hatching. So, the mage stole the serpent egg?'

'Yes, that's what the Devtakaris high priest said. Josmark, not Arric.'

'What else did he tell you?'

Cal shifted, rustling leaves.

She turned onto her side. 'I'll keep it secret.'

'The mage's name is Zanth. He posed as a royal messenger to steal the saphramurls.'

'That might have got him in the front door but not anywhere near the vault. The temple is more secure than the palace. It's a maze filled with the most powerful priests. How'd he get out?'

'Good question,' said Cal. 'I think he trained at the temple.'

When did the Resatrium turn him? 'Makes sense. Zanth used his knowledge of the temple and a disguise to get to the vault. Then, the anti-magic released from the serpent hatching brought down the barrier, and he grabbed the saphramurls.' She slid onto her back. 'We should get some sleep. Night.'

'Night.'

A pair of glowing eyes peeked out from a shrub outside the barrier. She yawned, the sound joining countless others in the insomnious forest. There were clicks, hisses and calls, along with the odd snarl or roar. Branches creaked above, mixing with the flutter of wings unseen.

Something didn't sit right. She pulled on different threads of thought until she found the issue. It couldn't just be a big coincidence that, earlier on the day of the theft of the gems, a hazzurus had attacked near the glade.

All four priests died. So, you can't know it was a hazzurus. It's no different to the end of Daslercia: no one left alive, so all conjecture and speculation. Or a convenient cover story.

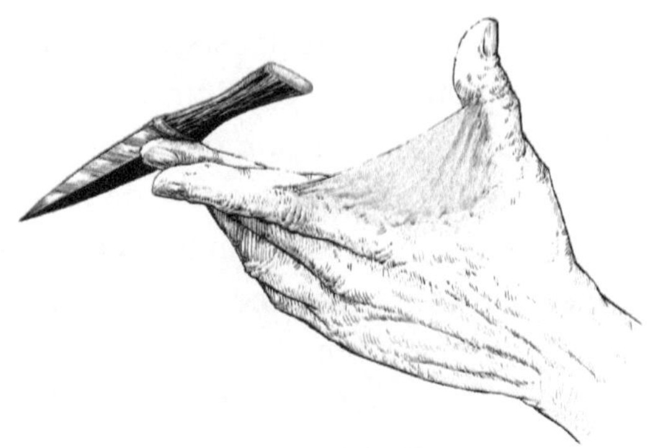

Eaten Alive

Birds sang in chorus, musical and high-pitched. A far more pleasant way to wake than the animal cry and crunch of bones from last night. At least the canopy had hidden the moon; Cal would be married on the next one.

He pushed himself up and rubbed sleep from his eyes. His neck was stiff. Most of the group were still in the land of dreams. Antarna sat cross-legged, each foot on the opposite thigh. Her knees touched the ground, her face serene.

Meditating or trying to connect with a past life?

The bites on his leg begged to be scratched. Instead, he dug into his bag for the salve his mum had packed. Cal applied it liberally.

It wasn't long before Antarna opened her eyes. She looked awake and refreshed. *Clearly a morning person.*

'How'd you sleep?' he asked.

'Well enough, thanks. It looks like those kept you awake.' She indicated to the red bites on his leg.

'Yes, those and something else. You and Farikarr lied to me.' He wasn't positive they had, but her reply would tell him. 'You know what apex predator attacked the mages.' If he'd had more sleep, maybe he'd have found a softer way to test his suspicion.

She clasped her hands and then separated them. 'Yes, we know. I'm sorry. I'm sworn to secrecy, though.'

'Look at where we are.' Cal stood and resisted the urge to add, "You can't keep secrets, not here." He kept a few of his own, of course, but they didn't speak to the reason that they were in this godforsaken forest. With his life on the line, he had to understand the full context of that reason.

'I don't have a choice.'

'Well, that makes mine easy. Time to return home. Good luck with the quest.' He closed his fist around his keys.

She rose.

He stuffed items into his pack. *Am I bluffing? You can't know if I don't.*

Antarna stood awkwardly—which, until now, he hadn't known was possible. Her mouth was a stubborn oyster shell, refusing to open.

'Garlin.' With his pack over his shoulder, Cal walked towards the oldest woodsmen.

'Fine,' she said. 'Can you keep a secret and never tell a soul, not even your chancellor?'

'I can, but for this, I'm not willing to.'

She took a deep breath, perhaps as a substitute for cursing him. 'Use your discretion, please.' Antarna approached and whispered into his ear, 'The priests in the glade died killing a hazzurus.'

'Am I a child that needs frightening?'

'I'm serious.'

'You know what's just as convenient as not knowing the creature? One we can't prove exists. Do you think I gobble up wild stories?'

She tilted her head and raised her brows.

'I'm sorry.' He brought his hands over the crown of his head. 'Who gave you the information?'

'My father.' Her words were as stiff as her back.

'The information is only as good as the person that told him. Do you believe it?'

'Would I've told you if I didn't?'

'Yes, and you'd likely answer a question with a question.' A memory surfaced; dots connected. 'The first time we met, when you teleported in and we were walking home, you mentioned a hazzurus. You wanted to gauge my reaction.'

She shifted her weight.

'You were still making up your mind. You've had doubts?'

'Yes.'

'Good.' Cal plonked his pack down and dug into it. Locating the jerky, he offered it to her.

She took a step towards him, a positive start. 'No, thanks.'

He rummaged again and pulled out some dried cinertin. *I know you like fruit.*

'Yes, please.' She raised her hands, ready to catch it.

He threw the dried fruit over. *Oh, I'm a jelly-brained mudfish.* Realisation hit him, and there was nowhere to hide—his pack could only fit an arm, maybe two. 'Of course ... You're vegetarian, from your time at the mountain temples.'

'I am. Not that my father has realised.'

Farikarr clapped twice. 'Let's get a move on.'

Garlin stood. 'Remember, single file and keep an eye out for delusians. They're silver flowers shaped like butterflies. One sniff will take your mind, then the forest will claim your body.'

Cal shook out his blanket, rolled it up and put it away. He was more concerned with creatures for which he was a meal, or a snack, than hallucination-inducing flowers. *Remember why you're here.* True Seer would be nice, but he'd settle for keeping his eyes, his livelihood and his mother safe.

Garlin resumed the lead. They walked past a wengoloc tree. It was covered in dead flower heads that uncannily resembled human skulls. Each was of a size about right for a baby. They hung in long ribbons, as if made into trophies. Cal was behind Hinn, whose feet effortlessly found the right place to step. Despite his careful attention, Cal couldn't seem to stop crunching, rustling and cracking.

Hinn pointed out a mound of dirt, larger than a bush. 'Spitting anthill,' he mouthed.

Given the amount they'd dug out to make space for their tunnels and nest chamber, the colony must have been massive.

On the opposite side, a low, continuous buzzing started. Garlin darted to Orrsin and whispered into his ear. After drawing forth two dulls, the priest formed a dark cloud of smoke. He sent this forward, dispersing it through the trees. The buzzing faded.

Cal kept his distance from Biesan. He'd foreseen people die before, but he'd never spent every moment with them until they passed away. The man's death may have been easier to swallow if he didn't have a family and if he had longer to live than a day or two. Still, Cal couldn't break his oath, not for him or anyone else.

As the morning progressed, mushrooms became few and far between. Flowers multiplied though, so much so that green was dethroned by its fellow colours. The air was heavy with their scent, stronger even than Kat's perfume. Garlin led them between the trees in a manner that was uncomfortably snakelike.

Orrsin overtook Antarna to come up behind Cal. He drew energy from a madrilik to write words into Cal's head. 'I'm informed that Josmark talked to you about helping to find Zanth?'

Cal pictured a quill and replied. 'That's right.'

'I received an update.' Orrsin tapped his temple: telepathy. 'Yesterday, Zanth used madriliks stored in the urlire to try to kill Arric.'

'In broad daylight?'

'Yes, he challenged Arric. They fought on the rim of the crater. Zanth lost and fled.'

'And you're worried he'll strike again? Or pursue us?'

'We're hoping you may be able to tell us.'

Cal turned his mind back to his conversation with High Priest Josmark. One remark stood out: still has his arms.

Yes, Zanth was one of yours.

Cal didn't like his chances of finding Zanth. His vision of Morsirel's murder hadn't even shown the killer's face. And, he'd had nothing more recent on Zanth.

The connection with Orrsin faded. If Cal raised a finger, the armless would reestablish it, and Cal could ask the question he needed the answer to: can you teleport a saphramurl? If the gems couldn't be teleported, the furthest they'd get would be the lake island. No one had ever made it from the lake island to the crater on foot—and a few had been crazy enough to try. Even if they reached the crater, the journey to the mountain temples would take months through the treacherous forest. A death sentence. If they found the saphramurls, and they couldn't be teleported, only the lake island would benefit. A chill swept through Cal. If the chancellor had realised the flaw in the plan, he'd had no incentive to speak up.

Unless the gems could be teleported, the quest was pointless. They'd never save the injured at the mountain temples. Although … it would appease the chancellor, keeping Cal and Mum safe. Not that he should think like that.

He resolved to ask Antarna soon, at the right moment. Then, she could question Orrsin.

They entered a clump of multicoloured trees. Their trunks and branches featured every shade, tint and tone of blue, red and purple. These colours ran up each tree in long strips of varying lengths, without any discernible pattern. No two trees were the same. This diversity was contrasted by the abundant foliage, a uniform vibrant yellow that stretched above them. The eye could not discern where the leaves of one tree ended and the next tree started, so seamlessly did they meld. Sunlight filtered through the leaves, bathing them in divine golden light.

'Have you been painting trees too?' Antarna asked.

Cal chuckled. 'I wish I could claim the credit for this, for they sure are a masterpiece.'

'That they are,' she said, her voice full of wonder.

'It's the distinctive way in which the bark sheds over time. The inner bark changes colour as the tree ages and is unveiled at different times.'

'Shut up,' Biesan whispered.

'Sorry,' Cal mouthed. *Oops.* He exchanged a look with Antarna.

To his left, a sturdy tree was covered in half-spheres. They ran up its trunk and along the underside of its branches. *Hives?* He stopped. They did not appear to have any entry or exit points. *Cocoons then? I'm glad we're not sticking around to find out.*

Antarna had overtaken him. A stick—hidden under leaves—snapped under Cal's foot. Yesterday, Antarna had also made her fair share of noise in the forest. But now, she moved more like the hunters and woodsmen.

As a swarm of elradorite beetles approached, she extended an arm. The iridescent creatures did not take up her invitation to land on her. Instead, they busied themselves sampling and collecting pollen. Bunches of closed flowers opened, making an exception for the special guests. One unfurled beside Antarna, flaunting silver petals.

Cal lunged forwards and grabbed her shoulder. On turning her neck, her jaw brushed his finger.

From the ground up, darkness consumed all.

We barely touched.

Not now, Goddess, please.

It happened as it always did: first, specks of light, then zigzagging between them at breakneck pace before smashing into one.

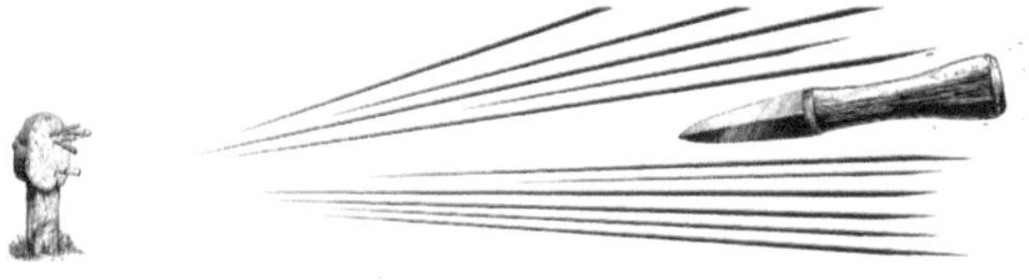

Antarna lay sprawled on the dirt. As a huge man approached, his skin dark with ink, she struggled to her feet. Her back was to Cal.

No, no. Let me see his death, not hers. Please.

A cacophony of clashing weapons, screams and rapid footfalls filled the air.

Blood ran from a nasty gash on Antarna's upper arm. On the second attempt, Antarna managed to raise her sword. In the distance, half-standing buildings stood silhouetted against an orange sky thick with pregnant clouds.

'My poison was just getting started, but your pain is almost over,' the man said. Flickering torchlight illuminated his tattoos. Above his forearm guard, lightning struck a cactus growing from a cracked skull. The lines were thin, clean and crisp. His other arm featured a gaping mouth. The highly saturated maroon emphasised the rows of pointed teeth. A rotting face slid down his neck, crawling with maggots.

He swung a strange weapon with both hands—like a spear with an axe added below the tip and a hook on the other side.

Antarna stepped clear, down a dirt slope. Stone walls rose on either side. At the bottom of the incline was an enormous pit, also lined with stone. It had metal bars.

Where is this? Daslercia?

Using the momentum from his last strike, he brought his weapon around again.

She ducked under it.

'You're a disgrace to your family.' He directed the next blow to her body, biceps bulging.

The axe blade deflected off her shield—slanted to avoid its full force.

No sooner than it did, he reversed the motion. The backside hook caught her shield. He yanked it free, and she fell onto her knees.

Get up. Get up! No, *Goddess, please.*

The man drove the spear tip through her armour, into her heart.

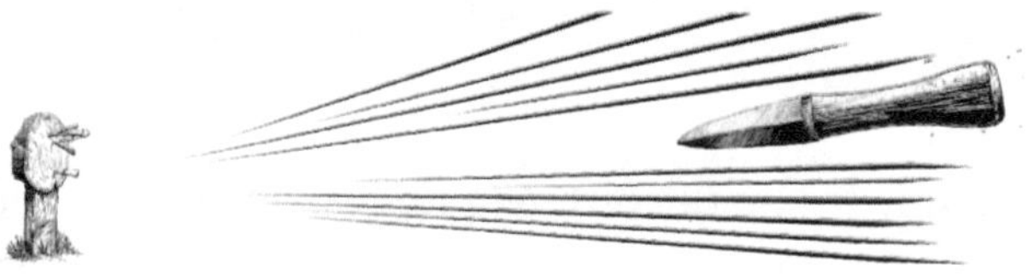

A warm hand lay upon Cal's arm.

Antarna.

The spike pierced your heart. You died.

The vision was too vivid. It would happen.

Antarna knelt beside him, her dark eyes warm.

He covered his face with his hand. She was kneeling just as she had been when she was killed.

I can't warn you. I can't change this.

'Are you alright, Cal?'

'Yes, thanks. Just a vision. I'm used to it. Let's keep moving. Avoid that flower.' He pointed to the silver delusian.

'Well spotted. Thanks.' She offered him a hand.

'Probably shouldn't, sorry.' He stood.

They passed through the all-coloured trees. Over and over, he saw the spike pierce her heart. He slowed, dropping back into the pack, putting her out of eyesight. The images came still.

Who is that desert warrior? And where does it take place?

The group had stopped. Cal and the last hunter, Nol, joined the others.

'Let's grab a quick drink then keep moving. We're going to need the light,' said Cal, keeping his voice low.

'Agreed,' said Farikarr.

Not long after, they were back in single file, following Garlin's lead. Cal brought up the rear. A butterfly with two eyes painted on each wing landed on a closed flower. Long and slender petals tapered to a pointed tip.

Again, the spike of that unusual weapon pierced her heart. He couldn't seem to banish the image.

Trees thinned ahead, and patches of sand-coloured stone caught the light. Cal and Rundlud joined the group that had stopped at the edge of the forest. Nature was well on the way to reclaiming the legendary city of Daslercia. Trees grew right up to the wall. Compared to the gnarled, wide trees that they had been walking through, these were mere youths.

The perimeter wall was cracked and crumbling, conquered by all manner of climbing plants. Behind it, tall, jagged structures persisted, hinting at the city's former glory. Cal pictured the city in all its grandeur, completing walls, adding roofs and clearing vegetation. It put the lake island, or the crater for that matter, to shame. The city could have held the populace of all four races and more.

Antarna sprang up from a branch. 'Thanks for getting us here, Garlin. Can you think of any places where a guard would've spent some time?'

Garlin turned to look over the ruins. 'We could try the armoury?'

'Good plan,' said Farikarr. 'We stick together. We don't know what we may come across.'

The thin undergrowth made for an easy walk. Stone blocks lay amongst the vegetation, longer than adults were tall. There was no order to them; rather, they were scattered like handfuls of thrown dice.

One tree grew on top of a block, its network of roots strangling the stone before finding the ground.

The group climbed through a missing section of the northern wall. Cal used it to get his bearings. Like the southern wall, it ran precisely east-west. They connected with the western and eastern walls to make a perfect square, aligned with the four cardinal directions.

More youthful trees greeted them. They grew amongst piles of rubble. A lonely column was the only stone standing with the trees.

Garlin took them left, alongside the wall. When they had walked half its length, they turned for the heart of the former city.

Grass as tall as his knees claimed the wide street. Cal paused before it, wary of the creatures that might stalk within and of the vision he'd had of grass like this. Garlin waved him on. They waded through the grass, passing under an arch. Not only did the topmost blocks seem to hang impossibly, but it was a wonder that the arch still stood. The walls of the houses that once lined the street were lucky to rise above the grass.

Tumbledown walls slowly grew in height, casting shadows over the group. Soon, they hinted at second storeys. Moss and vines called them home. Beneath and between the green, exotic symbols and designs were carved into the stone.

In the intersection between their street and another, a statue of a bare-chested man or god stood in the middle of some type of bowl. Its sides reached to Cal's thighs, and it was a good fifteen steps from one side to the other. The statue echoed these proportions; it was as large as an ilunger. Muscles rippled along its legs, torso and arms. It was missing its hands, anything that those once held, and its nose. The curls in its hair and full beard had been captured in stunning detail.

A *fountain*! He recalled reading of them. It would've been filled with water—not for bathing or drinking, but for honouring the gods and wish-making. This was a decadent use for a city two days from water. Daslercia lay equidistant between two rivers, the Blue River that drained from the lake of Cal's people and the Far River, a smaller one to the west.

Hopefully, we come across a wetway. He'd only seen a drawing of the wall-like stone structure that cut through the forest, carrying water from the Far River to Daslercia.

A madrilik twirled above the statue. Once, they would have gathered in staggering numbers deep underneath the city. It was said to have been a place of power to rival the mountain temples.

They turned left at the fountain. The grass was even longer. Something snapped under his boot. He bent down, parting the grass. Next to his foot, a skull looked up at him. Human, its temple caved in. Cracks ran along its length. He didn't lift his foot to examine what he'd broken. Cal's next step was tentative; it landed on soft earth. A dozen off-white objects as thick as his wrist rose from the grass, arranged in two rows of six, curving in towards each other.

A rib cage—a reminder of Daslercia's mysterious downfall.

The ribs clawed at the sky. The creature's backbone must've been hidden in the grass. After dying on its back, the creature would've cooled and stiffened. If it hadn't become a scavenger's meal, it would've bloated and smelt. Insects never missed their opportunity. Flies would've laid their eggs; maggots would've wriggled over the rotting form. After the tissue had liquified and the skin blackened, it would slowly have collapsed in on itself and melted into the earth. Wind and rain would've cleaned the bone.

The chancellor sometimes put a dead animal on display in his gardens, an exhibition in decay. It was as unsightly as it was odious.

They passed the skeleton and stopped in front of a solid building with stone walls twice as thick as the others. Other than missing its front door, roof and a chunk from the third floor, it seemed to be in good repair.

Cal walked up to Antarna. She had her shield hand on her hip and shoulders back. A posture of confidence or, more accurately, someone trying to find some. He wanted to question her plan to teleport the anti-magic gems, if they found them. But he couldn't distract her at this critical junction. Cal simply asked, 'How do you feel?'

'Hopeful.'

'I think you mean worried.' Everything rested on her having another vision of the cave.

'Maybe a little of both.'

'Would it make you feel better if I told you that I've seen you get us there?'

'Of course.' Antarna tilted her head. 'Have you?'

'Uh, not yet.'

She laughed, short but mirthful. 'Well, that's a lot of help, thanks.'

'Anytime. Shall we go in with you?'

'No, thanks.' With that, she entered the former armoury.

Cal sat. A four-tentacled face peered out from beneath a leaf. The slug gradually emerged, crawling forth like time was its most generous friend.

Do you perceive time the way I do?

Light gleamed off a lengthening trail of slime. A beetle landed beside the slug and folded its brown, translucent wings into its black body. It grabbed the boneless, shell-less creature and dragged it onto its side. The beetle hacked into its meal with its dagger-like mandibles, freeing a bite-sized piece.

Poor slug. Eaten alive.

Death was part of life. *Sorry, Biesan.*

Antarna strode through the doorway; another he'd foreseen die.

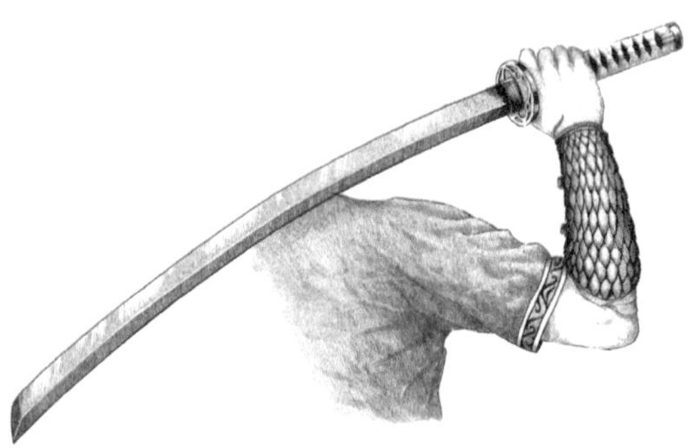

29. I Severed My Arms

Antarna pocketed her onyx vial, burdened by her failure. She'd fought the shadow opponent and travelled to her soul, but her past lives had resisted her when she'd needed them the most. And in that lay the likely cause: she'd put too much pressure on herself. Still, with reason and deduction, she'd formed a plan.

Sunlight brushed her skin, and she concentrated on its warmth to feed a gentle smile, carefully chosen. Antarna stepped out of the former armoury.

With a hand on each thigh, Cal pushed himself to his feet. 'What did you see?'

'Enough,' she lied. 'We follow their wetway, then head downriver.'

She'd given a crumb. It was enough for most. Cal clearly wanted the whole loaf of bread. It was written all over his twitching mouth.

Curiosity costs a tongue.

Cal held his, for now. No doubt he'd try to pull details out of her when they were alone.

'Well,' said Farikarr, 'you heard the princess. Let's move.'

The group headed for the west wall. A stairway led to nowhere. Faded tiles of a bird strutting its elaborate feathers clung to an internal wall. When a few more fell, the mural would be unrecognisable. The buildings progressively faded back to rubble. Seven columns persisted to her right. They were covered with dazzling delusians.

Doubt gnawed at her. If she led them the wrong way, the time they'd lose could cost Tozias his life. When she'd started training under Gil, she'd been drawn in by the prospect of the untapped power within her soul—with it, she'd never be defenceless or helpless again. But now, instead of unnatural strength or speed, what she truly needed was the knowledge held by her past lives.

Enthriff strangled her wrist. Antarna drew her sword and dagger. 'Something's coming.'

A gust of wind made the knee-high grass bow.

'Thanks for the warning,' said Hinn. The group laughed, all bar Cal. His pity was worse, though.

Biesan stood with a hand half-covering his smirking mouth. The next instant, he disappeared into the grass. His scream was cut short, replaced by a heavy thump.

Antarna broke into a sprint. Grass rustled ahead. There was a flash of human skin and a foreign green. Something had Biesan by the legs. A tail undulated, thin and spiked.

She pointed her sword. 'Orrsin, there!'

A crushing pressure returned to her wrist, only on the right side. She launched off her front foot, springing into the air.

Wide jaws came out of the grass. All teeth. The creature's body followed, a blur of solid muscle. A line of feathers ran down its back, marking it as a canenisk.

Airborne, Antarna lifted her legs to safety and arced her sword down. The canenisk passed below her. Its neck was short and thick.

No. She couldn't bring herself to take a life. As her blade was about to make contact, she altered her blow, slicing instead through the tough hide and muscle of its shoulder. Her steel bit into bone, jarring to a halt. Dark blood inundated the gash. The canenisk howled in rage or pain. Flying over the creature as it rushed right to left, all she could do was hang onto the hilt. A moment later and the force was too much; the sword slid from her grip. Antarna tucked her chin, curved her spine and rolled as she landed. The canenisk skidded to a halt, turned and charged afresh. It bounded at her a little lopsided as it took some pressure off its injured front left foot.

Yes. *Bring my sword.*

She leapt to her right. The creature swerved for her, now a body length away. She landed on the ball of her foot, coiled, then jumped again, this time to her left. The canenisk turned its neck, snapping its jaws shut. But she was clear. Grabbing the hilt, she unleashed a brutal kick. Her sword came free. She swung it around and lopped off the creature's tail, releasing a spray of blood. Warm liquid splattered her cheek and again, the canenisk howled. The tail wriggled, as if clinging to life despite having been cleaved free.

Antarna cut the air with her sword, then beat it upon her shield. *Give up.*

The creature limped away.

Bones snapped behind her. The initial canenisk levitated above the grass. It was dead, its neck turned at an unnatural angle. Biesan hung limp in its locked maw, dangling by his legs. Orrsin lowered the canenisk and wrenched open its upper jaw. Blood ran forth. Gaping puncture wounds covered the woodsman's legs. Garlin and Hinn were first to his side.

'We're here, Biesan. Open your eyes,' said Hinn.

Garlin supported Biesan's head and pressed two fingers onto his neck.

Please. Antarna held her breath.

Garlin shook his head, blinking.

Hinn turned to Orrsin. 'Heal him. Save him.'

'Even if I knew healing magic, he's gone. I'm sorry.'

Lowering her head, Antarna said a silent prayer for Biesan. She drew alongside Garlin and Hinn.

Cal joined them. 'Let's get Biesan out of there.'

They bent to lift him. Biesan's blood dripped from the canenisk's upper jaw. Parts of his flesh clung to the backside of its curved teeth. While the leading edge was smooth, the opposite side was jagged.

'Wait,' said Antarna. 'The teeth are serrated.'

Garlin knelt. 'Well spotted. We'll lift him off following the curvature of the teeth. With those serrations, it's not going to be pretty.'

Cal held down the lower jaw. The others lifted Biesan off to the sound of tearing flesh.

Hinn drove his spear into the canenisk. He patterned the carcass with gory holes and covered himself red. He threw the spear to the ground, panting heavily. Garlin put a hand on his shoulder.

Oh, his poor wife and twins. She pictured them huddled together, cheeks wet with tears. The girls would grow up without a father.

What are we even doing? What am I doing? Leading them under a lie ...

Hinn held up his bloodied hands. He turned them over and then back again.

Antarna grabbed her bladder. 'Hinn, here, let me.' Stepping close, she emptied water onto them.

After a pause, he rubbed his hands. 'We need to wash Biesan. He needs to go back to the lake. His place is there now.'

Maybe that's for the best. But Tozias ... and Evireny ... and the crater.

She locked eyes with Orrsin. He connected with her mind. 'Can you teleport him back?' she said, sending him her thoughts.

'No, sorry.'

She'd expected as much, given it'd taken four priests at each end to teleport her to the crater and, subsequently, the lake island. 'Take the group back then. I'll go on alone.'

Orrsin subtly shook his head.

'If we turn back now, his death is for nothing,' said Farikarr. 'This is hard, but we must go on.'

Hinn glared at him. 'You wouldn't understand. How could you? You feed your dead to a plant.'

Cal stepped between them. 'Yes, Biesan now belongs in the water. That is our way. But we are going to a river. There may be a suitable place there or at the Lost Cave, below the waterfall.'

'Wise thoughts, Seer,' said Garlin. 'Yes, let's find a suitable resting place for Biesan ahead and honour his death by completing the quest.'

Spears and a cloak were fashioned into a stretcher, and Biesan was placed upon it.

The group set off again. Garlin set a slow pace. This time, they avoided the grass where possible. Rubble made for unsecure footing, though. This was especially difficult for Cal and Hinn, who held the stretcher. The silence helped perpetuate their sombre mood. Even if she could speak, Antarna didn't know what she'd say.

The decrepit western outer wall loomed ahead and, beyond that, the forest. A welcome change. *Who knew I'd think that about the forest?*

The afternoon sun glinted off something to their right. Garlin's path led them closer. Steel bars stretched across a wide, deep pit.

On one side, the earth slanted downward into the pit. At the bottom was a huge steel door. The cage was lined with leaves and branches. But what had it been made to contain?

Not humans. There was enough space that a person could fit sideways between the bars.

Dirty stone walls lined the entry slope and the pit. Stone made sense; it'd stop a creature from being able to dig out.

'Hintal, let's put this down for a bit,' came Cal's voice behind her.

She turned. His skin was even paler than normal. 'What's wrong?'

'Nothing, just sweaty palms.' He didn't take his eyes from the pit.

What aren't you telling me?

He shook out his hands. 'Let's keep moving.'

A line of broken rock extended from the outer wall, unnaturally straight. It didn't make sense for it to also have been a wall. There had to be a logical reason for it ...

The wetway! Nice one, Garlin.

They passed through a gap in the outer wall. As they got deeper into the forest, the condition of the wetway improved. At its tallest, it stood around head height. A channel ran along the top, long since dry. Occasionally, a light ceramic tile still lay upon the top. They followed the wetway as the afternoon sun tired.

In the last of the light, they set up camp and checked themselves for blood suckers. Orrsin raised a protective barrier. The presence of Biesan's cloaked body weighed heavy upon the group.

Beside her, Cal kicked a twig clear of his sleeping area. 'When I say "magic", what is the first word that comes to mind?'

Distraction. What else could a question like this be? He was kind to try.

Death. 'I don't know. Maybe, danger.'

'Why is that?' He seemed genuinely interested.

'Madriliks devastated the mountain temples.' It had killed so many, including Gil. She couldn't let it take any more lives. 'Without the stones, more at my temple will die. Each moment we spend searching is one they spend suffering. Then there's Zanth. The previous Resatrium mage, Layaury, would've wiped out the royal line if Arric hadn't saved them.' Her past life had taken part in that plot; if he'd succeeded, she'd never have been born.

Cal shook out his blanket. 'I've seen that in a vision. I felt Arric step in front of your grandfather, into the beam of madriliks. It lit every nerve on fire. Anyone else would've died, but he was lucky to be born with not just a deep reservoir, but two. Not that he knew that.'

'Which makes it even more courageous.'

'Absolutely. And look what he did after. He became the most powerful mage of the four races, rose to high priest and now works with your king and father.' His mouth twitched, then opened. 'I understand why you said "danger". I think there may be another reason.'

The poison in the soup had come from the honey horn mushroom. Ordinarily, they had a foul taste and smell. But the Resatrium assassin had used magic to extract the poison, rendering it undetectable.

She sat, keeping her thoughts to herself. 'What about you? In a word, how would you describe magic?'

'Hope.'

Antarna leant forwards. The word sounded strange after the day they'd had. But maybe it was exactly what they needed.

'In this dark and dangerous world of ours, magic is a beacon of hope.' Passion inflected his voice. 'It protects our cities just as it keeps us safe tonight. My mum may not have survived my birth without the healing of magic. I wouldn't be a seer without it. It's a blessing for my people.' He smiled wryly. 'Even if it torments my dreams.'

'All good points.' Without magic, she couldn't have gotten to the crater or from there to the lake island. She took a drink from her cup. It was half empty, though Cal would take a different view.

Before lying down for the night, she meditated. It did little good. She couldn't shake the image of Biesan hanging in the canenisk's jaws. His wife was now a widow, and his twin girls would grow up without their father. She had some understanding of the hole that left.

Antarna turned onto her side, then tried the other. Soon, she lay on her stomach. If only she had a distraction—Cal had been on the right track earlier, but abstract discussions of magic wouldn't cut it.

It wasn't a hazzurus that attacked near the glade. She struggled to maintain her concentration but persisted.

What if the Resatrium struck?

Birdsong woke her, not long before first light.

A muted sound, part-rub and part-scrape, came from her right. Cal swept the tip of a charcoal stick back and forth across a sheet of parchment. It wasn't like him to be up so early.

She stretched. 'Morning.'

He must've been so absorbed in his work that he hadn't heard her. One of his eyelids snapped closed—a spasm; no one blinks with one eye. His weary, bloodshot eyes remained trained on the parchment. Had he even slept?

'What are you drawing?'

Cal turned the sheet around. A canenisk leapt from the parchment, its sinister jaws strained wide. Captured in terrifying detail from the bunched muscles of its shoulder to the sharp, curved claws reaching for her. She resisted the urge to pull away.

'Cal,' she said, her voice gentle, 'I'm so sorry about Biesan.'

'Me too.' He swallowed, then drew a breath.

She wasn't going to like what he was about to say.

'Given what happened, there's something I need to know.' He put down the parchment. 'The gems are anti-magic, so how can you teleport them?'

'It's recorded—'

'I don't have any faith in a dusty old scroll.'

The bitterness in his tone cut her. She tried not to take offence; he was tired, worried and understandably upset. Answers would calm him quicker than anything else.

She tried again. 'High Priest Effain—'

He snapped the charcoal, and she fell backwards.

'Sorry.' Abashed, he placed a hand atop his head. What energy he had seemed to leave him.

The group slumbered on, except for Orrsin. Just the person she needed. Antarna beckoned him over.

The armless took a seat opposite her.

She nodded her thanks. 'To confirm my understanding, the saphramurls can be teleported, right?'

'Steel is difficult to move. I can't imagine being able to teleport an anti-magic gem.'

He had to be mistaken. Surely. The trees loomed over her, their twisted branches reaching down hungrily. A root dug into her upper leg.

Why had no one raised this? Why hadn't she? Tozias would die. They all would.

'More supplies for this quest are easy to teleport,' said Orrsin. 'And we can teleport you back to the crater when you're ready, of course.'

'You can teleport people,' Cal said as if thinking out loud, his voice soft.

Even children knew the armless could do that. Cal certainly did; he'd been there when Antarna, Farikarr and Kathrina had landed at the lake island. Enthriff emerged and tried to comfort her.

Cal smiled as if the world wasn't falling apart. 'We can walk the gems back to the lake island and teleport the injured to meet us.'

She tipped her head back and closed her eyes. It was a perfect plan. When they arrived at the lake island with the gems, mages could materialise Tozias, Letti and the others to meet them—all without ever having to teleport the saphramurls. By goddess, it would all work out.

'Certainly,' said Orrsin.

Cal shuffled back, lay down and closed his eyes.

Tozias would only open his eyes if Antarna got a saphramurl to him in time. Was he doing better or worse? She recalled Orrsin's voice coming into her head when they'd encountered the pride of yalluts.

Before the armless got to his feet, she asked, 'Who can you contact using telepathy?'

'Anyone within eyesight, and those that I have an established relationship with.'

'You've never been to the mountain temples?' If he had, he should be able to provide an update on Tozias and the others.

His features softened. 'Sorry, no.' He shifted his weight. 'However, Arric may know how they are faring.'

Antarna would have gushed her thanks, but she sensed that he'd already started the spell.

Each moment dragged like it had when she'd put two fingers to Tozias's neck on the summit, afraid he may have passed on.

Maybe under Elgerin's care, the injured were on the mend. Or maybe she'd already taken too long.

Finally, Orrsin spoke. 'A child in a coma and an elderly priest passed on, but the others cling to life.'

Her chest tightened, a dozen faces flashing through her mind.

Cling to life.

She had to hurry.

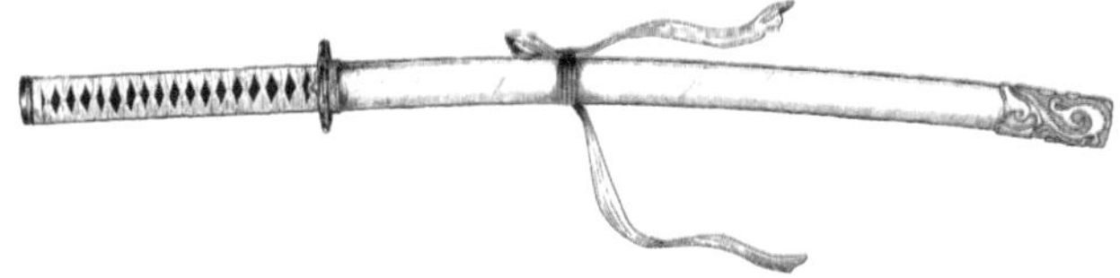

THE group broke camp. Hinn yawned beside her, closing his sunken eyes. She'd offered to help carry the stretcher, but he'd knocked her back. They continued to follow the wetway. By mid-morning, it was little more than rubble.

We getting close?

She heard Far River before she saw it, the gentle murmuring of water over rocks. Dirty brown water churned white as it hurled itself over smooth, grey boulders. Fallen leaves flowed past, tumbling and twirling.

Many were caught by a large branch that clogged the river. The edges were lined with ferns. The largest of the fronds almost stretched its width.

Exactly as I thought. There is only one reason the wetway makes sense.

'We made it,' said Cal.

Not why I was smiling. 'Let's find Biesan a resting place downriver. What are we looking for?'

'A deep pool. See that'—he pointed to a rough, choppy patch—'it's probably shallow. We're looking for swirling water. The current carves holes out of the bottom on the outside bends. Look out for a high bank. On the inside bends, the river offloads its sand and fine gravel, forming shallow bars.'

Further down, they found their swirling water around a rockime tree that'd fallen into the water. Its wood was too hard to cut—a stone axe head would shatter upon it, and you'd blunt steel before making any progress. Garlin, Hinn and Cal began the preparations. Farikarr took the three hunters in search of small game. After a not-too-subtle glare from Hinn, Antarna and Orrsin left the lake islanders to their funeral. They would wash the body twice, weigh it and drop him into the river.

She ducked under a low-hanging branch. 'Orrsin, how did the Resatrium mage learn magic?' *Zanth, not that I'm meant to know his name.*

'Probably at one of the temples. But if he did, he never became a priest.' Orrsin maintained an even tone, forcibly calm.

A poor liar. It supported Cal's theory: Zanth had trained at the temple of magic. 'How'd you pass your trial to priesthood? I've never understood how anyone survives ...' *removing their own arms.*

He stopped in a patch of filtered sunlight. 'Strategy and determination. It starts and ends at the temple. I set off through the forest to a tree scarred by lightning, the turn-around point. I knew that once I reached it, I only had until nightfall to surrender my arms. So, I made sure to arrive in the morning. This gave me time to make it to the glade. There, I severed my arms with searing hot blades of fire, both at once. The fire stopped me from bleeding out. I fainted but was safe in the glade from animal attacks. When I woke, my madriliks were replenished. This just left killing a creature no smaller than me and carrying it back to the crater, which I did.'

‘I guess you’d never know the depth of your courage or conviction until you’re tested like that.’ She caressed Enthriff.

‘Yes. I was far stronger upon my return. A year later, I was twice the mage I was before the test. I’d a different relationship with magic and understanding. It’s hard to explain. I—’

He turned. Leaves rustled.

Enthriff was unperturbed.

A spear tip extended above a bush, a ruby ribbon fluttering from it.

Farikarr.

The trio headed back together. The hunters hadn’t had any luck. By the river, the lake islanders were drying off. The stretcher was empty.

‘How was it?’ Orrsin asked.

‘He’s at peace,’ said Garlin.

The group continued, following the river. A high-pitched trill burst from a frog on a lily pad amongst a bunch of grey rocks. No sooner had it finished than a chorus of croaks sprang up around them. A frog sailed through the air, limbs extended and webbed hands and feet splayed. Like sails, its membranes caught the air, slowing its descent. The frog’s hands were as big as its head, and its feet larger still. It landed, with a splash, in the shallows. Another two frogs glided down from the treetops. One overshot a lily pad, while the other stuck the landing. It croaked loud and proud.

The female was twice their size. Behind her, a head surfaced. A tongue shot out of its beaked mouth. It struck like lightning, pushing the frog into the water. The predator erupted from the water, its long tail swishing. A grey shell encapsulated its body. She’d mistaken it to be a river rock, as the frogs must have too.

A *turtaculum.*

The predator extended its long neck and closed its beak around the frog. At the same time, two fellow turtaculums broke their cover. One caught its prey. The other just missed. The surviving male frog jumped from lily pad to lily pad, fleeing to the riverbank. It was fast, but not fast enough.

The frogs should’ve stayed up in the trees. Maybe she shouldn’t have left the mountain temple. Biesan’s death cast a heavy shadow over her, and her lies to the group deepened the darkness.

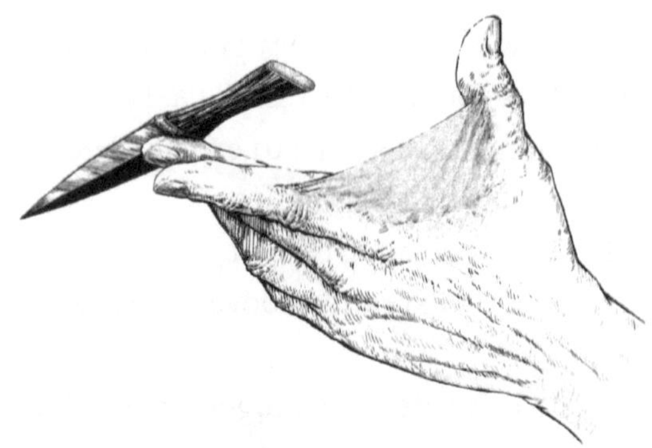

30. A Rotting Face

Cal glanced over his shoulder again. Branches swayed and creaked. Shadows moved in the trees. He couldn't shake the feeling that something or someone was following them. Although it might be the crushing weight of Antarna's fate on his shoulders.

They came around another bend. Bright blobs of pink stretched up the trunks of a clump of trees ahead. He hung at the back of the group with Hinn. Up ahead, Antarna ducked under a tree limb that Rundlud simply walked straight under. The taller women of the lake island often stooped, but not Antarna. When the forest permitted, she walked with a straight back. But today, her steps were smaller, her energy subdued.

The pink turned out to be a fungus enveloping the trunks. Glistening, blood-like drops of fluid hung in it. They pulled up beside the fungus for a quick drink from their water skins.

He approached Antarna. 'Are you level?'

'Yes.'

'I don't think you are.'

She sighed. 'I feel responsible ... for Biesan's death.'

He should've guessed. 'You couldn't have got to him any sooner. And anyway, he died when his head hit the ground, which was quick and painless.'

'But he wouldn't have even been out here if it wasn't for me.'

'You can't blame yourself. His death is not on you.' *You're not the one who foresaw it and stayed quiet.*

Fallen leaves tumbled across the ground and bumped into his boots. His shirt clung to his back. He flapped it, inviting the breeze in—yet it was neither cool nor crisp like those at the lake island. A winged bloodsucker tried to enter as well, and he swatted it away.

The group pressed on. The forest sounded different. His companions made the same noises, with their footfalls, breathing, swish of clothing and the like. Insects buzzed and chirped, birds tweeted and called, and leaves rustled overhead. The river gurgled. None of that had changed. Something had been added, and it took Cal a frustrating while to figure out what. A distant sound grew gradually louder, an incessant whisper that spoke of power.

Orrsin quickened his pace. Cal did too, and the whisper became a thrum, then a rumble. The group broke into a jog, packs jostling. They passed a pride of grazing yalluts, larger than the family they'd encountered two days ago. Two bore antlers.

The roar of water drowned out the sounds of the forest. Trees, shrubs and other pesky greenery continued to block his view. His pack bounced with each stride, pulling at his shoulders, aggravating his neck and tightening his back.

The trees parted, and Cal stopped. The river curved for a final time, ending in a heavy haze of white mist. Water plunged into a sinkhole large enough to swallow his residence, but not the chancellor's. Tumbling fearlessly over the edge, the brown water cascaded white.

Cal approached the edge, standing next to Hinn. Vivid moss lined the vertical walls. It fought for purchase and light against a selection of creeping and draping plants. The mist shrouded the bottom—if it even had one.

Antarna knelt, forefinger across her lips. He followed her line of sight. There was a black patch to the left of the waterfall. It sat above the mist, obscured by it and hanging greenery. The cave or dark rock?

Antarna stood, tapped Farikarr on the shoulder and moved back from the sinkhole. Cal followed, bringing Hinn with him. The others joined them.

'We made it, and I think I see it,' Antarna said, the corners of her mouth upturned.

Cal took half a step forwards. 'Lower me down. I'll take first look.'

'No.' Garlin pulled him back. 'We're not risking you, Seer.'

'I'll go down,' said Hinn.

'I'm not risking anyone else,' said Antarna. 'I'm pulling rank. I'm going.'

'That's—' started Garlin.

'Happening,' she said. 'This requires climbing skills. I summited a mountain every day. We're not talking about crossing a lake or a forest here. Plus, I'm the only one that's been in the cave. If there is a cave, we need to know if it is the Lost Cave.'

Cal put his hand out, palm up. 'Let's—'

'Let her go,' said Farikarr. 'It makes sense. We'll tie her off. Any issues, we'll pull her up.' He sent his hunters to find a suitable vine. Eryx led them out.

Antarna's gaze appeared to fall to Cal's neck.

He placed a hand over the two sword-shaped keys. 'How will we communicate with you down there?'

'I doubt that telepathy will work,' said Orrsin. 'If it's the Lost Cave, it'll block magic.'

Farikarr untied the ribbon from his spear. 'If you want to come up, just wave this.'

A chill scampered down Cal's spine.

The hunters returned. A thick vine was coiled from Rundlud's shoulder to his opposite hip. His steps were small and rigid. A load weighty enough for two had fallen to him, the youngest of them. Nol and Eryx lifted the vine off him and tied one end around Antarna. She'd lined up to the side of the cave, away from the torrent of water.

'You sure about this?' Cal asked her.

'Of course.' She rolled up her sleeves.

'Stay safe. Use the red ribbon if you need.'

Farikarr and his hunters gripped the vine, not trusting any outside the crater with the princess.

Antarna removed her sword and shield. 'Keep some slack on the vine, please. Trust me.' She found her first foothold. Descending, her movements were slow and considered. She relocated her arm, tested the handhold and, once satisfied, moved her leg. In this way, she kept three connections with the wall.

She edged closer to the waterfall, only to retreat away from it. Her hand slipped off a mossy rock, but she stayed on the wall. If she swore, the crashing water took her words. Finding another place for her hand, she continued. Water glistened on her face and tensed arms. She loaded her right leg as she stretched her other down. The rock under her foot came free and fell. Antarna did too, her hands sliding from their purchase. If Cal could have flown, he'd have leapt off the edge and wrapped her in his arms. It should have been him down there. The vine snapped taut, and she collided with the wall. A rock cut into her. Something small and dark slid from her torn pocket, perhaps a vial.

'Bring her up,' shouted Cal.

'Wait,' said Farikarr.

They peered over the edge. Antarna held her elbow. Her legs were perpendicular to the rockface. Farikarr waved at her. When he had her attention, he raised his hand three times. She shook her head and pointed down.

The hunters let the vine out. With feet shoulder-width apart and knees bent, she walked gingerly down the wall. Her hands gripped the vine. She leant backwards against it, allowing it to take her weight.

Soon, she was only a body length above the cave.

A thump and pained groan met his ears in quick succession. Hinn landed on his face beside Cal. An arrow shaft protruded from his back. On the opposite side of the sinkhole, an arrow sliced into Rundlud. Cal leapt to the side. An arrow flew above him and arced into the waterfall.

The earth shook, opened and swallowed Orrsin. *Magic.*

Rocks rained down upon Antarna. She covered her head with her arms.

A score of attackers broke from cover. They converged on the sinkhole from all sides. Tattoos marked them as desert folk. Cal drew his knives. Garlin caught an arrow on his shield.

Diving out of the way of a javelin, Rundlud released his grip on the vine. The other hunters took his load but not before jolting Antarna.

One attacker stood above the others. A rotting face covered in writhing maggots stretched down his neck. That ink, that man, had haunted Cal since his vision.

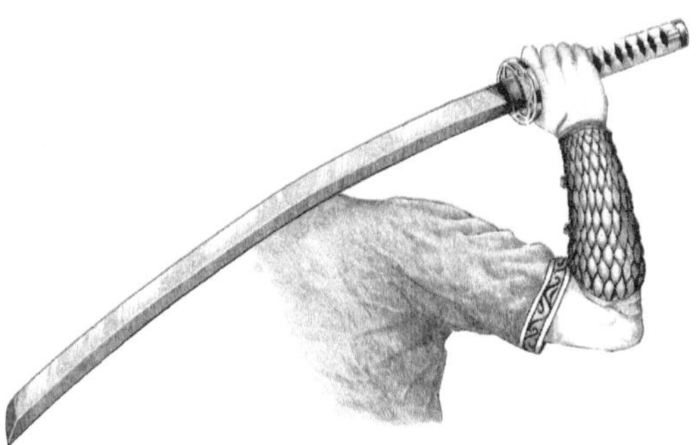

31. It Dripped Red

An unrelenting spray of water assailed Antarna. It stung the cuts on her arms and carried away the blood. Within a day or two, her battered skin would turn bluish-purple or maybe even black.

She'd managed to dodge the larger rocks. Otherwise, her arm guards had taken the bulk of the assault. What really hurt was losing her shadow vial. *Will I be able to access another soul memory without it?*

The rim of the sinkhole was vacant. Last time she'd looked up, Farikarr was above her, with Hinn, Cal and Garlin on the opposite edge.

She thought she'd heard a scream. But hearing anything above the rolling thunder of the waterfall was nigh impossible.

The cave was a mere body length below her, mockingly out of reach. Antarna hung with her feet against the wall and hands on the vine. Water ran down her legs, gathering in her boots.

Force was applied to the vine, pulling her up. No. She pushed off the mossy rock.

She would've screamed if they had a chance of hearing her. The rim was still empty. Dark clouds gathered. Antarna passed the spot where the rock had declined to take her weight. Her elbow hadn't forgiven her or the rock.

She cupped her hands to her mouth as green flashed by. 'Wait! Stop!'

Her head rose above the rock wall. There were too many figures: more than a dozen. An animal skin she didn't recognise armoured their shins, forearms and torsos. Ink covered their exposed skin. Desert warriors.

Blood marked Cal's upper lip. He knelt in a row alongside Farikarr and the hunters, each with their hands behind their back, likely bound. Men stood over them, weapons raised. Her shield and sword lay where she'd left them.

Four enemies yanked on the vine attached to Antarna.

Cutting it would get her a watery death, nothing more. She jammed her heels under a rock and drew her dagger. After resisting, Antarna released her foothold. This launched her into the air. She landed, rolled and opened the inked thigh of the closest man. He staggered back, tripping over her weapons. Antarna scooped them up, slid her shield on and drew her sword. Gripping it gave her strength.

Where are Orrsin, Garlin and Hinn?

Dead, most probably.

A thick-necked warrior with dual axes advanced. A scar ran from his forehead to his left cheek, crossing his eye. Scratches marked his well-worn armour. The other pair who'd held the vine moved to flank her. Trained killers, each of them. Not fat watchmen who bullied the malnourished and the old.

She'd still back herself against these three, but then what? There were twenty or so more, and they had Cal at knifepoint. Cornered, surrounded, and in the middle of the forest she wouldn't last a day alone in, how could she escape and save the captives?

The axe-wielder swiped at her, and she slid back and to the side. A few more steps would take her into the sinkhole. Mist from the waterfall settled on the nape of her neck. The men flanking her drew within two body lengths, a spear and a club raised. They too bore battle scars.

Behind them, an archer nocked an arrow. With the axe-wielder between them, he didn't have a clear shot. She'd have to keep him in mind, though, especially if she ran. That seemed as futile as fighting a whole kill squad.

Unless she didn't have to fight them all.

Their leader stood tall and broad, halberd in hand—a Daslercian weapon, like her sword. His spiked helmet, devoid of even a nose guard, left his face exposed. Tattoos, intricate and fierce, covered his skin. Black ink filled the whites of eyes. Matted rope-like strands of dark hair escaped from the back of his helmet.

She pointed her sword at the man. 'I, Antarna of the mountain temples, challenge you!'

'Surrender or I kill your friends.'

At that, his warriors pressed blades against the throats of Cal, Farikarr and the three hunters.

She approached the leader, brushing past the axeman without a nod or glance. With the challenge issued, she *should* be safe until it was accepted or refused. Enthriff would warn her if anyone tried anything. 'But where would be the honour in that for you?'

'You think hired blades have honour?'

Hired by whom? 'You're afraid to fight me.'

'Nice try. Drop your weapons, or I'll drop your friends.'

A scarlet bead formed below the knife and slid down Cal's neck. His breathing was short and shallow.

Antarna stepped closer. 'But where would be the fun in that for either of us?'

'Oh, we can still have plenty of fun when you're tied up.' He passed his forked tongue over his lips.

His men burst into raucous laughter.

'Why not have twice the fun? I've never known one of the desert to slink from single combat. Are you a scorpion without a sting?' She laced the accusation with equal parts venom and mockery.

'Without a sting?' He looked up to the versatile steel head of his halberd. An axe blade opposed a nasty hook, and these were topped by a sharp spike. A predatory grin spread across his face, putting red-stained teeth on display and giving her a glimpse of the darkness within him. Ruthless. Rotten to the core.

'I, Snarlark of the desert, accept your challenge.' He gestured towards a circular patch of fresh, crumbly dirt, as if someone had dug a mass grave and recently covered it.

Off to the side, a royal-purple leaf bobbed in the frothing water. That colour had dominated her early childhood. And yet the words had slid so easily off her tongue: "Antarna of the mountain temples". The leaf fell below the turbulent surface.

Focus.

With the pole of his halberd as long as she was tall, he had the reach advantage. She'd need to get close, and that'd be no easy feat. Despite his size, there was a lightness in his step, an ease to his movements. Scars didn't mark his visible skin, nor scratches his armour. He'd be confident. Overconfident. That she could use.

She followed Snarlark into the circle of dirt, and his warriors formed up around them.

His gaze bore into her. Antarna met it, staring into his silver-grey pupils, as hard as steel. The blacks of his eyes threatened to send a shiver down her spine. One of his large hands could squeeze the life out of her, and he'd probably sleep better for it. Not that she'd give him the chance. She'd been trained by the best.

She glanced away, trying her best to look intimidated.

'Your friends are watching.' He pointed to some bushes in the opposite direction to the captives.

Garlin's head was perpendicular to his body, attached by a meagre flap of neck skin. An arrow jutted out of another woodsman's back.

Anger built inside her, eclipsing the grief that wrenched her gut. Either emotion could get her killed. She tramped them down, determined to stay in control. Snarlark wanted her distracted.

The gaping mouth inked on his bicep widened as he raised his halberd.

She took an amateur stance and hefted her sword as if assessing its weight—though it was as familiar to her as Enthriff. *Underestimate me.* She only needed one opening.

Coins clinked as his men placed bets on how fast she'd lose. If she won, all captives and injured and bodies should be handed over, together with their weapons and coin. They were far from the desert, though, and honour may mean little to them.

Antarna slipped his first thrust, not trusting muscle memory with her sword to give away her training. She made a deliberately clumsy attempt to cut the pole of his weapon. Dipping it, he denied her the contact.

A spattering of chuckles followed at the obvious mismatch.

Snarlark ripped the axe head towards her shield. Instead of deflecting it, she took the full force of the powerful blow, jolting her miserable elbow.

The crowd enjoyed her pain, as did her opponent.

She dropped her shield arm, and he took the bait. Antarna launched off her back foot, flew past the steel head of his halberd and arched her sword down to his exposed lead arm. Her blade would take him above his forearm guard.

In a blur of motion, he twisted sharply. Her steel severed a strip of his sleeve. The fabric floated down and settled upon the dirt.

She couldn't believe her eyes. No one could move that fast.

Snarlark bared his teeth. A coldness emanated from him.

He came at her, ferocious. She deflected a diagonal strike and dodged a thrust that would've impaled her head, his steel whipping by her hair. Snarlark rained down lightning-quick blows. One slipped through and smashed into her amour, taking her breath. It took all she had to stay on her feet and alive. She was the desperate frog, and he the turtaculum. There was no riverbank though. No escape, only the circle.

His kill squad screamed their encouragement, anticipating the axe blade severing a limb, the hook tearing out her calf or the spike taking her eye. Any moment now could be her last.

On the back foot, sliding away from another flowing strike, she neared the edge of the circle. A warrior kicked at her. Enthriff warned her, and she sprang forwards. Snarlark thrust the halberd past her guard and cut her leg.

A blinding pain overwhelmed her as if a canenisk had sunk a full mouth of teeth into her thigh. Looking down, she expected a deep gash. Inexplicably, only a shallow wound traversed her skin. She dropped to one knee, gritting her teeth.

'Poison?' she whispered.

Enthriff gave two quick pulses: yes.

Her past burst from its locked box. For the seventh time, she begged her brother to join her at dinner. Someone carried her from the dining hall. Father kissed her forehead before she was teleported to the mountain temples. The memories hit her, one after the other, even with her eyes open. Snarlark hadn't moved a muscle since she'd taken a knee.

A blink brought the next memory. The infirmary ceiling was no more interesting than it had been two months earlier.

'Get up, Antarna!' said Cal.

The poison hadn't needed time to spread through her system. It was like salt in a wound, only far worse. Perhaps pain was its purpose.

Enthriff glided over her skin. She focused on him, exhaled and stood. 'Only a coward brings a poisoned blade to a duel.'

The corners of his mouth fell, and half of his top lip tugged upwards, revealing a couple of stained teeth. 'Says the coward afraid of a little poison.'

She ducked a thrust, but not fast enough, and his steel sliced her ear. An intense heat spread down her ear canal and neck. It seized her scalp too. Antarna rammed her tongue into the roof of her mouth. The next blow burst through her defences and slammed into her armoured chest. She flew backwards, shoulders slamming into the ground a fraction before her head. Dirt spattered her. When she opened her eyes, the halberd spike hovered above her nose.

His warriors disarmed her, taking her sword, dagger and shield. One even removed her boots. At least she kept her armour.

'Turn over,' another said.

She lay on her stomach. The pain receded, but reality hit, hard and brutal. Losing the fight doomed not only her but also Cal, the hunters, Tozias, Letti and all the injured depending on her. Unless ... unless she escaped.

A knife came out of its sheath. Cool bronze crept down her forearm and under Enthriff.

Good luck with that. 'It's just my wristband.'

The man sawed back and forth, nicking Antarna.

'Balls.' Giving up, the warrior wiped his knife on her and put it away. He bound her wrists with vine, tighter than needed. Then, he set to work on her legs, tying them with a vine long enough to allow her to walk but not kick.

After hauling her up, he marched her next to Cal. On the way, she caught the piece of Snarlark's fabric between her toes and gripped tight.

She took to her knees beside Cal. His cheek was red. Like her, his feet were bare.

'Are you level?' Cal whispered.

She inclined her chin.

'No need to act so stoic.'

Yet, with the fear in his eyes, that's exactly what he needed from her. And what she needed in herself.

Two warriors carried a rope ladder to a thick tree. They tied one end to the trunk and then unrolled it towards the sinkhole.

Snarlark rested his halberd on Cal's shoulder, axe blade next to his neck. He leant close, ripped Cal's necklace off and threw it to a man with a field of skulls tattooed on his arms. 'You know what to do, Ragud.'

The man left for the cave with five others.

Antarna leant back and transferred the fabric from her foot to her hands.

Snarlark hefted his halberd. 'I don't want the scent of blood too close to the falls. Take them upriver then kill them, all bar the seer and Farikarr. The seer can watch. Farikarr stays here.' He turned to follow Ragud.

Rough hands pulled Antarna to her feet. Cal stumbled. Rundlud's legs shook, the arrow still embedded in his back. Eryx and Nol, the two older hunters, were in more control.

The butt of a spear jabbed into her side. A dozen from the desert marched them along the river. Her fingers tingled. She couldn't break the vine binding her wrists or reach it with her fingernails. Enthriff brushed against her skin. With his smooth body, he wouldn't be able to cut through the vines. Maybe he could weaken them though.

Soft grass cushioned her steps.

Unshod. Unarmed. Outnumbered. Bound.

She stepped over a log. 'Since I'm going to die, who hired you? The Resatrium?'

'No talking.' His voice was gruff.

'My uncle is the king. He'll double whatever you're being paid.'

Something hard smashed against the back of her head. Antarna fell, twisting to land on the shoulder of her uninjured arm instead of her face. For a moment, her ears rang. A rock sat beside her, half the size of her palm. She rolled onto her back and clasped it. The edges were regrettably smooth.

A man stood over her. Half of his face—split vertically down the length of his nose—was tattooed with desert symbols of power, courage and strength. 'Speak again and I'll cut your tongue out before killing you.'

She pressed her lips together.

He pointed his club at her. 'Get up, and there had better not be anything in your hands.'

Antarna released the rock, letting it clatter against another so he knew she'd complied. She crossed her legs and stood, ready to hide the strip of fabric if the man checked her hands. But he didn't.

The family of yalluts that they'd passed on the way to the cave looked up, then retreated to the trees, spike-adorned tails swaying behind them.

Rundlud turned to face the closest captor, whose skin was covered in tattoo scales. 'You've got the cave; just let us go.'

'We're not worth the effort,' said Nol.

'There is no need to get blood on your hands,' added Eryx.

The scaled man swung his axe. With a nauseating crack, the weapon collided with Rundlud's head. Birds rose into the air. Life faded from Rundlud's umber eyes, slowly at first, then all at once. Blood gushed from the wound. It soaked his hair and covered the axe head. This couldn't be happening. Not to someone so young. Antarna's throat constricted.

Nol turned and ran, and Eryx launched himself at the killer.

Antarna fought against her wrist bonds with all her strength, every muscle tensed. Her arms shook. *Break.* The vines refused. Three warriors formed a triangle around her. They held their weapons at the ready: a spear, club and short sword.

Eryx drove his shoulder into the scaled man, and they fell. An arrow tore into the back of Nol's neck, to the side of his spinal column. Her eyes stung. *Greet him well, Zentrina.*

A warrior with a forehead scar that divided an eyebrow drew a knife against Cal's throat. 'Freeze or I'll kill him.'

Whether from this threat or the spear tip in his face, Eryx paused halfway to his feet. Cal got down on his knees.

Antarna did too. 'We're complying.'

The scaled man approached Eryx from behind. He put his left hand on the hunter's shoulder. With his other, he plunged his dagger into the side of Eryx's throat and tore it sideways. This severed the vocal cords and opened a ragged hole. Crimson liquid spurted from the puncture and fell like a curtain from the slice. Bound, he could not stem the torrential flow. Eryx sought to take a breath. He gargled and choked, then began to cough.

The sound cut Antarna to her core. It was more chilling than any scream. Her hands could not cover her ears, nor wrap around her body. Cal gagged.

Eryx tried for another breath. And another. And another. Then, mercifully, he lost consciousness.

Snarlark approached. His men would already be in the cave.

The scaled man put his boot on Rundlud's head and ripped his axe free. It dripped red. He met Antarna's glare with cold eyes. 'Kill her.'

'Do it yourself,' she replied.

The spearman thrust at her. She launched off her toes towards him, under the strike. After a roll, she swept his legs. Out of the triangle, Antarna ran with short steps toward Cal and the warrior with the forehead scar. His knife at Cal's throat was an empty threat. It was twelve to one, she was still bound and Snarlark was watching.

Scar-face pushed Cal to the side and lunged at her. At the same time, bending her elbows, Antarna brought her hands up her back, then shot them down. She wrenched her hands apart, and the vines snapped.

Thanks, Enthriff. He must have been squeezing the vines tighter and tighter, crushing them.

She stepped to the outside of the blade and, pivoting on her lead leg, swung a clenched fist at scar-face's jaw. The left hook connected, bone colliding with bone. She grabbed his knife hand with her right. Opening her left, she clawed at his eyes and dragged him to the ground. Her shin found his face. She sank her nails into his wrist and face. Screaming, he dropped the knife, and she pounced on it.

Snarlark jogged towards them, his stride easy and relaxed. His men had her encircled and were quickly closing in. The family of yalluts had disappeared into the trees, apart from a curious youngster who watched from their edge.

Jumping up, Antarna cut the vine connecting her ankles, then the one binding Cal. She grabbed out the piece of Snarlark's fabric, tied it to the knife hilt and handed it to him. 'Throw it!' Antarna pointed at the young yallut.

Cal stepped forwards and released the knife. It cut between two desert warriors. The yallut turned away. The knife buried into its behind. The creature released a high-pitched yelp.

First, the trees shook. Then, the ground. A pride of yalluts burst from the edge of the forest. Two males led the charge, antlers undulating with their furious gallop. One took a sniff of the knife as he passed his offspring. Behind them stretched a wedge of much larger females. They kicked grass and dirt into the air.

The warriors scattered.

The lead yallut caught up to a warrior and threw him into the air. He spun before landing in a heap.

The next closest faced the yalluts, club swinging. In recompense, an antler pierced his chest and burst out of his back with a splatter of blood. The yallut shook him free, stomped the ground, snorted and stampeded for Snarlark. Antarna, Cal and the remaining desert warriors were caught in the middle. Snarlark dropped his halberd and sprinted for the river. The warriors followed his lead.

Not so brave now.

The yalluts turned towards the river. Antarna took off the other way, racing for the edge of the forest with Cal. The scaled man gave chase.

The pride bore down on them. They trampled three warriors—crumpling armour, crushing chests, mashing flesh.

The forest was too far, the yalluts too fast, their line too long.

The scaled man gained on her. Against every instinct to keep running, she pulled up and faced him.

'What are you doing?' asked Cal, breathless. He too slowed to a stop. 'What are we going to do?'

'Stay behind me and be ready.'

She raised her hands and slid a leg back. The warrior's knuckles were white. He advanced with a slice of his axe, well out of range.

No helpful terrain. No weapon.

She circled, and he did likewise, as if they were in a sparring match instead of moments away from being flattened. When his back was to the pride, she rushed in. He was all too happy to join her. Antarna started a jab but looped it back. Her feint drew a strike. She leant away. The axe blade swept by, and she jumped towards him, knee up. Mid-air, she extended her leg into a kick. The ball of her foot struck him in the chest. He flew backwards, his beige hair flapping over his ears. He blinked, closing his wide grey eyes that were flecked with green.

No. What have I done?

Her goddess valued every life.

A yallut swerved to head butt the warrior. This created a gap in the wedge.

'Now!' Antarna dived for it, praying Cal was on her tail.

Hooves tore the earth. The sound was deafening.

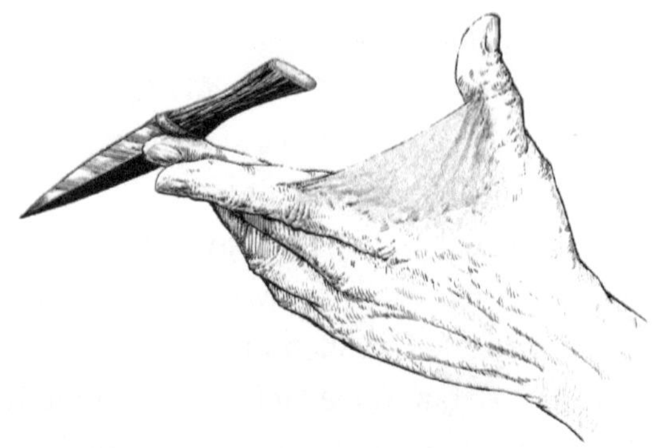

32. The Last Breath

DIRT splattered Cal. Thick dust suffocated him. A hoof landed beside his head, then another. In the thunderous chaos, he made himself small. Raw primal terror gripped him.

The stampede surged past. Cal lifted his chin and pulled his hands out of his hair. He coughed, the dust still thick in the air. *I'm alive*. It didn't seem real. Cal allowed himself a relieved grin.

Antarna lay on her side, curled into a ball. Thankfully, his saviour didn't appear injured.

'You level?' Cal's voice shook. He rose and brushed away the dirt.

With biceps flexed, Antarna's arms were clasped over her head. Her elbows touched her tucked knees.

'Antarna, what's wrong?'

Creases gathered around the corner of her eye, her face scrunched tight.

'Antarna, talk to me.'

Cal turned around.

The man covered in scale tattoos was prostrate upon the ground. Half his chest had been crushed. The back of his head lay open, ragged flaps of skin hanging loosely.

Cal brought his hand up to shield his vision.

I get it. You wouldn't even kill that anchor leech.

Cal came around and knelt beside her. 'He killed Rundlud and Eryx. We were next. You saved us. You didn't do anything wrong.'

Her biceps relaxed as her hands fell to cover her face.

Snarlark waded through the river. It reached to his armpits. Four of his men had already joined him in the water. The rest ran to it or lay dead.

We need to move. He couldn't rush her though.

She spoke, but her words didn't rise above the pounding hooves. He leant in.

'I killed ...'

Cal took her in his arms, careful to avoid touching her skin. 'No, you didn't. The yallut did. And that man would've died anyway. We all would've. You saved us.'

She was limp.

He turned his head. A yallut knocked a warrior down with its lead hoof and flattened him with its next.

'Antarna, we're alive because of you. He's with Zentrina now.'

She stirred.

That's a start. 'We need to finish what we started. For your friend ... Tozias.'

Her hands left her face, and she looked at him with glistening eyes.

Cal squeezed her shoulder. 'Yes, let's get the gems. Now is our chance.'

She swallowed and nodded.

He rose and helped her up.

She followed him downriver. The sounds of men and beast slowly faded. They crossed the circle of fresh dirt. Cal shuddered. Orrsin had been buried alive. The ground had opened, he'd fallen in and it'd covered him.

Where's your mage? He'd seen a cloaked figure in the tree line. But they hadn't entered the cave or travelled upriver.

Cal stopped short of the lip of the sinkhole. 'Farikarr isn't here. Neither are our weapons.' Or boots. 'What's our plan?'

'We do what we came here for: we enter the cave.' The colour had returned to her cheeks.

'Wait.' He held up his hands. 'There are, what, six of them down there?'

'Yes, but we have the element of surprise. They think we're dead.' She took the rope ladder down.

Oh, had we finished talking? He stood on the rim for a moment, then followed her into danger. The rope was wet and slippery.

Antarna handled it one step at a time until she stretched her long legs and skipped a rung. A horde of water droplets battered him. Soon, he was soaked from head to toe.

Antarna disregarded another rung. Cal paused, counting them from the top. *Fourteenth. Was it the seventh that she also skipped?*

As he descended, it grew darker and colder. A faint light flickered within the cave. Antarna paused beside the entrance to the cave, peeking in. She turned to him and held up a lone finger.

One person in there? Where are the rest?

She stepped into the mouth of the cave, and he followed her inside. A man stood at the far end before a door. A body lay beside him. Light flashed off the steel key in his hand.

That's mine.

The light dimmed, wavered then brightened. A large cancryst sat on the cave floor. Five bodies sprawled around it, desert folk. There was no smell of death. Skin still held colour. They had died recently.

A skeleton's arm poked out from a pile of rubble off to the side.

The man with his key turned and bowed. Cal didn't return the bow. Neither did Antarna. She picked an axe up and Cal grabbed a spear.

The man advanced, hands up. He was a few years older than Cal. His dark skin and hair marked him as one born in the crater. Lengthening stubble covered his cheeks and jawline, and the skin above and below his lips, although he'd missed a couple of hairs below his lower lip during his last shave. He appeared unarmed and devoid of madriliks, but there was something unmistakably dangerous about him. Maybe it was his eyes, dark and troubled. Cal and Antarna met him in the centre of the room.

He lowered his hands. 'Welcome to the Lost Cave. My name is Danix. Seer, you may remember me from the lake island?'

'No.' Several from the crater lived at the lake island. They were afforded fewer opportunities and rights, including that they had no right to vote or seek Cal's counsel.

'That's disappointing. I lived there for many years. Our chancellor sent me. I'm a tracker, which is how I found you.'

'He wouldn't have sent you alone.'

'No. There were eight of us until we encountered a velengoric.' His head dropped.

'Sorry to hear that.' Antarna pointed to the bodies. 'And what happened here?'

Danix shrugged. 'They were like that when I arrived. I found this in the door.' He lifted Cal's key. 'They set off a trap.'

Antarna knelt and plucked a small, thin object from one of the dead. It was made of wood, with a sharp point at one end and fletching at the other, perhaps a thistle or animal fur.

The bodies were covered in blow darts.

'That wall is man-made,' said Danix. 'It's got tiny holes in it. There must be a secret to opening the door. I can't seem to figure it out.'

'Antarna, you'll be able to, right?' Cal asked. 'Did you see anything useful last time?'

She shot him a warning glance and stepped back towards the waterfall. He followed her.

Antarna leant in. 'What if he's working with the desert folk? Or hired them?'

'Really?'

'You don't find his timing suspicious? He supposedly took off from the lake island and arrived right after the keys were stolen from you and they died trying to use them?'

Cal found his finger on his lips. 'Good point. Let's test him.'

He approached Danix. 'How do we know you're telling the truth?'

'Ask me anything.'

'Instead, show me.' *Will a vision work with the saphramurls so close?* Cal laid down to avoid collapsing, then stretched up his hand.

The purported tracker took it.

His goddess, Thelia, granted Cal's request, which started with pinpricks of light in the darkness.

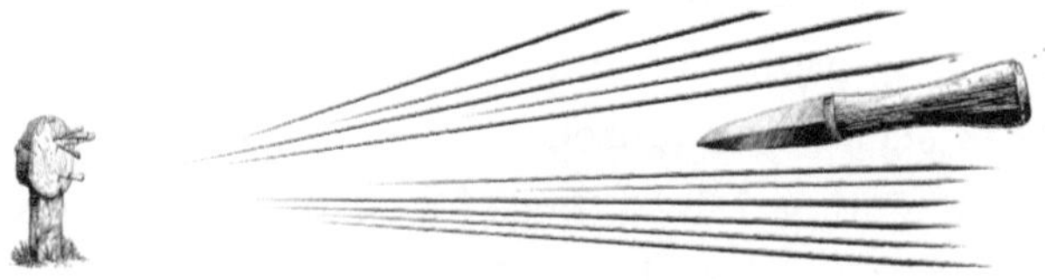

Danix balanced on one leg. His raised ankle was turned outward at a sickening angle. Sweat gathered in his unruly eyebrows and fell down his cheeks.

A dirt ramp fell away behind him, leading to a below-ground pit with steel bars. He stood at the edge.

Why am I here, where Antarna died? Cal couldn't make sense of it.

A spell shot for Danix.

But his chest cavity was dark. *Defenceless.*

Danix hopped back, circling his arms over his head. He landed in the dirt and slid down the slope. The bars caught him. Using them, he hauled himself up.

A man with a dagger appeared at the top of the stone retaining wall. Stitches were tattooed along his bicep, an ink tail disappearing into a gap between them. It was a simple work of black and grey. With only a dull in his reservoir, he was either a warrior or a spent mage. He took a javelin from his back and launched it.

Danix squeezed his eyes shut.

The javelin pierced Danix's chest, driving the last breath from his lungs and propelling him backwards through the bars.

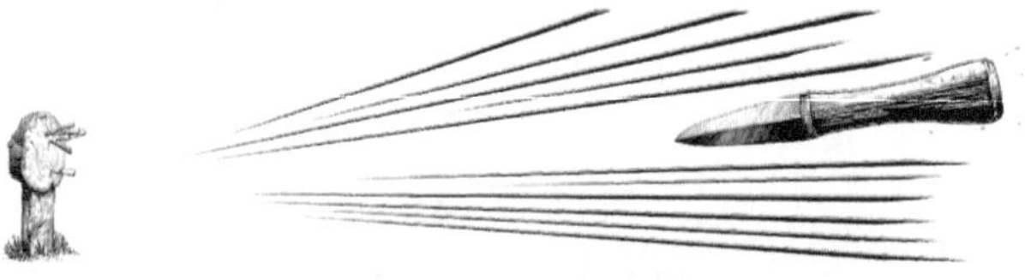

Another *death I can do nothing about.*

Cal released Danix's hand. 'He's not with them.'

'Then who are they with?' Antarna indicated to the corpses. 'Who hired them?'

'Best bet, the Resatrium,' said Danix.

She tilted her head. 'Could they afford it?'

'Apparently.'

'I'm not so sure.'

'What I'm sure of,' said Cal, 'is that the rest of their friends will be back soon. We need to get in and out. Starting with *that* door.'

The wood had an unusual grain, like swirling whirlpools fighting for domination.

Antarna crossed her arms.

'Danix, can you please give us a moment?' asked Cal.

He acquiesced, retreating to the entrance of the cave.

'Any ideas, Antarna?'

She ran a hand over the door. It was studded with small saphramurls, a reminder of what lay behind.

'You're not planning on chopping through it with that?' he asked. Her axe was more of a hatchet.

'I was tempted until I realised it's rockime.'

There was no cutting through wood as tough as rock. 'So, we need to find out how to open it. Can you try a vision?'

She fingered her torn pocket and shuffled back, dragging her feet. 'No, I lost my shadow vial.'

There had to be another way. 'How did your mentor access his soul?'

'He had such mastery that he could do so with just a meditative mindset.'

'Is it worth attempting meditation?'

She turned over a stray rock with her toes. 'I can try.'

Antarna crossed her legs and lowered herself to the cave floor. Once seated, she picked up one foot and moved it to the opposite thigh, near her hip crease. The sole of her foot faced up. She repeated the process with her other leg. On a deep exhale, she closed her eyes.

A shallow recess had been carved at shoulder height along the closest wall. It featured a series of white pearls and night-black pyramids no taller than the length of his hand. On the set closest to the waterfall, the pearl lay near the pyramid. The next one along had the pearl touching the foot of the pyramid. Progressively, the pearl was shown to climb the pyramid until, close by the locked door, the pearl balanced upon the pointed top.

Climbing to the summit.

Like a river climbing a mountain? Probably not.

Antarna's face was relaxed but robbed of tranquillity. By the entrance, Danix paced. They were short on time. Snarlark would be out of the river and coming for them. The cancryst went out, then came back.

Antarna opened her eyes and shook her head. 'I can't do it.'

'You've done it twice before. Your first vision got us to the ruins. There, your vision got us to this cave. Just take a few breaths and try again. I believe in you.'

Antarna glanced at Danix.

'He can't hear us by the waterfall. It's too loud. What's wrong?'

She blinked. 'There's something I must confess. Perhaps best if you sit.' She waited for him to do so. 'At the ruins, I never had a vision.'

'W-what?'

'Answer me this: why build a wetway to the Far River, instead of the much larger and cleaner Blue River? Daslercia is right in the middle of them.'

'Don't know. Lay of the land? Superstition?'

'No: to syphon water away from the sinkhole, so you can mine the gems easily.'

The cave was just to the side of the waterfall. And it hadn't rained in days, which was unusual. After a good downpour, the cave would be inaccessible.

Cal dragged his fingers through his hair and rested his hands on the back of his neck. 'You figured this out at the armoury, then lied to us about having a vision?'

'Yes. I'm awfully sorry.'

'What if you'd been wrong?'

'I couldn't let Biesan's death be in vain.'

He stood and turned his back on her.

'Cal ...'

The image of Biesan waving to his wife and twin girls came without warning.

'I know what you must be thinking,' she said.

He faced her. 'I, too, have something to confess. I saw Biesan die in a vision. So, stop blaming yourself.'

Antarna opened her mouth and then closed it.

Wondering if I knew about Garlin, Hinn or Orrsin? No.

She stepped towards him. 'But you couldn't say or do anything?'

'No. The primary commandment of my goddess, that lies at the core of my oath as a seer, is that I can't change the moment of one's death.'

'Why see a death you can't change?'

He shrugged. 'Thelia has her reasons.'

'Is it hard to follow a rule without understanding the reason for it?'

'Maybe, at times.' *You die. He does too. At the same place.* 'We're getting off track. We need to focus on getting through that door.'

Danix approached. He stopped when Cal held up his hand. The light flickered. Antarna looked blankly at a point between the door and the side wall. Enthriff wound around and around her still wrist.

Antarna, repeat after me: we're not dying here. Oh, real positive, Cal. He laid a hand upon her shoulder. 'What is it about the shadow from the vial that meditation doesn't provide?'

'My grandfather duelled against the shadow as a child, as did my father, then my brother. I used to love watching him.' Her arms softened and voice warmed. 'After his training session, father would retire, and I'd beg my brother to teach me a new move. No matter how tired he was, he always did.'

There was a quiet beauty in her openness and in the strength of her bond to her family—not to mention the way her dark hair framed her face. 'And you harness those fond memories to bring you into the right frame of mind?'

'Yes, I duel the shadow like he did, and instead of following the memory of that to my brain, I pursue it into my soul.'

Cal scratched the back of his neck. 'You've lost me.'

'Sure.' The edges of her lips upturned as she finished the word. 'Our experiences are not just recorded in our heads, but also in our souls. When we die, it's our soul that Zentrina reads. It contains our life story and that of our past lives. It's there I must go.'

The rockime door was smooth to Cal's touch. 'While you can't duel a shadow, you can still replicate a fight. That may be enough.'

'Perhaps.' She inserted a finger into a circular hole in the rock. 'And inserting a key may help provoke the memory.'

'Great.' Cal turned to Danix, who stood with one foot on a rock and hands on his raised knee. 'I need my keys.'

Danix threw them to him.

Cal handed the keys to Antarna. 'You can do this.'

Her mouth twitched. She looked like she was about to toss the small axe aside but instead threw it at the door. The stone axe head shattered against the rockime. Fragments battered Antarna and Cal. He covered his face. The harsh sound of breaking rock echoed around the cave. In a cloud of dust, Antarna coughed, then laughed. She reached down to the body by her feet. Fastened on the man's belt was a sheathed dagger. She drew the weapon and held the steel up to the light.

Ready now? Cal retreated to the cave's entrance. The rope ladder was empty, but it wouldn't stay that way.

Enthriff entwined himself around the smaller key and then stretched out along it, mirroring its shape. Something that looked like a snake could never be cute, but the creature was growing on him.

Antarna slid her right foot back and raised her hands. One moment, she was still; the next, she launched forwards. She feinted a low stab, then whipped the blade up. Cal raised a hand to his throat, picturing it sinking in. Antarna swirled to face another imaginary opponent. Dodging and slashing, she circled one way, then the other. She mixed up her angles of attack. Amongst the brutality, there was a beautiful elegance.

She was in constant motion from her feet to her head. Unlike a bird taking flight, she wasn't gathering speed. Rather, it came in frightful bursts. It was the same speed that had kept her alive against Snarlark.

A final stab ended the sequence. She inserted the key into the door, sat and slammed a hand over her heart space.

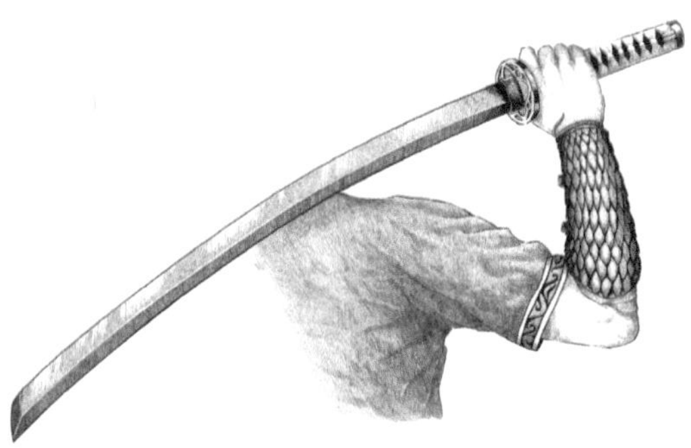

33. We're Going to Die

Horcil knelt beside Waslok, extending two fingers to his neck. There were no signs of life.

Redgwid stirred, then spat his necklace out of his mouth. Bite marks indented the leather. 'What was that?'

'No idea.' Horcil closed a hand around his saphramurl pendant. He moved to Abulap and shut the man's milky-blue eyes. There was nothing to be done about the body or the blood that pooled around it. Only a sliver of his neck remained; the stalactite had taken the rest. He collected the keys from Abulap's pocket.

Rocks lay scattered over the floor. The sack of saphramurls was buried beneath them, somewhere. Horcil stepped over a pyramid of pebbles, picking his way to the cave's entrance. The vine ladder was gone.

He dragged himself back to Redgwid and offered his hand. 'We can't stay here. We have to move.'

Redgwid rose and hobbled to the shelf.

Horcil inserted the smaller key into the door. He turned and Redgwid leant casually on the first pearl in the sequence. With a twist of his wrist and a clink, Horcil unlocked the door.

Antarna sprang up and bounded towards the shelf.

Cal followed, a lightness in his step. 'It worked?'

'Yes.' When she'd first connected with Horcil in Zentrina's temple in the crater, the sound of the waterfall had calmed her, and she'd been curious about a past life beyond Salorann. It was that type of mindset she needed for her visions, free of her fear of the Resatrium and the pressure to save Tozias.

The shelf stretched before her. She took a deep breath then forced it out through a narrow opening between her lips. Dust thickened the air, and she waved it away. A thin line encircled the base of the pearl.

'Press the pearl when I insert the key into the door,' she said.

'Will do.'

Antarna slid a large shield off the arm of a fallen desert folk. She threw it to Danix. 'Put it on and stand in front of Cal.'

Cal gulped. His gaze fell on the bodies covered in darts. The cancryst flickered as if it shared his nerves.

'Just a precaution.' Antarna slid the smaller key into the lock. *Please, Zentrina.*

Cal pushed down on the pearl. It depressed into the shelf.

Wincing, she turned the key. The click was more of a clunk. She pulled the door open to an ink-black space. Cool, damp air swirled around her. Anticipation rose within. She walked back, avoiding the sharp rocks, and collected the cancryst.

'Cal, we're going to need boots.' After selecting the tallest of the bodies, she removed his shoes and fought her feet into them. Her toes scrunched against the front.

Returning to the open doorway, she held up the cancryst. Wet, glistening walls narrowed. Iridescent green and blue veins criss-crossed the dark stone. Halfway down the passageway, she hunched her back and lowered her head. Antarna weaved between stalactites and stalagmites, keeping her steps short on the slippery rock.

Dripping water resounded through the cave. The three of them added to the tune. With each rise of their feet, droplets fell from their boots. Each step ended with a splash. They turned the corner, and the floor disappeared underwater. It rose to her mid-calf, then to her knee. Before long, she was waist deep. Something brushed her leg, and she froze, ready to bring her dagger down, but Enthriff didn't stir. The water was dark, the light of the cancryst reflecting off the surface instead of penetrating it.

'You level?' Cal whispered.

She slid her leg slowly forwards, finding nothing. 'Yes.'

The path descended. Ahead, the cave roof met the water.

'Allow me.' Cal held up his webbed hands. 'Who wouldn't want to go for a swim in a nice, dark cave filled with who knows what?'

She handed him the cancryst. 'Thanks. Be careful.'

He slid gracefully under the water. The ball of light grew faint then disappeared. She put two fingers to her neck.

One.

Danix's breath was short and shallow. The rhythmic throb of her blood continued against her fingertips. From her ribs down, the water sapped her heat.

Where are you? Her pulse quickened, her count at forty-two.

Part of her called to get out. A larger part wanted nothing more than to dive in after Cal.

The darkness was absolute. She rearranged her grip on the dagger, missing the comfort her weapons provided.

A light appeared in the water, so faint that she doubted herself. But it grew stronger. There was an arm. Like a banner in a gentle breeze, blond hair streamed out behind Cal.

He broke the water and pushed the hair from his face. 'Come on, you have to see this. Take a big breath.' Cal dived back under.

Antarna patted Enthriff, wishing she had something to wrap him with to protect him from the cold, and followed. Light waxed and waned—but even at its strongest, it did little to illuminate the passageway. The sounds of her hammering heart and the bubbles she blew accompanied her.

The cancryst was stationary. Cal held it next to his hip, near the surface of the water. The top half of his body was distorted.

She planted a boot on the stone floor and resisted the urge to use it to explode out of the water. Instead, she rose as silently as possible. Antarna wiped the water from her eyes and took a deep breath. The chamber was too vast for the meagre light source.

When Danix surfaced, Cal lifted the crystal high. This pulled the veil of darkness back from the closest two walls. In every cleft, crevasse and hollow, there was something ovate, thin and spiked. Most were about the size of her hand. Some were lucky to be half that. They were reddish-brown.

Cal stepped out of the water with a crunch that echoed through the chamber. He gingerly lifted his foot. Bending down, he picked up the victim of his boot. Nine limbs extended from an oval-shaped shell. There were four on each side and one tail. The front two limbs narrowed into sharp points. The tail ended in a pincer, like a crab. The shell was covered in spikes. Luckily, the sole of the boot had outmatched them.

Cal rotated the shell. It was empty, translucent. An outgrown shell.

Danix went over to the wall. 'They're crustrearons.'

'Asleep or dead?' Cal tiptoed towards the walls they couldn't yet see.

'Not dead.'

Given the dust on them, they'd been asleep for weeks, if not months or years.

As Cal moved towards the centre of the chamber, with Antarna right behind him, the black veil fell once more over the two walls. The floor was littered with abandoned shells and small bones. The chamber could have been barely larger than their hemisphere of light or as big as the crater. Antarna rested her hand on Enthriff, waiting for him to react to a threat.

The rock rose in front of them, then flattened. Crustrearons covered the surface. These averaged the size of a feasting plate, and their shells shimmered with gold flecks. *Larger, like the warrior ants of a colony?*

Above this was another shelf. Similar crustrearons blanketed the surface. A *tiered structure? What's at the top?*

Cal paused ahead of her, struggling to find somewhere safe to land his next step. The discarded shells and stray bones were more sizeable here. He jumped to a free space, then leapt to one that could accommodate both his feet.

The light revealed two more tiers. Resting at the top was an immense crustrearon. It would've made a crested littridon look like a lap pet. *Your queen.* The gold flecks were arranged in swirling constellations.

Part of her wanted to move closer, but the rest was ready to bolt. She'd trained to breathe through fear and harness it. Cal had had no such training she was aware of. Small bumps dotted the skin on his arm. A tremor overtook his hand. He steadied it with his other.

The spikes on the queen were as long as a sword. A segmented tail wrapped around the queen's shell. The tail constricted. *Lower the light.* Cal stumbled back, trampling molted shells and cracking old bones. His feet seemed incapable of finding the gaps. Every noise panicked him further.

'Stop.' She held out a hand.

Cal froze. The sounds lingered, then faded. 'Sorry,' he mouthed.

A short, high-pitched cry broke above them. Wings took to the air. Cal lifted his chin and turned his neck and torso towards the sound.

Enthriff was silent. *Great, thanks, bud.*

To the right of the tiered rock, there was an opening likely large enough for the queen. Antarna pointed to it and then led the way. Against the wall sat a human skeleton. Scraps of clothing draped the bones. Armour covered the chest and clung to one forearm. A braided string hung from the collarbone, a necklace without a neck. Its pendant was cracked and chipped. A lonely, pale orange light fluttered within.

She stepped back. *Horcil. You didn't make it out. I'm sorry.* Time had taken any clues as to what had happened to him.

Thick timber buttressed the passageway. Black painted planks ran along the roof. Each were longer than she was tall.

Danix took a sharp, short breath. He stood at the end of the passageway, parting a curtain of long, ribbon-like leaves that fell from the ceiling.

A sunset-orange glow emanated from a pile of rocks in the centre of the next chamber. The rocks ranged from the size of a human head to that of a torso. Each bore one or more glowing saphramurls. Inside these, plentiful lights danced and played, having their own party.

We made it. She twirled on the spot and pictured handing a bag of gems to Elgerin for those under his care. She had so much to tell Tozias.

Enthriff pinched her.

Antarna froze. 'Careful. Hold up.'

Danix's walk became a scurry. Cal slowed but continued to follow.

Take your eyes off the prize and open them. She chased after them.

The centre pile reminded her of the carnivorous pirrocical plant, with its orange, pitcher-shaped traps. Enthriff crushed her wrist.

'Stop.' She squeezed the word out between tight lips.

This time, they obeyed.

Cal turned. 'What's wrong?'

'We're not alone.'

Holes covered the walls, floor to ceiling, like honeycomb but with no discernible pattern. They could be shallow resting places for dust or the entry to a hidden world of interconnected tunnels or burrows. Most could swallow a fist. Only one was sizable enough to accommodate a person. Carved into the wall opposite, it started above head height.

In this hole, eight orbs burst to life, the same orange as the saphramurls. Arranged two wide and four high. More a pyramid than a tower: each pair below the top were a little larger, growing from the size of an iris to that of a pupil. Their light only showed a dozen rows of scales on a slender limb or tail.

The orbs blurred, shaken from side-to-side. Colliding, they emitted a harsh rattle. Yellow, slit-like eyes emerged from the hole. Four of them. A two-headed ciltrilian serpent slithered forth. Each head was wide and triangular. Its forked tongues flicked in and out. Rough, raised scales covered its body.

Antarna knew better than to move or speak, wary of provoking the creature. Was there any way to escape with their lives and some gems?

She spared a thought for Cal, whose greatest fear had just come to life. He was deadly still.

'Flay me,' Danix whispered. He took a step towards the bristly creature, raising his arms, making himself big.

No, *no. What are you doing?*

The serpent hissed. All around them, rattles flared then shook—thousands of them. The sound would've intimidated a thunderstorm.

Cal stooped. He raised and crossed his arms—forming a barrier to protect him from, and reject, the outside world. The rattling subsided. Cal spun and sprinted for the opening that they'd come through earlier.

Antarna took off after him. She caught him after only a few steps, grabbing his arm. 'Look.'

Above the opening stretched a line of coiled serpents, jaws agape. These were the only serpents not streaming from the rock. The rest converged on them from all sides. A couple of short breaths later, they'd blocked off the opening.

'We're going to die,' said Cal. 'Oh, did I say that out loud?'

They were surrounded. Nowhere to go. She had but a dagger. Next to her, Cal trembled. Behind them, the tracker climbed the mound of rock. With a gradual slope that peaked at shoulder height, the mound would be lucky to keep him out of the path of a toddler.

She backed Cal up to it, keeping herself between him and the serpents. Cal lost his balance, sending a loose rock tumbling. He caught himself on her outstretched arm.

'I need your dagger,' said Danix.

She leapt up the pile and handed it to him, hilt first. It wasn't much of a weapon against the threat, but it was all she had.

A thick ring of serpents closed in, over halfway to them now. A spattering featured two heads; the rest had one.

Danix clamped his foot on a rock and sank the tip of the blade next to the saphramurl trapped within it. Wiggling the blade, he buried the steel deeper. He brought his second hand on top of his first and wrenched down. The saphramurl popped free. Danix swiped at it but missed.

Antarna caught the smooth, multifaceted gem. Looking through, it turned the world orange. Under different circumstances, maybe this moment would have felt triumphant.

'Hold it out to me.' Danix slipped her dagger into his belt and shaped his hands into a circle over the centre of his chest.

By goddess, that's my blade. She extended the gem towards him.

'Both hands.'

She complied. He clenched his jaw, narrowed his eyes and held his breath.

What takes this much effort?

Danix released his breath. She turned her cheek to the hot air. The closest serpent was only three body lengths from the foot of the pile.

Danix looked to his feet. 'Not here.' He started clambering down. 'Come.'

'What's the plan?'

At the bottom, he closed his eyes. 'Yes, better.' His voice was little more than a whisper.

'What are you trying to do?'

'Hold it out. Brace yourself.'

She dropped one foot back and tensed.

A spark appeared inside the circle of his hands. Something shoved her back, an invisible force that would win a wrestle against a blizzard. She resisted, bending at the waist and bringing her arms in front of her face. The tight boots found plenty of purchase on the rough stone, but still she slid.

The serpents fled, scurrying and darting to their holes as if a flock of minderels plunged with talons extended.

Sweat dotted Danix's brow. A smile broke across his face. The spark faded and the force stopped.

Antarna stood. 'What was that?'

'Magic.' Cal descended the pile.

Magic?

34. It's Worth it

Zanth wiped his sleeve along his forehead. *So much for simple Danix.* The ruse wouldn't need to last much longer; it had almost served its purpose.

'You can do magic?' Antarna frowned.

'Only a little.'

Cal shook his head. 'No. It would take a powerful mage to cast a spell in a cave filled with anti-magic gems.'

'Luck is less demanding than the hard, weary road of skill. I was fortunate to manage a spark next to my chest. I don't think I could pull it off again. We'd better go before they come back.' He gathered up a few rocks.

Antarna did likewise.

Cal planted his hands onto his hips. 'You're no tracker. Who are you?'

'A friend, here to help. An ally sent by our chancellor. I'm a tracker but spent my early years in a temple.' *And you'd be dead if I hadn't acted.* 'We can't stay here.'

The seer glanced around, then scooped up some rocks.

Zanth hurried to the opening, showing them his vulnerable back. 'Why do you think the chancellor selected me? It's partly because of my gift.'

'We already had a mage,' Cal replied.

'Yes, one loyal to Arric. And where is he now?'

Antarna lengthened her stride to come alongside him. 'But then why lie to us? Why not tell us you can do magic?'

'I'm a tracker. That's who I am. I didn't think my few tricks were relevant, especially not in the Lost Cave.' Using his elbow, he pulled back a bunch of leaves that had fallen over the opening. Their translucence and slimy texture were akin to kelp.

Antarna nodded her thanks.

'After you,' said Cal.

You still doubt me.

They passed through the passageway into the chamber. The crustrearons were still asleep. Their king sat in his place of honour.

'Why were the serpents so scared?' asked Antarna.

'They wouldn't have seen magic before, living where they do.'

'Your spell was for a spark. So, anti-magic pushed me back?' She slowed to walk again beside him.

'Yes, the repulsive force between magic and anti-magic.'

'What would've happened if your spark touched the gem?'

'The closer they get, the stronger the repulsion.' He brought his hands towards each other—fists closed, squeezing his muscles ever tighter—until a finger-width separated them.

'But let's say you could get them to touch.'

He chuckled. 'I don't know. No one does. You know why? Because it can't happen.' The lie came easily.

She nudged a loose stone with her boot. 'Orrsin said the same thing.' Her pocket bulged with the keys.

'Well, there you have it.'

The rockime door blocked their way. There was a keyhole on this side too.

They each had their hands full balancing a load of rocks against their chests.

Antarna started to bend her knees.

'No, allow me.' Zanth dropped his load. The rocks tumbled to the floor. *Trust ... how to build trust.* 'Thanks for the loan.' Zanth raised the dagger then slipped it into her empty sheath.

'Of course. Thanks for saving our lives back there.'

'Bit of luck never went astray. May I?' He indicated to the keys in her pocket.

'Yes, please.'

He fished them out, placed the smaller one in the door and turned. The door opened against the pressure of his shoulder. Antarna and Cal entered as he held the door. The keys would've sat nicely in his pocket, but he resisted.

She dropped her load and then returned the favour, holding the door while Zanth fetched the rocks he'd let go of.

Mist moistened his face. Zanth released his rocks onto the pile with the others, then held up the pair of keys. 'Back to Antarna?' He had to raise his voice over the roar of the waterfall.

'I'll take those,' said Cal. He took them from Zanth without a "please" or a "thank you".

Antarna found a bag amongst the corpses. She started to transfer the rocks into it. They didn't have time to free the gems from each. Zanth bent down to help her.

'Why can't I see your madriliks?' asked Cal.

'Because I'm wearing this.' Zanth reached into his shirt and drew out his nalitroite pendant.

'And that hides madriliks?'

'Exactly. Let me show you.' He summoned almost all his madriliks into the hand that clasped the gem, hiding them from Cal—knowing he needn't worry about Antarna. When this was done, he slipped his necklace off and held it wide of his chest, completing the deception. 'See?'

'I do.'

Antarna put the last rock in the bag. 'Cal, what are you seeing?'

'He has ten dulls—low energy madriliks. Ten makes sense for a novice who's recently used some. You have three inside you at present. That's good for a normal person.'

'Oh, I'm just a normal person, am I?' asked Antarna.

Cal blushed. 'No, ah, not what I meant.'

She laughed.

The more time these two spent staring into each other's eyes, the less they spent examining him, and that only worked in his favour.

Zanth put his necklace back on. With his fist on his chest and under the cover of the nalitroite, he returned his madriliks to his reservoir. Plenty more than a paltry ten. 'We need to get out of here. Let me go up first. With my tracking and basic magic, I'll be able to see if we're ascending into a trap. They have a mage, right? I'll take the saphramurls up for defence.'

'No.' Cal shook his head. 'Not happening.'

'You still don't trust me? I didn't lie or betray you. I saved our lives. You've seen my future.' Luck must've been on his side then, or perhaps even the goddess of sight. 'If it's not enough, I don't know what is. They could come down that ladder at any time. That's what's concerning me. What are you worried about?'

The ladder fluttered by the entrance. Cal looked from Zanth to it and then back again. 'I'm worried you'll betray us.'

'That doesn't make any sense. If I don't return with you, our chancellor will drown me. Putting aside the "why", let's talk about the "how". If I'm carrying the saphramurls, I can't do magic. I don't have a weapon since returning the dagger. I also gave you back the keys, the only way to get into the cave. The keys are far more valuable than the bunch of rocks we collected, given how many saphramurls are left back there.'

Cal turned to Antarna.

'We don't have time for this,' she said. 'It needs to be one of you: I can't see madriliks.'

Cal scratched his head. 'Fine, you can check it out. Then Antarna. I'll come up last with the keys.'

'Sure.' Zanth put the bag over one shoulder.

The ladder was soaked through. The rope squished under his grip, releasing water. The saphramurls churned his stomach and the strap of the bag dug into his skin. *It's worth it.*

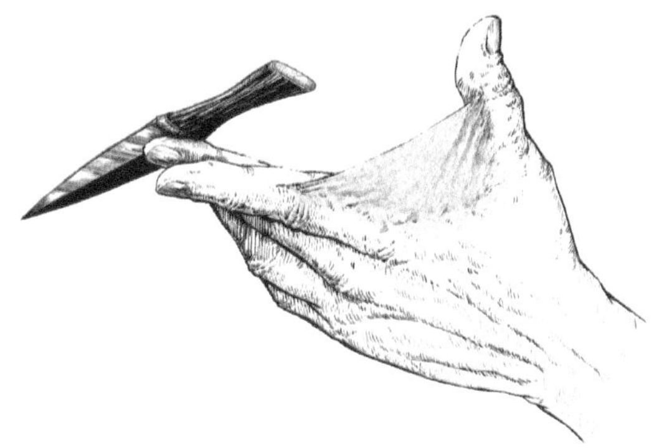

Pit of Blackness

Cal twirled the keys around his finger. 'I've a bad feeling about this.'

'You could've gone up instead.' Antarna pushed off the wall.

'And left you alone with him?'

'I can take care of myself. We can trust your vision, right?'

He caught the keys in his palm. 'Definitely.'

Danix reached the top of the ladder. There, he paused. His lips moved.

Who's up there with you?

The tracker grounded his hands and pushed off the ladder. He took off the bag and spun to face them.

A potent force ripped the keys from Cal's hand. He lunged for them, but the keys changed direction and then ascended alongside the waterfall. Cal jumped onto the ladder and climbed.

'Get down,' Antarna screamed.

No chance. He pushed his legs and arms, drawing closer to his keys.

'Cal!'

Danix brandished an axe. He cut one of the side ropes.

The rungs collapsed, limp and unsupported. Cal lost his footing. He clung to the rope with all his might.

It wasn't meant to end like this.

The axe sliced the last rope.

The ladder dropped. Cal's hands were locked around the rung.

A black pit awaited.

He fell.

Sorry, Mum.

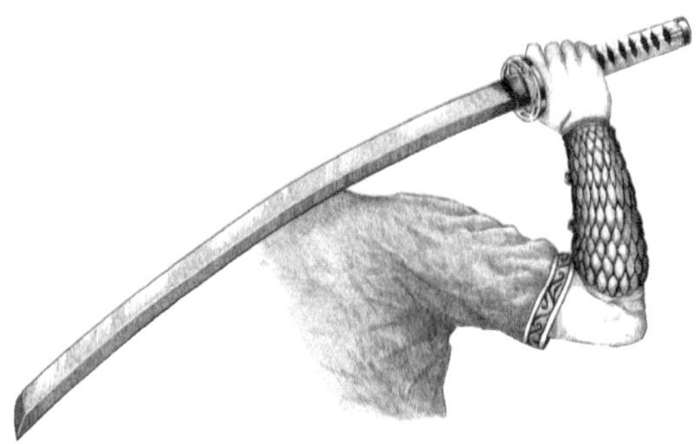

36. A Piercing Scream

ANTARNA sprinted to the edge.

Cal descended into the abyss. His knuckles were paler than his fair skin. A death grip.

The ladder! It trailed away from her.

She clawed at the undulating rope. It was out of reach. A pebble under her feet dropped into the gloom. Antarna raised her back leg for balance. With one hand gripping the cave wall, she snatched again at the ladder.

Enthriff glided along the back of her hand, secured himself to two fingers and stretched out. He caught the rope and dragged it into her grip.

She didn't miss a beat. Antarna bolted into the mouth of the cave, pulling up the slack.

The ladder drew taut. It yanked her back, heavy and determined. The weight was reassuring, though: Cal was still attached.

She slid. Her back foot found purchase in a depression, and she came to a halt. She pictured Cal arcing towards the rock wall, fast.

A piercing scream rose above the thunderous cascade of water. The pressure dropped off the rope.

Cal!

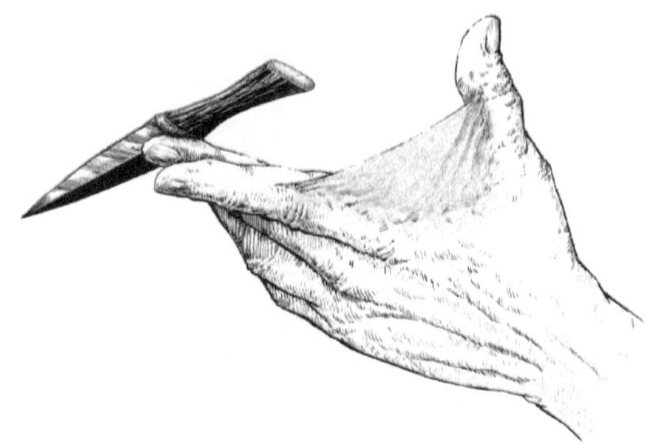

37. Blistering Fire

Cal's hair whipped against his face. Once more, he fell. Weightless. Spiralling into the terrible dark.

He reached desperately for the rope but found only air. A jagged cut burned his other hand.

The world tilted. Cal lashed out with his boot. It caught a rung. He pulled his toes back and came to a jarring stop. Inverted, he floundered, seeking to grab the ladder. His ankle howled.

The wet rope slid down and off his boot. He dropped head-first until a leg once again found a rung. Cal seized the rope, rewarded with a fresh bout of pain in his injured hand.

A scream broke above him. The ladder ascended. She was pulling him up. His saviour.

The rope cut into the back of his knee and his hands stung. Upside down, too terrified to try righting himself, his head pounded. But anything was better than the black pit below him.

On reaching the top, he collapsed on blessedly solid rock. 'Thank you.'

Sweat dripped off her flushed face. She jogged to his side. 'I thought I lost you. Twice.'

'I thought I was gone. Twice.'

'Oh, I heard.'

He rolled onto his back. 'Fell twice but only screamed once. You impressed?'

'Very. And I've never heard a more masculine scream.'

They laughed.

She offered him her hand. 'What happened the second time?'

Cal grabbed her forearm guard with his good hand and rose. 'First, this.' He held up his bloody hand. 'I lost my grip but managed to get hold again with my leg.'

'You were dangling upside down by one leg?' She tore a strip of fabric off her top and wrapped it around his hand.

'To get more blood to my head. It really helps you think. You should try it.'

She tilted her head back, looking up. Her face hardened. 'He betrayed us.'

The rim was empty. Danix—if that was even his real name—was gone, along with the stones and his keys. He couldn't be working with the desert folk, not given what Cal had seen in the vision. If the chancellor had sent him, had he ordered Danix to dispose of Cal and the others and return with the gems? Any which way, Cal was a jelly-brained mudfish.

With neither the ladder nor keys, they were trapped.

A hooded figure approached the rim, his torso bright with madriliks. Several middlers left his reservoir. In their place, an angry ball of white-blue flames grew.

'Run!' He turned, grabbing at Antarna.

She took off like prey from a diving flyer. His hand swiped only air.

The blazing orb was brighter than any star. It streaked towards them, rapidly closing the gap. A whistling shriek galloped ahead; a sound like nothing he'd ever heard.

Cal leapt over a corpse. Antarna reached the door and stopped.

What are you doing?

Blistering fire filled the cave's mouth. Antarna spun and rushed straight at him. She tackled him to the ground, behind a woefully small pile of rubble. A skeleton's arm snared and tore his sleeve.

Searing heat washed over them. He squeezed his eyes shut against the blinding light. In Antarna's embrace, he awaited the end.

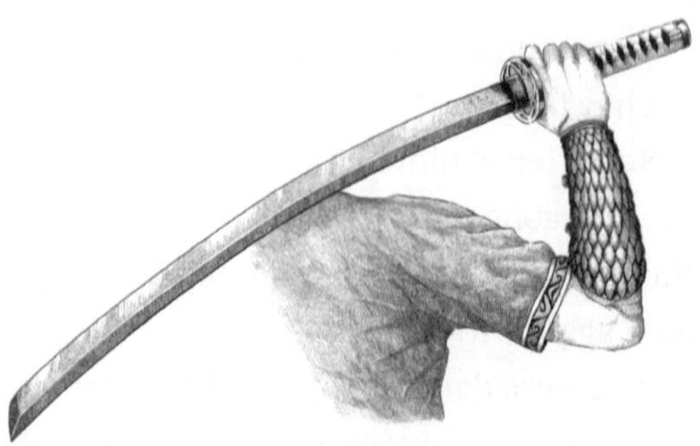

38. Enthriff

Antarna shielded Cal with her body. She wrapped her hand around Enthriff. Fire engulfed the cave. Her ears were the first to burn. She buried her face in Cal's back. The heat brought her back to an earlier time.

She was seven, her skin hot and sweaty. The white stone of the infirmary stretched above. Antarna slid off the bed. The stone floor sapped her heat.

One hundred and seventeen: the number of blocks making up the roof. She shivered. Like a scroll determined to roll back up, her knees begged to sink into her chest. But flat she lay, limbs spread.

High Priest Inhaloc entered with her father. She pulled her aching body to a sitting position.

'Burning up, again?' Inhaloc put a hand on her forehead.

Father dropped to a knee beside her, big and broad and solid. Wind had tousled his dark hair. In place of his usual scale armour, he wore a silver-grey tunic. 'I have a gift for you.' He held out a box made of light-coloured wood with a curving grain. Inside, a slender creature wriggled, snake-like. 'This lilreneer will protect you. He can sense anyone sneaking into your room. He can even detect poison. Let me show you.'

Father shut the box and took a small bladder and three cups from his bag. Into one he squeezed clear liquid from the bladder; the others he filled with water from her nightstand. Next to the water sat her dinner, untouched from last night.

'The bladder is poisoned, but it's not deadly, and Inhaloc has the antidote in his pocket.'

She drew her knees up and sank her chin into them.

After opening the box, Father coaxed the cute creature onto his little finger. The lilreneer wrapped around the finger but wasn't long enough to reach all the way.

Father drank from the first cup, then the second. He slid the creature up his finger and then back. The skin was all the same colour.

She hugged her shins as he reached out for the final cup.

'Ouch.' He smiled then brought his finger to the box. The creature unwound itself and dropped. A pale line extended around his finger. Gradually, the colour returned. 'See. He'll keep you safe.'

She lifted her head. 'What's his name?'

'He doesn't have one yet. What would you like to call him?'

Her mind raced. Scales? Ripple? She bit her cheek. 'Enthriff.'

'Your brother's middle name. Yes, that's perfect.' His voice cracked, and he looked briefly away. 'Now, he needs to be kept warm. So, how about we get you off this floor and back to bed.' He picked her up gently, embraced her in his thick arms and laid her down.

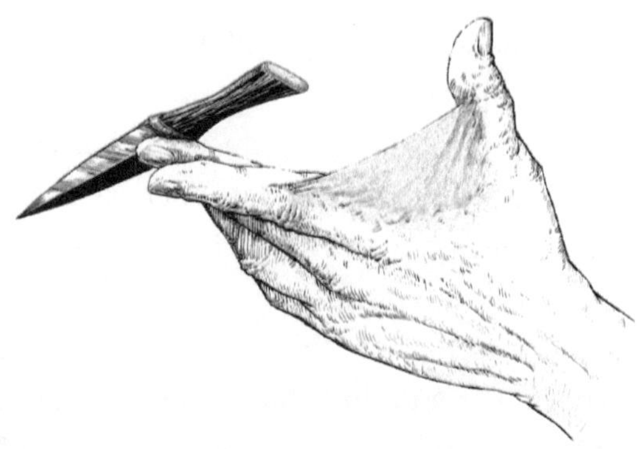

39. Dimples

An explosion shook the cave. A blast of wind tore at Cal. His ears rang. A rock pelted his arm. No doubt many more struck Antarna, heavy on top of him.

The heat intensified. Breathing in scorched his nostrils. The air, thick with the sharp scents of smoke and burnt earth, clawed at his throat.

Isn't my life meant to flash before my eyes?

The world drew quiet. His arm stopped complaining. The weight came off him.

'Cal, you're alright.'

He patted his arms and touched his face.

With a grimace, Antarna pulled a sharp rock shard out of her leg. This released a dribble of red. Her pet slithered around her wrist.

The fireball had dug a blackened hole in the middle of the cave floor. It had devoured three of the bodies. Another had been thrown halfway up the wall and rested on a slender shelf. The fifth was burnt and charred beyond recognition. A flame danced on its lower leg. The meat still sizzled. An acrid aroma assaulted him. It clogged his nostrils and filled his mouth, more a physical taste than a smell. He gagged, reminded of Brayan's eye gouging. But there was a strong scent of rotten eggs. *Burnt hair?*

She didn't offer her hand.

He stood. 'How are we alive?'

'Tell me what you saw.' She turned, eyes aflame.

'What?'

'When you took his hand, what did you see?'

'I saw his death. A desert warrior kills him. So, it was clear that he wasn't working with them.'

'You fool.' She turned her back, knotted her hands over the crown of her head and looked up. 'The gift of sight, and yet you're blind.'

'What? Explain it to me.'

'That man, Danix, or whatever his name really is, he's an underling. He fulfilled his purpose. He got into the cave. Now he's a loose end. Now he's disposable. It makes sense that they'd kill him.'

You trusted him too.

She walked towards the waterfall. 'I thought you saw us returning with the saphramurls or your chancellor throwing him and you a banquet or … something more …'

You didn't trust him. You trusted me.

'Thank you for saving me, again. I don't understand how we're not looking like that.' He kicked out towards the blackened corpse.

Antarna returned to stand next to the pile she'd tackled him behind. 'Help me dig.' She lifted a rock and threw it aside. Apparently, a reason would not be offered.

They worked in silence, but their busy hands kept most of the awkwardness away. He went for the smaller rocks, those he could manage with one hand.

Why'd I trust him? Halfwit.

Foresight, not bitter hindsight. That's what I'm meant to be good at.

He kicked a stone clear. Underneath was a crusty brown sack. The material was rough and stiff. On picking it up, saphramurls tumbled out the bottom, scattering amongst the rocks.

These kept the fire away. 'You knew they were buried there?'

'Yes, I saw them in my first vision of the cave.'

The floor swayed under him. The edges of his vision blurred. A faint buzzing arose, like an insect trapped within his skull ears. He laid down and coughed. His throat was parched. 'What a day. My head can't take much more.'

'Or your vocal cords.'

'I don't know what you mean.' Admittedly, his last scream may have been more of a squeal. 'We can both agree, that's enough danger for a lifetime.'

'Yes, so shall we just wait for someone to rescue us?' She pocketed a saphramurl.

'No one is coming. Not in time.' *Are you poking fun?*

'Would you say climbing that sheer wall of slippery rock is dangerous?' Her cheeks dimpled.

'With no ladder and an injured hand? The same wall you couldn't make it down with a vine tied around you?'

'That only leaves us going through that door, past the crustrearons and the serpents, to find the way out.' Her dimples were gone.

'No. I'm not going back in there.' Cal took a step back. 'Not even if I was dying of thirst in the desert and you promised me all the water in the lake. That's certain death.'

She approached the door as if he'd just agreed to her deranged plan.

'It's locked.' *And he stole my keys.*

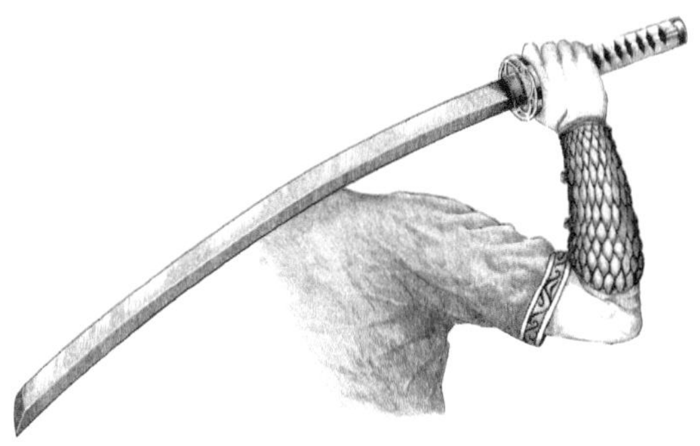

40. Paralysed

Antarna ran her fingers over the lock. Fire had shunned the door. She slid her hand down to a line of tiny saphramurl studs. She'd been running to the door until she realised Cal wasn't going to make it.

Cal coughed again. 'The chamber is a dead end. There was a single way in and out.'

'No. One hole was large enough for us, on the opposite wall just above head height.'

'That's a death trap. You've no idea that it goes anywhere at all. It likely ends shortly after it begins.'

'The Daslercians in my vision were trapped too. They couldn't climb up, so they went through. Horcil died, but the last man must have made it out. I know this because your keys ended up at the lake island.'

'Several entered but only one made it out?'

'That's better odds than us climbing.' *Although the crustrearons and serpents probably moved in after the mining stopped.*

'We still have that ladder. Just tie it around yourself, climb up, secure it, and I'll climb up the ladder. I'd do it for you if I wasn't injured.'

'Let no one say that chivalry is dead.'

He withdrew his hands from his temples and sat up. 'I don't know why we're arguing. We can't get through that door.'

'You count to five. If I don't have it open in that time, I'll climb up. If I do, we go through. Deal?'

'Deal.' Cal stood. 'One.'

She patted Enthriff. *Ready when you are.* He made his way onto her open palm and twisted his body into the shape of the smaller key. *Good thing you'd measured it up earlier, otherwise I'd be climbing.*

Cal stamped. 'No, that's cheating.'

'Press the pearl.'

She inserted Enthriff into the lock and turned. The door emitted the click that was almost a clunk. 'Let's go. And grab the ladder.'

It lay intact on the floor by the entrance. The fire had landed further in, and the rope had been soaked through.

He rolled up the ladder. 'What's the plan?'

'I'll show you.' She led him past the sleeping crustrearons and into the passageway.

Eleven wooden planks lined the roof. Cracks weakened five of them. Water had beaten the paint to bloat another. A pair by the side showed signs of rot and another two had been warped by time.

I only need one.

Like the others, the last board was secured to the supports by nails at both ends and in the middle. Antarna dug the blade of her dagger under the first nail and pried it loose. After all the nails were removed, the board still held its place, snug against its neighbours. Taking hold of each end, Antarna and Cal pulled it free.

'What now?' Cal asked.

'We attach the ladder so we can climb up the board to the opening.'

Cal removed the ladder, and they laid it along the wood. As it was far longer than the board, Antarna trimmed the ladder down to size. Next, they reinserted the nails, hammering them through the rope and back into their holes with the butt of the dagger. It would've been easier if the nails weren't all bent from the extraction. To finish, she flipped the board over and bent the ends of the nails against the wood.

Cal took a deep breath, eyes on the veil of leaves. 'Tell me you've got some clever distraction planned for the serpents.'

'Of course. I thought I'd get you to wake the crustrearon queen and invite her to help.'

'Oh, now you've got jokes?'

'We're just going to be quiet and quick. Grab the other end and let's go.'

Cal muttered something under his breath and then lifted the board.

Antarna took one hand off to slowly part the ribbon-like leaves. The serpents had retreated to their holes. She set a brisk pace. The board quivered in Cal's hands.

At least I don't need to worry about you advancing on a serpent, arms raised.

They circled the central pile.

The tail of a serpent glowed orange. Cal dropped the board. She waited for the crash against the stone floor, but it never came. He'd caught the end on the top of his boot. When it was back in hand, Antarna dragged him onwards. For the first few steps, Cal limped.

The tail swayed. Four more came ablaze.

Cal whimpered.

They raised the board up against the wall. It only reached the hole below their target. *Close enough.*

She stepped onto the wood.

The five tails shook, emitting short, sharp knocking sounds. Orange light and yellow eyes multiplied exponentially. So did the sound. Every serpent joined in, a whole chamber of them.

The rope ladder provided plenty of purchase. Hissing rose while she climbed. In no time, she reached the top.

A coiled serpent held its mouth agape. A pair of wicked fangs glistened within.

Enthriff tightened his grip.

The serpent uncoiled. She leant back. The jaws snapped shut just shy of her face. In readiness for another attack, the creature pulled back. The only option was forwards. There was no backup plan. Antarna leapt over the reptile, landing in front of the only hole large enough to be a way out. Cal waved for her to come back down. His legs shook.

She beckoned him up. Cal hovered his foot over the board. Enthriff signalled another warning.

A serpent whipped its head forwards. She slipped it like she would a punch—engaging her legs and hips to move her head off the centre line for the shot to whistle past. A yellow iris spiderwebbed with gold drew level with her face, a malevolent slit pupil dividing the eye in two. The head shot back almost as fast as it had come at her.

Three steps onto the board, Cal froze. A serpent wrapped itself around the top end and then began to descend. Antarna lowered her weight, ready to jump onto the board between the serpent and Cal. She pictured the wood snapping as she landed.

Below, several serpents crawled over each other. Even if Cal got past the one on the board, he'd have these to deal with too.

Her own problems multiplied. Now, there were seven of them: three on the left, two on the right, one below and one above. *Of course, seven.* Thousands more rushed towards her.

She picked up a rock.

A gust of cool air kissed her cheek. The dark passageway called to her.

Three hissing creatures hurled themselves at her.

She jumped—not into the safe passageway out of this nightmare, but off the rock wall. While airborne, she threw the rock at the entangled serpents milling around the top of the board. They scattered, the rock exploded, and she landed in the dust cloud.

They came at her with heightened fury. She dodged the first and gave the second a taste of her boot.

Cal was still yet to move. *Paralysed by fear or indecision?* If he could pass just one serpent, they could have stood shoulder to shoulder. But that one may as well have been a hundred.

Fangs came for her. She raised her arm. The long, curved pair of teeth shattered against her forearm guard.

Scores of serpents scaled the rock face, encircling her. She backed into the damp wall. The ledge was full, but still they came. They slithered over each other and pressed forwards.

A dozen streamed down the plank.

Cal.

Galvanised into action, he leapt from the board, looked up at her and then sprinted for the exit.

Save yourself.

There was nothing he could do for her.

The serpents reared their wide heads and flicked their forked tongues.

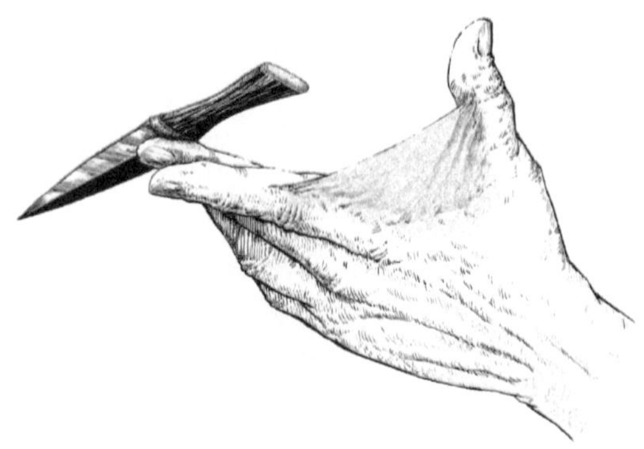

41. Ethereal Glow

Cal launched off the balls of his feet, exerting as much pressure as he could muster down to the ground. His arms pumped in time with his legs.

His life depended on it. Antarna's did too. He wouldn't lose her the same way he'd lost his father—skin punctured, poison flooding veins.

He had a plan. A crazy plan. A plan a madman would laugh at with not even a hint of appreciation. To start, he needed a rock.

The hurricane of hisses and rattles drowned out his footfalls. He tore through the ribbon-like leaves and down the passage. A rock the size of his foot was patiently waiting for him to find. He scooped it up and was pleased by its weight. It would serve as the perfect invitation.

Tiers of crustrearon emerged from the gloom. He turned sideways, took the rock back, aimed using his front hand and let the missile fly.

This is bad idea. A very bad idea. But he didn't have any others.

The rock arced towards the queen. Her words returned to him once more: *I thought I'd get you to wake the crustrearon queen and invite her to help.*

Cal raised the cancryst. The rock dipped too soon. It landed on a sizeable crustrearon on the second top tier. A segmented tail unwrapped itself from around the spiked shell. Eight limbs extended, lifting the body. Dust flew as the shell shook. The pincer snapped open then shut. The creature cast about and quickly settled all four of its raised eyes on Cal. Its tail rose above the shell of its neighbour.

The pincer came down, anything but gentle. It smashed against the shell three times—like someone locked out in the pouring rain, desperately pounding on the front door. The neighbour stirred.

The floor was covered in molted shells. Pebbles were nestled amongst them. *Why's it so hard to find a real rock in a cave?*

Two sets of thumping disturbed his search. The second crustrearon was awake and already at work on rousing another. *Not good.* He needed the queen, with her imposing size and intimidating presence.

A palm-sized rock rested by the wall. Cal picked it up, finding comfort in its good weight, and jogged towards the tiered structure. The four crustrearons raised their tails and menaced their sharp front limbs. After crossing one leg behind the other, Cal pointed at the queen, transferred his weight to his front leg and launched his missile.

The rock spun, edges blurring. The flight looked true. It peaked and began its downward trajectory. As it neared the queen, the crustrearons snapped at it with their tails. But the rock sailed above them. It crashed into the queen, fragmenting on impact. Her tail twitched.

Wakey, wakey.

The four crustrearons walked off the edge of the tier and dropped onto their brothers. These woke with a start. The crustrearons clicked their back legs together in some form of communication. Thirty-two eyes turned on him. Together, the creatures tumbled off the tier.

Eight crustrearons landed on eight more with a heavy thud accompanied by several sharp cracks. Four eyes rose from the queen's body. One after the other they opened: burning red irises, dark pupils bordered by an angry orange. She extended her legs, lifting her humungous shell.

What are you waiting for? Me to bring you breakfast?

He scrambled around for another rock, located one and threw it.

She batted it away with her tail, sending it soaring into the far wall. Her back legs smacked together, releasing a heavy, deadened sound. Again, the limbs collided, but this time, it gave off a sharp clack. All around, crustrearons stirred. Turquoise bubbles rose atop her shell then began to burst. A vomit-like smell burnt his nose. Cal's eyes itched.

Your morning odour? On a more serious note, it was probably some type of alarm—which suited him just fine. The bigger the crowd, the larger the sound.

The queen drove her front pointed limbs into the floor. Rocks went flying. The ground shook. Cracks zigzagged down the tiers. Crustrearons tumbled and fell. Some landed on their backs, legs flailing. She extracted her front limbs from the rock and ambled awkwardly down the fractured tiers. All four of her eyes were fixed on Cal.

He turned and bolted, heading back to Antarna. Not that he needed extra motivation, but the deafening clatter behind him urged him on. Bodies thudded to the floor, shells scraped together, pincers snapped. None of that compared to the frenetic scuttling—countless legs on rock. He could practically hear them arguing over who'd get the first bite. He glanced over his shoulder.

Crustrearons scurried out of the queen's path and surged towards Cal. Most moved sideways with their tails curled overhead. The larger ones, flecked with gold, shoved their way to the front.

Cal entered the passageway and passed the skeleton Antarna had been interested in. He took another look behind him. The queen had overtaken the others. Her massive form filled the space. Tentacles extended from her mouth.

Her pincer shot towards his head.

Cal threw himself against the rough wall of the passageway. The pincer bit shut in the space he'd just vacated. As he set off again, his foot slipped on a loose stone. He landed hard on his outstretched palms, ripping layers of skin from his hands and reopening his recent wound. Her open pincer lined with serrated teeth came for him. Cal rolled to the side, pushed himself up and flung his body forwards. His breath quickened, lungs insatiable.

He burst through the leaves and into the chamber.

Antarna's leg spasmed. The rest of her was hidden behind a wall of serpents. They turned to face him, jaws wide.

Cal didn't dare stop. His stinging hands were the least of his problems. The ground shook, jumping loose stones into the air. A serpent

fell from the crowded ledge. The queen emerged from the passageway, jabbing her spear-like limbs and raising her tail high. Her entire horde followed. Beads of sweat ran down his forehead, gathering in his eyebrows. His heart palpitated wildly.

Around the chamber, serpents scattered, fleeing into the darkest holes. A two-headed serpent was wrapped tightly around Antarna, its body as thick as her forearms. Each of Antarna's hands wrestled a head.

The plank still rested against the ledge. With the queen right behind, Cal crossed the chamber and leapt onto the wood. It wobbled under his feet. He sprinted its length—there was no time to climb with his hands. The serpent constricting Antarna turned one of its heads. Antarna brought her hands together, colliding the two heads. The coils around her loosened. Wrenching the serpent off, she flung it over the edge. The queen's pincer intercepted the creature mid-flight and sliced it in two.

'Let's go,' Cal said. 'We've overstayed our welcome.'

She cupped her hands. He put one foot into them, grabbed the shelf and lifted himself.

The tentacles around the queen's mouth twisted and elongated. Froth thickened on her shell. Under her feet, a swarming mass of crustrearons covered the chamber floor.

Cal offered Antarna his hand. She took it with a firm grip. A sharp, conical limb hurtled for Antarna. It would impale her. Her armour didn't stand a chance.

She released her grip and fell.

The limb buried itself in the rockface, jolting the cavern. Antarna boldly put a boot onto the limb and sprang off it for the shelf. The queen stabbed with her other arm.

Cal caught Antarna and heaved. She tucked her legs, and the queen missed again. They stood.

Antarna shoved him. His shoulder hit the wall. A huge pincer snapped shut where he'd been standing. He gulped.

'Run!' She took off into the dark tunnel, slightly crouched.

Cal pursued.

When I get back to the island, I'm eating crab.

A chorus of tapping rose behind them.

Crustrearons chased, hundreds of them. The tunnel wasn't large enough for the queen, but it was plenty big for her guards.

A burst of wind howled down the tunnel. Cal bent over, fighting against it. The wind didn't seem to bother the crustrearons. They closed in.

The air was fresher. It breathed new life into his legs. A small circle of light graced the floor. Antarna ran into it, glanced up, then continued. Cal was only a few steps behind. The light streamed down a shaft, wide and rough enough to climb. He squinted.

'Wait! Wrong way.'

'You're injured and they can climb faster than us. We have no choice.'

His hand was awash with blood. Crustrearons scuttled sideways along the walls.

Leaves on slender vines cascaded from the roof. They filled the tunnel, floor to ceiling and side to side. He plunged into their thick, slimy folds, keeping one hand on the rock wall and the other in front of his face. They tugged at his limbs and pulled at his hair. He waded through, picturing crustrearon pincers clamping down upon his ankle.

The wall curved. He turned the corner. The sound of rowdy, crashing water overtook the rustling of the leaves. Cal emerged and wiped slime from his face.

Antarna stood at the end of the tunnel, engulfed by mist from a waterfall. It had nothing on the power or volume of the one at the sinkhole, but it was far from trifling. A flowering vine ran down the wall opposite the waterfall. The lip-coloured stigmas were encircled by fine blue and white filaments.

A stone came at him. She'd hurled it. Cal flinched, and the stone flew by his hip. It landed with a hollow crack—not the sound of rock on rock. A crustrearon toppled from the wall and landed on its shell, legs up in the air. He kicked it back into the mass of leaves then jogged to Antarna's side.

The waterfall ended in a small pool. Cal leant over the edge. The water frothed and foamed, churning white. 'How deep do you think it is?'

'Deep enough.'

'What's in there?'

The leaves behind them parted for scores of crustrearons.

'Trust me.' She bent her knees. 'We jump.'

He grabbed her shoulder. 'Then what? There's no way out.'

Antarna's arms shot out, open palms landing on his chest. He fell.

Seriously? Cal took a deep breath.

She jumped after him, arms crossed over her chest.

Closing his eyes, he hit the pool boots first. Cold, turbulent water swirled around him. Kicking hard stopped his descent, though his boots felt like stone weights. He circled his arms from overhead to his sides. Water pulled against the webbing on one hand. The other clenched his cancryst. With a final surge, Cal broke the choppy surface.

Crustrearons descended the rock wall alongside the waterfall. One fell. Its spiked shell landed beside Cal, too close for comfort. Small squirming tentacles rimmed its mouth. The white water took the creature. The others continued to climb, unperturbed and determined.

'Follow me,' Antarna screamed over the noise. She disappeared into the water.

Cal ducked his head under. He blinked. A dark boot kicked ahead, and he chased after it.

An ethereal glow greeted them. At first, just wisps of it. Two strokes later and they were surrounded by it. *Kelp*? It lined a tight passageway. Antarna entered first. He extended his arms, making himself long and narrow. The kelp fluttered, the colour of a clear winter sky.

The passageway narrowed. Cal fluttered his feet. Silky kelp kissed his nose. At a fork, Antarna took the one that led upwards. The kelp thinned then faded. Cal passed the cancryst to Antarna. He let the light guide him. They continued to swim skyward.

She stopped. Cal pulled up alongside her. Rock. He beat a fist upon the dead end, forming a mass of bubbles. The urge to breathe nudged him.

Antarna flipped, tucking her knees into her chest. Her feet landed on the wall. With a strong push and a twist, she darted back the way they'd come. Cal copied her lead. Kelp reappeared, then the fork. This time, they took the downward one.

Swimming deeper didn't bode well. His need for air thrashed inside him, and his empty lungs burned. They took long strokes as the passageway widened. Finally, it turned upwards. Antarna's strokes quickened.

A soft ray of light pierced the water. Urgency claimed Cal's limbs. He caught up to Antarna, and they broke the surface together. Never had air tasted sweeter. They took large gulps as they made their way to dry rock.

Spiky mushrooms littered the floor instead of molted shells. The walls were rough but not covered in holes. Above, light entered through an opening large enough for a couple of adults. It was higher than the top of the sinkhole from the Lost Cave. His hand throbbed.

Antarna embraced him, sudden and strong. She trapped his arms against his sides with her own. The best he could do was to awkwardly lift his forearms to grip her waist. Her breasts dug into his chest, her scaled armour coarse and bumpy against his wet shirt. 'You came back for me.'

I'M WEARING HER SKIN

ANTARNA released her hug. For a moment, the cavern seemed colder and darker.

He dropped his hands and stepped back. 'Of course. But it's nothing.'

'No, it's everything. You could have saved yourself.'

'I froze, then ran.'

'You could have run right by the crustrearons, through the door and started climbing. But you woke the queen and entered the serpent chamber with her snapping at your heels.'

'At my head, actually.' He rubbed his neck. 'It was your suggestion: I invited the queen.'

She laughed. He was one of a kind. 'I'll take half the credit then.'

'Half? You can have a quarter. I mean, did you see how fast I ran?'

'You know where that speed came from, don't you?'

'Fear.' He patted his heart, mimicking its rapid beat.

'Yes, your body helped. So did your soul. It gives new meaning to *inner strength*.' If she ever mastered her soul visions, Gil promised she'd be able to tap into this power. Instead of a window to her soul, it could be more like a doorway.

'My soul? I never knew that.' He looked pensive.

The light fell upon a strange translucent plant sprouting through moss-covered rock. It was long and cylindrical, like the stem of a mushroom that'd forgotten its cap. The opening high above would test their strength.

'While we have the light, we need to climb. How's your hand?'

He turned his palm towards himself. 'Nice and clean after our swim. It'll be fine.'

Liar.

She led them across the floor of the cave. Her feet squelched in her boots. Her wet clothes clung to her body.

Cal stepped over a troop of mushrooms. 'You know, I'm the one who needs to be thanking you. How many times have you saved me today?'

'It's nothing.'

'No, it's everything. You broke free of your bindings and saved us from the desert men and the yalluts.' He dropped two fingers down. 'After you warned me about pursuing the keys, you caught the ladder and dragged it up with me on it. Then you saved us from the fireball, got through the locked door without a key, pushed me out of the way of that pincer and led us here.' Seven fingers were down. A deep cut streaked across his palm. 'Oh, I forgot the crustrearon that you hit with the rock.'

'I almost drowned us. And you wouldn't even be here if it wasn't for me. You should be safe at home.' *Getting ready for your wedding.*

Her toes cramped in her boots. She was tempted to take her dagger to the front to free them.

They reached the wall below the opening and started climbing. If their legs were twice as long, the first half may have resembled a steep, uneven set of stairs.

'How'd you know the water was deep enough?' Cal asked.

'Did you notice the flowering vine? It's an uplaful. One grows by the crater's pond. The flowers don't grow where water has risen to in the last few years.'

'You knew the water hadn't climbed up to where the flowers were?'

'Yes. The flowers stretched low and there was a lot of water flowing. So, it drained well and had to go somewhere.'

Cal stopped, resting a hand against the wall. 'But it could have slipped through cracks.'

'We didn't have a choice.'

He exhaled, looking to the ceiling.

Antarna stood on the sixth ledge, one above him. She offered her forearm, and he took it with his good hand, rising to stand beside her.

Hold on, Tozias. Just a little longer.

Cal wiped his hand on his shirt, smearing it with dirt. 'What are you thinking about?'

'That we need to move.' She ran along the narrow shelf, leapt onto a rock jutting out from the wall, pushed off and landed two ledges up.

Cal cocked his head, then turned away from her, facing down the slope. He pointed at the first shelf. 'One.' He silently counted the others until his finger halted at the seventh, the one she'd skipped. 'What's with you and the number seven?'

'It's nothing.'

'I'm fairly sure that we've established that when we say, "it's nothing", it means that it's actually *everything*.' He climbed onto the seventh ledge.

That number. That memory. Time seemed to fold in on itself.

The pebbles of the Purple Path pressed through her delicate, thin shoes and into Antarna's feet. Above, a crimson-robed priest read a scroll by the open window.

As she approached, a pair of initiates heaved open the front gate to Devtakaris's temple. Her royal blood could get her through this door, yet others remained locked. Antarna bowed her head and entered.

She passed the stairs, heading towards the forest. Hunters lined the passageway, dirty and bloodied. Kyrak stripped off his jadrossil-hide armour. Blood marked his cheek.

A hunter lowered his hands into a pail of water. She snatched it and held one finger to her lips. He bit his tongue.

Antarna jumped onto a log and emptied the pail over her brother's head. He spun, spluttering and cursing.

She stepped back. 'Is that any way to talk in front of a princess?'

'All I see is a little monster. Did you eat the princess?' He peered at her belly.

'Yes, I ate her, and I'm wearing her skin. But I still smell better than you. Hurry up, let's go to dinner.'

'Not tonight, Tarna.'

'You must. It's my birthday tomorrow.'

'Oh, is it? Why am I just learning about this now?'

'Ha-ha.' She put her hands on her hips.

'How am I going to find a present by tomorrow?'

'You already have it; you better. Which means you're free to come to dinner.'

'Tomorrow, when it's actually your birthday.'

'Father's coming tonight.'

'How old are you turning?'

'Seriously? Seven.'

'Well, if you say please for every year, yes, I'll come.'

'Please, please, please, please, please, please, please.'

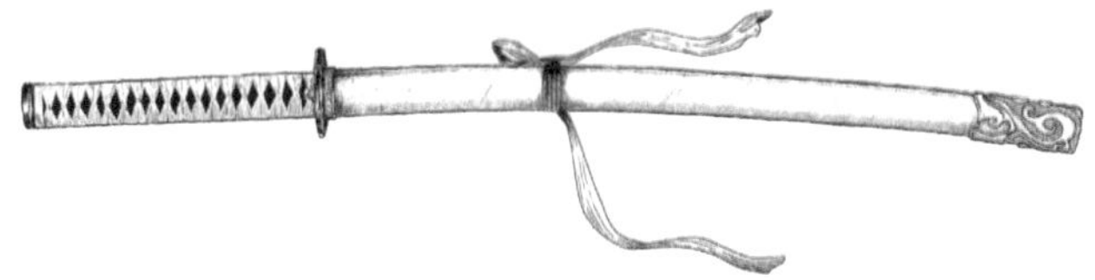

Cal laid a hand on her shoulder, having ascended to her shelf.

'My brother didn't plan to come to dinner that night,' she said. 'I pleaded with him, seven times.'

'You can't blame yourself. You didn't poison him.'

'I know.' She'd said what Cal needed to hear. Antarna put her boot into a foothold and reached up.

They climbed to the sound of their laboured breathing. Cal's injured hand made for slow going.

Her body moved steadily, and her mind whirled. The man that'd called himself Danix had said he could only do a little magic.

Lie.

'I'm a tracker.'

Lie.

She grabbed Cal's arm and hauled him up. 'Could Danix be a powerful mage?'

'Only if he found a way to hide his madriliks from me.'

She could strangle Cal. 'Sounds like something a powerful mage might know.'

Cal winced at the acid in her voice. 'The chancellor sure didn't send him. Who is he? A mage, born in the crater, after saphramurls and that—'

'Zanth!'

'So, the Resatrium have the gems. And they hired the desert folk.'

'That makes the most sense. But with what Zanth said, it makes me feel like it's not the case.'

'Then who paid them?'

43. Blood Pooled

Zanth's bound hands had stopped tingling some time ago; he could no longer feel them. Trivial, really ... Antarna and Cal had burned alive mistakenly believing he'd cast the fireball. His own death was imminent. The Lost Cave would fall into the wrong hands.

A bag of saphramurls bounced against his chest, clinking. It sat directly over his madriliks—putting their power beyond his reach. The coarse string of the bag rubbed against his neck.

The man who'd taken Zanth's nalitroite necklace picked a strange fruit. A tattoo of a tentacled skull covered his inner forearm. He ripped off its fibrous husk, revealing the sticky flesh inside. The first bite left him spitting seeds.

Each step aggravated Zanth's stomach. Still, he walked heavily, taking every opportunity to leave the outline of his boot or the imprint of his heel.

They're not going to take these saphramurls off until I'm dead. Why keep me alive?

The group marched east. The ruins lay in that direction. It could've been a coincidence, a rest stop, or the destination. There was no use in asking.

The snap of a stick joined the orchestra of the rainforest; the desert men walked lightly but not with the grace or familiarity of a hunter. The humid air was heavy with birdsong and clicking insects. Croaking frogs provided a steady beat. Something scuttled through the undergrowth.

A spiky branch of a bulbous tree clawed for him. He walked into it, letting it scratch his arm and snare the sleeve of his shirt. The branch bent, then gave a satisfying little crack. Fibres clung to it.

Where are the reinforcements, Prann? Ten desert warriors walked in single file ahead. And there were at least that many tailing Zanth. Dark clouds menaced, threatening to wash away their tracks. His dry, scratchy throat had a different opinion of the clouds.

A while later, the group stopped to rest. A foot slammed into the back of his knees, sending Zanth to ground. Water bladders came out, though none came his way. He shuffled to a tree and picked at the rope around his wrists with his nails. If only there was a sharp rock he could use instead. He made little progress before the group were back on their feet.

'Get up.' The butt of a spear jabbed into his back.

The group continued to trek east, single file. The clouds blackened and his mood threatened to match them. There was still no sign of the Resatrium. He'd die before they found him.

A band of birds shrieked and then took flight. Insects and frogs ceased their calls. Wind whispered in the topmost leaves, as if it was privy to what was to come. The group halted. Distant shouts intensified, quickly saturating the forest. He couldn't make out any words. A ferocious roar drowned out the shouts.

Branches broke. Feet pounded the ground. Something came towards them, something large. Zanth crept behind a tree. The warriors drew their weapons and advanced in the shape of a semicircle. A man with a heavy club stayed behind, close to Zanth.

A pair of spiralling horns flashed above a bush that was taller than most boys. The creature leapt the bush with ease, leading with its hooves. It had a thick, shaggy mane. Wide, serrated teeth filled its open mouth.

A velengoric.

Zanth pressed himself against the tree.

That'll teach me for lying about one earlier.

Something hard and heavy impacted the back of his head. His cheek collided with the tree trunk, pain exploding through him. He crumpled to the ground. Bright flashes of light overtook his vision. A branch dug into his hip, but he didn't dare move. At least it provided a distraction from his pulsating head. Someone prodded him, and he feigned unconsciousness. Footsteps fell away, so he opened his eyes. The world around him was a blur of greens and browns.

Zanth rolled to his side and pulled his legs into his chest. Using his elbow, he pushed himself onto his knees. He let his face fall forwards. The necklace caught the underside of his chin, its bag of gems reaching for his feet. Zanth shook his head, but dizzying pain was his only reward; it refused to budge. He stood and rubbed his binding against a rough branch, resisting the urge to run. If he could free his hands, he'd be able to take the bag of saphramurls off and access his magic.

An arrow bounced off the creature's scaled hide. Another pack of tattooed warriors pursued the velengoric. The creature swerved to avoid a javelin. A fin-shaped membrane rose vertically from its long tail, translucent like the webbing of a lake islander.

His captors tightened their circle.

Bark covered Zanth's hands. He shook it free. The vine was wearing down the branch instead of the other way around. *Leave it.* Zanth ran, ducking under branches and jumping giant roots. Leaves whipped his face, his arms unable to protect him. The bag of gems jingled like brass bells newly gifted to a small child. He waited for an arrow to pierce his back.

Nearby, a mage fashioned madriliks into a spell. A desert warrior dived out of the way of the velengoric's snapping jaws. The creature's tail smashed into another, sending him sprawling. A warrior drove his spear into a hind leg, only for the shaft to snap.

Zanth tripped. His body reacted by trying to extend his hands, forgetting that they were bound behind his back. A bush slowed his fall, thorns embedding into his shoulder. His forehead smacked against the ground. Something solid scraped his knee. He scrunched his eyes shut as his face dug a short ditch in fallen leaves.

The mage cast. The spell hurtled into the velengoric, dropping it.

Zanth scrambled to his feet. An arrow thudded into the tree beside him.

'The next one goes in your back.'

He froze.

'Smart choice. On your knees.'

Zanth turned to face the archer and obeyed.

He had a leather guard on the inside of his bow-arm. The man looked down the shaft of his nocked arrow. A half-full quiver sat against his back.

Another desert warrior approached with splayed feet, bronze dagger in one hand and a couple of lengths of vine in the other. He had an oversized head, thin lips and a scraggy beard with an ugly patch missing. His lips narrowed, near disappearing.

Behind him, others lashed the velengoric's front legs to its horns. This streamlined the body. Next, they tied the back legs and tail together.

The warrior raised the dagger.

Zanth met his intense gaze. The man shifted his weight and arced the pommel down.

Zanth flinched, expecting that to be the end of it: a show of power. The pommel struck his cheek. His head whipped back. He hit the dirt, eyes watering. Blood pooled in his mouth. His cheek stung and a deep throbbing grew in his skull.

The man tied Zanth's feet, allowing enough vine so he'd be able to shuffle along. Woozy, Zanth enlisted a tree to help him rise.

Vines ran from the horns to a cut sapling held by four warriors. They dragged the creature behind them.

What do you need a velengoric and me for?

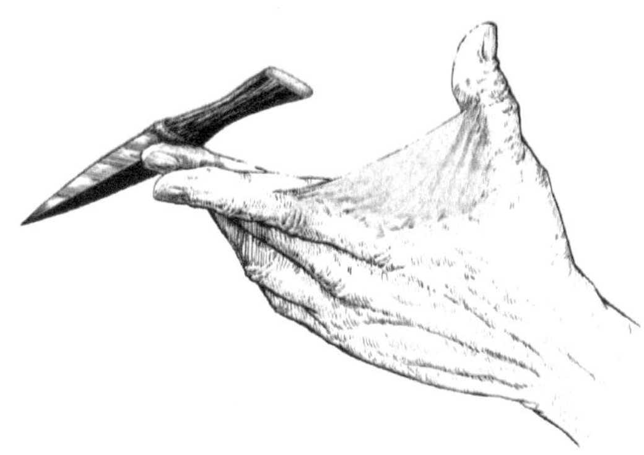

44. Halfwit

Cal crawled out of the cave onto the moist forest floor. He collapsed onto his back, chest rising and falling. The piles of leaves had a musky-sweet smell; it was intoxicating. Rays of sunlight snuck between dark-grey clouds and exploited a gap in the dense canopy, only to be swallowed by the cave. As *if the cave lured them. Or as if light is called to battle the dark.*

Antarna emerged and knelt beside him. Sunlight kissed her face, highlighting her cheekbones. 'Did you miss the forest?'

'I dreamt of the lake. But for now, I'll settle for fresh air and being outside.' He rubbed the base of his neck. *I need my key back.*

She rose and offered her forearm. 'Let's go get it.'

Withdrawing his hand from his skin, he took her forearm. *Am I that obvious?* 'My key and your gems. Which way?'

'I don't know where they're going. But you should. You saw Zanth die. Where did they kill him?'

The same place you die.

A sprinkle of rain pitter-pattered against the crowns of the trees. Wind rustled leaves and swayed the treetops. A branch snapped and tumbled down—the tree trying to catch its own but fumbling again.

'Cal, where did they kill him?'

Why can't I change your fate? 'Outside the ruins. Beside that pit.'

'That's a day's hike from here. And they've got a head start.' She made a quarter turn and then led them on.

I should've lied.

Large, incessant water drops beat upon layers of foliage. The clouds must have grown weary of carrying their load. The trees were also reluctant to bear it. Water dripped down in increasing volumes. A fat drop landed on his shoulder, soaking into the fabric.

She held back a branch for him. 'Question for you.'

'Hit me.' *Bad choice of words.*

She didn't release the branch. 'Do you believe in fate or destiny?'

'I believe that some things are meant to be. Sometimes, I blame fate: outside forces pulling strings to walk one along their pre-ordained path. Other times, it feels like destiny, where a person's choices and actions have led them to a particular moment. Why do you ask?'

'I was wondering if Zanth shapes his own destiny or is a puppet in the hands of fate.' She brushed the petals of a cheerful flower.

'He's responsible for his decisions; we all are.'

Her fingers left the flower to dance along an undulating ridged leaf. Water spilled from it. Her hands kept busy. If it was any indication of her mind, then that was racing.

You wondering about Zanth or yourself?

The falling darkness stole the wind from the sails of the shadows. They lost their definition and contrast. The darkness also ebbed away the colour of the forest. If he was painting the scene, he'd be mixing in more and more black.

Cal stopped beside a bush heavy with plump berries grouped together in shapes reminiscent of nine-legged starfish. He picked one. The rain stopped. *Take it as a sign?* He raised the berry to his lips.

'You can't see your own future, can you?'

Fruity and floral notes teased him. He threw the fruit away. 'No.'

'This one's safe, but I can't vouch for the taste.' She threw him a fuzzy fruit, then ate one herself.

Cal caught it and popped it in. The fur tickled the roof of his mouth. He bit down cautiously. It had neither seed nor flavour. *At least it's juicy.*

They gathered a bunch then continued. He finished his berries before Antarna was even halfway through hers. She savoured the berries, not that there was any reason to.

In the dying light, tiny birds with puffed out chests flitted from branch to branch. Antarna was two strides ahead of him. Sooner or later—sooner, if Antarna kept this up—they'd reach their destination. Unfortunately, he'd seen what would happen there.

He stepped where she stepped. 'Question for you this time.'

'Sure.'

'When you die, what happens to your soul?'

'My soul resides in the spiritual plane, tethered to my body at the head and the heart. When I die, these tethers break and my soul returns to Zentrina.' She paused as a pack of winged insects buzzed by. 'Souls are our eternal records. Zentrina will study mine. Then she'll allocate my soul to one of five rooms, if you will, to wait for re-embodiment.'

'Reincarnation.' He swatted away something that hungered for his blood.

'At the right time, in the right body, my goddess will reincarnate me.'

A branch cloaked in the darkness clawed for him, almost taking his eye. 'And how does she determine what's right?'

'Some people believe that their deeds determine it. That if they are good, kind, pious and generous, then they will be reborn to a healthy body with lovely, wealthy parents. They're mistaken.'

'How is it, then?'

'It's not a system of reward and punishment, but of learning and achievement. For example, you may be reborn to learn something that you failed to grasp before or finish a job that you started in a past life. Or, to help another do one of these.'

Leaves smacked his face. 'So, in this life, what are you trying to learn or complete?'

'My last life, Salorann, died trying to wipe out the royal line.' She slowed and looked up, as if to beg the gods for a sign, or perhaps to curse them. 'I need to stop the Resatrium threat.' But the words sounded hollow and lacking in conviction.

An old proverb came to mind: *Sometimes, it's the simple things that are the hardest to see.* The matter didn't merit further thought, though—she didn't have the time left to find or walk her path.

The canopy kept the view of the moon to itself. Only the odd ray of moonlight snuck through. Something grabbed his ankle and he fell, landing with arms outstretched. Leaves broke his fall. Cal freed his foot from the twisting root. A couple of snot-green mushrooms glowed to the side, but too softly to be of use to him. A dark, viscous liquid dripped from the rim of each cap.

He pulled out the cancryst. 'Light, please.'

Antarna spun and shook her head, shielding her eyes from the light.

The cancryst illuminated a hemisphere. He jumped over a moss-covered rock and squeezed between two trees. With the crystal on, he could move again with speed and confidence.

A pair of red glowing eyes stared at him from a bush on his left. The horizontally elongated pupils disappeared for a moment as the creature blinked.

He stepped back.

A pack of flying insects banked towards Cal. Each was as large as his face, sporting four wings, oversized mandibles at the front and stingers at their rear. He dropped the cancryst and backed away from it. The insects descended, swarming the crystal and smothering its light.

'Light off,' said Antarna.

Wings fluttered away.

Impenetrable darkness consumed the forest. He waved his arms in front of himself. *Halfwit.* He only had himself to blame. Cal stood waiting for his night vision to return. 'Did you see those eyes?'

'Those were not the eyes of a predator. The next pair might be.'

'Reassuring.'

Trees creaked and moaned in the wind, and leaves murmured. Insects communicated incessantly, trilling, clicking, rattling and drumming. Birdsong had faded with the light, but the distinctive chirp of a lolangal punctuated the night air. The faint sounds of scratching and scurrying were present too.

Slowly, the outlines of twisted trees returned. He stared at the spot where the cancryst should be. Some long moments later, it emerged.

Cal picked it up and tucked it away. 'Let's continue but look for somewhere to get some shut-eye?'

'As long as we're up before first light.'

The trees above them had long, thin branches. The clump of trees to the right had thicker limbs, but they started halfway up the trunks, which were smooth and straight.

Further on, an ancient oparitoon rose above the dense treetops of the canopy. Dozens of roundish burls covered the tree. The wartlike lumpy growths would make for easy climbing to branches that could easily support their weight.

Antarna turned to face him. 'No, the tallest are lightning risks.' After a couple of backward steps without looking where she was going, she spun back around.

How? Her grace was effortless.

He rested his hand against a trunk as he stepped over a rock covered in finger-shaped fungi. The damp bark moistened his skin.

As if the forest was determined to illustrate Antarna's earlier point, a massive tree lay split through the middle. Rot and decay had claimed one of the two charred halves. The other was in better shape, resting against a pile of boulders.

Cal pulled out the cancryst and approached. This time, he wrapped the crystal, leaving only a sliver exposed. 'Light, please.' A narrow beam stretched under the log. An elongated, multi-legged creature scuttled away, its segmented body undulating.

'Thoughts?' he asked. A yawn broke free.

'Looks dry, but tight.'

'We could take turns sleeping or find somewhere else?'

'It'll be fine. And Enthriff can keep watch for us. Let's grab some sleep.' She extended her arm. 'After you.'

Cal dropped to his knees, but the log was too low to crawl under. Instead, he lay under it and shuffled himself deeper, until his shoulder met rock. 'Light off.' Faint golden-green flecks of light remained, the moss resisting the pull of the night.

After collecting some stray strips of fallen bark, Antarna entered and dragged the bark over the gap. Her arm brushed his. 'Night.'

'Sleep well.'

She crossed her arms over her stomach. Her breathing slowed.

Enthriff unwound from her wrist.

Where do you think you're going?

It climbed up his hip and made its way along his chest, moving like a snake. Cal shivered.

Go back to her. It's your last night together.

Enthriff raised his body up.

We can't help her. I can't. Unless he broke his oath ...

It had never been clear to him if there were shades of grey between the black of breaking his oath and the white of upholding it. In the past, he'd confided his visions of death in Brayan, his mum and the chancellor—not to mention the occasional quill hound, countless canvases and a deaf man with his back turned. None of those had changed the moment of the death he'd foreseen for someone.

But what about telling someone after they promised not to interfere with the death of their acquaintance and without a vision to contradict that promise? Or telling a distant friend of the soon-to-be-deceased, believing them powerless to change the death?

Enthriff curled higher.

Antarna shifted in her sleep, and her dark hair fell across her cheek. His fingers itched to loop it back behind her ear, but he resisted, letting the moment pass.

He remembered her words: "Why see a death you can't change?"

Cal had to do something, anything. Of all people, she deserved it. There were shades of grey so light they looked white.

45. A River Climbing a Mountain

Antarna sat on the cold floor of the temple, in the fourth of five rings. All faced Zentrina's towering liquid form, which rippled in the middle of the room.

High Priest Inhaloc rose from the innermost ring. 'Last night, we lost another. Zentrina has already received his soul. Today, we will give her his body.'

Priest Weslutch struck a small gong.

Two priests and two priestesses entered carrying Tozias's body. His eyes were closed. The mark of Zentrina was still on his inner forearm, the sacred text never to move again.

She'd promised to be back as soon she could and to do anything in her power to get the saphramurls. But she hadn't kept her word.

His feet disappeared first into the shimmering charcoal liquid. A choked sob tore from her throat. The statue claimed his upper legs, then hips, then stomach. Time had slowed to a crawl. When his chest and shoulders disappeared, only his head was left. With one final, inevitable motion, it too was plunged into the liquid, fiery hair and all. She held onto the image of his face in her mind, only to find it a poor substitute.

A grey seed came from the statue. Inhaloc caught it and held the seed aloft.

Enthriff gripped her wrist. Hard. Something didn't feel right. He squeezed again. But not from this place.

She woke with a start. Darkness enshrouded her. She resisted the urge to sit up, knowing that there was a reason but not being able to remember it—

The log.

Cal snored softly with gentle inhales and exhales.

Enthriff unwound himself from her wrist.

Why'd you wake me?

The fog around her mind lifted.

Muted footsteps approached. *Padded feet? Something heavy? A predator?*

The fallen tree, rocks and bark kept them out of sight, but nothing hid their smell or the sound of their breathing. Moving the bark should let her see what's coming for them, but it would also guarantee discovery. She left it.

The creature drew closer. Antarna readied a kick, glad she'd left her boots on.

A growl cut the air, low and guttural. But not from right outside; it came from further away.

Footsteps receded.

She said a prayer to Veritonan, the god of luck, and patted Enthriff with long, full-length strokes. After waiting long enough to let the creature get clear, Antarna lowered the bark. Palm-sized beetles flew in clumsy patterns around a tree with pale, drooping flowers. There was nothing larger in sight. A star winked through a small hole in the foliage.

Her heartbeat slowed. She ran her fingers through her hair, pulling two leaves and a twig free. The scent of rich earth was inescapable. Hopefully, it came from the forest floor and not herself.

Impending daybreak started to pull the sheath of darkness from the forest. She bent down and shook Cal's shoulder. He opened his deep blue eyes only to close them again as he stretched his hands over his head.

This is going to take a while.

She lifted a leg onto a boulder and bent forwards at the hip, keeping her spine straight. To deepen the stretch along her hamstring, she extended her arms and gripped her boots.

In the stillness, she had time and space to think. The mystery of what had happened in the glade on the day her temple suffered continued to trouble her. The four priests hadn't died defending the crater against a hazzurus. The Resatrium had the means with the enchanted orbs they'd amassed. And the attack would've drawn mages from the temple and thrown it into chaos ... Perfect for breaking into the vault or murdering Arric. But something didn't add up: why attack the priests in the glade where they'd be at their most powerful?

Cal pushed himself upright and dragged up his sleeve. Three bites dotted his arm, the skin red and raised around them. He raised and lowered the shoulder of that arm—a one-armed shrug. It fitted with his look, which said, "Well, what else can you expect walking in the rainforest?" His eyelids drooped closed, the bags under his eyes too low to provide a cushion.

They departed for the pit outside the ruins. A spikey yellow fruit looked promising for breakfast, but Enthriff wasn't impressed with it. Strangely, Cal didn't grumble or complain. His brooding eyes barely left the forest floor.

'Are there many madriliks around us?' she asked.

He checked their surroundings, following one as though viewing a butterfly. 'Only a few.'

'Who has the greatest store of madriliks?'

'Arric, by far.'

'So, he's easily recognisable to another mage?' She stepped between twisting roots, wishing she'd been born with the ability to see madriliks.

'Absolutely.'

Energy surging through her, Antarna jumped onto fallen log. 'Then you couldn't confuse Arric with Morsirel?'

His eyes widened. Cal joined her up on the log. 'No. Anyone with training and sight wouldn't make that mistake. Zanth wouldn't.'

'If Zanth didn't kill Morsirel, then who did?'

'Someone powerful with access to the high priest's room. So, another priest?'

'Why? What's the motive?'

He scratched the back of his neck. 'Good question. It'd help if we knew more about Morsirel.'

Pale red fruit ladened the tree to their left. Each tapered fruit was formed from a collection of spiralling cones. They reminded her of the three wooden minderels nesting one inside the other on the shelf of her old bedroom.

Cal stepped towards it. 'Please tell me that's edible.'

'It's dead man's fruit.'

'It kills you?'

'When you break it open, the smell is powerful enough to wake the dead.'

Cal moved on.

She picked a few.

He looked back. 'That better not be to wake me tomorrow.'

'I can't make any promises.' She slipped them into her pocket. 'Morsirel's death is linked to everything here, I feel it. No doubt he had enemies.'

'His body was drained of madriliks.'

'Are they valuable?'

'To a mage, yes. It is far quicker and easier than filling up elsewhere, even at the glade.'

The sun was overhead by the time the stone of the wetway peeked through the trees ahead. They followed it to the western outer wall, located a gap and then crouched.

Ten men sat eating lunch under a shady tree. A lone warrior sharpened his knife in front of a pile of supplies. Her sword rested at the top. She scratched her right palm.

Footsteps approached. Antarna ducked and held her breath as a pair of desert warriors passed their position.

Another pair stood over a velengoric with closed eyes by the entrance to the pit. Its front legs were tied to its long horns. Vine also secured its snout and back legs. The rise and fall of its chest showed that it was alive.

They watched and they waited. Three more pairs passed them before the first came by again. All walked north beside the wall.

That made four pairs patrolling the perimeter and twenty-one men in total, all heavily armed. Not a priest or mage amongst them. Snarlark was also absent. *Need to strike soon, before any return.*

After the next patrol passed, Antarna crept through the gap in the wall, staying low and avoiding loose stones. Cal followed.

She led them through a thicket of bushes, circling away from the group of ten. At the other side, they darted to take cover behind a toppled wall. Only the bottom third stood, but that was sufficient. Hunched over, they walked its length.

Her sword was a mere dozen steps away. Behind the mound of supplies, vines bound Zanth to a stone column, the first of seven. His chin fell to his chest. Midway between his chin and abdomen rested the bag of saphramurls. A warrior with misshapen ears sat close by, whittling a dark piece of wood. Just like Tozias loved to. He had a punch dagger sheathed on his hip, made distinctive by its H-shaped grip, which kept the blade in line with the forearm.

'Stay here.' She pointed down. 'I'll distract them. Grab our weapons, then meet me at the columns.'

Antarna turned before Cal could reply. On hands and knees, she crawled through the thick grass. Wind stirred the field, disguising her passage. Biesan had died not far from here, in grass like this. His short scream reverberated in her skull.

Neither of the men guarding the velengoric paid it any attention. They were engrossed in a game of chance, taking turns rolling an eight-sided die. The die resembled two tiny square pyramids attached base to base. Its triangular faces were covered in desert symbols. The guards' beards spoke volumes. With crisp lines, one was carefully groomed and manicured, the hair lengthening as it progressed down the cheeks. A forest of facial growth overwhelmed the other, tangled and bushy.

Ego and Wild.

The dead man's fruit pressed against her thigh. She took them out and waited. A gust of warm wind snatched at the leaves of the shady tree, failing to rip them free. Holding her breath, Antarna broke the fruit open one by one. Inside, the soft flesh was a translucent white. She quickly threw them. One got a bad bounce off a rock. Another snared in a spiderweb. The remaining two landed close and rolled up towards the velengoric's head. A guard stood, looked about, then sat.

The velengoric's nostrils flared. Its snout twitched. The tight bonds minimised a tremor that ran down its powerful legs. Its eyes sprang open: merciless black slits cutting vertically down sun-yellow irises. Bony protrusions rimmed the forward-facing eyes.

Muscles corded down its neck. The bonds around its snout held, for now. Dragging its face along the ground freed all but one of the loops of vine. Meanwhile, the guards focused on their die. If they kept it up, they wouldn't notice the threat until it was swallowing their feet.

The creature shifted its legs and pulled at its tail. Bit by bit, the long, slender tail came free; this extended over its body, grabbed the last vine around its snout and pulled it free. Its sharp teeth couldn't reach the binding securing its front legs to its horns. Snorting, the velengoric batted away the dead man's fruit with its tail, sending them into the grass—and hiding her actions. Its tail then got to work on the vines around its back legs.

Wild stood, swearing. He pointed a dirty finger at Ego's sharp nose. Smirking, Ego swatted it away. Wild picked up the die and threw it at his companion. It bounced off Ego's armoured chest.

The velengoric struggled with the vine.

A warrior under the tree looked over. 'It's awake!'

Ego scrambled to his feet. Wild grabbed his spear. The warrior by Zanth kept whittling. But the guard by the supplies sprang to help with four from the perimeter and the same number from those having lunch.

You're up, Cal.

Wild lowered the spear at the creature's open mouth. His breath quickened. The velengoric snapped at him. Startled, Wild stabbed out. The predator turned its head, and the blade sliced through the vine tying a horn to a front leg.

Ego had circled around the back of the creature. He took another step closer, axe raised as if he intended to lop off its rippling tail.

The velengoric drew its legs in. Maybe Ego mistook it for an opportunity or a sign of submission, for he drew closer still. Two hooves slammed into Ego's lead leg, either side of his knee. Bone snapped.

Ego's shinbone tore through his skin. He flew backwards and landed in a crumpled heap. The other hoof had punctured his thigh, exposing the muscle and leaving jagged flaps of skin. Crimson gushed forth. Howling, he clutched at his leg.

This lit a fire under the desert warriors. As the creature fought to rise on three legs, they surrounded it and rushed to Ego.

Antarna stole away to the stone columns. She approached the first from the rear, staying clear of the silver delusians covering the other six. On each side of the column, Zanth's fingers twitched. Vine secured each wrist, pulling his arms taut, wrapping them around the upright. Zanth's feet and hips were also wrapped to the column.

'Do you prefer Danix or Zanth?' she asked.

He stiffened and then turned his head. 'That can't be what you came to ask.'

'Look down, not at me. Pretend you're muttering to yourself.' She kept herself hidden behind the stone column, out of sight from the warriors. 'Confess. You stole the gems from the crater and murdered Morsirel in Arric's office.'

'I stole the gems, but I'm no murderer. I was too busy trying to get out with the gems and my life. I don't care about Morsirel.'

'But you do want to kill Arric?' The cold stone column soothed her elbow.

'Of course, though I'm not going to mistake Arric for Morsirel. Or attempt that on the same night as I'm stealing the saphramurls. Plus, if I have the gems, I can't do magic.' He further inclined his head towards the full bag on his chest.

Then who killed Morsirel? A more important question burnt on her tongue. 'What happened in the glade?'

'Magic met anti-magic—as neither the gods nor nature intended. Their collision led to their mutual annihilation. You felt the shockwaves in your mountain temple. My theft of the saphramurls was too late to stop the weapons test.' He sighed. 'But it would've prevented further events if you hadn't found the Lost Cave.'

'Lies ...' Yet every word rang true. Antarna slid down the column. *The four armless tested a new weapon near the glade. The resulting explosion killed them. Not a hazzurus. Not the Resatrium.* Was the king or Arric behind it? Did Father know?

Judging by the constant swearing and screaming coming from the desert warriors, the velengoric had their measure—for now.

Cal approached in a low crouch, carrying her sword, shield and dagger. He whispered, 'You look as if you've seen a ghost.'

'What would happen if madriliks touched a saphramurl?'

'No one knows.'

It happened before, leading to the destruction of the once-great Daslercia. 'Best guess?'

'Something violent and terrible. It'd take an incredible amount of power. And be wholly unnatural. Like …' Realisation broke over Cal's face. 'A river climbing a mountain.'

Zanth tugged at the vines around his wrists. 'You ready to set me free?'

Cal stood. 'We can't trust you.'

'The Resatrium killed my mother and brother.' Antarna slid on her shield.

'Why would we do that?' Zanth asked. 'The king and his policies are at the heart of our issue: Ithranned is even worse than his father. Targeting your family would only inflame the situation. It wasn't us.'

She risked peering around the column, and Zanth turned his head. His honey-brown eyes met her gaze and held it. Firm. Fierce, even.

Her confidence in the truth she'd clung to shattered, and the sharp edges of her grief and anger cut her anew.

With a thud, the velengoric slumped to the ground. A desert warrior lifted a double-handed bronze hammer onto his shoulder. Two of his companions lay unmoving, blood pooling. The rest closed in on the creature and set to work with vines.

Time's up.

The pommel of her dagger was larger than that on her sword. She transferred the dagger to her favoured hand. Short hair covered Zanth's chin and bottom lip. *One clean strike for lights out.* The bag of saphramurls sat plump and ripe on his chest. She raised her weapon. Zanth squeezed his eyes shut.

'Princess, there you are. I've been looking all over for you.' Arric advanced from the trees, his robes streaming out behind him. 'The king and your father will be relieved.'

A desert warrior drew his axe and looked to Arric. The high priest shook his head, and the man lowered his weapon.

But that'd mean–

'Nothing to worry about. They're now working for the king, not the Resatrium. I defeated their leader, who fled, then offered to pay them double. You don't need to worry about them.' His level voice had transitioned to a soothing tone.

'What's going on? What are they doing with a velengoric?'

'They captured the creature to sell, I imagine. But that's in the past. You found the Lost Cave. Your king and father will be so proud of you. I am.'

'Arric's going to kill you,' Zanth said. 'Antarna, you've embarrassed the king, and you know too much. Cal, you too will have to die. The crater won't share the saphramurls. They'll pretend the cave was never found.'

Arric took a heavy step closer. 'Says the man who'd say anything if it helped his traitorous cause.'

'Ending a reign of terror isn't traitorous. I'm loyal to the people of the crater.' Zanth turned to her, fighting against his bonds. 'Did you like what you saw when you returned to the crater? Having been born into royalty doesn't mean you have to blindly follow the king.'

Loyal to the people? Is that what motivated Salorann? Is this what motivates Evireny? Is that what the Resatrium are?

46. Dancing Flames

Zanth's red, raw wrists stung. Yet still he tugged at the vine, angling his body towards Antarna.

Trust me. Cut my bindings. Everything depended on what she did next. He readied himself to tear the bag of saphramurls off and cast at Arric. *I'll melt your face.*

Her dagger flashed. It came at him all wrong: pommel first, towards his gut. At the last moment, he braced. The steel struck. He started to double over, but his binds held him back.

Antarna spun on her heel and walked away from him. 'If I'm hungry, Cal must be starving. Have you had lunch yet, High Priest?'

'No. Good idea. Let's eat.'

Cal hurried after her.

Nothing to say, Cal? Unusual.

His guard returned—regrettably unscratched—from helping with the velengoric, fingers lingering on his punch dagger's distinctive handle. He tore at Zanth's shirt, ripping off two strips. 'Open your mouth.'

Zanth did so, but snapped his teeth shut as the man brought up one of the strips.

Knuckles from a fierce backhand slammed into his cheekbone. 'Sometime soon, they'll order me to kill you. I'm going to enjoy it.'

His vision lost focus. Waiting for it to come back, Zanth stretched out his jaw. Cloth clogged his mouth, invading deep and from cheek to cheek. Tasting dirt and his own sweat, he gagged.

Rough hands closed his mouth and tied the other strip over it and around his head. He didn't resist further. When the warrior finished, he perched to whittle. His ears, knotted and lumpy, told a story of trauma.

Arric, Antarna and Cal sat under an old tree. Leaves only clung to three of its branches. These rose skywards before turning around to come back the way they'd come. It was as if the branches had made a conscious decision to shun the sun. A *fitting seat for you, Antarna. Rejecting your people in favour of your royal blood.*

A desert warrior brought the trio a selection of cold meats, cheese, bread, chutney, pickled vegetables and freshly foraged fruit. If Zanth's mouth wasn't bone dry, it would've watered. They filled their bellies in the shade. The sun beat down upon him, and Zanth's stomach growled but no longer hurt. *Did you pull that strike, Antarna?*

Arric floated the keys out of his pocket and towards Cal. 'These belong to you.'

Cal swallowed his mouthful. 'Thank you.' He closed his hands over the keys.

'I'm still coming to terms with you two finding the Lost Cave. It's momentous.'

'The injured at the mountain temples need the saphramurls. My friends are dying.' Antarna put down a pickled vegetable. 'Will you escort us back to the lake island and help to teleport the injured there?'

'Of course, it would be my pleasure,' said Arric.

Antarna's face lit up. The poor, gullible girl. What a fool.

Twisting his body, Cal swivelled his head from side to side. 'Where's Farikarr? Have you seen him, High Priest?'

'No. I was out looking for you and was hoping to find him with you. When did you last see him?' He levitated a piece of dark-yellow cheese onto his bread and chutney.

'By the sinkhole,' said Antarna. 'Snarlark held him back while others marched us off to die.'

'Maybe I shouldn't have killed him so hastily.'

'How did he die?'

'Screaming as he burnt alive.'

Antarna nodded.

Would she be as gullible if she wasn't being told what she wanted to hear?

Cal put down his food and advanced upon Zanth. 'What did you do with Farikarr?'

'Nothing.' The gag muffled and garbled the word.

'What?' Cal ripped down the strip around his mouth.

Zanth tried to spit the wad out of his mouth. It was jammed in tight. His tongue barely budged it. With two fingers, Cal grabbed the fabric and pulled. Zanth's cheeks depressed. Sweet, fresh air rushed in. The ball of cloth fell to the ground.

Cal wiped his fingers clean. 'Where is Farikarr?'

'Arric probably had him killed.' His former mentor could've learnt that Farikarr had been working with Zanth. *How do you think I found you?*

Cal balled his fist and clenched his jaw.

'It's a waste of breath,' Antarna said. She motioned for him to return. 'Considering how much practice he's had, you'd think he'd be a better liar.'

'True.' Cal joined them.

Zanth's guard picked up the cloth and drew a punch dagger. The double-edged blade extending above the man's knuckles went against his balls. Zanth opened his mouth, and the gag was reinserted. A piece of grit fell under his tongue. He tried to fight his way around the fabric to get to it, but his tongue couldn't free enough room to dip under itself.

'While we have the light, I'm going to take the hired blades and look for Farikarr,' said Arric.

What's your real objective?

Cal put his palms on his knees, preparing to rise.

Arric shook his head. 'You must be exhausted from your journey. How about you rest and keep an eye on Zanth?'

Antarna laid a hand on Cal's shoulder. 'Thank you, High Priest. Yes, we'll do that.'

'Excellent. We'll be back before dark.' Arric strode over to the velengoric and, deploying madriliks, rose it off the ground. With the struggling creature floating in front of him, he made his way to the excavated cage. Its roof of bars was at ground height.

A warrior rushed down the slope to the cage door and lifted the heavy latch. It took two more desert warriors and a blow with a hammer to loosen the hinges and heave it open. The creature landed heavy, snapping branches and crunching leaves that lined the cage floor. It made it to the door a moment after the steel clanged shut.

Arric's robe streamed out behind him as he ascended the slope. The fabric clung to his thighs, revealing a rectangular bulge against his right: a box. It was about the size of an adult hand. The standard temple robes featured no pocket there. The high priest must have made or requested it. There was no opening on the outside of the robe.

Closing his eyes, Zanth concentrated on the object. The saphramurls around his neck hindered him. But, still, he could've sworn there was something unusual about the box.

Arric approached the old tree. 'Shall I leave a guard for Zanth?'

'He's tied up. We'll be fine, thanks,' Antarna replied.

Cal turned to her. 'Shall we join the search?'

'They've got over twenty men. I'm tired. I'm injured. As are you. Let's tend to our wounds.'

'Sure.'

'Rest up,' Arric said. 'We'll find him.'

'Thanks.'

Arric and the desert warriors faded into the forest. *What are you up to?*

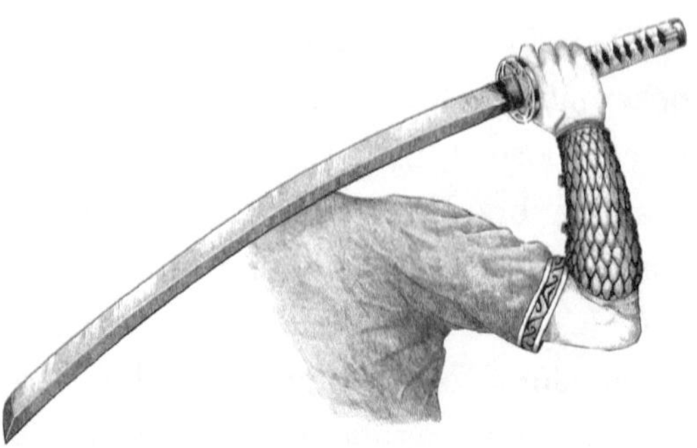

47. Fatal Strike

'Arric's lying.' She cursed how blind she'd been to the truth.

Cal leant away from her. 'What? You were just nodding and agreeing with him.'

And she'd hated every moment of it, but what else was she to do? 'I believe Zanth. He stole the saphramurls to prevent them from being used in a new weapon: the explosive might of magic and anti-magic. I even believe him when he says that he didn't kill Morsirel.'

'Then who killed him?'

'Four priests died in the glade and shockwaves hit the mountain temples. What if Morsirel was angry about this and came to Arric's office to confront him?'

'Right. Threatening to expose the truth. Or to shut it all down. You're saying Arric killed Morsirel?' Cal scanned the trees, probably checking them for the man they'd just eaten with.

She ran a hand through her hair. 'I know how crazy it sounds. By goddess, he's the reason my father and uncle are still alive.' Antarna jogged over to Zanth and removed the gag.

Zanth took a deep breath. 'That was his first taste of power. Imagine it. Arric woke up a dirt-poor orphan. He ended the day famous, a hero with the new king his biggest supporter. Not just that, but he had magic, and talent for it.'

'And he rose to the rank of high priest. Behind the king and my father, he's the most powerful man in the crater.'

'You think that's quenched his thirst? Where does he go from here? The temple is so busy keeping up the sky barrier and joining hunting parties, it can do little else.'

'You're saying he's a megalomaniac?' she asked.

'You just called him a murderer. Is this such a leap?'

'Do his motives matter?' Cal circled around to Zanth's back. 'Even if he has the crater's interests at heart, what he's doing is wrong. It goes against nature, and it's too dangerous.' He readied a knife to cut Zanth free.

Arric didn't leave to find Farikarr. He's watching. This was a test and siding with Zanth failed it. Antarna lifted her hand. 'Stop.'

Enthriff squeezed.

Cal blurred. He split into hazy droplets. They hung, then fell to the ground. None landed, though; they simply vanished.

'Cal!' Antarna drew her sword. She'd find him, whatever it took. Arric wouldn't have teleported him far. The spell must've cost him a steep sum of madriliks, not to mention the strain of it. The sheer magnitude of his power was almost incomprehensible.

'Cut me free,' said Zanth. 'I'll help you save him.'

She took a cautious step forward.

A towering wall of flame cut between her and Zanth. Another arose parallel to it, trapping her between them. She turned her face from the searing heat. Fire ran up a tree trunk and enveloped the crown. Smoke billowed from cracking leaves. She coughed.

At the start of the walls, Arric stood firmly grounded. Dancing flames reflected in his eyes. He bent his knees further as he summoned lightning and fashioned it into a spear. The bright bolts buzzed and hissed.

She reached for the item she'd claimed from the cave.

Arric launched the lightning at her. A sharp clap of thunder eclipsed all other sounds.

Antarna leapt into the fire, shield-first. It parted before the saphramurl in her left hand. As she landed, the opening closed behind her.

Lightning decimated a tree to her left. Had the gem diverted it? Branches crashed to the ground. Flames sprang up.

Antarna hurried towards Zanth. She needed to have the man fight magic with magic. The earth trembled, and Zanth hugged the column, eyes closed. Sharp rocks tore through the soil in front of her. She sprang to the side.

You'll never let me reach him.

The walls of fire went out. Arric strode towards them, desert warriors emerging behind him. One nocked an arrow, drew and released. The man's aim was off. The flightpath changed suddenly, correcting to hit her. Antarna turned and ran.

The arrow tore over Zanth, accelerating. Antarna veered behind a tree, heading to the mound of supplies. Twenty steps away may as well have been two hundred. Swerving around the tree, the arrow pursued. After a glance over her shoulder, Antarna turned left, then right. The arrow zigzagged behind her, changing direction quicker than she had. Antarna launched off a rock and, spinning in the air, slashed at the missile. It spiralled away from her arcing steel, heading for her heart. Still rotating, Antarna extended her shield, saphramurl in hand. Bronze arrowhead met jadrossil hide with a thud, and she landed, chest heaving.

Crouching, she scooped up the arrow, managing to add it to the hand that gripped the shield strap and saphramurl. Desert warriors converged on her position.

A harsh, grating roar burst forth from behind Zanth. A cloud of dust enveloped him. Huge shapes moved within. Light and shadow alternated. The dust dissipated, revealing four stone columns flying horizontally at Antarna.

Not bad, but you'll have to do better than that.

She sprinted to the mound of supplies, only for them to erupt in flames. Ahead of her, a deep crack split along the base of the crumbling wall. It too rose into the air. Antarna turned right, towards the large tree that the warriors had eaten under. The wall glided to block her path, then rushed at her.

A bearded warrior led the charge, a javelin held beside his head with arm bent. After two skips, side-on, he extended his arm back then rotated his shoulders to initiate the release. The missile hurtled towards Antarna.

Ducking under it, she burst forwards, planning to meet the wall head-on. Antarna lengthened her stride. Her sword and shield dragged at her arms.

Warriors closed in from both sides. Behind her, so did the columns. The four hunks of stone formed a wall of their own, flying at her horizontally, one on top of the other.

A kill box. They had her right where they wanted her. But they didn't know what she did.

The wall hastened to her.

The faster the better.

The mortar crumbled between bricks. Moss covered half the wall. A climbing plant clung tight, its roots dragging along the ground.

She pictured two male yalluts crashing together in the forest, antlers locked, females observing but feigning disinterest.

The wall dipped to skim the grass. Perhaps enough room to roll under. Most likely not, and that didn't matter.

She bent her knee, dipped her arms, then exploded upwards. Her leap carried her towards the top of the wall—knowing she'd be unable to clear it. Bracing her shoulder against her shield, she made herself small behind it.

Air buffeted her. A gale of it, galloping ahead of the wall.

Shield met stone. At force.

Vibrations from the impact travelled through her body. She compacted, like a jacket getting stuffed into Cal's already bulging backpack. Her shoulder took the brunt of it.

As Antarna burst through the weaker top section, the wall tore by her. It slammed into the airborne columns and shattered.

After landing, she dashed for the forest. The shadow of the columns chased her down; the wall had done little to delay them.

Three warriors blocked her path. Thick, scaled hide covered their shins, forearms and torsos. Bronze helmets exposed only their eyes and mouths.

Ankles, thighs, elbow and knee joints, upper arms, armpits.

The man on the left advanced, spear at the ready. Though he was taller than her and sinewy, his movements were surprisingly fluid and fast. The warrior on her right swung his mace—its strong, wooden shaft featuring a thick, bronze head. Lumbering forwards set his generous layers of fat into a jiggle. This hid powerful muscles; just one blow could incapacitate her. The third man bounced on the balls of his feet, an axe in hand. A long, slender nose and thin eyebrows perched above a nasty grin. *Picturing your axe in my skull? Good luck with that.*

Antarna held her course. The axeman's smile grew. His eyes darted from her to the pursuing columns.

Three steps out, she deviated to face the man with the mace. He turned his hips and rolled his hands. Having drawn the strike, she sprang clear. An axe arched towards her. It hit her shield aslant, deflecting. Not bothering to counter, Antarna burst through the gap between them.

The columns dipped for her. They should've flattened her attackers. She waited for the screams.

They did not come. Nor did bones snap.

Two of the three materialised in front of her, hazy droplets rushing together. No *fair.* The spearman stumbled, only to catch himself with his weapon. The man with the mace stretched out his arms, his upper body rocking side to side. There was no trace of the axeman.

Antarna closed the gap.

The spearman thrust, now looking lanky. She sidestepped and opened his bicep.

A mace came for her. Ducking under its menacing bronze head, she cut the large man's thigh.

And with that, she took off, leaving them howling.

Sickening crunches cut them short.

Ten steps. The forest beckoned, offering its protection.

Stone flew at her, already flecked with red. She extended her stride, leapt off a rock and curved her back. The column passed underneath her tucked legs. It suddenly froze just off the ground—Arric, the puppet master, not yet done.

Antarna dipped, as if she planned to vault it.

The stone rose.

She slid under. Turning her head, Antarna skinned her cheek against the rough surface.

Emerging into sunlight, she jumped.

The column crashed down, shaking the earth.

Another overtook it.

She dived behind a thick tree.

The column struck. Stone fractured. Wood splintered. Bark and rock whipped by her, along with the two halves of the column, hurtling into the forest. Roots rose around her feet. The trunk split. As it fell, she raised her shield over her head. Leaves rained down around her.

Column versus tree. Both had lost.

She crouched in a triangle of space, the base of the trunk at her back and the rest of it forming a roof over her head. Branches tore at her as she crawled out. She ran into the forest. It blurred around her. Deeper and deeper she plunged. Her dagger banged against her thigh. Warriors pursued, shouting. But with her head start, they stayed out of sight.

When the shouts were but a mere whisper, she stopped. Her arms ached. She set her shield down and lay her sword on top. The saphramurl went into a pocket. Setting her hands on her head, she opened her chest. She slowed her rapid breath, focusing on a long, deep inhale and steady exhale. Seven clumps of moss stretched along a log, staring at her. Antarna turned her back on them.

Five fungi clung to a trunk, half circles, like little shelves. Five; her mistress was with her.

The fungi were rigid, tough.

I ran. I fled.

She couldn't find the words to describe the blue of the mushrooms.

Cal wouldn't struggle with this. Is he alive? She couldn't fight Arric, but Zanth could. More importantly, he could find Cal.

Antarna collected her weapons and began retracing her steps. Birds trilled overhead, still able to find some happiness in this world. Picturing Cal lying bleeding, she picked up the pace.

A pair of small lizards scampered down a branch. Eight thin structures rose along their backs, one after the other. They curved gently, like her sword. They may have been formed similar to the shaft of a feather, or perhaps they were an adaptation of a scale.

What would Cal see when he looked at them? Masts without sails? Flagpoles without flags?

Yes, because masts and flagpoles are curved ... Fool.

The lizards stopped at their prize: dangling ebekkis. The last time she'd eaten one, she'd been a child. Antarna jumped and pulled an ebekki free. The oblong fruit gave a little under her grip. Enthriff lay unmoving. She bit down. While her tongue shrank from the rind, the pulp was sweet and sticky.

An eerie silence fell over the forest. Other than her chewing and footfalls, only a soft buzz rose from a few brave insects.

She kept low, weaving between the odd mushroom almost as large as her. Trees thinned. A dozen desert warriors ringed the pit, each with their back to it. Three pairs patrolled along the edge of the clearing. Another stood by Zanth, whose head hung low. But they wouldn't have been guarding him unless he was still alive.

Within the circle of warriors, a boulder rose into the air, revealing four feet, shins then knees. One wore the crimson robes of Devtakaris, rimmed in black. The other had greaves made from the tough skin of a creature she still couldn't place. As the boulder hovered towards the pit, Snarlark and Arric emerged from behind it. With a thud, the boulder landed beside the pit. A palm-sized circle glowed red on its surface. Molten rock ran from the hole, hissing upon contact with the ground. A tuft of grass caught fire. Earth parted to swallow it.

A warrior brought forth a thin pole, three times as long as Snarlark's halberd and made of neither wood nor metal but something else entirely. It disappeared into the rear side of the boulder only to reappear from the newly fashioned hole moments later. From there, it proceeded to descend into the pit, angled downward.

What would a weapon that harnesses the explosive combination of magic and anti-magic look like? Testing it in a pit in the ground, far from the crater and lake island made perfect sense. The pole could help direct madriliks, with the rock holding it in place.

Arric cut a section of a fallen column into a four-sided pyramid. This rose to his waist. The apex flattened then caved in, leaving a bowl-like depression.

To hold what?

A muscular warrior with deformed ears approached Zanth, punching the air with his unusual dagger. He drew his arm back, preparing to deliver a fatal strike. The exposed neck was the most likely target. There was nothing Antarna could do.

Zanth squeezed his eyes shut. The blade rushed harmlessly by the side of his head. With his fun had, the warrior reached into the bag resting on Zanth's chest and drew out a saphramurl. It was the right size for the depression at the top of the small pyramid.

The pyramid was nowhere to be seen. Its maker stood at the rim of the pit, looking down. Behind him, Arric drew a box from his robes. Strange symbols covered its surface, glowing faintly.

Saphramurl in hand, the warrior proceeded down the ramp. The velengoric growled, only for this to become something more akin to a yelp. A patrol passed her position. Antarna paused and then slunk along the edge of the forest until she was lined up with the ramp. Two men held the door open. A wall of flames separated the creature from the warrior inside the pit.

Poor thing. Probably the first time such words had ever been used to describe a velengoric. She recalled the fierce heat and acrid smoke of the walls Arric had raised against her.

The warrior placed the saphramurl on the pyramid and left. The end of the dark rod that pierced the boulder stopped just short of the saphramurl, pointing directly at it.

Leaves crunched behind her. A shape moved behind a bush. A spear tip bobbed above. Another patrol?

Bronze glinted to her left. An archer nocked an arrow—his umber, uninked skin identifying him as one of the crater. He wouldn't have been hiding so if he was with the high priest.

The Resatrium.

The rebels didn't stand a chance against Arric, not without a mage. Odds were, Zanth was the only one they had. Their plan would thus involve part of her own: free Zanth. Arric would never let the Resatrium get close enough. But the high priest would have a much harder time stopping her. She put her hand into her pocket, and her fingers found the smooth surface of the gem.

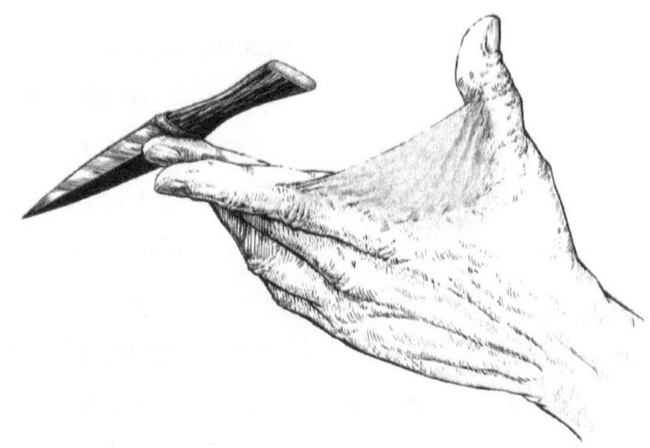

48. Sceptical

THE cold stone column at Cal's back sapped his heat, and he shivered. Vines and tendrils coiled tighter around him, stilling his limbs. The climbing plant had embraced him moments after Arric had teleported him here. Wherever here was.

Six columns rose around him, wrapped in vines. Flowers dotted them—white or silver, it was hard to tell. His vision blurred. Dizziness overtook him, his head light and buoyant. Only his bindings kept him from falling, and for that, Cal was thankful.

Maybe I'm bleeding out? He'd lost feeling in his legs some time ago. He could be cut and not know it, his life leaking from his thigh or calf. That should've disturbed him, but he'd spent too much of his life worrying. Life was for living. Perhaps the smooth vines gripped him so tightly to stop the bleeding and save his life.

The vine's leaves flaunted their beauty, a vivid green beyond compare. The sweet fragrance of the flowers caressed his nostrils.

Bleeding out can't feel like this. If the vines were preventing blood from reaching his legs, maybe he had too much going to his head. But that didn't seem right either.

The nearby clash of weapons and screams of anger and pain pulled at the veil of tranquillity, threatening to dislodge it. Cal turned his head towards the commotion—one of the few parts of his body he could move. The sounds cleared his mind. Arric hadn't teleported him far. *Are you alive, Tarna?* She was a survivor, bold and strong. If anyone could make it through, it'd be her.

Last night, he'd broken his oath to his goddess when he'd taken steps to save Antarna from her fated death. *Sorry, Thelia.* Maybe his goddess could find it in herself to forgive him—after all, he'd intervened while Antarna slept, without speaking to her, writing to her or touching her. Last night seemed like a faint dream.

A man materialised on a rock before Cal, solidifying in the shimmering air. Armour covered his body and tattoos his skin. He ducked, shielding his head with his arms from a blow that never came. The man looked behind him. 'The column ... was going to crush me.' He dropped to his knees and then noticed Cal. 'You!'

'Me?'

'You're that seer.' He grounded the handle of his axe and used it to help him rise to his feet. Thin cracks ran up the wood. A nick marred the blade.

'Yes.' The word bought him a precious moment to think. 'Which is why I know Arric teleported you here to bring me back to him.'

'Is that so?' He seemed sceptical.

What reason would I have to lie to you? That sounded bad enough in his head and would only get worse if he voiced it. Being tied up in the middle of nowhere didn't put him in a strong position—like trying to sell expensive wares wearing rags and with squid ink smeared on your cheeks.

Cal's silence must have played to his favour, for the warrior dusted himself off and approached, unsteady on his feet. He had long limbs and a slender, elongated nose.

Silver pollen drifted in the air, reminiscent of stardust shimmering in the night sky. A sweeter perfume he'd never smelt.

A vine slithered for the warrior, and he had the sense to step back. 'Arric teleported me for a reason. Maybe I'm meant to kill you.'

Cal laughed, loud and free. He couldn't stop. The sound rushed out of his mouth, gracing the heavens.

The man chuckled, then joined him in roaring laughter.

Obliterated

Zanth lifted his head. The ring of desert warriors expanded, putting some more distance between them and the saphramurl in the pit.

He'd expected something more sophisticated than a rod through a rock pointing at an anti-magic gem in a pit. Other designs sprang to mind, each employing magic in a different manner—like a box containing a bright madrilik and a saphramurl that shrinks until they're forced to touch. And yet, therein lay the supremacy of Arric's approach: it used raw madriliks and not a single spell. The rod allowed the high priest to channel madriliks to the saphramurl from a safer distance. The saphramurl would resist the madriliks. But Arric could launch ten thousand specks of power at it: a never-ending torrent of arrows, each perfectly on target. One would find its mark. The pit would help to contain the ensuing explosion and put Arric above the blast.

If Arric could unlock the immense power unleashed by magic and anti-magic annihilating each other, the possibilities were endless. A small blast to take out a nest of predators, even those with hides typically resistant to magic. A large one for mining. The threat of the ungodly weapon would be enough to crush the Resatrium and to extort tribute from the lake island, desert and cavern.

He remembered Arric's earlier words: "Too few are born with magic." With sufficient experimentation, a mage may have been able to create a device with a single madrilik and sliver of a saphramurl inside it and hand it to a warrior to set off at the appropriate time—a portable explosive to rival the most powerful magic.

None of this should have been possible. When a spy within the palace had warned the Resatrium of the impending weapons test in the glade, Zanth had been tasked with stealing the saphramurls. And, against all odds, he'd done so.

Yet here we are. It was all for naught.

The guard nearby him blew wood shavings off his wooden carving of a scorpion. He pocketed the piece, threw his knife into the air and caught it. It would only be a matter of time before they turned the knife on him for information on the Resatrium. It was ironic how dispensable he'd been while in the Order, but valuable now.

I'm not going to tell you a thing. Or maybe I'll just lie through my teeth. Though, if Arric handled the torture, he'd force his way into Zanth's mind.

Dark clouds threatened to swallow his last sunset.

A warrior screamed, pointing up. Arrows filled the sky. Those with shields took cover behind them. A score of armed men of the crater and lake island burst from the forest. The Resatrium. His brothers in arms and cause.

You did it, Prann.

Salvation. Freedom. Revenge. All were within his grasp.

His weariness dissipated. Zanth strained anew against his bonds. He welcomed the stinging, the chafing.

Arric swept the arrows off course with a blast of wind and then uprooted a tree, felling it onto three attackers. Several more of his Resatrium brothers fell under arrows and javelins unleashed by desert warriors. *Zentrina will reward your bravery and sacrifice.*

The two groups charged at each other. Battle cries overtook the screams of the injured. The masses of bodies drew closer and then collided. Heavy. Brutal.

A hammer went through a desert warrior's skull.

One of his brothers was lifted clear into the air, impaled by a spear.

A club snapped a shield. A knife broke against armour. An axe took an ear.

The Resatrium had the numbers, for now.

Two of its members broke through.

Cut me free! Zanth knew better than to shout it.

The pair slumped to the ground, eyes rolling into the backs of their heads. Hopefully, Arric's spell had only knocked them out. The high priest was never going to let the Resatrium reach him. Without anyone to oppose his former mentor, this was far from a fair fight.

Arric turned to the guard beside Zanth. 'Kill him, *then* take the saphramurls.'

Not so valuable after all.

'Told you this was coming. I'm going to enjoy this.' The warrior advanced, closing a fist-like grip over the crossbars of his punch dagger and drawing it from its sheath.

Zanth emptied his lungs and closed his eyes. Out of the darkness, Silisa emerged, radiant in white. A smile bloomed across her heart-shaped face. The dark freckles atop her lifted cheeks were the same colour as her loosely curled hair. She wrapped her warm arms around him, exploring his back. Raising onto tippytoes, she leant in, mouth parting. Her hand rose along the back of his neck, into his hair. He met her soft lips.

Something brushed by his arm. Silisa dissipated, a shadow into mist. *Don't go, my love.*

The dagger came for his neck.

Steel flashed by, opening his guard's arm. A boot crunched into the man's face, silencing his scream.

Antarna stood beside him, resolute. Her next swing cut his bindings.

A curse flew towards her. Zanth ripped the bag of saphramurls from his neck and lunged forwards, holding it at full stretch. The curse disbanded before the power of the anti-magic gems.

'Don't think that makes us even.' Antarna snatched the bag from him and pocketed it. 'Where's Cal?'

'We've got bigger problems.' Without his nalitroite necklace, Arric could see Zanth's meagre store. The high priest's chest shone.

'No, we don't.'

Snarlark summited a pile of rubble, blood dripping from his weapon. Antarna tensed beside Zanth. The desert warrior rushed down the slope, and Antarna cut a path to meet him.

Widening his stance, Arric raised a defensive ward around himself and his abomination of a device.

Zanth walked towards Arric, doing his best to appear calm. 'Everyone will find out what you're doing here.' He drew upon a middler to establish a protective barrier.

'They will find out what we tell them. And they will honour Devtakaris for it.'

'Yes, lie to them and claim the glory for yourself. That's about right.' Zanth drained another middler to add a second layer to his defence, saving his brights. 'What did you tell the families of the priests that died in the glade? The lie about the hazzurus?'

'Zentrina embraced them warmly. She will not do the same to you.' An intense flash burst from Arric.

A direct block would be costly on his reserves. Saving his madriliks, Zanth threw himself out of the way of the disintegration spell. His outstretched arms landed first, absorbing some of the impact. Rocks dug into him as he rolled on the ground. Behind Zanth, the spell struck a magnificent tree. The leaves faded first, leaving the long branches bare. Next, the bark, stripping the last of the tree's dignity. The rest of the tree dissolved without a sound or a shudder, until only a gaping hole in the earth remained. Zanth drew upon a dull to rise to his feet and propel himself towards Arric.

As the high priest released a pair of dark hexes, a large desert warrior charged Zanth, leading with his spear.

Yes, come make yourself useful. Zanth lifted the spearman in front of him. The hexes struck the man and twisted his body like someone wringing water from a wet shirt. Bones snapped. The chest caved in, and his head spun backwards. Blood rained down.

Zanth caught the man's spear. The wooden shaft was reassuring in his hand. He pictured driving the point into Arric's cold heart.

A jagged bolt of lightning tore through the sky above Zanth and, before he could react, broke through his outer defensive barrier. But his inner layer held. Only three body lengths separated Arric from him.

He sprinted, closing the gap. With the disparity in madriliks, he'd be a fool to trade spells with the high priest. If he could just get close ...

Curved talons materialised in front of Zanth—floating talons longer than his legs. They raked the face of his barrier, which wavered and then shattered. He dispelled the talons.

One body length. Dipping into his madriliks, Zanth depleted three brights and unleashed a fierce torrent of orange-yellow fire. His knees bent under the exertion of the spell. With luck, his former mentor would think he was making the same mistake he'd made in their last encounter. But the flames concealed the real threat: the weapon in his hands that Zanth was almost close enough to plunge into the man's chest.

Arric fought fire with fire. Blazing blue flames burst forth from him, hotter and stronger than Zanth's. The spear caught fire, and with it his plan. *Flay me.* Zanth dropped the weapon and redoubled his efforts, his body straining together with his mind. The intense heat burnt his hands and baked his lungs. His feet slid backwards in the face of the onslaught. The blue inferno closed in around Zanth, searing his cheeks. Death had never been closer.

With his last bright, Zanth threw up a shield and leapt wide. Fire battered the magical barrier, threatening to tear through. His face hit the ground, and, finally, the flames stopped. The bitter earth tasted better than his fear and his failure.

Blood, gore and death surrounded him. His Resatrium brothers were overwhelmed—but refusing to retreat. Antarna and Snarlark circled each other.

The ground quaked. Across the clearing, thrashing roots burst from the earth. Zanth rolled wide of one. Yet, up close, it was insubstantial, a mere illusion cast by Arric. That man had used half of his madriliks. Zanth's reservoir held but a measly trio of middlers.

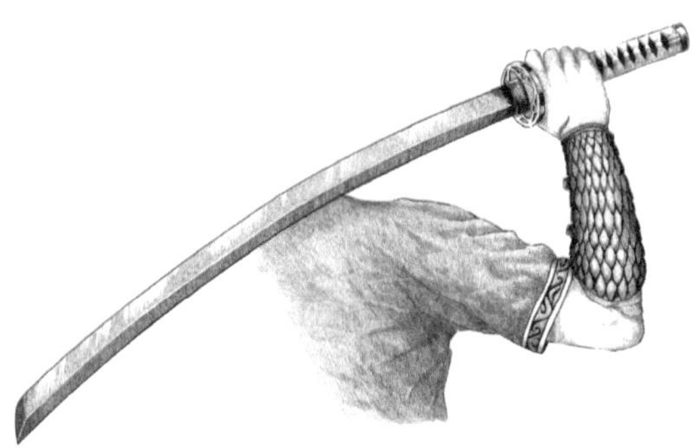

50. Poison

A twisting vine stretched for her. Antarna readied her sword, but strangely, Enthriff seemed unperturbed.

Opposite her, Snarlark slashed at a vine. His weapon passed right through the plant—unless her eyes deceived her.

An illusion.

Antarna accelerated towards Snarlark. On the back foot, he defended well. In her haste to land a strike, she accidentally stepped through a false vine. The deception broke.

Snarlark yelled the truth out to his men. With a series of diagonal strikes, he advanced, alternating between the axe blade and the hook. She tried to find a way through, but his reach advantage was too much. It was as though she held a knife, not a sword.

She withdrew and adjusted her grip. 'Where is Cal, the lake island seer? Did you kill him?'

Snaking out his forked tongue, Snarlark licked his lips. His dark eyes were like wet, smooth obsidian glinting in the sun. A shiver ran through him. 'Your pain, it's delicious.'

'I hope you enjoy your own.' He reminded her of Revertika standing in the fighting ring after having broken Uloron's nose, delighting in his opponent's agony. *Another pain empath.* It explained Snarlark's choice of poison: one that heightened suffering. She'd have to minimise the damage she took.

As she moved to flank him, he sidestepped, the tip of the halberd trained on her. Before she could get within range, he thrust, fluid and precise. She changed directions, avoiding it. Within a blink, Snarlark had withdrawn the shaft and reset, ready to strike again.

Antarna pressed forwards only for the space to be occupied by the point of the halberd. And so it continued, Snarlark keeping her in front of him. She tried a height change, but with reach came leverage, and it only took a small movement at the back end of the shaft to generate a large movement at the point.

After three more strikes, his sweeping blow struck her jadrossil-hide shield. The impact reverberated through her. She struggled to keep her arm up and her legs under her.

The next attack came swiftly, while her limbs still shook. She sought to deflect it, but his two-handed strike ripped through her defence, opening her shoulder. Searing pain tore through her like a wildfire backed by a gale. The deep wound swam with blood.

He unleashed a fluid combination, whipping the steel tip into a blur. Dodging and ducking, Antarna retreated. Still, she had no answers to his speed. Having drawn blood, Snarlark was the predator, and she was the injured prey. He directed her back and to her left. Try as she might, there was nothing she could do to avoid it. Her next step was longer than she'd expected. Antarna was on the edge of a sloped path. It led to the animal cage: a dead end.

That's a shortcut to the grave.

Snarlark sliced at her.

Anticipating it, she ducked under the blade and leapt to close the gap.

He rushed his hands up the shaft—shortening the weapon—and reversed the slice. Torchlight glinted off the hook of the halberd.

Antarna got ahead of it, blocking with her sword where the head met the shaft. Vibrations travelled along her blade and down her tensed arm. The smouldering fire in her shoulder burst into flame, high and savage. The clash of steel filled her ears. She slid her sword down the shaft towards his unprotected hands.

Enthriff squeezed her wrist.

Snarlark had one foot planted, the other loaded. He kicked, muscles flexing.

There was no time to react. His heavy boot slammed into her chest. It knocked the breath out of her and propelled her into the air. Antarna landed on her bloodied shoulder. Her head smashed into the dirt. She tumbled over and over.

Everything blurred. The world. Her thoughts. Time.

She couldn't breathe.

Her shoulder was a raging inferno.

A powerful force squeezed her skull.

All storms pass.

Wherever the thought had come from, it brought her back. Her shield was still attached to her arm, and her dagger and sword were close. She collected them and struggled to her feet, sword heavy in her hand. Raising it up, she fought the pain. It was stronger than her. She gritted her teeth, dropping her arm but refusing to release the sword.

Snarlark sauntered down the slope.

You can't always wait out a storm.

She hauled up her sword, pitting her full determination against the agony.

'My poison was just getting started, but your pain is almost over.' Snarlark swept at her.

On unsteady legs, Antarna stepped back.

'You're a disgrace to your family.' He brought the next blow to her torso.

She deflected it off her slanted shield.

He reversed the motion. The backside hook caught her shield. He pulled with the force of three men. Antarna released her grip, dropping her dagger in the process, but the strap caught awkwardly on her arm. He yanked it free. She fell forwards onto her knees.

Snarlark sank the halberd's spike into her chest.

51. Eerie Silence

Zanth nursed his tender, stinging hands as he staggered to his feet. The red, uneven skin had begun to swell. Grasping a middler, he drained it and flung a particularly nasty curse at Arric—one to melt the flesh and addle the mind.

Arric deflected it towards a bulky Resatrium warrior, forcing Zanth to untie the curse before it struck.

A root erupted from the ground, snared Zanth's leg and wrenched him down. Another curled around his throat and squeezed, taking his next breath. He clawed at the tough root, unable to get his fingers under it. Darkness narrowed his vision. Desperate for air, Zanth called upon his magic, but it refused his call. With the last of his focus, he tried again. A middler answered, and he used it to obliterate the roots. Zanth sagged to the ground, gasping.

Arric's illusion now made sense: it'd been cover for him to call actual roots to do his bidding. One tiny light floated within Zanth's chest, all that was left of his stores.

Behind him, a ramp led down to the entry to the cage. Snarlark kicked Antarna off the tip of his weapon. She tumbled, body limp, lifeless.

Arric drained more madriliks from his reservoir than Zanth had used in this battle. A pair of dark curses formed, wrapped in a hex and then encased in a jinx. With intricate detail and confusing complexity, the curses were unidentifiable to Zanth.

C.U.B.E. A lone middler wasn't enough to mount a Counterattack with. The incoming spells were too powerful to Untie or Block. Zanth didn't like his chances of being able to Evade; Arric would redirect the spell.

But that gave him an idea. He relinquished his defensive barrier, already weakened by the fire. Using his last madrilik, Zanth spewed fog from his burnt fingertips. The thick cloud obscured visibility, and, with his reservoir dry, he'd be hard to find on the magical plane.

Two steps backwards took him to the edge of the ramp. Snarlark had departed. As the curse-hex-jinx bundle burst through the fog, he circled his arms over his head, leaping back. The spells separated, searching for their target.

He fell.

Not fast enough.

The hex collided with his foot. White-hot pain shot up his leg. An explosion seared the air. It shoved him to the ground and battered him with wind. A harsh echo hammered at his ears.

The echo gave way to eerie silence. He slid down the slope, gathering speed. Twisting, Zanth faced his feet downhill. Blood oozed from a toeless lump of raw flesh and jagged skin. Pieces of the hex scurried over the surface, reassembling.

A voracious flesh eater.

His good foot landed on a steel bar, halting his fall. Gritting his teeth, Zanth grabbed the bars and hauled himself to standing. Clinging to the steel, four fingers blurred into eight, before multiplying again. He blinked and turned at a faint noise behind him.

A tattooed warrior stepped onto the stone retaining wall. He slid his dagger into its sheath and took a javelin from his back.

Not like this.

A vine erupted from the ground and wrapped around Zanth's waist, securing him against a bar.

The warrior released the javelin. It flew true.

Zanth squeezed his eyes shut.

Contact. Square on his chest.

He flew backwards through the bars, and the vine snapped.

I'm coming, Silisa.

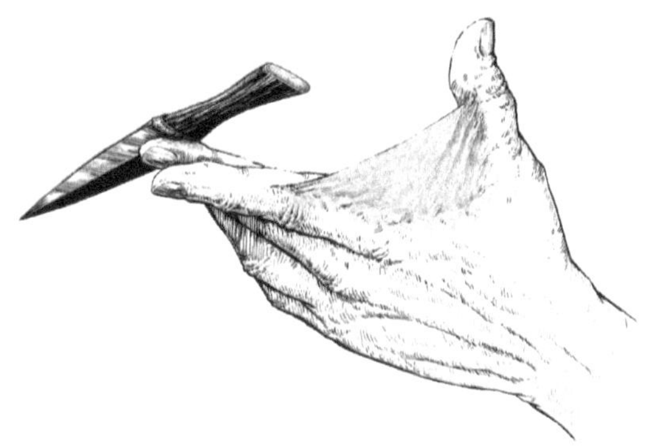

52. The End

THE vines held Cal prisoner. Were they carnivorous and feeding on him out of sight? How he'd ever thought they were friendly was beyond him.

Colour had leached from the world. Shadows stalked him, and they were everywhere.

'Maybe I'm meant to kill you.' The desert warrior pointed his axe at Cal. Its metallic head came in and out of focus.

It wasn't funny this time, not in the slightest. 'What if you're meant to guard me?'

'Only Arric and the gods know that.' He looked up. 'Yes, the gods will guide me.' The man fished into his pocket and withdrew a coin. He showed Cal the two sides: a desert creature with a stinger on one and a criss-crossing pattern on the other. 'If you're meant to live, this will land pattern-side up.'

'Wait! Let's be rational.'

He loaded the coin onto his thumbnail, almost dropping it in the process.

'No, stop.' Cal struggled against nature's binds. Sweat trickled down his forehead and stung his eyes.

The man flicked the coin into the air. It spun, life on one side, death on the other. The coin reached its zenith and hung suspended, the moment dragging long. Then it fell.

Panic gripped Cal tighter than the vines. *This can't be the end.* He had yet to fall in love, buy his mum a house or paint his dad's portrait as it should be.

The coin landed on the warrior's outstretched hand. Cal couldn't breathe. The warrior advanced, one leg straying in front of the other, and the back foot dragging on the ground. He used his axe like a walking stick. Even still, he staggered—and it wasn't just Cal's vision.

Leaning on his axe, the man extended his swaying palm.

Cal hesitated, then looked down. The face of the coin depicted a desert creature with a stinger. Death. A fitting punishment for breaking his oath to his goddess. He met the warrior's gaze; his dilated pupils had almost swallowed his irises.

The warrior curled his lips and took his coin-hand to his axe.

53. A Cup of Tea

Antarna rolled off Zanth and dug her fingers into the earth. 'You're still with us.'

Her shoulder had hit his chest before the weapon. The javelin stuck out from the earth behind them, its tip buried deep.

The halberd hadn't missed her, though. *How am I alive?* Her fingers found the slice in her armour and sensitive skin underneath. The weapon should've pierced her heart, but she wasn't even cut. It made no sense.

Zanth screamed, hands stretching towards his misshapen foot. Not a single toe. His muscles, veins and the odd bone lay exposed between a patchwork of blistered skin.

Must stop the bleeding. She rose to a knee beside him.

Bloodied, but not dripping from the foot, nor pooling under it. It had yet to clot but did not flow.

Strange.

Brown smoke rose from the end of the foot. It smelt like the kitchen of the royal palace before a feast, fat dripping from the spit roast onto the fire.

A piece of skin shrank. It didn't curl in on itself, it was plainly disappearing.

'Can you stop the spell?'

He shook his head with a grimace. Tucking his chin, his eyes rose from foot to chest. 'Empty.'

Enthriff applied pressure.

A deep growl rose from the shadows. Primal.

Zanth crawled to hide behind the saphramurl-topped pyramid.

Spiralling horns emerged first. Longer than her dagger, shorter than her sword. Sharp enough to gut her with a casual flick.

Dark slits cut down vivid yellow eyes. Trained on her. The velengoric tossed its head, sending its mane flying.

'I set you free, remember.' Slowly, Antarna laid her sword down. She could barely hold it anyway.

'What are you doing?' Zanth asked out of the corner of his mouth.

After a snort, the creature advanced parallel to them, showing off just how large it was. Its weight must have been that of ten men. Widening its stance, the predator lowered its head. Its tail rippled.

Antarna slunk away from Zanth. Large hooves pawed the earth. Bending at the knees, she readied herself.

The velengoric charged. Its powerful legs quickly closed the gap.

Antarna feigned left. *Follow me.*

The creature adjusted course.

That's it. She leapt right.

Turning with greater agility than should be possible for something of its size, the velengoric pursued.

Antarna dipped then exploded up, arms stretching for the bars. She wasn't sure if she'd reach them; it'd be close. Her fingertips brushed the steel, and her hands closed around the bars.

The creature's horns lunged for her. With a swift, desperate movement, she lifted her legs up and to the side. The velengoric thundered by, dangerously close.

She landed softly, absorbing the impact. As the creature spun, she grabbed the javelin and raised its point.

They circled.

'What a show,' said Arric from the top of the pit, beside the boulder and the dark rod. 'I'd enjoy seeing you ripped to shreds. But I need test subjects.' A box floated out from his robe. The lid rose, yet the box appeared empty. She turned to Zanth.

He jerked his head back and blinked.

'What?' she asked.

'Madriliks. Morsirel's store. Others too. Hiding on him, out of sight.'

She pictured the box brimming with dazzling specks—raw power at the high priest's disposal.

Head low, the velengoric shrank back.

Streaks of vermillion ran down the length of the rod from top to bottom. Arric must have been channelling madriliks down the rod. It had begun, a battle of opposites: magic vs anti-magic. If they touched, it would be all over.

The saphramurl glowed, brighter and brighter. It sat snugly in a depression at the apex of the pyramid. Zanth tore a hand from his leg and raised it in front of his eyes to guard against the onslaught of blinding light.

Wind lashed her and Zanth. Violent, it burst from the narrow gap between the madriliks and saphramurl. She hunched against it. A fierce heat radiated from the gemstone. Pressure built in Antarna's skull. Her feet slid backwards, and she dug her boot into the soil. Liquid ran from her nose onto her lips. She snaked out her tongue. Blood.

Deep inside her ears, discomfort grew. As she would climbing the summit, she pinched her nose and blew air into them. Instead of a satisfying little pop, the rhythmic thump of her heart filled her head. Then came a wetness. She touched her earlobe, coming away with red fingertips.

The gale snatched the smoke from Zanth's calf. His head fell limply to the side. His body relaxed.

She shook Zanth's shoulder. 'Wake up.'

Above, Arric stood, tense. She'd never reach him.

With the force pounding upon the saphramurl and its heat, even if she could reach it, she didn't stand a chance of freeing it. But if she could sever the rod ... It looked tough and crystal-like. There was only one way to know whether the material was a match for steel. Antarna raised her sword.

'That'll kill you, Princess.' Arric's voice invaded her head.

She smiled, arcing her sword. Her arm fell, all her might behind it. Steel struck the rod.

A force slammed into her, lifting her clean into the air. More powerful than if she'd taken a bucking velengoric's hind hooves square in the chest. Vibrations racked her body. Clinging to her blade, she tumbled over and over. Antarna plunged her sword into the ground.

Wind rushed by, escaping up the ramp. She could too. It would even carry her out.

Out to Cal … If you're alive.

Back to Tozias … If you're alive.

The rod bore but a faint scratch.

The squall intensified. And the heat. The light, too.

It's over.

She'd thought the same, grappling a serpent head with each hand, having the life squeezed out of her, alone in the cavern. But Cal had burst in, the queen and her horde right behind, and had proved her wrong.

Antarna took a step forwards. Then another. And another. A wave of nausea rose. She dropped to a knee and retreated into her mind. There, Tozias handed her a cup of tea and took a seat at the long table where Parsannon laughed with the youngsters.

She rose. For Tozias and for Cal.

The last of Zanth's calf faded, eaten.

Five more steps.

54. Diseased Rodents

Zanth woke to heat. Scorching heat.

Madriliks poured into him, a waterfall of them from the rod. A crushing force on his rib cage. Bright and hot and powerful. Beautiful, even. The specks filled his reservoir and pinned him to the pyramid. The saphramurl dug into his back. It sat silent. Wedged between the end of the rod and pyramid, his body shielded the gemstone.

Antarna lay beside by his remaining foot, unmoving. He pictured her battling the wind, facing the heat, hauling him up against the pressure. She'd saved them, stopping the explosion he'd thought was inevitable. And with madriliks in his chest again, she'd given them a fighting chance.

The curse ate at his thigh like a hungry pack of diseased rodents.

He called to a middler inside him. It responded, but then a bright crashed into it, and the middler disappeared into the churning mass of madriliks. He shifted his focus to the bright only for it to ignore him, overwhelmed and overexcited. *Come on.* Zanth tried again, unsuccessfully.

Tilting back his head, he screamed, channelling his hurt and frustration.

Zanth shoved the madriliks. They slid from his chest to his stomach before bouncing back. Not letting them settle, he pushed again. They dropped to his hips. *Once more*. This time, they fell to his thighs. Caught in the frenzy of madriliks, the curse disbanded. The excruciating pain began to release its stranglehold.

At the source of the madriliks stood the high priest.

Uncanny. Life had come full circle. Arric had ruined the Resatrium's plans by jumping into the stream of madriliks that Layaury saturated the king with.

'Don't look so smug,' Arric said telepathically. 'Why haven't I pulled back?'

You ... have the same intention as Layaury.

His reservoir had been bone-dry. Now it was close to bursting.

Stretching an arm wide, he grabbed the edge of the pyramid. His hand pulled away from the scorching stone. *If I could just use magic*. After shaking it cool, he clamped his hand down and heaved. He peeled his other shoulder off the pyramid and reached across his body.

Madriliks pummelled him back, refusing to release him. Even though he could no longer contain them. Overflowing and drunk on energy, their every movement built heat inside him. Drenched in sweat, he grabbed the apex of the pyramid, hooked his foot on the corner of the side, and tried to pry himself free. To no avail.

The symbol-covered box fell to the ground, empty. Arric released madriliks in his chest, hurtling them down the rod.

A crack ran down Zanth's reservoir. Then another.

His body too was on the edge. At any moment, his ribs could fracture or skull rupture.

Blood spilled from his nose. As it had in the glade those years ago, immersed in madriliks at the bottom of the pond. He'd shrunk in fear then. He wouldn't now.

Clenching his fists, bending at the knees, Zanth threw his will into reinforcing the sides of his reservoir. But not the base. Instead, he pulled at that crack. Urged the madriliks into it. Forced them ever down.

The crack spread. It widened. Tears ran down his cheeks.

The madriliks breached.

And flowed down to a second reservoir. *I have one*. Six years ago, he hadn't believed Arric. He hadn't believed in himself.

'You underestimate me,' Zanth said. 'I'm not who I once was.'

'You're not so different.' Arric stoppered the flow of his madriliks.

As he did so, Zanth grabbed hold of the stream and yanked. Compelling it forwards. Calling it into him.

The stopper burst free. Arric fell to a knee, madriliks pouring forth again. 'I invented that move before I knew I had the gift. Before you were even born.' He bared his teeth and sealed his supply.

Antarna stirred beside Zanth. He lifted them out of the pit, landing on the grass. A little magic kept him steady on one leg.

Thunder boomed.

Arric turned a tree branch into sharp stakes and launched these at him. Zanth separated the flying wooden stakes, as Arric had done to him on the rim of the crater. The high priest was mocking him, recreating that attack.

Zanth wiped sweat from his brow. Arric's words echoed in his head: '*Fear of the test kept you awake. Fear of dying. That's why you fled.*' He remembered Lisoun's and Ezro's bravery, taking on the high priest with orb and arrow. Around him, Resatrium warriors gave their lives for the cause. He had to be fearless.

Grabbing handfuls of brights, Zanth clawed at the sky above Arric and away from Antarna.

The fabric of the sky frayed and stretched, then tore. Fist-sized. Ink-black. Unworldly. Opening to a place of certain death—an airless, lifeless nothingness.

The hole inhaled. A dagger took to the air and disappeared. A branch followed. Next, a helmet.

Arric summoned vines to wrap around his legs, securing himself to the ground, and raised a protective shield.

The vines ran deep. Zanth withered them, and Arric's foot came off the earth. Then Zanth slashed at the edges of the hole, opening it wider.

With a desperate scream, a flailing warrior was sucked into the insatiable blackness.

The high priest left the ground. Shining threads of energy spiralled from the stumps of his shoulders and wrapped around Zanth's chest. With a sudden yank, they dragged him into the air. Tethered together, the vortex pulled them ever closer. Zanth sent a crackling bolt toward Arric, but the high priest's magic intercepted it with a brilliant flash. One after the other, spells clashed, sending shockwaves through the damaged sky. Even with all the madriliks at Zanth's disposal, he couldn't seize the upper hand. He hurtled backwards towards the vortex with his former master further out.

Arric had the audacity to grin. Of all things, to grin. As if Zanth had never been his match. As if Arric had been right all along.

Zanth wrenched upon the tether and simultaneously gave in to the vortex's pull. He dragged Arric towards him, the man's dark eyes bulging and nostrils flaring. When only a body-length separated them, the high priest severed the binding.

Close to the suffocating blackness, the whirlwind grabbed them, fiercer now. A freezing cold cut through Zanth, seeping out from the lifeless darkness. Nothing could survive in there. Not even a powerful mage.

Arric desperately poured his magic into closing the hole. Zanth turned his to widening it. The hole constricted, expanded, then constricted again. They were locked in a battle of might, a battle of wills, and Zanth was losing.

Amidst the chaos, the obscure barrier between planes came into focus. Shimmering fractures radiated out from the hole, slowly repairing themselves.

Death catches the stagnant.

Siphoning as much power as he could muster, Zanth unleashed it at a single fracture. One running by him towards Arric.

Silisa, find me in my next life.

A violent tremor spread along the fractures, and they ruptured, bursting open. The sky folded inwards, helpless against the endless void that drained air and life and warmth.

Horrified, Arric opened his mouth to scream or curse, but it was too late.

Darkness devoured them.

55. A Cup of Blood

The great gash in the sky shuddered closed. The dark veins that had spread from it faded. As the gale ceased, an airborne corpse thudded to the ground. The wind hadn't troubled Antarna though, not with the vortex facing away from her. If she'd had a rope, maybe she could've saved Zanth. *Greet him well, Zentrina.*

Snarlark advanced, alternating stances, weapon high. Slow. Cautious. 'But I killed you?'

'You tried.'

'I drove this point into your heart.' He raised it high.

'Zentrina sent me back for you,' she lied. The mystery of her survival could wait for the battle to finish.

'Your goddess didn't think that through. You can barely hold that sword.'

Circling, she kept her shield forwards. The shield handle and dagger, point down, fitted snugly in her good hand.

I am water.

He swung, the halberd's axe blade rushing at her. She deflected it off her shield and slashed. Snarlark brought the back hook for her leg. Her dagger and shield were waiting, but with unnatural speed, he lifted the strike over them.

Redirecting her slash, Antarna blocked the attack with her sword, halting the hook just shy of her eye. Her shoulder screamed. Reopened, her wound dribbled blood down her chest and arm.

With blades locked, he pushed against her. She angled her weapon, sending his high as she ducked under.

His foul tongue flicked out, and his eyes lingered on her injured shoulder. There was no hiding pain from an empath.

The faintest streak of poison glistened on the axe blade. A memory crawled from a dark recess: she wriggled under the table towards her convulsing brother, only for her own limbs to spasm. But she couldn't change the past. Not her own or Salorann's.

Antarna tucked her elbow to her ribs. *Be fluid.*

Snarlark feigned to her shield, then struck for her right side.

She sidestepped.

Pressing forwards, he came for her injured arm. Like a true predator.

After half a dozen strikes, he ripped her blade from her weak grip. It tumbled along the ground, coming to rest beside a decapitated body.

Be adaptable. She transferred her dagger to her right hand.

The muscles in his arms tensed.

I am wind.

He thrust.

Antarna withdrew.

A high sweeping strike came next. She avoided contact and advanced to counter. But Snarlark cross-stepped and thrust to her face. Ducking and retreating, she kept moving.

His attacks grew faster. Stronger. Ever closer to connecting.

Her dagger felt as though it had the weight of a longsword and the reach of a table knife.

Around them, Resatrium warriors fell, one by one.

Her shirt clung to her, soaked through. She'd lost at least a cup of blood. The cut was a ravine, deep and narrow. Her pain demanded to be heard. She listened, letting it fill her up, and lowered the dagger to rest the butt upon her hip.

His body dipped. Snarlark thrust high, taking the lure.

Her pain was nothing—nothing compared to what she'd been through and what was at stake.

I am fire.

She slipped the halberd's point, like she would a punch. As it passed her ear, she caught the inside edge of the axe blade with her dagger. Her other hand shot for the shaft and grabbed tight.

They struggled. She lifted her leg and stomped on his knee. He let go of the halberd, and she did, too.

Stepping forwards, Antarna stabbed low, below his body armour. Her dagger sank into the meat of his thigh. He bled red; she'd almost been expecting another colour.

Snarlark drew his knife and swiped at her. She took a step back and to the side, keeping herself between him and the resting halberd. For the first time, she had the reach advantage—her blade half again as long as his. With a hand on his injured leg, Snarlark glanced at his fallen halberd and then behind him towards the swirling fog that had come from Zanth's fingertips. Masking his pain and with his blood slicking his hand, Snarlark lacked his characteristic confidence.

And then it returned, his chin held high. 'Follow me if you dare.' He limped into the fog.

I dare.

Fog encircled her legs, reaching for her midsection. Moist like a cloud but not as cold as those that often enveloped the mountain peak. Shadows danced in the thick, white haze. Antarna proceeded slowly, carefully. The fog devoured her. Part of her hungered to kill; the image of Garlin's near-decapitated head would forever haunt her. But a deeper part resisted—ever loyal to the teachings of Zentrina.

Taunt me. Be foolish. Open your mouth and give away your position. No, this was no fireside tale. Either Snarlark stood still or moved as she did.

He'd know where she was by the throbbing of her shoulder. *Damn empath. Well, since you're aware …* 'I knew you were a coward. I told you so in our first fight.'

Enthriff applied gentle pressure.

Hand raised before her, she slid it across her body. *Which way*? He paused then pulsed. She turned to expose her back. His grip tightened.

Just a little closer.

She tensed, aggravating her shoulder. Enthriff eased.

'Where are you?' She cleaved the fog to her right.

The force on her wrist grew again. Snarlark lunged, coming at her from the side. She spun and slashed his weapon hand.

Dropping the knife, he reached for it with his other hand. Another slice from her forced him to withdraw it.

With her blade pointing at his chest, she advanced. Snarlark retreated out of the fog. The cage sat at his back. She manoeuvred him towards it, just as he'd done before driving the halberd's spike for her heart.

Snarlark unleashed a shin kick. She checked it with her foot and then kicked him square in the chest. Snarlark fell, dropping between the bars.

He caught one, halting his fall.

A growl reverberated from the pit.

The velengoric leapt from the shadows, horns first. Its mouth snapped closed around Snarlark's lower body, teeth piercing flesh. A tortured scream burst from Snarlark.

She turned away.

A heavy thud. Bones snapped. His screams ended.

She waited for the remorse or relief to hit her, but a different thought dominated: *Cal, where are you?*

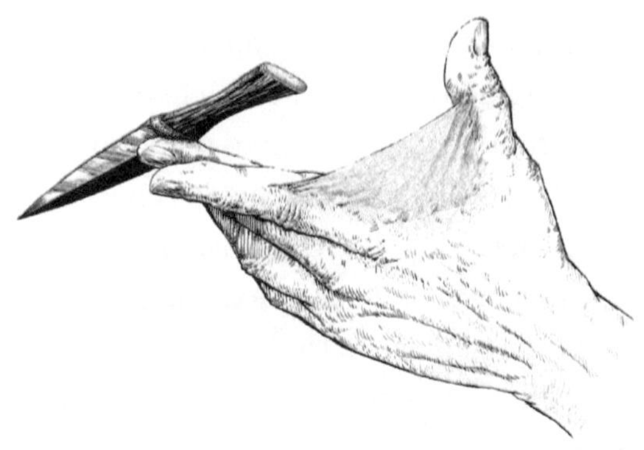

HIGHER

CAL lay on his stomach, hands under his chin. The cloud was fluffy and soft under him.

Cuddly.

Curvy.

Calm.

The words rose in him like bubbles floating to the surface. The cloud was carefree. And so was he.

As he floated towards the heavens, the lake island shrank. He traced its outline.

A flock of birds in wedge formation passed below him. They were white, like his cloud, apart from naked yellow skin around their eyes and beaks.

It would've been peaceful, if not for the racket someone was making. Harsh, jarring, loud: a mix he couldn't place. No matter. It would fade soon.

Higher he climbed.

He flipped onto his back and closed his eyes.

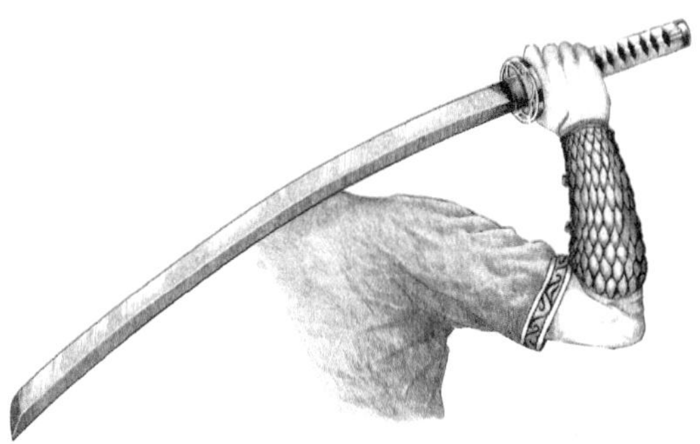

57. Bones Crunched

REUNITED with her sword, Antarna wiped the blade clean. She limped towards the columns where she'd last seen Cal before he'd split into hazy droplets. It seemed as good of a starting point as any. While Arric could have teleported him anywhere, maybe he'd thought to keep Cal close.

She stepped around a discarded, broken shield. A small box covered in strange symbols lay on its side, half-buried in dirt. Arric's.

Focus. Where is Cal?

She jogged towards the ruins. Saphramurls clinked in her pocket. The only one missing from the bag rested on the pyramid, and she sure wasn't going to go down there to fetch it.

A fat water droplet splattered upon her hand. The heavens opened. Before long, she was saturated. No amount of rain could wash away what had happened.

'Cal? Cal!'

Where is he, Enthriff?

An aftershock rocked the earth. She managed to keep on her feet.

Somewhere ahead, stone crashed down. A sharp cry rose above the hammering rain.

'Cal?' Antarna entered the ruins.

Cracks climbed pillars and traversed walls. The vines looped around them probably kept them standing.

Loose pebbles rolled from a pile of rubble. She ran through an arch, ready to jump clear if it fell. 'Cal?'

'Antarna?' The voice was male, but not Cal's. It was older. Familiar. 'I'm here.'

'Farikarr?'

'Yes. Hurry.' Pain pulled at his voice.

Slowing before a doorway, she peered through. Rope lashed Farikarr to a faceless statue gripping a spear with its only remaining arm. The hunt commander's ankles, waist and shoulders were secured to the stone. They'd used enough rope to restrain five men. The rope around his midsection secured his arms to his sides but left his hands free.

A fallen column lay up to Farikarr's knee. If he was lucky, it'd only crushed his toes. Or perhaps it had shattered his shinbone, and he was bleeding out.

Desert warriors had long departed—unless they were lying in wait. An ambush seemed unlikely, though, with Arric and Snarlark defeated. Passing through the doorway, Antarna jogged towards Farikarr.

Fighting against his bindings, he did his best to turn to face her. 'I was so worried for you.'

'Who are you working for?'

'What do you mean?' Farikarr looked surprised. Maybe he was.

'Let's try this another way. Why are you tied up?'

'Because we're their enemy. Now stop playing games and free me.'

'Not until you start talking. That's the reason you're still alive and tied up, isn't it?'

'Antarna, I have no idea what you're on about.'

Lie. She walked by him.

'We both know you're not going to leave me here.'

Do we? The tops of another row of columns peeked over a wall. Enthriff brushed over her skin, energetic. *What's got you excited?*

'Fine. I'm Resatrium.'

'Tell me something I don't know.' She approached the wall. A breeze could take it at any moment.

'Zanth hid behind a secret panel in my house after stealing the gems.'

She paused.

'I'm still loyal to your father. The king has taken things too far. You know that. Come back. At least roll this stone off my foot.'

Antarna took a step back, then another, but stayed facing the wall. Was something back there?

A flock of birds took flight.

She lowered her stance and shifted her weight forward.

Everything shook: ground, stone and even sky. A jagged fissure opened below her, rock splitting and earth parting. She jumped for solid ground. As she landed, Farikarr screamed. The wall tumbled down, a cascade of bricks and cloud of dust.

She turned to the hunt commander. The fallen column still trapped his leg, though he appeared to be in a bit more pain. Enthriff slithered down her arm, along her forefinger and drew it straight. He had her pointing to the dust cloud. *What's there?*

The column emerged through the settling dust. Next, a figure, secured to the middle one. His chin lay almost on his chest. Hair covered his face. 'Cal!'

The ground shifted under her as she ran to him. Dust assailed her eyes, then her nose. A small price to pay.

Please be alive. She reached for a pulse, as she'd done with Tozias. *Don't make me wait.*

Blood rushed under her fingertips.

'Cal, wake up. Please.' She shook his shoulder. Vines covered all apart from his shoulder, face and one foot.

Enthriff squeezed. She stepped back. Silver flowers shaped like butterflies sprawled above him. Delusians.

To the side, a male body lay face-down, his head in a bouquet of flowers and his hand on an axe handle. A rock had broken the warrior's back. Of the three desert warriors that should've been crushed by the airborne column, Arric had teleported two ahead of her, but the axeman hadn't reappeared. The High Priest must've sent him here, then the flowers had claimed him.

'Cal's fine,' said Farikarr. 'Come roll this off me.'

She brought her sword down. The vines fled. Her steel cracked against the stone, sending up sparks. Vibrations overtook her arm. A crack in the stone extended its reach.

Blind fool. Rivulets of blue ran along the length of the vine.

'The lake islander can wait.'

No, *you can.*

A vine snaked for her foot. Sword in hand, she menaced it.

Cal's eyelids fluttered.

'That's it. Wake up.' With her fingers resting on his jaw, she ran her thumb over his cheek.

He looked at her. 'You're pretty.'

A delightful warmth filled her. 'Do continue.'

'You're pretty like that flower.'

Antarna twisted. A dull flower clung to its last three petals. She laughed. 'You're high.'

His pupils were dilated.

She recalled when Cal had grabbed her shoulder in the forest before she came too close to a delusian. That would've been right before he'd had the vision of her death.

A rumble tore through the forest. Animals shrieked. The earth shuddered. Vines fled up the column. The base crumbled and then fell, taking Cal with it.

The column crashed down, landing on its side. It rolled towards a huge slab of stone. Leaping, Antarna put herself between them. The rough surface scraped her hands. Her feet slid back. Cal's outstretched arm rotated into the collision zone. His body was next. He struggled against the vines.

Her heel hit the slab behind her. *This is it.* Slipping her palms into a groove in the column, she pushed anew. A grunt came out from deep down.

The column started to slow. Her knees threatened to buckle. Antarna's arms shook, and her wound wailed.

Half a moment from being flattened, she dropped to the ground. Time slowed. The column rolled above her. Cal's arm—blue veins traversing gorgeous pale skin—turned with it. Caught between the two hunks of stone, his forearm compressed and long fingers clenched.

An animalistic howl hurtled from Cal's lips. A large part of her wanted to calm him, maybe with her hand again on his shoulder and another on his cheek. Instead, she launched up and pushed. Her muscles strained.

The column budged ever so slightly. Cal grew silent. Even with the extra space, he still couldn't free his arm. The column grew heavier, impossibly heavy. She fought it until her strength gave out.

He screamed anew.

'I'm sorry,' she said. 'I'm so sorry.'

Looking to the heavens, he appeared to be trying to stuff the pain down. 'Don't be. I'm surprised to be breathing. And thankful you are too.'

Something about the way he said that gave her pause.

Cal's hand and forearm were eerily pale. If she didn't restore blood flow soon, he'd lose them. He may lose them anyway. She pushed away the image of severing his arm to free him. *I'll find another way.*

She wriggled out from below the stone. 'Zanth didn't make it. He took Arric with him.'

'Brave.'

'Cal, I'm glad to hear your voice,' said Farikarr. 'Antarna, free me, and I'll help you get my future son-in-law out.'

She jogged over to Farikarr. Several cuts later and his bindings dropped to the ground.

'Thanks.' He rubbed his forearms then felt around the calf of his trapped foot. His fingers came away red.

'How much blood have you lost?'

'Enough.'

'Can you move your toes?'

'No.'

The column pinning him down was the same size as the one Cal was attached to. Their roundness meant that they'd be easier to move than the statue or the slab.

How do I move them?

Rust had claimed the statue's spearhead: brown, red and flaky. But the wooden shaft had weathered fine.

One slash of her sword freed the spear from the stone hand. Hopefully, Cal wasn't watching. She caught the shaft as it fell.

Farikarr straightened. 'Smart thinking.'

'I'll come back for you. You can't climb onto the slab with that leg, but Cal can help me free you.' *And the spear may not hold to do both of you.* She turned.

'Wait. No. I'm right here and he'll only have one arm to help with.'

'You'll only have one leg.'

'I'm stronger.'

'But I trust him.'

'You can trust me.'

She leapt onto the slab, a feat Farikarr would be unable to manage.

'I have so many secrets to share. Secrets to your most troubling questions.'

Secrets or lies?

He continued, his voice richer and smoother, his confidence returning. 'I can tell you who Arric was working with.'

She turned her back to him.

'Don't you want to know who killed your mother and brother? Without that, you're as trapped as me. Free me, and I'll free you.'

'You're serious?' She glanced over her shoulder.

'Yes.' Farikarr nodded as he spoke.

You lowlife. Antarna balled her fist.

'It's fine,' said Cal. 'Save him first.'

She slotted the butt of the spear into the gap beside Cal's trapped arm. 'What, free the man who threatened me, not the one that saved my life earlier today?' She spread her hands and adjusted her grip.

'You deserve answers.'

'And you deserve to paint with that hand.' Antarna planted her feet and heaved, applying her weight and every scrap of strength. The wood groaned. *Hold.*

As the column stirred, the shaft splintered then snapped. She fell back. After rising, she dusted herself off.

'Cut it off.' Cal inclined his head to the trapped half of his arm.

'I'm not ... it won't come to that.'

'We're out of options.'

She bit her lip and shook her head.

'It's fine.'

I should be the one reassuring you. 'You're a painter.'

'I'm a seer.'

'You're an artist who enjoys swimming and throwing knives.'

'I've got another hand.' He gave it a wave.

'No need to act so stoic.'

'Ouch. Using my own words against me.'

A bird fluttered through a hole in a tumbledown wall, not two steps from an open doorway. It was like a child climbing out of her bedroom window when the parents weren't home. *Windows and doors.* 'There may be a way.'

'I'm not going anywhere.'

She put down her weapons and closed her eyes, embracing the dark. Rock provided a solid base under her. Sliding her feet into a fighting stance, she raised her hands.

Rocks clattered.

Farikarr crouched then froze, unblinking.

A snout emerged from behind a block of stone, nostrils flared. Its mouth opened to reveal its slicing whites.

She sealed her lips and collected her weapons.

The velengoric advanced upon Farikarr, tail swishing. With his leg trapped, he couldn't hide properly. Even if he could, his scent would've given him away.

Alone, her odds against the creature were about as high as steel making friends with water.

Cal groaned. Vines constricted his chest and crept for his throat. They retreated before her steel.

The velengoric changed course, heading for Cal and her.

There was no time to free his arm now. She couldn't sever it either: even if they could stop the bleeding, the blood would make the creature murderous and attract other predators.

'Here.' She passed him her dagger, stood in front of his trapped arm and drew her sword.

Cal straightened. 'Right. Act like we're more trouble than we're worth.'

The velengoric turned its head and raked its horns across the trunk of a dead tree. Farikarr shrank lower at the sound. Two parallel gashes marred the wood.

Intimidation? Or a challenge?

As the creature drew closer, the dagger in Cal's hand quivered. She'd reassure him if she knew how. Maybe standing in front was enough.

Bronze did little against thick scales. Her steel could draw blood, but few blows would be anything more than flesh wounds. In this way, large beasts and heavily armoured warriors were similar. The joints and eyes made the best targets. Simple enough in theory. The writers of that theory had a full hunting party, including a senior priest brimming with madriliks. And even then, such groups typically returned with casualties and a mere plant-eater as their prize.

The velengoric passed by Farikarr. But he wasn't out of danger, and he knew it. The hunt commander grabbed his knee and tried to twist his leg free. His life and Cal's lay heavy in her hands.

She clanged the flat of her blade against her shield. The next time, off-centre, and the metallic reverberation hung longer in the air.

After a twist of its head, the creature spun to face Farikarr. That wasn't why she'd made the noise. Perhaps pain had a scent. Several bounding steps brought the velengoric within striking distance. Its jaws snapped shut over one of his outstretched arms. The arm offered the same resistance as small game: none. Blood spurted from Farikarr's shoulder. The velengoric swallowed the arm whole, not bothering to chew. The next bite took his head, ending his scream.

It'd happened so fast. Any answers he once held had perished with him. Had he really known who killed her mother and brother?

'Antarna. Tarna.' Cal touched her arm. 'I'd ask you to run—'

'But you know I won't.' She closed her eyes, preparing to enter her soul. 'Let's get you out.'

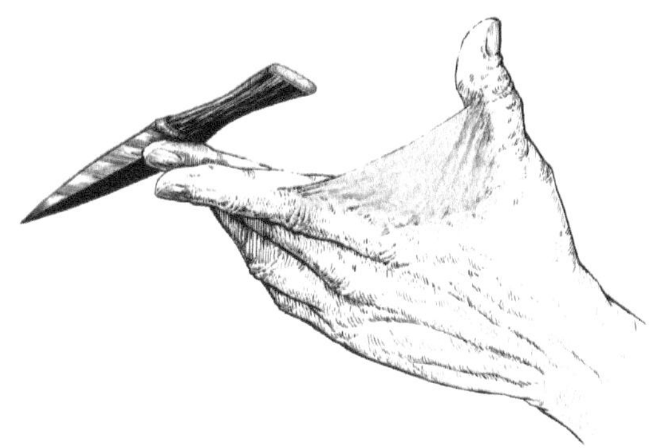

58. Another Mouthful

THE chomping made Cal's skin crawl and stomach roil. A bone snapped. The velengoric's sharp teeth sliced and tore at Farikarr's flesh. The headless body, missing an arm and stained with blood, barely looked human.

Slow down. Take your time. Not nice thoughts, but the man was already dead, and Cal had no idea how long Antarna would need.

Cal drew strength from her presence. There was no one he'd rather have by his side. Guilt rose within Cal; she'd chosen him over the closure she needed. The origin of Kat's warning made perfect sense now. What else does a Resatrium parent say to their child but not to trust royals?

The creature claimed Farikarr's right foot and shin and munched down, chewing with its mouth open.

His mum had taught him better. Odds were, he'd never see her again. His death would break her poor heart. She'd barely held things together when his father passed.

Tugging at his trapped arm was useless, but hard to resist.

The velengoric took another mouthful.

There's hope still. Antarna's eyes danced below her closed eyelids.

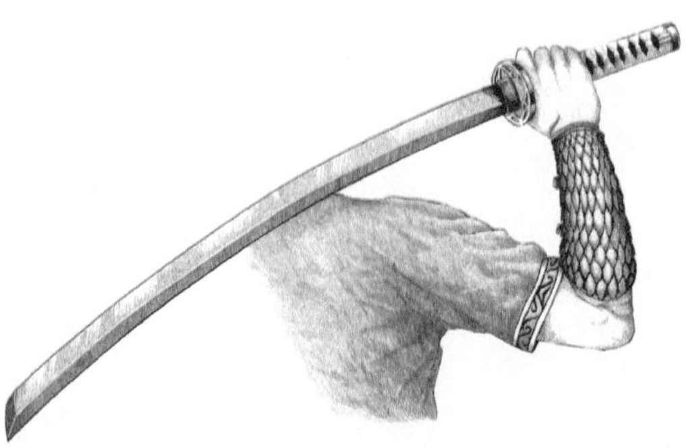

59. Lard-stick

Antarna descended inside herself, picturing Salorann's face. Three freckles sat in a straight line across his cheek.

She hadn't the time or means to duel a shadow, nor to replicate a mock fight. But maybe she didn't need to, not anymore.

A seemingly endless network of spheres surrounded her. Parts were familiar from her training under Gil. But they lay on the other side of a labyrinth.

She reached for Salorann. His face faded, but his presence grew. Salorann had attempted to kill Antarna's father and her uncle. The Resatrium mage almost took out her grandfather. Yet he had not been motivated by bloodlust or a thirst for power. She could see that now. The Unjust Uprising was a desperate attempt to end the abuse of the lower class. The Resatrium were doing what they thought was right, or at least, Salorann had been. Antarna neither liked nor agreed with it, but she could understand it.

Something drew her deeper inside of herself. More than a feeling, less than a path. She followed it. Each sphere sat quieter than the last.

Antarna lost count of the threads she flew down and the spheres she passed through. The feeling grew stronger. Surely, it led her to her soul.

Snow-white mist swirled around her, obscuring the sphere.

While she didn't know where the next passageway was, her feet seemed to. Soft, dry grass cushioned her steps. A dense hedge stretched before her. Approaching, she extended her hand. The wide leaves fluttered under her touch. Antarna turned right.

A silver door, smooth and handleless, broke the wall of green. Antarna pushed, and it pushed back. A *test of strength*? She launched off the balls of her feet. Her shoulder collided with the wall. It retaliated with greater force, hurling her into the mist. The ground hid from her until the last moment. Pain felt different here, more like making a horrible mistake than getting punched or kicked.

A gentle breeze stirred her hair. A bird could fight the wind all day and get nowhere, or it could soar great distances with it.

Antarna placed her hand onto the lustrous metallic door, which yielded slightly under her touch. *I'm ready. Let me enter.* Her arm sank into the silver. She stepped through.

Blinding light. Blistering heat. She raised her arms and tucked her chin. Her foot slid back into the door.

No, I'm not leaving without what I came for.

Spreading her arms, she lifted her face to the light. 'Salorann, I respect you and accept our connection.'

The assault on her eyelids eased; she opened her eyes.

Salorann stood, radiant like a star.

Her bond with him pulsated, the connection stronger than ever. He was a part of her—not just of her history—as were the past lives that came before him.

We need to save Cal. I can't do it without you: all of you, all of us.

She brought a collection of memories to the surface. Cal paddling in the canoe on the lake, hiding his worry behind long, confident strokes. Their laughter. Cal scrambling away from Enthriff, the anchor leech on his thigh. Serpents releasing their grip, slithering from her to reveal Cal charging into the cavern with the queen on his heels. Their warm embrace.

Moisture gathered in her eyes, even here.

Help me. Please.

A long moment passed. Doubt wanted to take hold, but she refused it.

Strength coursed through her. An exhilarating power, demanding to be used.

Antarna bolted back the way she'd come, feet barely touching the ground. Door after door. Higher and higher until she returned.

Cal brandished her dagger.

Fresh blood covered the velengoric's face. It approached.

'I'd hope you'd no longer be hungry,' Cal muttered.

'That's awful.'

He cringed. 'You weren't meant to hear that.'

'Let's get you out.' She scooped up the two halves of the broken spear. With one in each hand, Antarna leapt onto the top of the slab. Again, she slotted the wood into the gap beside his trapped arm. After filling her lungs, she wrenched, giving it everything. Her muscles, at their limit. Her jaw, clenched.

Salorann heaved with her, as did their innumerable past lives.

A splinter came from the wood.

Not again.

The column rolled and Cal's arm dropped free. He clutched it to his chest like a mother reunited with her lost baby.

The velengoric snarled. Its largest teeth rivalled her middle finger in length.

'Cal, back away, slowly.' She pictured throwing the broken weapon in her hands and hitting the creature. The rusted metal tip would shatter; it would bounce harmlessly off and only enrage the predator. She discarded the ancient spear halves and drew her steel. Her connection with Salorann faded.

Spiralling horns dropped to point at her chest.

Joints and eyes.

Dark slit pupils drank her in. If she managed to avoid being skewered by its horns, going for the eyes put her far too close to its jaws.

Cloven hooves pawed the ground.

We've been here before. She had no bars to grab, though. Even if she did, the creature wouldn't make the same mistake twice. No doubt it would be wary of her now.

It charged.

She rushed forwards.

Loose stones rattled.

Leaping wide, Antarna arched her blade towards the rear of the creature's lead knee.

Horns swept across and collided with her steel. Her sword bounced off, bending her elbow and testing her grip. The force of the impact flowed down her arm. In mid-air, she shifted to soften her landing and avoid stabbing herself. Landing on her shoulders set off her wound.

The velengoric spun and tore towards her, muscles rippling.

Cal threw a rock. 'Hey, lard-stick, over here.'

Scrambling up, she suppressed a smile.

The rock fell short. The predator closed the gap.

You're lucky I saved your dominant hand. She jumped from a block to the top of a wall. The narrow surface restricted her pace.

Hurtling towards her, the creature looked like it intended to ram the wall. If so, it'd punch right through. A solid plan.

Two body lengths out.

One.

The velengoric turned, but its hoof slipped on the stone. Skidding sideways, it slammed into the wall.

As the wall toppled, Antarna sprang clear. A roll eased the landing. Rising to a knee, she reached out to Salorann; but he'd withdrawn deep within. Enthriff alerted her to danger.

Something grabbed her ankle and yanked her back. A vine pulled her towards a writhing mass of its kin. With a precise swing of her sword, she broke free. This incensed the plant into a frenzy. Vines lashed the air like whips.

The predator burst through the dust, jaws snapping. She sprinted toward it. Vines stretched for her heels, a second threat to deal with. She'd trained against multiple opponents in the fighting ring, learning to manipulate their movements. She needed to use one against the other.

Joints and eyes. Skipping into a fighting stance, she launched forwards, making a half-cut right. Drawing a turn of the creature's head, she rotated her wrist to cut left. Her sword struck a bony protrusion above its eye.

A horn hit her shield, and she let its power push her sideways, away from the reaching vines.

The creature pursued, quickly catching up.

Antarna ducked below its horns and raised her blade. The undercut connected with its cheek, opening a shallow wound. Another strike or two, and she'd force the creature into the way of the vines.

Its scaled snout bashed into her shield. A flick of its head threw her into an airborne spin.

Two rows of serrated teeth separated, making room for her.

With her back to its mouth, she swung her arms to hasten her rotation. Its hot breath assailed her neck. If only she'd given the saphramurls in her pocket to Cal. She tried to flick Enthriff off her, but he refused to budge.

A rusted spear tip atop a broken shaft tore towards the velengoric, heading for its eye. A perfect throw, until the predator extended its neck.

The tip struck scales behind the eye and shattered—as she'd pictured. Jaws started to close around her.

Great flecks of rust pelted the predator's face and eye. Its eyelid dropped, and its head turned.

Antarna kicked off the side of a tooth. The upper jaw dropped. Tucking her legs, she pulled her feet free. Not a moment too soon.

The muscles in the velengoric's neck corded, readying to strike again.

The creature fell face-first. Vines bound its legs. Roaring, it struggled. Further vines secured the prize, dragging it back to the heart of the plant.

After landing and sheathing her sword, Antarna slid a hand into her pocket. The smooth saphramurls rested, calm and safe. With her other hand, she patted Enthriff.

A flock of minderels settled into a nearby patch of trees. They filled the ruins with trilling birdsong.

Cal rushed towards her, cradling his hand. A wide, triumphant smile lit up his face.

'Nice throw.' She moved to meet him.

'What was it Zanth said? "Luck is less demanding than the hard, weary road of skill." Not that he believed that.'

Behind them, the creature snarled and thrashed, teeth and claw cutting through vines.

Cal retreated. 'It will break free.'

A creature so proud and strong deserved to. 'Not for a while. And when it does, it'll be too tired to come after us.'

Enthriff constricted. The minderels took to the air.

'What now?' He sighed. 'Did the gods put a price on our heads?'

She drew her sword.

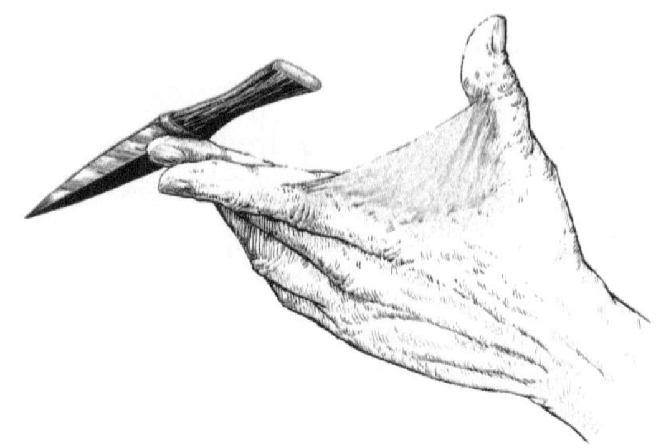

60. Bronze Hook

CAL turned to face the multicoloured light. 'Magic.' *Too much for one mage.*

'Back at the pit?' She stepped towards it.

'What are you doing?'

'Isn't it obvious?' Her strides lengthened.

'You're being reckless.' *Foolish even.*

Antarna paused but kept her back to him. 'Let me guess. Your plan is to flee into the ruins or forest?'

'Yes, to move away from danger.'

'Danger?' She spun, spreading her arms. 'That's all around us. We won't last out here alone.'

We've got each other.

The light intensified, and Antarna took off.

He followed. 'You remember the part where the high priest just tried to kill us? What if these are his disciples?'

She set a pace, clearly incapable of plodding, shuffling or ambling. He'd even take a saunter or stroll. But no, not Antarna. She was on a mission. Her mind was set.

He'd seen patched, tattered dolls at the orphanage in better condition than they were. Cleaner, too. What he'd have given for a swim.

We've made it this far. We'll make it back.

Antarna entered the clearing and stepped around a body. Bloodied. Young. Face down. Pausing, she turned to him. 'Which way?'

He pointed back the way they'd come.

She gave him a look. Oh, such a look. He mightn't have survived it if his mum hadn't desensitised him over the years. Maybe he should thank her. That probably wouldn't go down well ...

Cal straightened his good arm, this time towards the light she could not see. It gathered where the mound of supplies smouldered.

Without so much as a thank you, she pressed on. Each step took them further from the safety of the tree line. Finally, Antarna crouched behind some bushes.

The magic took a shape like a bell, large enough to fit several people inside of it.

A *portal*? If so, the Order of Devtakaris were about to come through. No one else had so many madriliks to spend. Cal couldn't even bring himself to say, "I told you so." Sometimes, he hated being right.

A man draped in crimson stepped through. Armless, thin, sharp nose, beady eyes. Another priest of Devtakaris joined him. Two chins, protruding ears. They surveyed the carnage and then established a defensive barrier.

Two is already two too many. He nudged her foot and whispered, 'Let's go.'

But apparently, he'd spoken to a statue. *Where do you get this stubbornness from?*

A man stepped out of the light, taller than even Antarna. Her father, Barrass Tarlqua, second in line to the throne after the king's son. They'd met once. Or, rather, they'd been in the same room once. Not that Barrass would remember him, tucked off to the side.

Royal guards emerged next. More than one dozen, less than two. Like Barrass, they wore scaled armour and bristled with weapons. A priestess and priest of Preslina were the last through.

Antarna started to rise.

Cal grabbed her wrist. 'We don't know who Arric was working with.' Kat's warning came back to him: *You can't trust the royals.*

'No, we don't. But my father would've never let me come if he was a part of this.'

Her wrist slipped through his fingers, leaving him crouching like a coward. She straightened, keeping her shoulders down, her head level and eyes forwards. Tall, but not stiff. Where did she find such strength?

Clearing her throat caused the royal guards to spin to face her, weapons up.

'Father, how'd you find me?'

'Tarna.' His features softened. He sheathed his sword. 'Are you alright?'

'Now I am.'

They embraced. Father and daughter. Her cheek against his neck. Arms at full reach, squeezing tight. Far superior to the awkward hug Cal and Antarna had shared after swimming free of the crustrearons. Not that that was his fault. She'd given no warning and pinned his arms to his sides.

'I've been so worried,' Barrass said.

No new threat emerged, sending a flock of birds into the air. The gods gave them this nice moment. If the portal had opened any later, Cal's moment with her wouldn't have been stolen.

As they separated, a man in grey robes trimmed in sky blue exited the light. A spattering of fine hairs clung to his head, a shade darker than his robe. The bell dissipated.

Do I stand? Awkwardness weighed on him.

'High Priest Effain.' Antarna gave a traditional greeting.

'Princess.' He returned the greeting.

'How's Tozias? And the others?'

'Holding on, but fading.'

She turned to her father. 'Effain helped you find me?'

'We lost contact with Orrsin and thus with you. Effain alerted me of a significant disturbance. We came to investigate, and I'd hoped to find you here.' Barrass surveyed the battle scene. 'What happened?'

'It's a long story. Very long.'

'You can tell me when we're home. Are there any other survivors?'

'Some fled into the forest. They won't want to be found. Otherwise, just me and Cal.'

Cal stood, regretting not doing so earlier.

Their gaze bore into him.

Maybe being eaten by a velengoric wouldn't have been so bad after all.

Cal moved to join them, discarding line after line of dialogue. *Hunt Master, you're looking well. Barrass, you should be proud of your daughter.* 'Antarna, have you told them the good news?' Eyes turned from him. The breeze carried away his worry.

Her smile faltered.

Cal's stomach dropped. *You didn't plan to tell them ... Do we trust them?*

'The cave is no longer lost.' She pulled a bag from her pocket and opened it to show off the saphramurls inside.

'You did it.' Barrass's voice brimmed with awe and pride.

'That's incredible.' Effain swallowed. 'Sorry, we can't bring saphramurls through a portal.'

'Yes.' Antarna dipped her head. 'Will you accompany us as we walk them back to the lake island, please?'

'What then?' her father asked.

'When we arrive at the lake island with the gems, we teleport the patients to us.'

The plan was solid.

Effain's face said otherwise. 'They wouldn't survive the trip. Teleportation is an intense spell involving substantial madriliks. In their weakened states, the injured couldn't handle that level of exposure. I'm sorry.'

They'd gone through all this for nothing. Cal was sorry too, a whole ocean full of sorry. His heart broke for Antarna. They'd found the unfindable, survived the unsurvivable, and still Tozias and the others would die. It wasn't fair or right or just.

'Then we ...' Antarna's arms fell, going loose. Her shoulders rounded.

Cal wished he could help. He'd comfort her, but he didn't know how, especially not in front of her father.

Antarna straightened, determination returning to her face. 'Then we bring the gems to them.'

Barrass and Effain each waited on the other to answer.

The high priest caved. 'Even if such a journey was possible, we wouldn't reach them in time. They haven't got long.'

'There's enough time to say goodbye,' Barrass added.

If he expected that to soften the blow, he didn't know his daughter.

Her hand dropped to her hilt. 'You've given up on them?'

'Of course not.' Barrass's arms floated in a lake of uncertainty between his hips and shoulders. 'You're bleeding. You must be exhausted. Let's get you back, and then we'll put our heads together, I promise.'

'I'm not leaving the gems.' She squeezed the hilt.

Her father bristled, drawing himself up to his full height.

She spoke first. 'Not until I've at least had a chance to think.'

'We can't stay here. Not with so much blood spilled.'

'It's a good thing you came prepared.'

'You've got until we patch you two up and check the bodies. Then we're leaving.'

A priest in white approached Antarna, and a priestess neared Cal. Sun had darkened her skin to the colour of moonlit reeds. Time had left its mark too, like a child dragging a stick back and forth through mud. Madriliks pranced within her chest.

'How are you, Seer?' She stretched out a hand.

'Fine now, thanks, other than this arm.'

She examined it tenderly. 'You were lucky the bone held.'

It was a miracle he still breathed. Actually, the real reason, a certain princess, sat on a nearby rock. The priest attending her finished applying numbing salve to Antarna's shoulder. He pulled a curved bronze hook from his bag to stitch her wound before he applied magic.

Cal couldn't bear to watch it pierce the skin. The priestess beside him called upon her magic, and it buried into his arm. The pain faded, and the swelling eased.

The guards checked the fallen, closing their eyes and bringing their hands to rest on their bellies. Another guard had fetched the saphramurl from the pit and brought it back to Barrass.

The priest had finished his stitches and examined Antarna's other wounds.

A cut ear. *Snarlark, from their first fight.*

A burn stretching up her neck onto her other ear. *When you shielded me from the magical fire.*

Horizontal marks developing on her neck. *Strangled by the two-headed serpent.*

The priestess turned her attention to the cut on Cal's hand from the rock after the ladder had been sliced. His hand tingled, skin knitting together. He resisted the urge to flex his fingers.

'Are those bothering you?' She pointed to his ankle.

Three bites formed a triangle with sides of similar length.

'Didn't notice them.'

'Good, dear. Is there anything else I can help with?'

'No, you've been amazing. Thank you.' He was curious about how the bites from the anchor leech were healing, but not enough to take off his pants.

Antarna stood and indicated for the priest to have her seat. Her ear and neck were healed. With a gesture of thanks, he took her offer. Sweat dripped down his face and stained his robe, turning patches from white to translucent.

Wind streamed her hair behind her and lifted a scab from her shoulder. Soft pink skin lay underneath. The stitches could probably come out. Physically, after a warm bath, hot meal and a long sleep, she'd be fine. Mentally, however, that'd take time. No spell could help. Mages had tried over the years—often with horrible results.

He recalled her curled into a ball, after having kicked that homicidal savage into the yallut's path.

Antarna zigzagged between the bodies.

'Time to go.' Barrass nodded to the armless.

'Not yet.' She spoke over her shoulder.

'We are leaving. You're coming, even if I must carry you myself.'

Her turned back spoke volumes.

What are you looking for, Tarna?

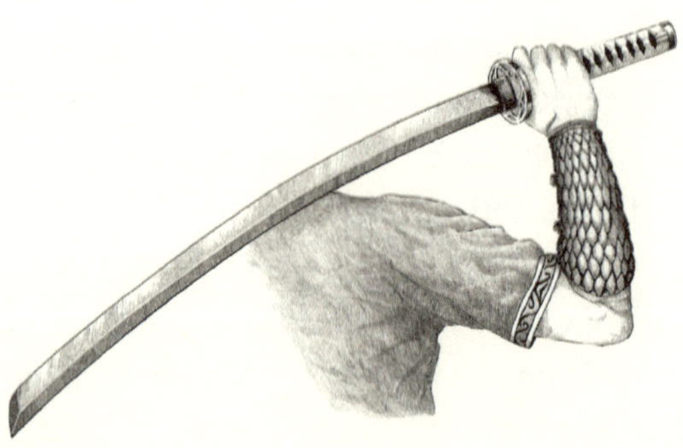

61. Sell my Soul

WHERE *is it?*

The idea had come to her when the priest had packed the salve and hook away in a small box. Antarna wasn't sure whether it would work. But no one had any useful thoughts, and time wasn't on her side.

She lifted her foot over a forgotten axe. The head rested unsullied. Maroon streaks curled around the handle, though, capturing the odd fingerprint.

To her right, an arrow shaft protruded from a body. Bone, wood and feather. Created for hunting beasts, used against one of its own. *Are we the true beasts? At least beasts kill to eat and feed their young.*

An arm stretched into her path, palm up, its surface ghostly pale. Settled blood had turned the bottom edges reddish-purple. Antarna squatted, her legs grumbling in protest. *Welcome them, Zentrina.* She lifted the sweaty limb—not expecting it to still be warm—and then lowered it to his chest. The man couldn't have been more than a couple of years older than her. His jaw hung open. Liquid pooled around his thighs.

'Tarna. Enough. We're leaving.'

Father's words struck like rocks. She took small steps away from them, passing two more bodies. Death filled her nose.

'Antarna Loreleif Tarlqua.' He came for her.

'I'm almost—'

A strange symbol peered out from amongst some rubble: a swirl resembling an eye. She dashed to it and pulled a box free. Runes covered its every side, and it drank in the light. A numbing feeling spread down her fingers and into her palms.

Father peered over her shoulder as only he could. 'What's that?'

'It was Arric's. I think he kept extra madriliks hidden in it.' *Like Morsirel's store.*

'Hidden?' He took the box, turned it over, then handed it to Effain.

The high priest almost dropped it. 'Fascinating. I've never seen it before. Seems similar to nalitroite but … more powerful.'

'If it can hide madriliks, could it do the same with anti-magic?' Antarna bit her lip.

'Only one way to find out.' Effain opened the lid.

She took the bag of saphramurls from her pocket and placed them inside.

The high priest lowered the lid as if it was made from eggshells.

'What do you sense?' *Please. Please.*

'Nothing.'

Hope spread its wings. 'It's comfortable to hold?'

'Yes, surprisingly.'

Hope took flight. She couldn't hold it back if she tried. 'Is it teleportable?'

'Only one way to know.' Father beckoned to the priests of the Order of Devtakaris.

One took the box from Effain, floating it in front of his chest. *Another good sign.* The other moved back, twenty paces or so. Grey had crept into his carefully trimmed beard.

If only I could see madriliks.

They stiffened. The older priest closed his eyes. His parted lips fluttered.

The box blurred, edges as nebulous as smoke. It flickered. And again.

Come on.

Sharpening, solidifying, it came back into focus. The priest lowered it to the ground and shook his head.

Hope had flown high, only to find the air too thin to breathe.

'Worth a try. Thank you.' Father turned to her. 'We're leaving.'

Cal leapt from one stone to another. 'I've an idea.' He picked up the box, lifted the lid and upended the bag. Saphramurls spilled out, clinking. Their orange light darted over the inside of the lid.

She drew alongside him, and he handed her the box. The sensation of holding it began to seep away, her fingers growing distant and dull. Cal picked up the largest gem and dropped it back into the bag. His slender fingers brushed over midnight blue surfaces. Scratches and the odd cut ran along his hands. Dirt darkened his skin and blackened the ends of his fingernails. A different set of hands than when they'd first met. Gem after gem filled up the bag, until only the smallest saphramurls sat in the box.

'There. Let's try that.' He made no attempt to hide his smile.

She held back her own with difficulty, given how infectious his was. What if the Daslercian mage that'd first transported the gems to the crater had teleported them using a similar means?

The pair of crimson-robed priests looked to Father. He waved them on, acquiescing. Again, the younger one took the box and the other backed away.

What little muscle they had tightened; fervently committing to a life of magic wasn't conducive to a strong body.

The box didn't soften or come out of focus. It just hovered. And hovered.

Is something wrong?

The next moment, it vanished and reappeared in front of the older priest.

Arms up, Antarna leapt into the air. *We're coming, Tozias.*

Wearing a smile even broader than before, Cal took a large step towards her. Almost as if he'd decided to close the distance and embrace. Instead, after glancing at her father, he brought his hands up and clapped, loud and strong. Guards joined in, as did she, followed even by Father. *Is it proper for us to clap when the priests have long given up their arms?*

'Let's go. We'll drop that off at the mountain temples?' She pointed to the box with its precious saphramurl inside.

Father crossed his arms. 'The king is expecting us. After we meet with him, you can head back to the temples.'

Antarna took the box from the old priest.

They gathered close.

I hate this part. From the hesitant faces around her, she wasn't alone in that.

Archaic words swirled around them, picking up pace.

Clenching, she waited for the force to strike from above. It hit like a yallut.

I killed that man. His crushed chest and gut-churning head wound was burnt into her mind's eye. She'd never be free of it; she didn't deserve to be.

Those tiny, unseen hands tugged at her. *Do your worst.* They tore her pieces from her, until they didn't. She hung in stagnant droplets. They fell. She fell.

A room spun, the floor unsteady.

'You level?' Cal stretched out a hand.

She took it. Warm. Gentle. Solid when nothing else was.

In the bowl of the crater, fields sat bare. Nothing more than friendship could grow between her and an engaged man. Releasing Cal's hand, she headed for the door.

Priests of the crater sucked in air, one on each corner of the square. Of course, they weren't Arric. But she saw a bit of him in each of them.

How much do you know? Where do your loyalties lie?

Enthriff slithered up her arm.

Outside, the royal guard waited beside an ornate palanquin and its four bearers. Eerily reminiscent of when she'd first arrived in the crater to request saphramurls from the king. Before she'd learnt that the gems had been stolen. Well before she'd understood that the Resatrium had stolen the gems to keep Arric from further testing his destructive weapon, not as a means of toppling her family. Maybe Farikarr had spilled the secret to them. But if he knew, then so did the king.

And my father?

Father strode past her. 'Let's not keep the king waiting.'

The royal guard snapped to attention.

Chin high, Antarna ascended the steps to the palanquin of royal purple and pristine white, which matched the flag fluttering on its roof. A bearer held back a gauzy curtain. It fell into place as she sank into a mountain of cushions. They swallowed her like quicksand.

Ridiculous. Is the traveller a fragile egg?

With poles resting on their shoulders, the bearers stood in unison. The oval pod rose.

The procession set off, pebbles of the Purple Path crunching under foot. Only she suffered the indignity of being carried. She patted down her torn and bloodstained clothes, but the crinkles resisted. *They're the least of my concerns.* At least all the pomp and ceremony would make it difficult for the king to try anything, if he were so inclined. Her knowledge was dangerous.

The pod swayed too gently to explain her rising nausea. The delicate walls pressed in around her. Her sword would make short work of them. Two slashes, maybe three, and she could see the sky, feel the breeze. Better yet, she'd leap down and walk like everyone else. Of course, Father wouldn't understand.

Finally, they stopped inside the palace gates. After extracting herself from the cushions, she took the stairs.

Her breath caught in her throat as three in crimson robes passed by. They entered and turned right, heading for the throne room.

Keep calm. One meeting with the king, then back to Tozias.

Under the herald's announcement, Father led them in. They passed the rib cage of a zarrleck, where Evireny had been held and searched. At the end of the aisle of bones, Antarna and Father bowed, while the others took to their knees.

King Ithranned clapped thrice atop his deep-purple throne. 'Well done. You found saphramurls. Let's see them.'

She took the steps and presented him with the box. 'The rest will be teleported shortly.'

'Brother, Antarna, Seer, join me for a celebratory drink.' His arm extended towards a small balcony.

Young and old toiled in the fields below. A line stretched to the pond. Stakes rose around Heltorne.

This must change.

A servant brought around a tray with large mugs of dark beer.

'To your success.' The king hefted his mug.

She raised hers to her lips but could not bring herself to drink.

'I need to make one thing clear.' The king focused on Cal before turning his gaze to her. 'You did not find the cave. It remains lost. It's safer that way.'

'But—'

'We understand,' Cal interjected.

Fighting the temptation to upend her beer over his ridiculous head, she put the mug down. 'What's next, Arric died a hero?'

'The high priest served our people,' the king said. 'He led the fight against Resatrium scum, giving his life in the process.'

'He caused all this. You know that, right? His priests tested the saphramurl in the glade and the shockwaves almost destroyed the mountain temples. Morsirel, a senior priest, confronted him, and so Arric killed him.'

'What proof do you have?'

'He flung a stone wall at me. He hired desert warriors to kill us. He locked me in that pit to again test his weapon.'

'None of that proves what happened in the glade, or to the temples or Morsirel. How do you know it wasn't Zanth?'

'Zanth couldn't have mistaken Arric for Morsirel. Their stores of madriliks are too different. And he wouldn't try an assassination on the same night of the theft. Nor could he use magic with the gems.'

The king didn't look convinced, but it was probably an act. 'He could have put the gems down. Angry as he was, who's to say that Zanth didn't risk both in the one night? When he found a senior priest instead of Arric, maybe he took his anger out on him.'

Cal took a small step forwards. 'I foresaw the death. Morsirel recognised his attacker and relaxed, that I know.'

And you couldn't say anything because of your oath. Did you break your oath to save me?

The king took a drink, buying himself time. 'But you don't know it was Arric he recognised?'

'No.' Cal shuffled back.

'So, you've no proof. What do you want? Glory for finding the cave?'

The truth. Antarna bit the words back, tempering her wrath. The truth hadn't died with Arric and Zanth, but it might as well have. If the king and Arric had plotted together, Ithranned would deny it to his last breath.

The king awaited her reply, scrutinising her as if his future depended on it.

Antarna raised her chin. 'A gem and teleportation to the temples. Evireny freed. Lining up for water stopped. The stakes around Heltorne removed. And staking abolished.'

'I grant all bar the last request.' He offered her back the box.

She accepted it—a smarter choice than challenging him to a duel. Heat surged in her chest, burning with all the words she wished to hurl.

'Whatever happened, I'm sure Arric had our people's best interests at heart, as do I.' The king attempted a gentle smile.

It was too much to take. 'The weak and the short-sighted cling to their good intentions.' She stormed out.

The door should've slammed behind her. Evidently, someone caught it.

'Antarna.' Cal's tone was a mixture of sympathy and pleading.

She whirled about. 'A cover-up! That's how he rules?'

He straightened his fingers and brought his palm parallel to the floor.

'No, I won't calm down.'

Cal opened the closest door.

They entered a sitting room.

She walked its length. 'Can you believe that?'

'Part of me can't. Part of me can.'

'They all died. Garlin, Hinn and Biesan. Rundlud, Nol and Eryx. Orrsin. Zanth.' She couldn't bring herself to name Farikarr or Arric. 'And for what?'

He stepped into her path and took her hands. 'We found the cave, stopped the weapon and brought back the gems. We'll always know the truth.'

He was right and wrong at the same time: the weapon didn't die with Arric. Another could recreate it. That couldn't be allowed to happen.

Cal looked at her in earnest. His hands were warm and reassuring.

Now was as good a time as any to ask what she'd been wanting to for some time. 'You had a vision of my death and broke your oath to tell Enthriff.' It was the only possibility that made sense. *Why? In return for me saving your life or because you have feelings for me?* 'When?' The question was a poor substitute for asking why.

Cal released her hands. 'While you were sleeping in the forest.'

'Thank you. Never have those two words been so inadequate.' She pictured him tormented over the decision, then breaking his oath to his goddess by whispering the manner of her death to Enthriff while she slept. Cal must've seen the spike of the halberd driven into her heart for him to tell Enthriff the location to guard. She patted Enthriff. The halberd hadn't pierced his scales, but it would've hurt a great deal. The point of the weapon would have skidded off him and continued into her unless he'd formed a cone shape or gripped it.

She met Cal's deep blue eyes. 'Will there be consequences?'

He dropped his gaze. 'It'll be fine.'

Lie.

'Speaking of thanks, I'm again in your debt for saving me and this arm.' He held up his painting hand. 'Especially as you could have finally known who was responsible for your mother's and brother's deaths.'

'I'd make the same choice again.' Farikarr would have said anything to save himself. *If* he'd known the truth, there was no guarantee he'd have parted with it—especially not if it implicated the Resatrium or himself.

'And that's what makes you, you.' Cal started for the door. 'We should see you off before the king changes his mind.'

'What about you? Heading back to the lake island?'

'Yes, after I see Kathrina to break the news of her father's death. Her house is near the temple. I'll see you off.'

The image of her sobbing into his chest formed.

They exited the palace without saying goodbye to her father. After refusing a palanquin, they walked the same way they'd arrived.

'Tozias must be strong,' Cal said, 'to hang on so long. With the gem, he'll make it.'

'Thanks. Distract me. What are you looking forward to on your return?' *Other than getting married. Please don't say that.*

'Swim, dinner with Mum, painting. The little things.'

'They're often the best.'

An initiate welcomed them to the temple and led the way to the teleportation room. 'The priests will be in shortly.'

'Thanks.' She turned to Cal. 'More importantly, thank you. I'm so glad we did this together.'

'Yes. You, me, Enthriff and the fallen.' He moved over to the window.

She couldn't bear to join, to see her people sweating in the heat.

In the silence, a chasm grew between them. One no words could bridge. Here, their paths forked.

I'm going to miss you. Words she couldn't voice. Not even if the room was hers alone.

'Come here.' His hand beckoned her too.

She approached.

Cal pointed. 'That's you, that's what you've done.'

People swelled around the pond. Repressed people. Her people. 'It's not enough.'

'It's a start.'

'I feel like I'm running away.'

'You're keeping a promise and returning to save lives. You're the bravest person I've ever met.'

Yet still, I asked you "when" instead of "why". 'You're pretty brave yourself.' She should end it there, but she couldn't help herself. 'I've never heard a more manly scream than yours.'

He bowed and they laughed.

'Until next time.' Cal opened his arms.

She entered.

Their bodies met. He clasped her tight, and she wrapped her arms around him in turn, melting into him. Cal bent his knees.

Wait. You're not going to—

Her feet left the floor. He smelled like the earth after a drizzle of rain.

A broad smile spread over his face.

As he lowered her, she planted a kiss onto his warm cheek. His eyes widened and a soft blush took to his face, gracing his pale skin.

The priests entered the room.

'Until next time,' she said.

The chanting, the tiny hands, the droplets, it happened just as before.

Crisp, cold air greeted her, as did High Priest Inhaloc.

She set the box down upon the unsteady stone floor. They each brought a pair of fingers to their third eye, lowered their hands to hearts and spread their fingers.

'Welcome home.' He signalled for an initiate to bring her a jacket.

Home. But already it felt different.

Accepting the jacket, she pictured Gil's face. *Too many lives lost.*

She picked up the box. 'How is he?'

'He's alive. You're not too late.'

'To save him?'

Inhaloc pursed his lips.

'To say goodbye?'

He reached to comfort her.

She sidestepped and ran past.

Ominous clouds withheld the sun's rays. Her boot slid across an icy rock, but her other found purchase. Still, she didn't dare slow. She couldn't.

Several babbling trees rose around Preslina's temple. Before the shockwaves hit, they'd encircled it. She entered through the front door, recalling the tree that'd blocked it when she came down from the peak with Tozias on her shoulders. Two corridors later, she bounded up the even numbered stairs. *Maybe next time ...*

No groans or cries came from the infirmary. Inside, Tozias, Letti and several others lay still. Rows of neatly made beds and a floor devoid of bodies stood in stark contrast to her last visit.

Antarna took his webbed hand. Despite layers of blankets, cool skin greeted hers. Warmer than when she'd found him at the peak, but that didn't say much. A fiery beard had overtaken his face.

'I'm here and with a saphramurl. You're going to be fine.' She opened the box and slid the gem under the back of his neck—to protect both head and heart. Madriliks would flee before the gem, not that she possessed the gift to see that taking place. Priests would bring further gems through for the others.

'You can't die, not after ...' *everything.*

Elgerin came by. Pleasantries and updates were exchanged, but about the only thing that mattered, there wasn't much to say. She didn't press for a promise he couldn't give.

Wind rattled the shutters. Antarna prayed, washed Tozias's arms and face with warm water, and then prayed again.

An initiate brought her a steaming bowl of hearty stew. Of course, she should eat. *Maybe later.* She lay on the bed next to his. The starting word of the tattoo on his arm rotated into alignment with his freckle. It took fifty-three slow breaths for the word to clear the freckle. It was like watching his beard grow.

The sun fled, and selfish clouds kept the moon's light to themselves. Her mind refused to submit to the darkness. Back on the mountain, memory after memory surfaced. Of prayer and practice, of snowball fights and stargazing. Tozias featured in most. *If I'd only gotten you the gem sooner.*

She turned from her left side to her right, tried her stomach and then flipped onto her back. After two breathing exercises, she got up and lay upon the stone floor as she had when she'd first arrived as a child, high with fever. The stone snatched at her heat. When Enthriff squeezed, she climbed back into bed. At some point, sleep finally claimed her.

Before dawn, she jerked awake from a nightmare of a velengoric with Snarlark's face standing between her and the gems. Opening the shutters revealed the peak menaced by clouds as dark as Snarlark's heart. The peak called to her, as it had always done.

Not ready to face it, she lay next to Tozias and started her account of the trip. When she finished telling of the fight with Angry and Dull, she kissed his forehead. 'I'll be back shortly.'

Antarna returned to Zentrina's temple before the first bell tolled, changed into her robes, prayed and stretched. Instead of joining them for breakfast, she made another trip to the temple of life. Standing over Tozias, she counted. This time, fifty-eight slow breaths passed before the first word cleared the freckle.

I'm too late. Antarna wrapped one hand around herself and dropped the other to Tozias's cheek. His skin was cold; she felt colder.

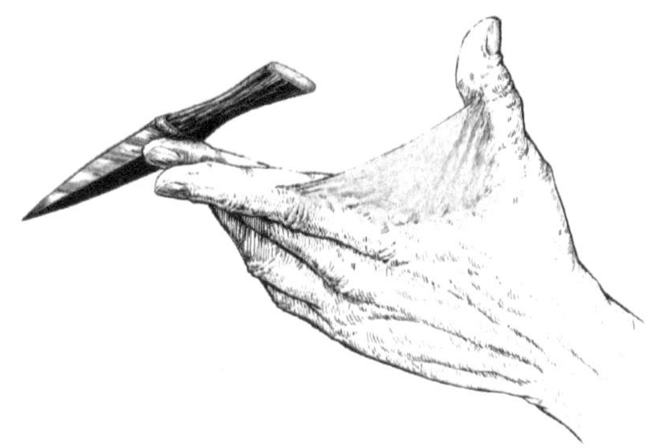

62. A Little Embellishment

Cal took a coin out of his pocket, reminded of when his life hung on one landing pattern-side-up. He flicked the coin into the dark alley between the temple of magic and Parliament Chamber, as Brayan used to do every day without fail.

A soiled hand snatched it out of the air. 'My thanks, Seer,' said Pegnic.

Seeing Brayan was high on Cal's list of priorities, along with making amends with his goddess and discussing his marriage with the chancellor. He had inquired about his former master, and the chancellor would summon him soon.

When Parliament fell behind him, out of sight, the tightness in his chest eased. Yesterday, on behalf of the chancellor, the commander of the woodsmen had barraged him with an endless stream of questions. The interrogation had outlasted the sunlight. He'd been half-delirious when he left.

Something gnawed at him. The commander hadn't batted an eyelid when Cal had told him that Farikarr was Resatrium. *Because the lake island already knew?*

A woman dripping in jewellery emerged onto a nearby balcony, followed closely by her husband.

If the chancellor knew, why have me marry Kat? It had always struck Cal as strange that the chancellor had refused to endorse his mum's first two choices of bride, each from a higher-born family. Perhaps his marriage was not to solidify the lake island's relationship with the crater, but with the Resatrium? Being a piece in the game was one thing, but it was entirely another to be lied to and used for the opposite purpose than you'd signed up for. Cal added this to the growing pile of reasons against the marriage.

A couple walked by him and dipped their heads. Cal returned the acknowledgement. He weaved his way east, keen to kick off his shoes, squish his toes into the sand and dive into the lake.

A fisherman loaded a net into a handcart. 'Morning, Seer.'

'Good morning.'

Something grabbed his naked arm—above the glove, below the sleeve—from behind. A small hand belonging to a thin boy who couldn't be much older than six.

Thelia didn't call to Cal.

His goddess hadn't granted him a vision in ages. Not since ... he'd told Enthriff of Antarna's fate. He'd been praying, though, more than he ever had, and his goddess would warm to him again.

The boy smiled, his grin missing his two front teeth. 'Will I change the world?'

'The world? Yes, I think you just might.'

The boy punched the air and ran down the street.

As Cal neared the beach, pressure mounted on his chest. Last night, he'd had a nightmare of a sickly green substance covering the surface of the lake, paint-like—just as algae had before they drowned the fifteenth seer. But it was only a nightmare, surely.

He hastened past vendors and pushed through the crowd. The lake stretched before him, the forest and sky reflecting off its perfect, flat surface. Dropping his hands to his hips, he exhaled. First, a swim, then he had a painting to finish.

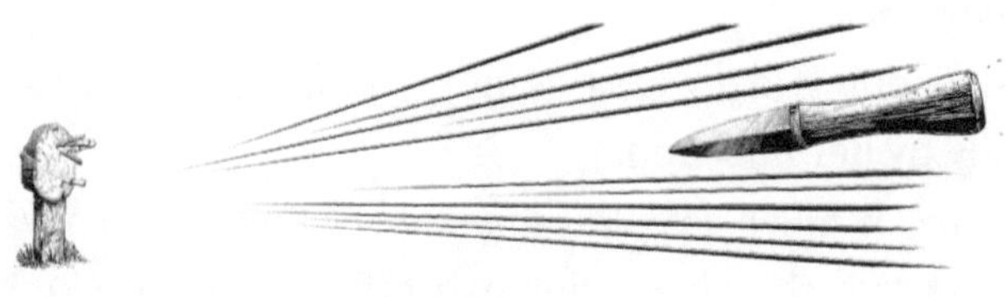

With long, flowing strokes, Cal added a further layer of paint to Antarna's hair. Over and over, as if his paintbrush was a comb. Her smooth hair fell just past her shoulders. The afternoon light revealed brown hues and showed off its gloss. Her hair gathered heat, drinking in the sun.

It had been warm upon his cheek during their embrace. His arms around her slender waist. Her smell enveloping him: soft but strong, sweet but fresh, more zesty than floral, hints of spice. Like nothing he'd ever smelt. Just straight intoxicating.

'What's got you smiling like *that*?' His mum stepped over a pillow, angling her neck to get a view of the work upon the easel.

He slid in front. 'It's not finished yet.'

'Since when does that bother you?'

'Close your eyes and stay there. I have something for you. For us.'

'Mysterious.' Her eyelids closed.

'Maybe you should be sitting for this.'

She crossed her feet and lowered herself to the floor.

Cal fetched a painting off the drying rack and held it up. 'Open wide.'

Her aquamarine eyes drank in his efforts. Tears seeped down her cheeks. 'It's ... gorgeous.' She swallowed, wiping her face. 'It's perfect. His eyes, how I've missed them. And you got his hair just right.'

The hair had given him the most trouble, even with the finest paints and brushes. Those loops and locks. The gold and honey hues.

Sniffling, his mum rose.

They walked through the courtyard and entered the prayer room. After passing the shrines to his goddess and to Antarna's, they stood before the one dedicated to his dad. His mum took the black and white portrait of her husband down. Holding his breath, Cal hung its replacement.

She looped her hand over Cal's shoulder. 'He'd be so proud of you.'

'Thanks, Mum.'

Retiring to the courtyard, they slid into a pair of padded chairs. Steam rose from mugs of tea on the small table between them. *Thanks, Nalgrid.* Warmth spread from the ceramic into his hands. His breath rippled the surface of the liquid. Taking a small sip, he let the smooth, deep tea roll over his tongue before swallowing. The liquid soothed his raw throat—a result of the interrogation yesterday, struggling to sleep after it, and the nightmares.

A confident knock on the front door reverberated down the hall. Nalgrid answered it and returned with a scroll. It bore the chancellor's triple initial monogram. Taking a deep breath, Cal broke the wax seal and unravelled it.

Seer,

The king of the crater has announced that High Priest Arric and Hunt Commander Farikarr died from their wounds after finding a bag of saphramurls and killing a hazzurus and a pack of velengoric. In honour of their heroism, their names have been carved on the wall of the crater.

Meet me shortly in my office.

Your chancellor

Suppressing a laugh, he passed the scroll to Mum.

She drew in a sharp breath. 'A hazzurus and a pack of velengoric?' Her vocals rose in pitch.

An embellishment. How he wished to speak that thought aloud. Or better yet, tell her the truth. But such knowledge was too dangerous.

'You're marrying the daughter of a hero.' Pride bloomed over her innocent face.

Cal's body tensed, and his face drew tight. Unable to hide his expression, he turned his back. Farikarr was no hero. Loyal only to the Resatrium, he'd lied to them all. If he'd shared what he'd known, how many lives could've been saved? And the man had demanded to be saved ahead of Cal. Even if Cal could pardon those wrongs, he'd never forgive Farikarr for holding Antarna to ransom for the answers she deserved. *How am I meant to look at your daughter without seeing your betrayal?*

'You'll need to give Kat lots of support,' his mother continued.

Cal had thought long and hard about this. He knew how tough it was to lose a father, but she'd have plenty of support from her friends and family, who all knew her far better than he did. And, as the daughter of a hero, she'd have her pick of suitors. She'd have a chance for love with one of those.

He pointed to the scroll. 'Gotta go.'

'Love you.'

'Love you too.'

The note failed to reveal why the chancellor wanted to meet. As to his mood, well, that was anyone's guess. Perhaps that he only requested Cal to meet him "shortly"—instead of "urgently" or "now"—was a good sign. And any note from a messenger was preferable to a box filled with cut webbing, or armed men come to haul him away to be drowned.

Cal recalled the chancellor levelling a menacing poker at Brayan's eye, ice-cold words dripping from his lips: "I don't tolerate failure." He couldn't be happy that his woodsmen were dead, along with Farikarr. Or that Cal hadn't betrayed Antarna. Thankfully, the short walk didn't allow too much for such thoughts. Painted clouds decorated Parliament's dome roof. Wispy ones of different shapes and sizes. Storm clouds would've been more fitting. A few turns later and he stood before Rayvic.

The herald opened the door to the chancellor's office. 'Calik Dyterog, the twenty-third seer and locator of saphramurls.'

Has a nice ring. Though we found the Lost Cave, not just saphramurls.

A small pyramid of saphramurls rose on his desk, each larger than the one set in his ring. The chancellor withdrew one from the base, sending the others toppling.

Cal stood beside the chair that Brayan had sat in when the chancellor took his eyes. He hadn't survived impossible odds only to come home and be blinded.

'Half the gems are here.' The chancellor rubbed his fat thumb over the surface of a saphramurl. 'Why does the crater have my other half?' He raised his small, hard, unblinking eyes to Cal.

'After we found the Lost Cave and stopped Arric, the king's brother arrived with armless, a priest and priestess of Preslina and over a dozen royal guards.'

The chancellor looked back to the saphramurl in his hand, perhaps conceding the point. Cal was just getting started.

'I knew'—Cal put his hand on his chest and then extended it towards the chancellor—'that you'd want to do everything possible to try to rectify the relationship with the crater after … well …'

'Spit it out.'

'After Farikarr betrayed the group and revealed to Antarna that he was a member of the Resatrium. Of all the people to confide in, my future father-in-law tells a member of the crater's royal family.'

'Is this your way of saying that you're not going through with the marriage?

Cal bowed. 'I was simply answering your question.' He lifted his chin, and the press of Antarna's soft lips still lingered upon his cheek. 'But, on that topic, I can only imagine your feelings towards the Resatrium. They spat in your face, stealing your urlire jewel and your serpent egg.' *If they hadn't, Brayan would still have his eyes.* 'Then the Resatrium turned on us again, seeking to claim the saphramurls for themselves.' Cal had left off that the chancellor had been supporting the Resatrium for years to weaken the crater.

'You are against this marriage.' The words came out slowly. His tone wasn't accusatory or judgemental. The chancellor leant back, his chair creaking, and appraised Cal with a newfound respect.

'Powers shift in the crater.'

The chancellor nodded. 'That they do.'

Cal dug his nails into his palm to keep from smiling.

'You've spent a lot of time with Antarna. Will she return to the crater?'

'She didn't say. But it's possible.' A large part of him hoped it was more than just possible. He couldn't stop thinking of her. His face may have betrayed him before he could bury his emotions.

A servant entered bearing a tray of refreshments. After serving the chancellor, the young boy offered the selection to Cal.

Fruit bobbed in pale liquid. Cal gripped a cool mug then took a long drink.

'If she returns to the crater, you'd seek to court her?'

Jamming his lips together prevented the liquid from fountaining over the chancellor. He gulped. A cough racked his body. Turning away from the chancellor, he covered his mouth. The cough shook him again and again, as though it was squeezing his lungs. Finally, it released its grip.

The question seemed out of character from the man that robbed his master of his foresight. And yet that same man had denied Cal's mum's first two choices of bride. This wasn't about romance, but power.

'So?' The chancellor spread his fingers, webbing drawing taut.

'I will give it some thought.' Not willing to risk another sip, he put the mug down.

Rayvic set foot into the room. 'The high priest is here.'

'We're almost done,' said the chancellor. He looked Cal over from head to toe. 'Congratulations, I'm promoting you to True Seer.'

What?

'This is where you thank me,' said the chancellor.

'I'm just … Thank you. I'm … honoured.'

'There'll be a ceremony next week. That'll be all.'

Cal didn't need to be told twice. He was out as fast as etiquette would allow—well, maybe a little faster.

True Seer.

He leapt off the top step and landed with bent knees. Home was too short a walk, so he turned instead towards the docks. A strengthening breeze urged him forwards. Sunlight kissed his skin, imparting its warmth, and it set the lake a-glitter.

He stopped dead, grabbing the trunk of a tree. *Did you make me True Seer because I deserved it, or to give me better standing if I'm to court Antarna?*

The wind changed, carrying the scent of drying fish towards him.

After dropping his forehead to bump against the wood, he dragged his feet forwards, keeping to the shadows cast by the buildings.

His stomach rumbled.

True Seer. Well, still a good excuse to eat crab.

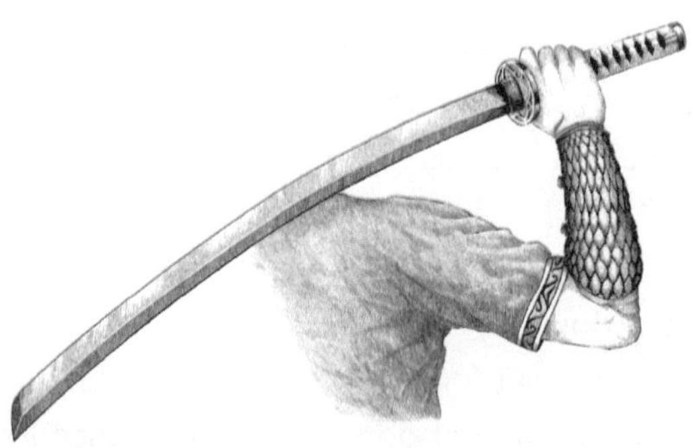

63. Soaring Gracefully

Antarna bowed to the immense grey form of Zentrina. So many bodies had disappeared into her undulating fluid-like substance. Too many.

A numbness had spread over her, slowing her mind and weighing her down. With heavy steps, she left the Sacred Hall. Grey surrounded her—the floor, walls and ceiling. Grey robed her, the people she passed and even the sky with its thick, solemn cloud cover. Never had the colour seemed more appropriate.

Her feet took her to the base of the main tower; they'd followed the same path that the priests and priestesses took when they carried the small grey seeds from Zentrina's likeness to the garden bed before her. Antarna's arms hung at her sides, slack, and she crossed them, hugging her body.

Narrow mature vines covered the grey stone of the tower, one for every death. She knelt. A vine shoot rose skyward. Despite only recently breaking the earth, it bore a blooming flower with thin, translucent petals that curled back on themselves. Luminous pollen wafted from its core, whispering of life and of hope. She reached out and caressed a smooth petal. Sensations awoke inside her, the deadness receding like the darkest night yielding to the radiance of the rising sun.

A flower already. Thanks to our goddess. It warms my heart that you've been reborn. Embrace your new gift of life, as I know you will.

I miss you. I treasure the time we had. This temple isn't the same without you.

Your new family and future friends are so fortunate. If I'm lucky, we'll meet again. Though if we do, your name won't be Gilverson.

Time slipped away. An ache grew in her knees. Dread coiled inside her once again. At any moment, Tozias could be next—his body offered to Zentrina and a seed emerging from her likeness to be buried here. He'd be reborn, of course, but with no memory of her other than that buried deep in his soul. She could search and search and never find his next incarnation. If she found him, he wouldn't recognise her. *Which is why you must live, Tozias.*

Antarna rose gingerly to her feet and left the temple, longing for the numbness to claim her again. Frigid air nipped at her exposed skin and filled her lungs. She jogged by the temple of Devtakaris, its dark stone so unnatural amongst this landscape. Any day now, a new high priest would be appointed to replace Arric. She chided herself for not having seen Arric for who he'd become earlier. He'd been well-known for wanting to raise the crater up to be like Daslercia. The end didn't excuse the means.

A group of Preslina's initiates and acolytes had cleared away the uprooted babbling trees and were beginning to plant saplings in their place. Dirt marked their white robes. Antarna joined them. They lowered waist-high saplings into holes, backfilled with the native soil, gave them a good watering and added mulch made from shredded leaves and wood chips. Fine slits adorned the slender, hollow trunks. When they finished up, she accompanied them into the temple and wove through the corridors to the infirmary.

High Priest Elgerin stood over Tozias.

Her steps quickened.

Tozias sat, propped up with pillows. He blinked.

She leapt onto the bed and wrapped her arms around him. He returned the embrace, sliding his arms under hers, encircling her waist. The details assured her that this was no dream. The brush of his fine forearm hairs against her skin. The firmness of his spine. The muscles of his shoulder. He leant his wild bearded cheek against her face, his chest rising and falling.

'Hey, sleepyhead,' she choked out, giving him a squeeze. He was solid, warm, alive—yes, alive—and awake.

Elgerin tapped her shoulder. 'Gentle, now.'

While she longed to linger in their embrace, she released him and wiped away a joyful tear.

Tozias ran a hand through his hair. 'How do I look?'

'Like you need some sun and a shave.'

Laughing, he dropped his hand to his beard. 'True.' He looked around, taking the infirmary in. 'What happened?'

'You were overexposed to madriliks, up at the peak. There was ... an event, a disaster.'

'How am I alive?'

'Stubbornness,' she replied, another tear falling.

He grinned.

'You kept strong and fought so hard. You hung on until we could get you what you needed.' Antarna pointed to the gem peeking out from beneath the pillow behind him.

'A saphramurl.' The words came out slowly. Tozias picked it up, clearly confused. 'From the crater?'

'No.'

His eyebrows scrunched further together.

'You've missed a lot. I might have a story or two for you.'

'Tell me everything.'

And she did. Tozias cackled when she told of Cal "inviting" the crustrearon queen to assist with the serpents, and he swore at Zanth's betrayal and at Arric's. He was a most attentive listener.

Her tale took them through the afternoon, and the sun peeked through the clouds. Tozias managed a short walk with her at his side, helping to take his weight.

While he enjoyed a bath, she got a fire going and fetched dinner.

Tozias sat and stretched his hands towards the crackling flames.

'Feeling more like yourself?' She handed him a bowl filled with curry and put a plate of flatbread between them. Spices perfumed the air.

'I am. How about you? You look ... different.'

'By goddess, I feel different. These robes do too.' She rubbed the hem of the grey fabric between two fingers. 'It's hard to explain.'

'After all you've been through, change is to be expected.' Balancing a mound of curry on his flatbread, he took a giant bite.

'I guess.'

'While I was in the bath, one question plagued me. Did the king know what Arric was up to?'

'I'm sure of it. The pair were too close for the king not to have known.' And it sounded like something the king would get behind: not just a weapon for the crater against the creatures that kept all bar the strongest and bravest within its walls, but a powerful threat and deterrent against the Resatrium he'd feared since they'd killed his father before him.

Someone had to keep an eye on the king to make sure this never happened again. Not just that, but her people needed help.

'I know that look,' he said.

'Do you now?'

'That I do. There's a problem no one else will address, and you're determined to fix it yourself.'

Antarna laughed. But, if she dared to be honest with herself, he was right. The truth had been cast into the light, and who would she be if she turned her face from it? She must return to the crater. While there, she'd find an excuse to see a certain lake islander who'd saved her life more than once.

Tozias reached out and took her hand. 'With my soul as my eternal record, may my actions be honourable, ring true and serve others.'

She repeated the last line of their daily prayer.

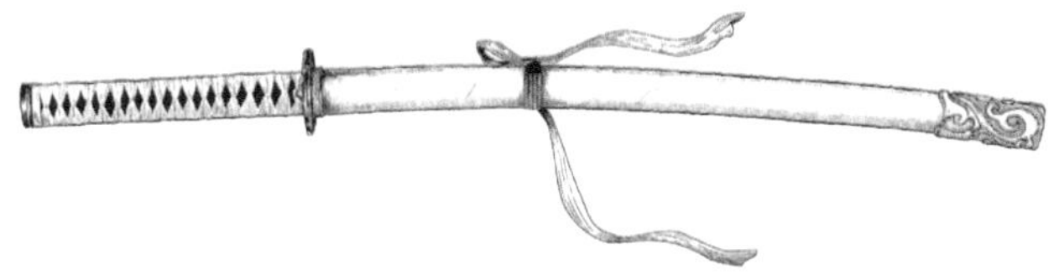

Antarna opened the shutters.

Soft moonlit clouds clung to the mountain peak, the closest point to the gods and goddesses who watched from above. There, earth and sky met in solitude.

Stay there; I'll join you.

She closed the door and made her way outside.

The path wound to the right, smoothed from those who came before her. Countless many would come after her.

The king had followed in the footsteps of his late father. Salorann and the Resatrium had taken an opposing path. She had her own to forge.

After breakfast, she'd connect again with Salorann. *The past has much to teach.*

A beetle with a rich purple-black shell flew by. Antarna lifted a flat rock. A many-legged creature with an exoskeleton like gnarly bark scuttled away.

As the path grew rougher, it demanded more of her attention. She planned her steps at least two or three in advance—another lesson from the mountain for her to remember on returning to the crater.

Jumping over a tuft of grass with blades finer than hair, Antarna landed on a boulder. She paused to draw two breaths of thin air through her scarf. Neighbouring snow-capped peaks rose around her. The murmuring wind died, creating a moment of stunning serenity. How she wished she could bottle it.

Pressing on, virgin snow crunched under her boots. Pristine white. Her footprints trailed her. The guide rope hung down a vertical rock face. She took it and rose hand over hand, feet ever searching for the next crack. The seventh knot sat above her grip. So close, yet so far.

The wind intensified, encouraging her. Enthriff added his, too.

She stretched out her hand and took the knot.

Her mother and brother stood with her; she could feel them. They'd never left. They would never leave.

Lighter now, Antarna continued upwards. A bird cut across the moon, soaring gracefully. She approached the top of the world. Memories flowed through her, and she let them. Grounded by the mountain, Antarna allowed herself to feel.

The temple grew smaller. The world larger. Sunrise closer.

A slender plant stood proud and resolute upon the summit, radiant with pristine white light punctuated by specks of delicate yellows and warm oranges and reds.

Hope had a most beautiful signpost.

Acknowledgements

I've always loved a good story. It helped that my mother was a teacher and a librarian, and my father was a born storyteller. Yes, the fish was "this big"—now stretch your arms wide... no, wider still.

This novel has occupied a place in my mind since I was a teenager. I fondly recall bouncing ideas for it off my brother while a soccer ball or table tennis ball arced between us. Four years ago (and twice the age I was back then), I sat down to write it in earnest. My brother, Lance, has been with me every step of the way, as have my parents and my wife. I'm grateful for their boundless love and support.

There's one name on the cover, but a small village of people whose contributions made it possible and brought my vision to life.

Anderson Magalhães from Design Unlikely is the talent responsible for the stunning front cover and internal artwork. His skill, creativity and attention to detail shine through in every aspect of his illustrations.

My heartfelt thanks go to my trio of extraordinary editors: Sarah Chorn (queen of clarity), Kathryn Harris (champion of emotion) and Nathan Hall (jack of all trades). Each played a crucial role in shaping, enriching and polishing the novel.

I would also like to acknowledge and express my appreciation for the invaluable comments and insights from my beta readers, manuscript assessors and others who lent their expertise—including Chelsea Lauren, Brandon Young, Michael R. Fletcher, Sally Odgers, Elisa Arnott, Kelly Esparza, Mikayla G, Tory Hunter, John Gunningham, Shannon Scown, Mikhaila Andrews, Evan Porchetta and Katie J. Thanks also to my eagle-eyed proofreaders, TJ Shiree, Lauren Elmore and Nicole Lindsay.

Last but certainly not least, a big shout out to Shelby Hild, Amy Karas, Lia Zambetti, Katherine Lykos, Darren Watt and Bron Morrison, for our wonderful SFF writing sessions and discussions.

Kane Williams

About the Author

Kane Williams believes that the pen is mightier than the sword (and asks that you kindly don't tell Excalibur he said that). Yet you'll often find his characters with sword in hand.

Perils of the Past is his debut novel. He also pens flash fiction and the occasional short story. Previously, he wrote non-fiction and was published by Thomson Reuters.

Website: kanew.au

www.ingramcontent.com/pod-product-compliance
Lightning Source LLC
Chambersburg PA
CBHW020245030826
48979CB00030B/2618/J

* 9 7 8 1 7 6 3 7 3 6 4 2 9 *